LAST
SNOW

LAST
SNOW

Eric Van Lustbader

A Tom Doherty Associates Book

New York

LAST SNOW

Copyright © 2010 by Eric Van Lustbader

A Forge Book
Published by Tom Doherty Associates, LLC
175 Fifth Avenue
New York, NY 10010

www.tor-forge.com

Forge® is a registered trademark of Tom Doherty Associates, LLC.

ISBN 978-0-7653-2515-0

First Edition: February 2010

Printed in the United States of America

0 9 8 7 6 5 4 3 2 1

LAST
SNOW

PROLOGUE

Capri | April 1

EVERYTHING COMES to an end. Love, hate, betrayal. The greed of wealth, the lust for power, the comfort in religion. In the final moment, everyone falls, even the kings of empires and the princes of darkness. In the silence of the tomb, we all get what we deserve.

Reassured that for him that particular moment is a long way off, he boards the cramped and crowded bus at Piazza Vittoria for the vertiginous ride down the mountainside into Capri village. The driver's square metal fare box is closed and locked and he will not take money for the ride. This is the Caprese version of a strike against management for higher pay. No marches, no shaking fists, no amplified rhetoric. Calm and considered, slow as the pace of the island itself, the protest has been going on for three years.

The two-lane road down which the bus wheezingly careens is steeply pitched, harrowingly twisting. Traffic whizzes by in the opposite lane so close the trucks appear ready to kiss the bus. The road is decorated on one side by sprays of brilliant bougainvillea, on the other by views of the Gulf of Naples, glittering in the sun. Occasionally, in the mysterious niches of the rock face, miniature painted plaster statues of the Virgin Mary can be seen, bedecked with wilted flowers. He has seen the open-air factory near the beautiful cemetery in Anacapri where the statues are made, white bisque with blank eyes turned out of rubber molds, ruffles of rough edges that must be removed with a knife. Many of the passengers, mostly the older women, touch forehead, chest, and shoulders in the sign of the cross as they pass these hallowed places where pedestrians were struck down.

All the orange plastic seats are occupied. Bags shifting between bare knees. Long hair floating on a hot breath of wind. Brief arias of Italian conversations, the loud, brutal bite of German. Handprints on the glass, greasy chromium poles, the stirring of silent bodies in the grip of the forces of gravity. He stands, staring out through the window at the cloudless sky, the cobalt water, the yachts and pleasure boats. He sees a packed hydrofoil cutting a scimitar swath through the bay from Naples and he wonders whether this is the one.

Watching the hydrofoil, it occurs to him that the port of Mergellina was the last real thing he can remember. When he himself stood on the eleven o'clock hydrofoil as it bounded across the bay, when frenzied Naples faded into the heat haze, when the steeply rising slopes of Capri had appeared as if from the deepest portion of his memory, he had entered a land of lost time. He felt as if he was seeing the rocky shore as Augustus Caesar had known it more than two thousand years ago. And just then he had caught a glimpse, high up atop the rocks, of the remains of the Villa Jovis and quite without conscious volition had projected himself either backward or forward in time into that palace of stone and grass and magnificent ruined baths.

A young man in a red-and-blue checkered swimsuit, taking full advantage of the unnaturally warm spring, dives off the bow of a sleek teak and fiberglass sailboat into the dark water. A brief creamy splash, then his blond head appears as he wipes water off his long Roman nose. He waves enthusiastically to a woman in large sunglasses and a wide-brimmed straw hat who has appeared on deck. Her feet are spread wide, one hand presses her hat to the top of her head to keep it from whirling away. Her swimsuit is comprised of three tiny yellow triangles.

Ten forty in the morning and already the back of his neck feels sticky. A line of sweat snakes down the indentation of his spine. His face itches. The bus lurches around a hairpin turn and a body is thrown against him. He smells a light citrus scent and turns, aware of the heat emitted from bare skin. A Caprese girl of eighteen or nineteen in a short, unnervingly tight turquoise skirt and a lime green sleeveless Lycra top that looks to him like underwear. The perfect curve of a tanned arm, and underneath the smooth hollow that leads inexorably down to the lift of the young breasts. So vulnerable and at the same time so remote, as if she is part of another lifetime, another universe. Which, of course, she is. This does not stop him from staring at the intimate dewlike sheen that licks the shadowed dell from which floats toward him the unmistakable aroma of freshly peeled lemons. Her face is partially hidden by the thick curtain of her long dark hair, but he can catch a glimpse of coffee eyes, a generous Sophia Loren mouth. And her ass. My God, the Caprese have magnificent buttocks! Even the mothers. All that climbing up and down steep inclines. All day, all night. Better than a StairMaster. The modern-day Romans are wrong to disdain the Caprese as peasants. But when you have your nose in the air it's difficult to appreciate the treasures that lie close to the earth.

A sudden longing pierces him, drawing him to her as if she is a lodestone, the very center of True North to which he has long ago become attuned. With the tension of a biologist encountering a potentially new species, he studies the tiny silken hairs on her taut forearm, and at the back of her neck as she lifts a slim hand to swing the waterfall of her hair out of the way, the long pale sea-creature cilia at the arching of her nape.

This Caprese girl, fresh as a *spremuta*. He wishes he was holding her hand, brushing against her rocking hips, listening to the music of her lithe legs as they walk side by side through the peaceful earthen aisles of the mountaintop cemetery. They would stop and silently watch the women on their knees, plunging their hands into buckets of soapy water, scrubbing down the carved marble of their family grave sites, arranging freshly cut flowers in green glass vases married to the cool surface of the tombstones by black iron rings. How he would love that and how utterly bored she would be. To judge by the blank look on her face, a bracing *macchiato* and a spin into Tod's is more her speed.

He is close to her, his thoughts caressing her as intimately as would a lover's hand. And yet she is utterly oblivious. Lips moist and half open, she cracks her chewing gum. He laughs silently, at her, at himself. How foolish fantasies are, and at the same time how compelling. He cannot imagine anything more powerful.

He inhales her deeply, recognizing an alchemical change: His reaction to her has released a powerful sensation inside himself. It is both exhilarating and frightening, an eely thing dredged up from the darkness of his youth when he wandered the debris-strewn streets of Manhattan at three in the morning with the Outsider's contempt for the humdrum world. How he cherished being other—a lone wolf watching the sheep all moving in the same direction. And how he feared the loneliness it brought with it. Possibly, he tells himself, he was searching for her, just this one, this perfect creature, but immediately he knows this as a conceit. There is no one that does everything for you, and so you keep searching beyond love, beyond companionship, because part of the human condition is not being satisfied, for if you were there would be nothing left save death. Dissatisfaction, he tells himself, is the engine that drives life.

This girl, this fantasy needs to be belted down neat like a triple scotch. She is there to make him forget, to help ease the pain inside him that has become an illness. This moment in time, this present, is for him little more than a dream. He is still living in the moment that occurred three hours ago but that continues like a whipping, devastating in its excoriation.

The creaking bus turns a corner and for a moment he can see the ribbon of road behind them, running up the steep, verdant mountainside to the Hotel Caesar Augustus. His heart seems to turn over in his chest like a dropped stone. Mia's final, brutal, horrifying sentence said it all, wrapping up the last two weeks in the soiled brown paper it deserves.

The bus, gears grinding ominously, staggers the last half kilometer into the open-air depot at Capri village, where he changes for the bus down to Marina Grande. Fifteen minutes later, he arrives. The bus begins to disgorge its load into a street clogged with people and vehicles all, it seems, needing to go to the same place at the same time. Those seven hateful words, the bland look on her face that revealed not a trace of bitterness or remorse, made him want to smash her face with his balled fist. He is filled with rage, a swamp through which he is struggling as he swings off the bus. He hits the pavement, his heart aching, his nerves raw.

Craning his neck, looking around for her, he feels the stir of resentment like a hungry dog's growl, sharp and craven. He hears Mia's closing line in his head, perfectly, devastatingly choreographed.

"Don't worry about me, I'm well fucked."

This woman, moving like a siren of the sea, circles him still like a hungry beast.

He wishes Cloe had come, because it would mean that she has forgiven him, that she'll take him back. He imagines what it would be like to catch sight of her through the crowd, to watch her walk toward him. He would find it a jolt to see her here, the open arms that the real world holds out to him in forgiveness. Yes, forgiveness.

He is thinking of what he will say to Cloe when he calls her this evening, the new beginning that might now be his; the betrayal that will be forgotten, because he's quite certain that Cloe would never hurt him as cruelly as Mia hurt him. He is imagining as if it is a film he is expertly splicing together: the mise-en-scène of betrayal, and he begins to wonder (because all good films are juggling acts of counter-balancing forces) what is the opposite of betrayal. He walks amid the squall of people. His steps quicken, his heart pounds as he takes out his cell phone. He'll call Cloe now, confess everything, tell her it's all over and done with, a bad dream consigned to history. She'll understand, of course she'll understand.

He sees what will happen reflected in the eyes of a wisp of a girl striding toward him, sees it an instant too late. He is still absorbing her look of horror when the narrow Caprese van strikes him full on and kills him instantly.

PART ONE

Lady Macbeth:
"The sleeping and the dead
are but as pictures."
—WILLIAM SHAKESPEARE,
  Macbeth

ONE

Moscow | April 5

JACK MCCLURE, cell phone to his ear, stood in his hotel suite, staring out at the arc-lit onion domes of Red Square. It was snowing. The last snow, it was predicted, of a protracted and, even for Russia, frigid winter. Red Square was nearly deserted. The swirling black wind swept the last of the tourists, shoulders hunched, digital cameras stuffed inside their long coats to protect them, back to their hotels where steaming cups of coffee waited, spiked with vodka or slivovitz. Jack had arrived here a week ago with the presidential entourage on a trip that was both politically necessary and culturally important, which was why the First Lady and the First Daughter had been invited along. The trip had been arranged—brokered might be a more accurate term—by General Atcheson Brandt, who had commanded a wing in the Gulf War. He was both a decorated veteran and, now that he'd retired, a revered military analyst for both CNN and ABC. He knew everyone in Washington who mattered. When he spoke, senior politicians of both parties listened. Though the former administration's mini cold war with Russia, and President Yukin in particular, had raged for eight years, General Brandt had made it his business to keep the private lines of communication with Yukin open. His public criticism of the former administration's hard line against Russia had led to a brief summit between Yukin and the former president. Though nothing of substance had come of it, General Brandt had been praised on both sides of the Senate aisles for his efforts.

However, at the moment General Brandt was far from Jack's mind. Jack hadn't said a word for the past three minutes and neither had Sharon. Rather, they were listening to each other breathe, as they often did when they lay in bed together in Jack's house in D.C. While Jack listened through the phone, he thought of her coming home after work, shedding her clothes layer by layer, until she was in her bra and the bikini underpants she always wore. He imagined her sliding into bed, pushing backward, feeling with her buttocks for that shallow indentation his absent body had left behind like a memory. He imagined her eyes closing as she drifted off to sleep. And then imagined she descended further. What did she dream of when all the artifice and layers demanded by civilization melted away, when she reverted to who she had been as a child, when she was certain no one was watching or, at least, able to pierce the veil of her sleep? He liked to imagine that she dreamed of him, but he had no way of knowing, just as he had no way of knowing who she really was, even though he knew her body almost as well as he knew his own, even though he'd observed over and over her every tiny motion, day and night.

He knew these questions assailed him because he was so far from home—traveling with the newly elected president of the United States, his longtime friend, Edward Harrison Carson, as Carson's strategic advisor.

"What does that title mean exactly?" he'd asked Carson, when the two had met the week following the inauguration.

The president had laughed. "Just like you, Jack, cutting to the quick of everything. I pulled you out of the ATF to find my daughter. You brought Alli back to me when no one else could. I and my family feel safest with you close."

"With all due respect, Edward, you have a platoon of perfectly competent Secret Service operatives better suited than I am to guard you and your family."

"You misunderstand me, Jack. I have far too much respect for you to offer you a babysitting job, even though nothing would please Alli more. Besides, on a practical level, your special abilities would be wasted in that capacity. I have no illusions about how difficult and perilous the next four years are going to be. As you can imagine, there are already no end of people who are clamoring to whisper advice in my ear. Part of my job is to allow them this access, but you're one person I'm inclined to listen to, because you're the one I trust absolutely.

"That's what 'strategic advisor' means."

SHARON HAD begun whispering, which meant, according to the routine their calls had fallen into over the week Jack had been in Moscow, it was time for them to talk. Jack turned and padded in bare feet past the table with the photos of her and Emma he took everywhere he went, across the carpet to the bathroom. He was about to turn on the water, in order to defeat the listening devices planted in every room. No fewer than four representatives of the Russian government swore there were no such listening devices. But ever since the first night when Secret Service personnel had discovered one, he and everyone in the president's service were warned to take precautions when speaking to anyone while in the rooms, even if the conversation seemed innocuous.

He heard voices rising up from the hot water pipes behind the toilet. Over the course of the week, he'd occasionally heard a drift of voices from the room on the floor below, but had never before been able to make out a single word. This time, a man's and a woman's voice were raised in altercation.

"I hate you!" the woman said, her raw emotion vibrating through the pipe. "I've always hated you."

"You told me you loved me," the man said, not plaintively, which might be expected, but with the guttural growl of a stalking male.

"Even then I hated you, I always hated you."

"When I was pinning you to the mattress?"

"Especially then."

"When I made you come?"

"And what was I screaming in my own language, do you think? 'I hate you, I'll see you in hell, I'll kill you!'"

"Jack?"

Sharon's voice in his ear caused him to twist on the water full force. He wasn't one to eavesdrop, but there was a vengeful, knife-edged sharpness to both voices that not only compelled listening, but made it almost impossible to stop.

"Jack, are you at a party?"

"In my room," he said. "The people downstairs are going at it tooth and nail. How are you?" An innocuous enough question, but not when you were forty-six hundred miles apart. When so much distance separated you, there was always a question in your mind: What is she doing, or, its more far-reaching corollary, what *has* she been doing? It was possible to tell himself that her day proceeded precisely as it did when he was there: She got up in the morning, showered, ate a quick breakfast standing at the kitchen counter, stacked the dishes in the sink because there was time to either wash them or put on her makeup but not do both, went to work, shopped for food, came home, put on Muddy Waters or Steve Earle while she prepared dinner and ate it, read an Anne Tyler or Richard Price novel or watched *30 Rock* if it was on, and went to bed.

But he couldn't help wondering if her day differed in some significant way, that it had been added to, that someone else might have inserted himself into her day or, far worse, her night, someone handsome, understanding, and available. Now he couldn't help wondering whether this fantasy was jealousy or wish fulfillment. When, three months ago, Sharon had moved back into his house, he was certain they had reconciled the differences that had driven them apart in the first place. The intense physical desire for her that had first drawn him to her had never truly been entirely extinguished. But the fact was, they were still the same people. Jack was dedicated to his work, which Sharon resented, because she had no such dedication. She'd tried several different careers, all without feeling the slightest attachment to them. At first, she'd set herself up as a painter, but though technically accomplished she lacked passion—and nothing good, or at least worthwhile, can be created without it. Typical of her, she'd then drifted into dealing art, figuring to make easy money, but again her lack of conviction, or even interest, predetermined her failure. Finally, she was hired by a friend who worked at the Corcoran but was let go after less than a year. As a result, she now toiled joylessly in real estate, work that was tied to the vagaries of the economy, which, he imagined, could only further stir the pot of her simmering anger—at him, at the world, at her life without their daughter. He couldn't help but think that she wanted him home for dinner every evening as a kind of revenge, for enjoying his job when she clearly didn't. This was a desire that made him feel as if he were being strangled. He had always been an outsider—from his dyslexia to his unorthodox upbringing he'd never fit in and, as he'd finally been able to admit to himself if not to anyone else besides Alli Carson, he didn't want to. One of the things that had bonded him with Alli was that they were both Outsiders. Sharon was conventional in most things; in all the others she was regressive. In the beginning, he'd loved her despite their differences, loved the smell of her, the sight of her both naked and clothed, the intense way she made love. Now Emma, or, more accurately, Emma's memory, stood between them like an immense, immovable shadow that limned their differences with a cutting edge that was painful.

"Who's that I hear whistling?" he said now.

"My mom. She arrived yesterday."

Sharon's mother had never liked him. She hadn't approved of the marriage, telling her daughter that it would end in tears, which of course it had. That triumph of hers was in no way mitigated by Sharon having returned to him. Their daughter—her granddaughter—Emma was dead, killed at age twenty in a car accident. As far as Sharon's mother was concerned it had all ended in tears, no matter what happened from now on.

"Jack, when are you coming home?"

"You asked me that yesterday and the day before."

"And yesterday and the day before you said you'd find out." She made that noise where her tongue struck the roof of her mouth. "Jack, what's the matter with you? Don't you want to come home?"

The subject, he suspected, would not be coming up so insistently if her mother hadn't arrived with all her pernicious baggage. "I told you when I signed on with Edward—"

"My mother said you never should have taken that job, and I have to say that I agree with her."

"What do you mean?"

"If you cared about me, if you cared about repairing the damage to our marriage, you would have found a job closer to home."

"Sharon, this is starting to feel like déjà vu all over again. I can't—"

"That's your answer to everything serious, isn't it, making jokes. Well, I can't take that anymore, Jack."

Silence on the line. He didn't know what to say or, rather, didn't want to say something he'd regret. It was strange how intimate conversations became attenuated—how emotions seemed muted, al-most murky—when transmitted over long distances, as if the phones themselves were having the conversation. Perhaps it was his alien surroundings—his present, and therefore his priorities so different from her familiar ones.

"You didn't answer my question." Her voice sounded thick, as if during the interim she'd been crying.

"I don't know. Something's come up."

"Something's always coming up." Her voice had sharpened like a knife at the strop. "But that's precisely what you want, isn't it? You—"

The rest of her acerbic response was drowned out by a sharp, in-sistent rapping on the door he had come to associate with the presi-dent's Secret Service staff.

He took the cell away from his ear and ducked back into the main room, which was at once anonymous and oppressive, a hallmark of what passed for modern Russian decor. It was on the top floor of the vast H-shaped hotel, whose somewhat faded hallways reminded Jack of *The Shining*. The entire floor was allocated to President Carson, his family, and his entourage.

Dick Bridges, the head of Carson's Secret Service detail, filled the doorway. He made no move to step inside, but silently mouthed *POTUS*, the Secret Service acronym for the President of the United States. Jack nodded, held up a forefinger in countersign: a moment. *Now*, Bridges mouthed, and Jack stepped back into the bathroom where the water was still running.

"Sharon, Edward needs me."

"Did you hear a word I said?"

He was in no mood for her mother-instigated bullshit. "I've got to go."

"Jack—"

He killed the connection. Back in the room, he stepped into his shoes and, without bothering to tie his laces, went out into the hallway.

President Carson, flanked by two agents, was standing in front of the metal fire door that led to the stairwell, which had been blocked off to the floor below. They had the aspect of men who had been talking together for some time: Their heads were tilted toward one another, their mouths were half open, and familiar glances were being exchanged. All of these small observations told Jack that something of significance had arisen at this late hour.

Therefore, he was on high alert when Bridges opened the fire door and they all trooped onto the unpainted concrete landing. There was an unfamiliar mineral odor, as sharp as it was unpleasant, but at least there were no electronic eavesdroppers.

"Jack, Lloyd Berns died in Capri four days ago," the president said without preamble. Lloyd Berns was Carson's minority whip in the Senate and, as such, his death was a serious blow to the president's ability to ram through legislation crucial to the new administration.

Now Jack understood why Carson and his bodyguards had been in conference. "What happened?"

"An accident. Hit and run."

"What was Berns doing in Capri and why did it take four days to find out he died?"

Carson sighed. "We're not sure, which is the problem. He was supposed to be on a fact-finding tour in Ukraine, up until ten days ago, that is. Then he disappeared. Best guess from our intelligence boys: He was taking time off from a failing marriage or—and this isn't unrelated—in Capri with someone else. He had no ID on him and everything grinds slowly in Capri. Three days passed before it occurred to someone in authority that he might be American, so finally a rep from the consulate was contacted and dispatched, and so on and so forth." He rubbed his hands together briskly. "Be that as it may, I've got to get back to D.C. to straighten out the political mess."

Jack nodded. "I'll get packed right away."

The president shook his head. "I'm wondering if you could stay with my wife and Alli. You know how important this accord with Yukin is. Once it's signed, Russia will no longer aid Iran's nuclear program, and American security will reach a new level. This is particularly imperative now because our armed forces are dangerously overextended, exhausted to the edge of endurance, and opening the current wars in Afghanistan, Iraq, and Somalia on yet another front would be disastrous. If my family leaves with me it could damage the fragile détente I've managed to form with President Yukin. I can't have that; he and I are only days away from finalizing and signing the accord, and my entire first year as president hinges on the signing."

The president seemed abruptly older, as if he'd aged five years since Jack last saw him, fifty minutes ago.

"And, Jack, on a private and very unpleasant note, Alli has begun to act out again—she's unnaturally willful, contrary, sometimes it seems to me irrational." His eyes seemed to be speaking another language entirely. "You're the only one that can make her see reason."

Alli had been psychologically traumatized. Her abduction was bad enough, but the man who had kidnapped her had also brainwashed her. Ever since Jack had brought her home, a team of psychologists had been working with her. But, more than that, she'd wanted Jack near her as much as was possible. The two of them had forged a close relationship and now, like her father, Alli trusted Jack over and above anyone else in the world, including her parents, with whom she'd always had a difficult and not altogether pleasant relationship.

Jack did, of course, understand. So even though he wanted to return to Washington to advise his old friend or, failing that, to be sent to Capri to find out the details of Lloyd Berns's death, he did not argue with Carson's suggestion.

"All right," he said.

The president nodded, and the Secret Service contingent left them alone in the putrid stairwell. It was at this point that Jack realized every detail of this clandestine meeting had been meticulously planned.

When the two men were alone, Carson took a step toward Jack and handed him a slip of paper. "This is a copy of Berns's itinerary in Ukraine. The cities I've marked are off the official itinerary, but it's Kiev that was his last stop. Also, remember this name: K. Rochev. Rochev was the last man he saw or was due to see before he abruptly left Ukraine for Capri."

Jack looked at him. "In other words, you have no idea what the hell he was doing in Kiev."

Carson nodded. His concern was evident in his eyes, but he said nothing more.

All at once, Jack understood that the babysitting assignment was for the Secret Service personnel's benefit. This was the real assignment. He smiled. It was part of Carson's genius to get what he wanted either by suggestion or by leading the other person to the conclusion he desired.

Jack did not look at the writing, which, because of his dyslexia, he'd have to concentrate on fully in order to read. "I guess I'm going to Ukraine to find out what Berns was doing and why he left."

"I think that's the best idea. There's a private jet with diplomatic privileges waiting for you at Sheremetyevo, but you can wait until tomorrow morning, if you wish." Carson squeezed Jack's shoulder. "I appreciate this."

"Part of my job description." Jack frowned. "Edward, do you suspect something?"

Carson shook his head. "Call it caution or paranoia, the choice is yours. In any event, as Dennis Paull has detailed in his most recent security briefing, my enemies from the previous administration are still powerful, and all of them have very long memories, especially when it comes to revenge. They fought like wild dogs against my nomination and, when I won it, they tried everything they could think of to undermine my candidacy. That they've made conciliatory statements in the press doesn't fool me for a minute. They're after my blood, and it seems damn lucky for them that Berns is dead, because they know better than anyone that without him I'm going to have the devil's own time with the Democratic-led Congress."

Jack did not say that killing Carson's right-hand man was an extreme way of crippling him, because he'd had firsthand experience with people within the previous administration. He knew what they were capable of and that their thinking did not exclude murder. They'd arranged for Alli to be kidnapped, had almost succeeded in an attack on Carson at the inauguration, and while the perpetrators were either dead or behind bars, the people who had calculatedly planned the attack remained safe to this day behind veils of plausible deniability that even Carson with all his might and power couldn't penetrate.

The president's grip on Jack's shoulder tightened. "Jack, I won't bullshit you, this could be a wild-goose chase, but if it's not, if Berns was killed or if he was involved in something that could turn into a scandal, you're the only one I can trust, you're my friend and you're apolitical. I want you on this until you can tell me whether I'm right or wrong." His eyes grew dark, indicating that he was deeply troubled. "And one other thing. No one is to know what you're up to, not even Dick."

"You don't trust Bridges?"

"I trust you, Jack," Carson said. "That's the beginning and the end of it."

Two

SLEEP WAS impossible after that disturbing conversation. Jack put on earbuds and fired up Emma's iPod, which he took with him wherever he went, and putting it on random play, listened to "I Call My Baby Pussycat" by Funkadelic and "Like Eating Glass" by Bloc Party, before he felt suddenly claustrophobic alone in his suite with his daughter's music and a half-dozen electronic listening devices, so he put the iPod aside and took the elevator down to the immense gilt-and-marble lobby with its overstuffed velvet furniture, musty samovars, and gimlet-eyed staff. He shivered slightly as he strode through the space, his steps echoing hollowly.

The bar was to the right, the room only slightly less imposing than the lobby itself. At least the lights were lower, the half-moon banquettes giving the illusion of intimacy. To his left was a curved bar of polished metal, macabrely lit from underneath, in front of which were twelve modernist stools. Not too long ago this bar and others like it all over Moscow were filled with free-spending oligarchs, businessmen who had made hundreds of millions of dollars buying up the huge corporations privatized during glasnost. Snapping up the companies for cents on the dollar, they'd been made rich beyond their wildest dreams virtually overnight. Yukin had ended all that when he'd decided to take back the corporations. Now the oligarchs were in a panic, scrambling to find the money to pay for the debts they had amassed while leveraging their nonexistent businesses when their short-lived power was at its zenith. Now the bar and others like it all over the city were as empty as a subway car at three in the morning.

Jack went past the bar itself and saw a Secret Service agent nursing a club soda. He turned his eye from an empty banquette at the rear at which he was planning to sit to the one the agent was keeping an eye on, and saw Alli Carson. She was sitting by herself next to a window that looked out onto the snow-covered square, occupied only by architecturally florid buildings, all of which had a history steeped in blood and power. She looked so small, almost lost, vulnerable against the high-back crescent, but he knew better. This part of her physical appearance was caused by Graves' disease, a form of hyperthyroidism that made her look sixteen rather than twenty-two. Beyond that illusion, she was tough as reinforced concrete and smarter than many people twice her years. Her skin was pale against the bloodred material. Clear green eyes below a thick fall of auburn hair dominated an oval face. A constellation of freckles danced across the bridge of her nose. She wore jeans and a T-shirt that read SEX IS DEAD across the front. She could not have looked more out of place.

"I'll have whatever she's having," he told the somnolent waiter as he slid into the banquette beside her.

Alli's slim fingers gripped the glass. "It's not a Shirley Temple," she said.

He grinned. "Good God, I hope not."

She laughed, which was the point.

"Where's your mom?"

"In bed," Alli said. "She might be asleep, or not. She only took the Xanax ten minutes ago."

"She still having trouble sleeping?"

"She hates it here. She says the Russian women are too piggy to be impressed with her."

The waiter came with Jack's drink, which turned out to be a White Russian, a bit sweet for him, but what the hell, he thought.

As he lifted his glass, she said, "You're not leaving, too, are you?"

He had learned early on not to lie to her; he'd needed to earn her trust. Besides, she was too quick to be gulled. "I'm not going with your father, no."

A ghost of a smile played around her generous mouth. "Which means you're going *somewhere*." Her gaze slid slyly sideways. "What are you doing for him?"

"You know I can't tell you."

"Whatever it is it's got to be more interesting than sitting around this dump."

"I thought you liked it here."

"Talking to Dad again? Didn't your bullshit meter go off? The Russian boys are Neanderthals and the Russian girls are sluts—what's to like?"

"There's a lot of history here."

"Which no one wants to talk about because it's been entirely rewritten," she said dryly. "I'm begging you, take me away from all this, Jack."

"I wish I could, Alli, really."

"Fuck. Fuck you!"

"Don't be like that."

"How would you like me to be?" Her eyes flashed. "Docile, meek, girlish?"

"Now you're confusing me with your father."

"How can you be friends with him?"

Then again, Jack thought, she could still be startlingly immature. "He's a good man, but that doesn't necessarily make him a good father."

As quickly as her anger had sparked, it winked out. "Fuck." But now her voice had softened. "I hate this life, Jack, really, it sucks beyond belief."

"How can I make it better?"

She kissed him tenderly on the cheek. "If only." Then she downed the last of her White Russian with such force the ice cubes clacked against her front teeth. "One day it'll get better, or it won't, right?"

She began to slide out of the banquette.

Against his better judgment, he said, "So how are you doing?"

Alli paused. "About as well as you."

It was a smart answer, Jack thought, or else it was a smart-aleck answer. Maybe, knowing Alli, it was both. "That would have made Emma laugh." Emma, who had been Alli's roommate, best friend, confidante, and closest ally against Alli's parents. "Remember the time I came to watch you in a relay race? You were the anchor, remember?"

"I remember."

"She let me sit next to her and though she didn't say a word I could see how proud of you she was. She didn't get to her feet, she didn't applaud like everyone else when you pulled away and won."

Alli was quiet for some time as if lost in the past. "That night when I came back from celebrating, the room was dark and I thought she was asleep. I went into the bathroom and undressed as quietly as I could. As I got into bed I saw there was a small box lying on the blanket. I moved it into a bar of light slanting through the window. Inside was a leaping silver cat on a chain.

"As I held it up, she said, 'It's a cheetah, the fastest fucking animal on four legs,' and turned over and went to sleep." Alli stood up. "I'll never stop missing her and neither will you."

He watched her walk away, but he was seeing Emma. Alli was right, he would never stop missing the daughter who he'd allowed to drift away from him, who'd called him right before she crashed her car into a tree and died on the spot. Although, improbably, there had been times afterward when she'd appeared to him, even talked to him.

Which opened up four possibilities: His extreme guilt had caused him to conjure her up from the depths of his unconscious, as the shrink he'd consulted suggested; he was insane; his dyslexic brain was playing tricks on him; or the incorporeal part of Emma had survived her physical death. Any one of those scenarios filled him with dread, but not for the same reasons. He wanted to believe that there was more to reality than life and death, which were, after all, man-made concepts. He wanted to believe that Emma still existed in some form. To him that was the definition of faith: to believe in something that science was unable to explain. When Emma had been killed he'd lost whatever faith he might have had; when she returned to him he'd regained it.

Alli and her escort had been swallowed up by the lobby, and he was alone in the bar. The hush of a mausoleum wrapped itself about the room. The lamps glimmered like shale in a riverbed. The snow tap-tap-tapped feebly against the windowpane, a starved beggar wanting in. He'd only taken a couple of sips of the cloying White Russian, and he pushed it away now. Catching the waiter between catnaps, he ordered a single-malt whisky with water on the side. Then he pulled out the slip of paper with Lloyd Berns's itinerary in Ukraine and concentrated on reading it.

Jack's dyslexia caused his brain to work thousands of times faster than what was considered normal. He could not understand, at least not easily, anything that wasn't in three dimensions, which meant that he could solve a Rubik's Cube in about ninety seconds, but writing, which was two-dimensional, was an arduous task. He had to decipher it as if it were a foreign language or a code. He'd been taught to master his disability by a minister who'd sheltered him after he'd run away from his father, who had constantly beaten him for being unable to learn at school. It was only later, as an adult, that he had discovered that his dyslexia could be a devastating asset in deconstructing crime scenes and crawling inside asocial and psychotic minds.

He was running down the list of unfamiliar city and street names when he heard someone order a vodka in a voice as sharp as it was familiar. Glancing up from his task, he saw a young blonde in a black dress and high heels, perched on one of the bar stools. Her hair was pulled back from her face in a ponytail that reached to the hollow between her shoulder blades. Though that hairstyle was most often used by women with thin hair, this was not the case with the blonde, whose hair was as thick as it was lustrous. Her large, slightly uptilted eyes were the mineral color of carnelian. She had wide lips that might have been sensual had they not been down-turned in a distinctly unattractive scowl.

She was sitting beside another woman of approximately the same age, with dark hair and eyes, dressed in a flashy dress of hunter-green, which was so short most of her thighs were pearled by the light. When the blonde spoke again, Jack racked his brain as to where he'd heard that voice before.

The blonde tossed her head. "So I said, 'I'll see you in hell.'"

And Jack knew hers was the female voice from the room below him.

"Then I threw the lamp in his face and the bulb burned his cheek."

The brunette laughed. "Fucker got off easy."

"You bet," the blonde with the carnelian eyes said. "If I see him again I swear I'll kick his balls into the other side of Red Square."

"Well, honey, here's your chance," her companion snickered.

The blonde turned toward the entrance and so did Jack. He saw a large, bearlike man with dark hair, oiled like an American gangster from the thirties. There was a ruddy burn on his cheek, no doubt from the lightbulb. He wore one of those gaudy silk suits that only Russians think are fashionable, a chunky gold watch, and an even chunkier gold pinkie ring. He held himself like Tony Soprano coming in heavy to a Mafia sit-down. Even Jack, who didn't know him from a hole in the wall, wanted to kick his balls into the other side of Red Square.

The blonde swiveled around to face her lover, or ex-lover, who, as he came toward them, was leering at her. Jack could see, if no one else in the bar could, that there was going to be serious trouble. He wished he'd left with Alli, because he had no desire to get involved in a fight that was none of his business. On the other hand, as the Soprano wannabe moved, Jack glimpsed the butt of a 9mm pistol in a chamois shoulder holster in his left armpit. He edged to the end of the banquette and turned halfway outward, giving him a clear field to get to his feet quickly if the need arose.

The man sauntered up to where the blonde and her girlfriend sat. The blonde was swinging her left leg as if in time to unheard music. Jack could see her smiling, but the smile seemed wicked, deadly even. The man, cocksure and armed to the teeth, appeared oblivious to the bloodlust in her heart, or possibly he felt invulnerable meeting with her in this public space. After all, what would she dare do to him that he—or his 9mm—couldn't handle?

He was about to say something to her when, with an upswing, she buried the toe of her high-heeled shoe in his groin. He grimaced, making a face not that different from his leer, and bent over almost double. Because he was on the man's left side, Jack could see what the blonde couldn't: Her lover reached for the 9mm.

Jack was out of the banquette. He took two long strides to the bar and brought the edge of one hand down on the man's hairy wrist. The gun clattered to the floor, the waiter jumped back, and the bartender signaled for security.

The blonde's lover lunged clumsily past Jack, the fingers of his right hand grabbing the woman's throat, throttling her. She gave a soft gurgle, like an infant at the breast. Jack punched the man in the throat, and that was the end of him or, more accurately, the fight in him. By that time, two of the hotel's security team had arrived. One of them dragged the ex-lover away while the other picked up the 9mm with his bare hand. He seemed unconcerned with leaving his fingerprints. Obviously, they did things differently in Moscow, Jack thought, wondering fleetingly what the Russian crime scene unit was called. This thought took his mind off the murderous look the blonde's ex-lover shot him as he was dragged away.

"Are you all right?" Jack said to the blonde, whose hands tentatively fingered her throat.

"Yes, thank you."

He nodded, about to move away, when she added: "My name is Annika, and this is Jelena. We were about to go clubbing. Why don't you join us?"

"It's been a long day and I was just on my way up to my room."

"Please. I'd like to repay your kindness." She gestured at the empty stool beside her. "The least I can offer is a drink."

Jack really wanted to get back to his room and prepare for the assignment he'd been given, but it would be rude to refuse. "One drink."

She nodded. "One drink only. Then, if you like, I myself will escort you to the elevators. I'm staying here, too."

"Yeah, I couldn't help hearing the shouting match earlier this evening."

She made a face. "Jelena said that everyone in the hotel must've heard Ivan and me."

He sat on the indicated stool and nodded after the departing figures. "I guess we'll need to give statements to the police."

At this, both women laughed. "I see you haven't been in Moscow
long," Jelena said. "The police are too busy shaking down businesses
and taking American dollars from people like Annika's boyfriend—"

"Ex-boyfriend," Annika interjected. "*Very* ex."

"Whatever." Jelena shrugged. She spoke English with no foreign
intonation at all, unlike Annika, whose English was freighted with a
heavy Russian accent.

"I see you have no trouble talking to strangers."

"If I did, I'd be out of a job," Jelena said. "I handle the hotel's
overseas bookings."

Annika signaled the bartender. "What will you have . . ."

"Jack," he said. "Jack McClure."

Annika nodded. "What's your poison, Jack McClure?"

"Single malt," Jack said to the bartender. "Oban, please."

"Right away, sir." The bartender went to retrieve the bottle of
scotch.

"I hope you have a strong constitution, Mr. McClure."

"Shut up, Jelena." Annika shot her friend a daggered look before
turning back to Jack. "Ignore her. She's developed a lurid imagination from reading too many American thrillers."

"I have no idea what the two of you are talking about."

The bartender set his drink in front of him, then backed away as
if they were all radiating plutonium.

"You might as well tell him, Annika."

"That seems like a good idea," he said, taking a sip of his Oban.

Annika sighed. "My ex—his name is Ivan Gurov—is a minor—
and I stress *minor*—member of a Russian *grupperovka*." Her eyes locked
on his. "You know this word?"

Jack did. "He's part of the Moscow mafia."

"He's a fucking criminal," Jelena said with more emotion than she'd shown up until now.

"As you can see, Jack, Jelena didn't approve of my involvement with Ivan."

"He's a bloodsucker," Jelena said, clearly warming to the topic. "He's trash washed up in the gutter, who'd as soon slit your throat as look twice at you. He gets more pleasure out of blood than vodka, that's for sure."

"My friend needs to learn to have an opinion," Annika said with a good-natured laugh.

"And you need to watch out behind you," Jelena said soberly. "You, too, Mr. McClure. I saw the look Ivan gave you."

"I take it that means he won't be thrown in jail."

"His friends would see he got out in a heartbeat," Annika said, "which is why the police won't bother pursuing the matter."

"More likely they don't want to wind up in an alley with a bullet in the back of the head," Jelena said. "They have a serious aversion to being taken out with the garbage."

Jack took another sip of his scotch. "Count me in on that group."

"Don't worry," Annika said. "Jelena tends to overstate the case when it comes to Ivan. He's pretty far down the *grupperovka* food chain."

Jelena made a derisive sound. "That doesn't stop him from killing people."

"You don't know that for a fact."

"I hear things, Annika, same as you." She shook her head. "You're so naïve sometimes."

Jack had had about enough Halloween stories for one evening. He had zero interest in seeing Ivan Gurov again, but he didn't have any expectation that he would, especially since by tomorrow morning he'd be in the air, on his way to Ukraine.

He finished his drink and stood up. "Ladies, it's been interesting, but all things considered it's time for me to leave."

"You see what you did, Jelena," Annika pouted, "you've driven away another man." She rose and threw some money on the bar. "I promised to make sure you got to your room."

"That's right," Jelena said with a sardonic edge. "That disgusting pig of yours might be hiding in the elevator."

Jack held up his hands. "Ladies, I like women fighting over me as much as the next guy, but, really, I can find my way upstairs by myself."

ALONE IN the elevator, he still felt Annika's cat's eyes following him, and he wondered whether she or Jelena had been seriously coming on to him. Maybe that was just male ego talking. Then again, it could be that both of them had been flirting with him, which had long been a fantasy of his, one he shared with about a billion other men. One thing was for certain, his brain and theirs had been vibrating on two distinct frequencies. Between the assignment in Ukraine, secret from even the president's staff, and the escalating friction with Sharon, his mind had no room for flirtatious Russian women, especially when one had a mobster for a boyfriend, ex- or otherwise.

He got off at the top floor, nodded to the Secret Service personnel on duty, and entered his room. Something about his talk with Carson in the stairwell bothered him. Why had he dismissed his bodyguards before he brought up the subject of Jack's assignment? When Jack had queried him, the president had said: "*I trust you, Jack. That's the beginning and the end of it.*"

Did Dennis Paull suspect a mole inside Edward's staff—in the president's own Secret Service detail? If true, it would be a devastating blow to Edward's work guiding the administration. What if his political enemies—who, as he said, were still powerful—knew his every move before he made it? Carson hadn't spoken their names, but Paull had: Miles Benson, the former director of the CIA, a hard-headed, take-no-prisoners war veteran; and Morgan Thomson, the former national security advisor, the last of the credible neocons, bellicose, nervy, with recently revealed ties to several companies manufacturing war materiel. Between them, the two men had almost sixty years of service and networking inside the Beltway, formidable opponents indeed. They could not only stymie the president's agenda, but also undermine his standing in the country. These days, polls were everything. The appearance of failure was all that was needed to send Carson's popularity skidding.

He thought about calling Sharon, but he needed something to calm him. Maybe a hot shower. As he stripped off his clothes and padded into the bathroom, he made a mental note to follow up on his line of reasoning, either with or without Carson's approval.

He turned on the shower, and had to wait for the hot water to come up, but a man's voice arrived before the heat did.

"Toss the entire fucking room."

Jack, listening closely, turned off the water and put his head near the pipe.

"I want to find her secrets, something I can use against her."

Ivan was speaking in Russian, a language Jack had learned while at the ATF because of his work with terrorists. He'd used Rosetta Stone to learn Russian, Arabic, and Farsi, all within an eight-month period. He already had been fluent in Spanish. As long as the foreign language was delivered aurally, his dyslexia allowed him to be an astonishingly quick learner. He was able to see the words, phrases, tenses, and colloquialisms in three dimensions as he heard them, and thus remember them instantly and without need for repetition.

He sat on the edge of the claw-foot tub, bent over, straining now to pick up every word. Clearly, Ivan hadn't been handed over to the police. So much for law and order in Russia.

"I thought you knew this bitch inside and out," another male voice said now.

"Do you know your bitches inside and out?" Ivan said irritably.

"My bitches are *tyolkas*. Young girls in heat are unknowable and, anyway, who the fuck cares? There's tons of new *tyolkas* at Bushfire every night— Hey, what's this?"

"What've you found?"

"Hmm, just a pair of sweaty panties. This bitch is a pig."

"If I know her, she left them there on purpose, just for prying eyes like yours," Ivan said. "Which means we've been looking in the wrong places."

"I already checked under the drawers and behind the toilet tank."

"Too obvious."

"Ah," said the second voice, "let's try the shower drain."

There was an answering grunt, then, a moment later: "Found something—look, a monofilament line tied to the drain, almost invisible in this light."

"What's on the other end of it, Milan Oskovich?" Ivan said in a hushed voice, made slurry by its journey up the pipe.

Jack leaned forward, the better to hear.

There was no sound from below, and for a moment, Jack was afraid the two men had left the bathroom. Then: "It's a necklace," Ivan said.

"A cameo," Milan corrected.

"No wonder she hid it, it must be worth a lot of money, especially on the black market."

From what Jack had seen of Annika's attitude and style, she did not seem the type to wear a cameo.

Apparently, Milan didn't think so either, because he said, "I'm not sure she hid it for its monetary value. Could the cameo be hiding something inside?"

Silence again, and Jack found that his muscles were tensed as if anticipating a blow.

"Fuck!" Milan said. "It's an ID."

"She's FSB." Ivan's voice held a note of incredulity.

Jack knew that the Federalnaya Sluzhba Bezopasnosti, the Federal Security Service or FSB for short, was the successor to the Soviet Union's KGB.

Milan was laughing. "You poor dope—you've been fucking an undercover FSB officer."

"Shut up!"

"You'd better not let Arsov get wind of this."

"I said shut the fuck up!"

Jack knew from his pretrip briefings that Kaolin Arsov was the head of the Izmaylovskaya *grupperovka* in Moscow.

"He'll have your nuts over an open flame."

Jack heard the sound of a brief scuffle, and he imagined the two thugs going at it. Why was he listening, this had nothing to do with him. But at once an image of Annika, blond hair and carnelian eyes, long legs crossed one over the other, flashed across his mind. He heard the silvery peal of her laughter, which morphed into Emma's last appeal: *"Dad, help me!"*

"Calm the fuck down." Milan was panting hard. "You can be sure I'm not going to tell anyone. It's the bitch you have to worry about, not me."

"I know that."

Silence again, then a length of unintelligible whispering. What was Ivan dreaming up, Jack wondered.

"Annika? It's Milan. . . . No, for God's sake, don't hang up. Ivan's been shot. . . . That's right, shot. He's alive, but . . . We're at Bushfire . . . on Tverskaya . . . That's right, near Red Square, just down the block from Nightflight. No, I haven't called anyone else. Ivan said to call . . . You'll come, then? All right, we're around back in the alley."

"Let's go!" Ivan said. "We'll only have a couple of minutes to beat her there."

THREE

THE SNOW had left a moon of dubious value, but the wind had picked up, turning the flakes that had settled into the gutters or at the base of stony walls shooting upward, striking Jack's face like grains of sand. With his hands deep in the pockets of his overcoat and his shoulders hunched against the near-arctic chill, he crossed Red Square on the diagonal, on his way to Bushfire, whose address he got from the leering concierge on his way out.

"Hold onto your wallet, *gospadin*," the concierge had said as he wrote on a slip of paper.

"Just tell me the address," Jack had told him, ignoring the useless paper.

As he'd crossed to the elevator on the top floor, his eyes had met those of Alli, who was leaning against the door to her room, smoking one of the clove cigarettes that were among her new passions.

"Go to bed," he said.

She exhaled a cloud of aromatic smoke. "I will when you do."

He glanced down to where she was looking, jammed the Sig Sauer P250 further down in his waistband.

The elevator door opened. "I won't be long."

"I'll wait up," she said as he stepped in. "You can tell me all about where you went."

The doors closed on her enigmatic smile. Jack shook his head, wondering what it would take to get the murk of her incarceration out of her system. Perhaps she'd never fully overcome what had been done to her; who knows what psychic damage the brilliantly deranged Morgan Herr had inflicted on her? Who knows how deep it went? Not her phalanx of shrinks, who had finally released her into her parents' custody because she either derided or ignored the therapists who had tried to get her to open up about her nightmare experience at Herr's hands. The only thing known for certain was that he hadn't raped her, which was a blessing. But what, exactly, had he done to her? That was the billion-dollar question.

The buildings, flood-lit from below, seemed even more monumental limned against the milk-and-ink sky. The darkness lent the onion domes a fairy-tale aspect that belied the structures' lugubrious history. But, then, as Alli had so rightly pointed out, history was being rewritten here every day. He walked quickly, but not with his head down as most people tend to do in such unpleasant weather. Instead, he was on the lookout for Ivan and Milan, though he was certain they had made it out of the hotel before he'd even had time to dress. More pressingly though, he was looking for Annika, because if he saw her he could cut her off, tell her what he'd overheard, and drag her away from heading into the ambush. But apart from an old babushka, thin and arched as a black alley cat, he saw no one.

Briefly, he asked himself what the hell he was doing. He was here on presidential business, he had a charter flight waiting to take him to Ukraine at Carson's request. It seemed the height of madness to be striding across Red Square in the dead of night toward an ambush between two Russian mafia hit men and an FSB agent. Part of him said that Annika could take care of herself, but another, deeper part— the part that had been permanently scarred by his daughter's death— said that unless he intervened she'd be found dead tomorrow morning with a bullet in the back of her head. If this were America he could phone the police, but as Annika herself had pointed out, this was Russia, and Russia had a very different set of rules that had little or nothing to do with the law. He'd have to get used to this new reality for as long as he remained here.

But, at the moment, there was a deeper issue at work. For him, the present was always infused with the past. What if he hadn't been too busy with a drug bust to listen to Emma when she'd called for his help? Would she still have lost control of her car? Would she have veered off the road and careened into the tree? He would never know, of course, but he could ensure nothing like that happened again. He knew it wasn't his job to save Annika; he scarcely knew her. He knew it was potentially a stupid thing he was trying to do, and yet he couldn't help himself. He knew she was going to die; he could never live with himself if he allowed that to happen.

On the far side of Red Square Jack found the street named Tver-skaya, and at once spotted the club's entrance due to the knot of young people and the lineup of panting *bombila*, the gypsy taxis that cruised Moscow's streets, tying up traffic. They either crawled along, nose to taillight, trolling for fares or, once they had one, hurtling at gut-wrenching speed to their destination. At those times, they were like living bombs, hence their name.

Bypassing this morass, he went around the block, cautiously ap-proaching the alley where Ivan and Milan lay in wait for Annika. He supposed she had been lured here at the thought of finding out more about the workings of the Izmaylovskaya from Ivan as he lay dying. Clearly, she had given up on him otherwise. Perhaps he was too far down in the hierarchy to be of continuing use to her. Having milked him of whatever he had whispered in her ear in the afterglow of sex she was prepared to move on—or, more accurately, upward.

At the head of the alley he drew his Sig and paused, both to allow his eyes to adjust to the gloom and to remain hidden from Ivan and Milan. He needed to pick them out of the murk or, failing that, to figure out where they might have secreted themselves. As his eyes adjusted, his brain began to compose a three-dimensional construct of the alley, complete with doorways, windows, two scarred metal Dumpsters backed against a building wall, piles of trash tied up in plastic bags, and the heavily stained ground itself, strewn with random bits of garbage, used condoms, and wads of dirty tissues in among the small drifts of snow, yellow where it wasn't already crusted with soot.

He'd tuned his ears not only for any sound of the two criminals, but also for the crunch of Annika's high heels, which, he realized now, would do her no good in the slippery alleyway. In fact, they would be a hindrance. He had mapped the entire scene now, had determined that the best and most likely place for Ivan and Milan to strike was the gap between the two Dumpsters. While it was cramped, especially for a man of Ivan's bulk, it had the twin advantages of being in heavy shadow and of being concealed from either end of the alley.

And that was the problem, because now a shadow fell tentatively across the far end of the alley, only to remove itself almost immediately. Jack knew it had to be Annika. For a moment, he considered running around the block in order to get to her before she entered the alley, but then he saw her moving in the uncertain light. She entered the mouth, and for a moment the blaze of light from the street behind her made it impossible to see even her outline, which winked in and out of existence like a ghost.

Jack had no choice now but to enter from his end and hope he got her attention before Ivan and Milan attacked her and he was forced to fire his pistol. As he moved toward the Dumpsters and

Annika, his eyes picked out a length of PVC pipe. It wasn't metal, but it would have to do. He scooped it up, then picked up his pace, waving the white pipe in the air to get Annika's attention. This he did, but it proved the wrong strategy because it both startled her and diverted her attention from Ivan and Milan who, hearing the sound her high heels made as they struck the ground, jumped out from the gap between the Dumpsters.

Jack saw the dull flash of Ivan's 9mm and threw the length of pipe at him. It struck him on the shoulder, and he turned his back on Annika, then squeezed off a shot at his attacker. Jack ducked down and fired off an answering shot. From his position, he saw Annika had one shoe in her hand. She slammed the end of the heel into Milan's head just above his hairline, and with a grunt he reeled back against the brick wall.

Hearing his compatriot's outcry, Ivan squeezed off another shot, possibly to keep Jack in place, then turned back to Annika. He was just leveling the 9mm at her when Jack leapt onto him. When the two men crashed heavily to the pavement, both the Sig and the 9mm clattered into the alley. Annika made a grab for the Sig, but with a herculean effort, Ivan kicked it away from her. The 9mm lay somewhere, hidden in shadow.

Jack drove his fist into Ivan's midsection, but the big man seemed to scarcely feel it. Instead, he grabbed hold of Jack's chin, pushed it upward, exposing his neck. Jack twisted away, and Ivan's fist struck him on the side of his neck. A split instant later and Ivan would have punctured his throat. The man was even bigger at close range, and his rage was palpable. Jack ducked and weaved, got in a punch here and there, but was being methodically beaten to a pulp. Out of the corner of his eye, he saw Annika make a run at Ivan. She hit him without visible effect. He lashed out at her with one massive arm, and she careened backward, crashed to the ground, and Jack knew there would be no more help from her.

In the moment after the swipe when Jack's attention was momentarily diverted, Ivan turned him, had him in a choke hold. Now he was trying to bend him backward. Jack put all his energy to moving forward, crawling with agonized slowness across the width of the alleyway to the shadowed spot where he surmised the Sig had fallen. Hand-to-hand, he was no match for the huge Russian. The handgun was his only hope now.

His breath came in shallow pants, his eyes felt as if they were bulging out of their sockets as Ivan increased the pressure on his windpipe. His mind was whirling, blinding flashes of light interspersed with vast reaches of blackness that threatened to pull him down into their unimaginable depths. The alley canted over, as if about to spill him out onto his ear. He could no longer distinguish up from down, right from left, and so was nearing the end of his ability to keep going. He was drifting, as if leaving one world on his way to another, and he heard her voice, Emma's voice, as he'd heard it several times after her death. Once, he had even seen her glimmering between the trees behind his house, the house at the end of Westmoreland Avenue, his sanctuary, where he'd once lived with Gus, the big, black pawn shop owner, after he'd run away from his abusive father.

"*Dad*," his daughter called. "*Dad, where are you?*"

"Emma . . . ?"

"*Dad, I'm looking for you and I can't see you. Where are you?*"

"I'm here, Emma. . . . Follow my voice. I feel like I'm very close to you."

"*I see you now, Dad.*"

He heard her gasp of dismay.

"*You have to go back . . .* "

"Go back where?"

"*You have to go back, Dad. . . . You're right near the gun. . . .* "

That was when he felt something metallic strike his knee. Scrabbling around with his right hand, he found not the Sig, but Ivan's

9mm. He gripped it, his finger on the trigger. He was right up against the alley wall, and he bent over as hard as he could. Ivan's forehead struck the wall, his grip on Jack's windpipe loosened enough for Jack to turn the 9mm around.

He fired two shots into Ivan's stomach.

THE NEXT thing he knew Annika was dragging him up out from under Ivan's inert bulk.

"Come on!" she said breathlessly, "we've got to get out of here!"

"What?"

"You shot a member of the Izmaylovskaya *grupperovka*."

"Only a minor member, you said." Gasping to fill his burning lungs, half dead, part of him still in that gossamer nowhere he'd drifted to, he was still only half aware of what had happened.

"You think that'll matter to Kaolin Arsov?" Annika's expression was grim. "He can't allow one of his men—any one—to be shot dead without immediate retribution. Like the heads of all the families, his reputation rises and falls on two things: discipline and revenge."

He took her proffered hand, began to stumble down the alley away from the body.

"Drop the gun!" she said. "For God's sake, drop the gun and let's get as far away from here as fast as we can!"

Jack, in awkward turns running and shambling, let go of the handgun, as he'd seen Michael Corleone do so many times in *The Godfather*. He stumbled over a leg, and noticed Milan sprawled facedown, as unmoving as Ivan. Were they both dead, he wondered briefly. Then they were back on the brightly lit street and Annika was hailing a *bombila*, wrenching open the back door, shoving Jack into the interior, and climbing in after him.

"We'll hole up in Jelena's apartment until I can make some calls," she said as she gave the driver an address.

"Emma?"

"Emma?" Annika echoed. "Who is Emma?"

Jack, tears in his eyes, averted his face. He'd almost said "my daughter," but instead replied, "No one."

He cranked down the window and pushed his face out into the night. *Emma, Emma, how I wish I could have saved you.*

"Hey, I'm already freezing my ass off," the driver protested.

But the bracingly cold wind was precisely what Jack needed to clear his head. The adrenalin was still pulsing through him, and he knew it would be some while before the pain Ivan inflicted on him would manifest itself. Meanwhile, there was the current situation to contend with. His brain, coming around, began to work at its usual lightning speed.

He hunched forward. "Forget that address," he shouted to the driver over the harsh whistle of the wind. "Take us to Sheremetyevo."

"The airport?" Annika said. "Why would we want to go there?"

Jack sat back as the *bombila* changed direction, heading for Ring Road. "Like you said, we need to get as far away from that alley as quickly as we can, and that's just what we're going to do."

FOUR

EVERYTHING IS in the process of being lost. That's what Emma's death had taught him. His marriage, too, for that matter. Even at the beginning, in the first ecstatic blossoming, the seeds of loss had been sown, predestined even, looked at in a clear-eyed manner.

These thoughts rolled once again through Jack's mind as he and Annika jounced along in the *bombila*. Once they were outside Ring Road and on their way to Sheremetyevo, Annika dug out her cell phone and made a call, he assumed to her superior at the FSB. However, it quite rapidly became clear that she wasn't getting the response she had expected. After she had accurately described in detail what had happened in the alley behind Bushfire, she was silent, listening intently, her face screwed up in a frown of concentration and, then, frustration. Finally, her voice rose and she began to speak Russian in quick-fire bursts that lost Jack near the beginning. All at once, she cut the conversation short and threw her cell phone onto the floor of the *bombila*.

"What's up?" Jack asked. Annika had said nothing to him after she'd queried him about their destination, not a thank-you for saving her life, nothing. Until the phone call, she had appeared sunk in contemplation without any sign of animation whatsoever, as if she were in the *bombila* by herself. Jack supposed her withdrawal was a reaction to the violence she had endured, the imminent threat to her life, the struggle to survive that required every ounce of energy. It wouldn't be at all out of place for her to be in shock. Assuming so, he had preferred to give her a chance to calm down before he started querying her. Now a new, ominous element had been added to the mix.

"I'll tell you what's up," she said. "We're screwed, totally and indelibly screwed."

"I don't see why. Ivan was a low-echelon thug and you're with the FSB."

She turned her head so sharply he could hear the crack of the vertebrae in her neck. "Where did you hear that?"

"The same place I learned about the ambush. Ivan and Milan were in your room, looking for revenge. They found the cameo you'd hidden in the drain."

"Fuck me!"

"Hiding your ID in a cameo was a mistake. A cameo is not your style at all."

"That cameo was my mother's." She stared out the window for a moment, her expression opaque. When she turned back to him, she said, "The problem isn't Ivan, it's Milan. Ivan knew nothing, which is why I broke it off with him, but he, you know, didn't want to let go."

"You're apparently very accomplished in bed."

She stared at him for a moment with her lambent eyes. This close to her, even in the dim light, he could see silver flecks flare in their mineral color as the *bombila* passed streetlamp after streetlamp.

Apparently deciding not to comment, she said, "It's Milan I was after, and once he discovered who I really was, he set the trap. Of course I took the bait, because it was he who called, because I knew he would be there, that with Ivan out of the way I could start on him."

"They fucked you six ways from Sunday."

She tilted her head. "I don't know that curious idiom, but I'm sure I catch your meaning."

They were on the final approach to the airport, and she bent down and retrieved her cell. "The real problem isn't even Milan, though that's bad enough. Milan was tied to a man named Batchuk. Oriel Jovovich Batchuk is a deputy prime minister, a close confidant of President Yukin's, they go back all the way to St. Petersburg, where they served together in the municipal government. Even in those days, Batchuk did all of Yukin's dirty work. The two developed a remarkably effective modus operandi. Yukin targeted successful businesses in the St. Petersburg area and sent Batchuk out, armed with paperwork that accused the company—its principal owner or its board—of malfeasance, of not being in compliance of arcane laws, whatever. Basically, it didn't matter because the charges were all phony, but the resulting shit storm landed the company or the individuals themselves in court, where judges owned by Yukin handed down decisions favorable to him. Unlike in America, here you can't lodge an appeal, or, more accurately, you can, but there isn't a judge who pays it the slightest attention."

The interior of the *bombila* was lit up in the sodium glare of Sheremetyevo's arc lights. Jack, leaning forward, told the driver where to drop them off.

"Yukin and Batchuk got rich as very young men," Annika continued. "Now both have risen to the ultimate level, and the same MO is being repeated, only on a national scale. Yukin is using Batchuk and the power of the federal courts to retrieve the largest, most lucrative privatized companies by finding arcane accounting discrepancies or fabricating multiple charges of fiduciary malfeasance against the officers and the oligarchs behind them, many of whom had skimmed off profits to pay him and his people. It started with the takeover of Gazprom and has only escalated from there."

"But what is a deputy prime minister doing with a high-level member of the Izmaylovskaya *grupperovka*? He must have every government agency on his payroll."

"Batchuk is far more than a simple deputy prime minister," Annika said. "He's at the head of a shadowy secret service agency that flies so far under anyone's radar it doesn't even have a name, or, at least so far as anyone can ascertain, anything other than a designation: *Trinadtsat*."

"The number thirteen, possibly Directorate Thirteen?"

"*Trinadtsat* is not a part of the FSB, it's over and above FSB and every other secret service agency controlled by the Kremlin." She made a face. "This is why my directorate cannot help me in this situation—and I cannot help you. Everyone above me is paralyzed with fear now that Milan Spiakov is dead. I am, as they say, radioactive. I cannot return to my job or to my normal life, from which I have been summarily expelled."

"I'm sorry, Annika, but I'm in somewhat of the same situation."

She shook her head. "No, no, you are American. Americans always have more options."

Which is why we're at this part of Sheremetyevo now, Jack thought. *It will be far easier for Edward to get me out of Ukraine than it will be from here. Besides, I still have my assignment.*

He could see the private plane Carson had set aside for him. Its cabin lights were on. As Edward promised, the crew was waiting for him. As he directed her to walk with him toward the plane, he said, "I want to get this straight. Thirteen is under Yukin's command alone."

She nodded. "Yukin and Batchuk's, yes. But perhaps *Trinadtsat* is not its name at all. What little is known is speculation, anecdotal, often contradictory, but one thing seems clear: Batchuk stands at the previously unthinkable nexus between an unknown arm of the federal secret service and the *grupperovka*."

"It's as if Yukin is covering all his bases."

Annika shook her head. "Again, I don't understand this idiom."

"I mean he's marshaling all the forces, even those who have traditionally been enemies."

"Yes, that's it exactly. He's presiding over an unholy alliance."

"But why? What purpose does Thirteen have?"

They'd arrived at their destination. Jack, having failed to agree on a price beforehand, was presented with an outrageously inflated fare. That was before Annika spent the next minute and a half berating the driver with a string of colloquial curses, the meanings of which were too obscure for Jack to fathom. However, the driver understood well enough, because Annika came back with a figure one-tenth of the one the driver had first presented. Jack paid and they climbed out of the huffing *bombila*.

"Who knows what Yukin and Batchuk are planning?" she said. "Something sinister, surely."

The night had turned mild. Whatever was left of the snow was either melting or being swept away by a moist southerly wind. A diadem of lights had constructed another sky—low, metallic, artificial, without the stitching of stars in the soft sky high above it.

"Now," she said, looking around, "please tell me why we are here."

He pointed. "You see that plane ahead of us? It's going to get us out of here."

She pulled up short. "Who are you, Mr. McClure?"

"We passed 'Mr. McClure' back in the hotel bar."

Her eyes were full of doubt. "You are someone with his own plane. An American oligarch."

"No, I'm not a businessman," Jack said, urging her to continue on toward the jet and its welcoming mobile stairs. He found it curious that an FSB agent didn't know who he was, that he worked for the President of the United States. "And the plane isn't mine. It belongs to a friend."

"A very rich and powerful friend. So you are his, what—vice president?"

Jack thought that was funny, though in truth there wasn't much to laugh about in their situation. "Let's just say that like Oriel Jovovich Batchuk, I'm a deputy prime minister."

She eyed him even more suspiciously. "America has no prime ministers."

"Well, not yet, anyway."

"YOU REALLY have no idea who I am or who I work for?" Jack said.

"Should I? If you're someone from the international pages of the newspaper you're beyond my field of expertise or even interest."

Having taken turns in the small restroom cleaning up as best they could, Jack and Annika were seated in the private jet as the cockpit crew went through their final checks. The captain had told Jack that he had his instructions, had submitted the flight plan to the airport personnel, and was otherwise ready to take off.

"I was wondering why you were at that hotel at the same time I was."

"Perhaps we're meant to have a passionate affair."

She said this with such an acid tongue Jack could think of no possible response.

"Yes, that's it," she said in the same knife-edged tone of voice. "I've followed you all the way from—where in America are you from, Jack McClure?"

"Washington—the city, not the state."

Annika, having made her point and clearly uninterested in his answer, turned away, stared out the small Perspex window at the airport.

There seemed to be an odd tension between them now, as if in the last several moments they had become antagonists. Jack was an unusually astute judge of character, but he found this woman unreadable, as if she had multiple personalities cycling around her brain clamoring to be heard. In this respect she reminded him of Alli.

At length, she said in a more modulated voice, "My focus is, or at least has been, on infiltrating the Izmaylovskaya *grupperovka*, with an eye toward gathering evidence against Arsov. Now I'm beginning to believe that someone felt threatened by the investigation, that I was set up to be taken out of the picture."

"They could have sent you to Siberia."

She turned back to him. The flecks in her eyes had turned the color of gunmetal. "The sudden outside pressure would have set off alarm bells inside the FSB and thus brought unwanted attention on Thirteen. No, this was a better way to handle me, making me a pariah." Her face was set in a grim mask. "Now I will be hunted, very possibly killed, by my own people."

"At the cost of Milan's death?"

She shrugged. "I'm quite certain there's already another ready to take his place. That's how these things work. Surely, you understand that people like Milan—people like me—get thrown under the wheels from one minute to the next."

Jack nodded. "It happens in my country, too." Then, without waiting to think about it, he said: "You haven't said anything about what happened in the alley." The moment he said it, however, he knew he'd made a mistake.

Annika turned to him, her full lips compressed into a line as thin and distant as the horizon. "What is there to say? Two men died and we're alive. What would you have me do, Jack McClure, break down and sob on your shoulder? Do you feel a need to comfort me? Do I look like I need comfort?"

"You look like you aren't used to comfort." With her friend

Jelena in the hotel bar she had seemed so flirty, *"We were about to go clubbing. Why don't you join us?"* But now she was all titanium and steel. "In fact, you were friendlier when we first met."

He could see that with this comment she had retracted her claws and was now plunged deep in thought. "It's just—" Her voice seemed to fail her and she cleared her throat, unsure for a moment whether to continue. "I'm sorry, but I get my back up when I'm frightened."

She had said this last with her face averted, as if ashamed of any emotion deep enough to crack her outer shell, even if only temporarily. "It's an ugly trait, I know, but I get frightened so infrequently, you see . . ." She had turned back, was laughing softly and much too briefly. She waved a hand as if her words were written on a blackboard, erasable. "I keep asking myself why you came after me. Why would you do that? After all, we're strangers, between us there is no obligation or, rather, there wasn't. Anyway, every time I asked myself this question I came up with the same answer. To you, I'm not a stranger because you must work for an American secret service agency." She glanced around. "Is this a CIA plane?"

"No, it isn't," he said, "and I'm not a Secret Service agent."

Annika regarded him levelly, trying to gauge the truthfulness of his words. "Would you tell me if you were?"

"I would now, yes."

She reached out a hand and he saw how pale it was, how long and tapered the fingers were. Was it a kind of benediction she was giving him or was he the recipient of a mysterious divination? "I believe you," she said, as if she had been able to read something that couldn't be seen, but which she nevertheless had conjured up with her white hand. She sighed then. "There's something else, something underneath, if you know what I mean." Her hands arranged themselves in her lap, crossed one over the other, as if tired from their recent work. "I suppose my prickliness is the result of spending too much time alone. Jelena is right. Damn her, she's almost always right, and isn't shy about bringing up her stellar record as often as possible. Anyway, I'm no good with people, at least not in my private life."

"What about Jelena?"

She gave him a small, wintry smile. "Jelena isn't a friend, she's like a sister or a priest who, despite her sharp tongue, chooses to hear my confession without judging me. And therein lies the other, better reason not to acquire friends. It's not what you do that is your life, it's what others think you've done, or not done, whatever the case. In this way, the truth becomes a lie, and eventually the lie takes on a life of its own, independent of you. Do you see how you lose control of your own life, because without quite knowing how it's happened you've become what other people think you are."

A shaft of light from the headlights of a moving vehicle outside on the tarmac briefly spotlighted Annika's face. She was really quite a striking woman, even when she was in full-bore diesel mode, but more so now when her lips had relaxed into their natural shape and a bit of color had returned to her cheeks.

"Being in the secret service plays a role in that, don't you think?" Jack said. "It erodes your sense of yourself. You become what your handlers want you to be, the lies you need to tell to accomplish your mission become the truth, and soon enough you lose the ability to tell the one from the other, you don't know any other way to act or react."

"You know about this difficulty." Her face clouded over with renewed suspicion. "I thought you said you weren't an agent."

"I'm not, but I know a number of people who are, and they all say the same thing. Well, if they don't admit to it I can see it in how they act."

For the first time since they had met in the bar, she showed a spark of genuine interest. "But in my case, the damage had been done long before I ever came to the FSB."

"Your father?" he guessed.

"A variation on a theme perpetrated over and over on women."
She pulled a cigarette out of the handbag she'd managed to pluck off
the muck of the alley, but then remembering where she was, she
dropped it back into the bag. She frowned. "My brother and I shared
a bedroom, not so very uncommon in this country. From the time I
was twelve, my brother raped me, night after night, with a hunting
knife at my throat. When he was finished, while he was still on me,
while he was still in me, he said, 'If you tell anyone I'll slit your
throat.' And then, to make his threat tangible, he nicked a place on
my body, made me taste my own blood. 'So that you never forget to
hold your tongue,' he said. Every night for eighteen months he cut
me afterward, as if I were an imbecile who couldn't learn."

The turbines moved to a higher pitch, the thrumming and vibration in the cabin becoming more noticeable, but Jack could see that
the movable stairs were still in place. His attention returned to
Annika. There wasn't a hint of self-pity in her voice.

"Where is he now?" Jack said.

"My brother? In hell, I trust. Not that I have the slightest interest
in finding out. I'm not a victim."

She said this last with a good deal of force, almost venom. Not
that Jack could blame her, but in this he suspected she was wrong,
because her brother's words—"*If you tell anyone I'll slit your throat*"—
whispered into her ear night after night had acted like a physician's
evil tincture, poisoning her against keeping anyone close, anyone who
could protect her, who could hurt him or interfere with his heinous
activities. So she kept her own counsel, closed herself off from anyone
who could help her—"*I'll slit your throat*"—so in that sense she had
succumbed to her brother, she was still his victim. Her strength,
which was both prodigious and multifaceted, was all in the hard shell
she had erected to protect the still vulnerable core.

In life, like often cleaves to like. He and Alli had bonded because
they were both Outsiders. He wondered whether he could make a

dent in Annika's armor, and thought it worth a try. "With me, it was my father," he said slowly and deliberately, putting equal weight on each word so that she would pay attention, so that she would understand the gravity of what he was saying. "He beat me because he said I was stupid, because he came home drunk every night, and I suppose because he hated himself and his life. One night, I'd had enough and left."

"Yes, of course, you're male." Annika's tone was resigned rather than bitter, as if she had contemplated this inequity so often it had become banal. "Males can move about at will, can't they, while women, well, where can they go? Even when a situation is atrocious, intolerable, there are only home and family, even though both are toxic, because slavery and death wait out on the street."

She shivered, as if from an intimate memory. Then she turned her head again, abruptly nervous once more. "Shouldn't we have taken off by now?"

At that moment, an aide came down the aisle toward them.

"I'm sorry for the delay, Mr. McClure," he said, "but there's someone who requires a word with you."

These aides of Carson's were always so proper, so formal, Jack thought, or perhaps that was just the way things were with any presidential staff, where deference and protocol were a way of life.

Annika looked alarmed. "Who—?"

"Relax," Jack said as he rose. "Whatever it is, I'll take care of it."

He was heading forward toward the door when Naomi Wilde, the head of Lyn Carson's Secret Service detail, stepped smartly into the cabin.

Damnit, Jack thought, *what the hell is she doing here? Has something happened to the First Lady?*

Wilde was smiling, though in an embarrassed fashion, as if she'd screwed the pooch in some way she couldn't mend. This was odd, because Naomi Wilde was a take-charge agent, a woman who was superbly trained. She had confidence enough for her entire team, but now she had the look of a fish on a riverbank, a woman who finds herself in a situation for which she has no answer or, rather, only one answer, which is not to her liking. She was breathing air when she should be breathing water.

"Sorry about holding you up, Mr. McClure," she said, "but as you'll see I had no choice." She stepped fully into the cabin as if impelled, and someone brushed by her as if she didn't exist or was of no further use.

At once, Jack understood Wilde's state of extreme discomfort. He thought, *Oh, Christ, no*, because he was staring into the grinning face of Alli Carson, the First Daughter.

FIVE

"HI, JACK, surprised to see me?" Alli said as soon as she stepped into the cabin.

Jack was staring at Naomi Wilde, who winced at the look, then resignedly shrugged her shoulders. It was astonishing how Alli could reduce people like Wilde—professional, superbly trained, loyal, and brave—to Silly Putty. This was her particular genius; in the interval after the inauguration and its immediate aftermath, she had learned to use her fragile mental state to get whatever she wanted. Take me out of school to go to Russia? Okay. Let me hang out with Jack instead of you and Mom? All right, honey. Jack could only imagine the conversation between Lyn and her daughter this time. Had she threatened to run away, a mental fugue state, a bout of depression so serious she might spiral down into suicide? All these possible symptoms of what she had been through had been meticulously explained to her by the doctors, psychiatrists, and therapists at Bethesda, the medical facility where presidents and their families were treated.

Obviously, she had absorbed the details, so that she could wield them like weapons on the field of her family battle. Edward had said that she had begun acting out again. God only knew what her real mental state was.

Regaining his composure, Jack stepped in front of Wilde so as to block her view of Annika. The last thing he needed was to answer awkward questions about who she was and why she was here and the fact that she hadn't been vetted.

"What the hell is she doing here?"

Wilde again winced visibly as she said, "She's going with you."

"What? She can't. It's not secure."

"You're preaching to the choir, Mr. McClure."

Just then, Jack's cell phone rang.

"You'd better take the call," Naomi Wilde said. "It's the FLOTUS." She meant the First Lady of the United States.

Jack put his cell to his ear with some trepidation. Alli's expressed preference to be with Jack had caused some friction between him and Lyn Carson. What he expected now was a severe dressing down, culminating in a stern order to send her daughter back with Wilde.

"Hello, Jack." Lyn's voice was cool in his ear.

"Ma'am, if I may, Alli can't come with me," he said. "It's out of the question."

"Good luck with that." Wilde gave a brief nod toward Alli. "I'll wait outside, Mr. McClure. I won't leave until you escort her to the limo or you take off."

"I'm afraid neither of us have a choice, Jack," Lyn Carson said. "Much as I hate to admit it, she's better off with you."

"Edward would never allow—"

"Edward's not here," the First Lady's curt voice cut in. "He's in the air on the way back to the States, he doesn't have to deal with his daughter or her threats to slip her guards and lose herself in the Moscow streets. Can you imagine what a nightmare that would be? And you know better than most why I don't dare keep her under lock and key."

"But Mrs. Carson, you can't expect me to take her now."

"I can and I do. Listen to me, Jack. I know we've had our differences, and maybe I've never told you how much I appreciate everything you've done—and are doing—for my daughter. But tonight I'm asking you to keep her safe. I have important state functions I need to attend over the next week. I don't want to be at any of them, but I have no choice, it's my job now and I have to do it. The same goes for you.

"Need I repeat that Alli has threatened to 'go off the reservation,' as she colorfully puts it. You know her, Jack, she doesn't make idle threats. The American press has been on her like flies ever since the . . . incident at the inauguration; they'll ask too many awkward questions and when she doesn't appear at the functions with me the Internet blogosphere will go ballistic."

Jack turned to see Alli walking down the aisle toward where Annika sat, swiveled around to face her.

"Jack is married. He told you that, didn't he?" she said to Annika.

"The subject never came up," Annika said. "Not that it matters."

"No?" Alli eyed her with one eyebrow arched. "I'd have thought otherwise. You look like you're ready to jump into the sack with the man who's standing closest."

Jack, feeling desperate, said, "Lyn, this is a very bad idea."

"If you have a better one, let's hear it," she said.

"Jump into the sack?" Annika repeated in confusion.

"Fuck," Alli said. "You understand the word 'fuck,' don't you?"

"Okay, okay." Jack felt boxed in by both Alli's impetuosity and her mother's inability to control her. "She stays with me."

"Thank you, Jack. I won't forget this kindness."

"It's hardly a kindness when—" But he was already talking to dead air. Snapping shut the phone he hurried back down the aisle.

Annika smiled placidly into Alli's scowling face and said, "Jack McClure, who is this delightful imp?"

Without hesitation, Jack said, "She's my surrogate daughter."

This sentence, spoken to a person Alli didn't know, had the same effect as Aladdin rubbing the grime off the magician's lamp. The real Alli, or rather the Alli Jack knew in their quiet, private moments together, appeared like a genie with the power to charm whoever laid eyes on her.

"My name's Alli. Jack's my father," Alli said, taking off her midnight blue parka and plopping herself down on the seat across from Annika.

"I'm Annika." She held out a hand, which Alli took briefly.

She looked Annika over critically, analytically, as if she were Anna Wintour interviewing a potential assistant. "But, really, you *are* thinking of him as a fuck puppet, aren't you?"

Annika appeared not to have taken offense at any of Alli's deliberate provocations. Not yet, anyway. "What makes you say that?"

"Look at you, I'd get a nosebleed in those fuck-me pumps. Look how you're dressed with the tops of your boobs popping out, look how you're made up with lips and nails the color of blood. And, my God, you smell like a well-used whorehouse."

"My friend and I were going clubbing," Annika said mildly.

Alli leaned across the aisle and leered at her. "Oh, yeah, that explains it."

"You know, I think this is your problem, not mine," Annika said. "You're acting like a jealous lover."

Alli recoiled as if bitten, which, in a sense, she had been. "What the fuck?"

"Yes, you have the best of both worlds. You have a father who isn't really your father." Annika pressed her advantage in a way that, though not quite cruel, led Jack to believe that in fact she had been stung, or at the very least had been made to feel that she had entered a field of battle. "It's okay to have a crush on this man, isn't it? To have fantasies about him, sexual and otherwise."

"You don't know me at all," Alli said as stiffly as a soldier addresses his superior.

"On the contrary," Annika replied, relentless, "I know you quite well. Unlike Mr. McClure, your real father is a constant shadow looming over you. You prefer to think of him as an impostor, even while you crave his approval and his love."

"Hello, ladies," Jack said, stepping between them, both literally and figuratively, "getting to know one another?"

"Fuck no," Alli said, standing up. "She's a stone-cold psycho."

Jack put his hand on her shoulder. "Sit down, Alli, we have some things to talk about."

"Mr. McClure," Annika said with a certain urgency, "it would be prudent to leave, don't you think?"

"In a moment," Jack said as soothingly as he could. "This situation has to be straightened out before we can take off."

"What situation?" Alli said. "Let's go. I'm ready, the psycho-bitch is ready, what's the problem?"

"You," Jack said. "You're not going with us."

Alli crossed her arms over her breasts. "Oh, but I am."

"Alli, be reasonable—"

"Not my strong suit."

Despite himself Jack allowed his anger to spill over. "Don't play the damaged girl card with me."

"I *am* damaged. You know that better than anyone else."

"You're too smart to be damaged in the way your doctors and your parents fear." Jack stared her down; someone had to be the alpha dog, otherwise things would remain out of control. "You know it and I know it, so let's cut the bullshit. You know the rules. Whatever mind games you play with other people you don't play with me."

She broke off the staring contest and gazed down at the floor.

"I'm dying back in that hotel room, Jack." Her voice had shrunk to the size of a grain of sand. "I can't go back. Please, I'm begging you."

"Where I'm going is too dangerous—"

"Not too dangerous to take the psycho-bitch, is it?" she said acidly.

"Apples and oranges," Jack said sternly. "Alli, set your mind to it, you're going back. I can't let anything bad happen to you."

She rose again, facing him, her face imploring. "But, don't you get it, if I stay one more night in that hotel room something bad *will* happen to me. I'm not kidding, no bullshit."

Jack hesitated, which was when Annika made a tactical mistake.

"Surely you don't believe her, Mr. McClure," she said. "You're not seriously considering letting her stay on board."

Alli remained silent, which was the smartest thing she could have done. In fact, thinking about it afterward, Jack suspected that she had played him and Annika perfectly. She knew how to get what she wanted in all kinds of weather, the heavier the better. At the moment, however, he was otherwise occupied. He knew her well, better than her parents and certainly better than her doctors, whom she delighted in tricking. The desperation in her eyes was genuine. He'd seen it before when he'd rescued her from the house where Morgan Herr had kept her imprisoned.

That look—the desperation—was utterly naked, unbridled, elemental, a world unto itself, and as such it had the ability to stop time, or, in a less fanciful description, to make the past manifest itself in the present. With that look she and Jack were hurtled back in time to the moment when he'd rescued her, when danger was as palpable a presence as a hand on the throat or the plucking of a sleeve from out of a nighttime crowd. There was an understanding between them that at that moment nothing was safe, nothing was certain, that all around them lay peril and the gaping unknown. There is no more powerful situation in which to forge true intimacy, a bond that cannot, or perhaps more accurately will not, be broken.

Which was why Jack now turned to the waiting aide and said, "Close the door and let's get under way."

Alli didn't look at Annika, she didn't gloat as she might well have done. Instead, she kissed Jack chastely on the cheek and murmured, "Thank you," in his ear, before returning to her seat and strapping herself in.

"Don't make me regret what I've done," he said in return, but in truth part of him was already regretting it. He was ready to ignore his promise to the First Lady. Even as they began to taxi out onto the runway he felt the urge to call the aide over, tell him to stop the plane. As he took a seat, he told himself that Wilde must have already departed in the limo, but whether this thought was a form of consolation in order to lessen the burden of guilt that was already beginning to weigh on him or an actual fact he never found out because he quite deliberately kept himself from looking out the window to see if, in fact, the limo had left and, with it, his other option. He'd made his choice, now he'd have to live with it.

SIX

"WHAT'S UP with you?" Jack said.

"What's up with the psycho-bitch?"

"Please don't call her that."

"I'll stop calling her a psycho-bitch when she stops acting like one," Alli said. "Which will be never."

Jack had taken Alli to the rear of the aircraft as soon as it had taken off and reached cruising altitude.

"Jack, what is she doing here? I mean, who is she, anyway?"

Jack glanced over her head, checking to see that Annika was still in her seat. "She and I got into some trouble, which is why she's here. She can't go back to Moscow, to her old life."

"You mean she fucked up her life, now she's going to fuck up yours."

"It's not that simple, Alli."

"Okay, then explain it to me."

"The less you know about this, the better, believe me."

"Now you sound like my father."

"Low blow," Jack said, and they both laughed at the same time. "Still," he said, sobering quickly, "two men were killed tonight, two criminals."

"So what's the problem? The police—"

"This is Russia, Alli. The police aren't to be trusted. They're in the pocket of either the Russian mafia or elements of the federal government, both of which are as corrupt as they come." He looked at her. "In any case, one of the criminals was so highly connected that Annika's bosses have turned their backs on her. They may even send people after her."

"To bring her back?"

"To kill her."

"You're kidding, right? Tell me this is a joke—I don't care how sick it is, maybe I deserve it, but just tell me—"

"It's no joke, Alli." He sighed heavily. "Now you know why I didn't want you coming with me."

She was silent for some time. The plane hit an air pocket and dipped unexpectedly, obliging them to hold on for a moment. Jack reached for one of the overhead bins, Alli grabbed on to him, pressing closer.

She bit her lip. "The only reason I fought to come on this boring trip was so I could be near you."

"Alli—"

"Listen to me. I feel safe only when I'm with you. It doesn't matter where you go, Jack. I can't be on my own now—I can't be with my parents or their handlers or the doctors. When I am, I'm filled with a nameless dread, or maybe it isn't so nameless, right? We know him— you and me and Emma."

"Morgan Herr is dead, Alli. You know that."

"And yet I *feel* him close to me, breathing against my neck, whispering horrible things in my ear."

Jack put his arms around her. "What kind of things?"

"Things from my past—people and places, things that only Emma and I knew, and sometimes not even Emma; things I'm deeply ashamed of, things I'd rather not remember, but he won't let me forget. It's like he crawled inside my head and somehow, I don't know how, he's still there, living and breathing, whispering to me, whispering . . ."

Her last words dissolved into racking sobs. She pushed her face into his chest and he rubbed her neck in order to soothe her and, in another sense, soothe himself because he felt her pain almost as if it was his own, a twin, two melancholy trains running along the same track, which led to Emma, perhaps only a memory of her, perhaps not; best friend to one, daughter to the other. But part of him wasn't sympathetic at all. He sensed that a good deal of her persistent anxiety stemmed from pushing down those very incidents in her past, because the more she turned away from them the more they tore at her, exacerbating her anxiety, stoking her fear. For the moment, at least, it was easier for her to believe that Morgan Herr was instigating those thoughts, rather than admit to herself that it was her own mind struggling to work through the most emotionally devastating days and nights of her past.

"I wish Emma were here," she said in her soft little girl's voice.

Jack stroked her hair absently. "Me, too."

"Sometimes I can't believe how much I miss her."

Alli said it, but it might just as well have been Jack. "She's in our memory, Alli, which is what makes memory so precious." He detached himself from her so that he could look her in the eye, to confirm to her, if she didn't already know, that they were traveling along the same track. "It's this same memory that holds your dark days— Emma's, too, for that matter, as well as mine—and I think you can figure out for yourself that it's all one, the dark days and the bright, shining ones. Of course we both want to remember Emma, and we do, but for you the cost of holding your dark days at bay has become too great. If you push them away then you risk losing Emma as well."

"It can't work that way—"

"But it does, Alli. Whatever's happened to you is a part of you; you can wish it hadn't happened, but you can't deny that it did."

"But every time I think about the dark days I break out into a cold sweat, I start to shake, and I hear a screaming inside myself I can't silence, and then I'm sure I'm losing my mind, and the fear starts to build until I can't stand it anymore, and I think . . ."

True to her word, she had started shaking, tiny beads of sweat appearing at her hairline. Jack held her close again. "I know what you think, honey, but you're never going to act on that thought. You understand that, don't you? You're not going to kill yourself, there's far too much life inside you."

He waited until he felt her nod wordlessly against him before going on. "Whatever happened to you, you're still who you always were. Morgan Herr didn't have the power to take that away from you. In fact, it was in those dark days that you found your own courage, you found out who you are."

"But he programmed me. I did what he wanted me to do."

She looked up at him, a little girl again, stripped of her tough young woman's armor, her smart mouth, her arrow-swift rejoinders learned in a culture that grew its children into adults before their time, a culture that moved far too swiftly, becoming fixated on the glossy surface of things. He saw her as her father never would, an unspeakable tragedy that Jack, a man who had lost his only child, was struck by more deeply than most.

"No one knows the future," he said, "we all accept that, but we don't really know the past very well, either. We know only what happened to us, not what happened to those around us. We have no idea, for instance, how what they did or didn't do affected us. Once you accept that we're aware of only a sliver of what happened, you can see how nothing is simply how we remember it. We create our own past, our own history, it's all fractured, pieced together, and yet this is who we become, imperfect but human."

"WE'LL BE landing inside of twenty minutes." Annika smiled into Jack's face. "I've made this flight before, a number of times."

"Then you know Ukraine."

"Intimately." She turned, looked back at Alli's sleeping form. "For a young girl—"

"She's twenty-two."

"She can't be just seven years younger than I am," Annika said. "She looks sixteen."

"Alli has Graves' disease. It screws around with the pituitary gland." He pointed to the side of his neck. "Her growth process was compromised when she was a teenager."

Annika showed some surprise, or perhaps it was pity, it was difficult to say with her, a woman trained to be guarded even when she didn't have to be.

Then she shrugged. "Well, no matter. I will be leaving you as soon as we set down."

"I don't think that's a good idea," Jack said.

She raised an eyebrow. "No? Why not?"

"You said yourself that the FSB might be sending people after you."

"I can take care of myself," she said stiffly.

"Of that I have no doubt." Jack pursed his lips in thought. "On the other hand, you'll be easier to track down if you're on your own."

Annika tossed her head, dismissing his words. "I have many friends in Ukraine."

"Friends or colleagues?" His pause was deliberate. "Ex-colleagues now. And if Batchuk is as powerful as you say, if he's even half as vengeful as most Russians in high places, he'll have compromised some, if not all, of your contacts."

In the ensuing silence, both became aware that the aircraft was slowly losing altitude. Annika had been right on the money as to the length of the flight.

A range of emotions passed across her face like clouds brushed by a freshening wind. She seemed to be digesting his words, or possibly considering the range of her next moves. "Do you have an alternative to suggest," she said slowly, "or are you simply stating a fact?"

"I'm doing both." Jack led her to glance at Alli again. "Look, maybe her coming aboard is a godsend for us."

Annika appeared on the verge of laughing in his face. "How could that possibly be?"

"We enter Ukraine as a family: mother, father, daughter. That will throw your FSB pals off the scent, at least for a while."

"Really?" Annika cocked her head to one side. "And what passports are we going to use, Mr. McClure?"

"I hadn't considered that."

"No, I thought not." Annika nodded. "But that's all right. I've been working out a plan while you and the girl were huddled together in the back. Assuming we're flying to Kiev . . ."

"We are."

"At least something's gone right tonight. I know someone there." She held up her hands, palms outward. "Don't worry, he's not an ex-colleague, he's someone I unearthed on my own, the head of the airport immigration staff, who's always in need of money to feed his gambling habit. You have money, I take it."

"Don't leave home without it."

"Dollars, not, God forbid, rubles, which don't do anyone any good, not even us Russians?"

Jack nodded.

"All right, then." She pulled out her cell phone. "Let me get to work. Once my greedy friend escorts us past Immigration, there's someone else I know who can forge us documents so we can become your mythical family and move about the city. Names?"

Jack thought a moment. "Mr. and Mrs. Charles. I'm Nicholas, you're Nora."

"Nora." Annika wrinkled up her nose. "I don't think I like this name."

"Would you prefer Brandi, or maybe Tiffany?"

"Nora it is," Annika said, already dialing. "And the girl?"

"Emma," Jack said without thinking, because in this instance thinking would be fatal; thinking would point out all the flaws in this insane plan, just as it would put into glaring headlines the terrible risks he'd chosen to take the moment he'd decided to try and protect Annika from Ivan and Milan.

They took their seats and strapped in as the Fasten Seatbelt sign came on. Annika was chattering away on her cell, which meant that she had at least been able to contact her immigration official. What if he hadn't been on duty, or was on vacation—though who in Ukraine took vacations at this time of the year?—or, worst of all, wasn't answering his phone? But another, more benign outcome seemed to be taking place, so for the moment Jack sat back and tried to look at the situation from all angles, as he worked on thinking his way out of this jam.

His first option, once they were on the ground, was to call Edward, but he didn't know whether that was the smartest option or the stupidest. The very last thing he wanted to do was to involve the President of the United States in what could turn out to be a major international incident. Relations with President Yukin were fragile enough as it was. Carson had spent the better part of this past week trying to undo the damage his predecessor had inflicted on U.S.-Russian relations over the past eight years. So in a clearheaded moment Jack decided that the man who could help him the most—the most powerful man in the free world—was also the most vulnerable and, therefore, off-limits to him.

His next option was to contact Dick Bridges and persuade him to use his clout in the Department of Defense to get him and Alli out of Kiev using a cadre of the clandestine agents from the CIA or the NSA. That plan also had its risks, not the least of which was Carson's own warning not to let Bridges know what Jack's mission was. If Bridges was working for Edward's enemies and Jack told him what was going on, Jack would personally sink Carson's administration before it even got rolling.

The third and last option he'd thought of involved calling Chief Rodney Bennett, his old boss at ATF. The problem there was that Bennett ran a regional office. Jack had no idea whether he had the contacts higher up to trust with this highly flammable information.

Precisely when had this situation become toxic, Jack wondered. When he'd overheard the conversation between Annika and Ivan? When Annika had been accosted by Ivan? When he'd become aware that Ivan and Milan had invaded Annika's room? Each increment of last night was like a tiny glass tile with its own color, shape, and texture, meaningless on its own, but when pieced together they had led him to this fugitive place, where only the unknown awaited.

The aircraft kissed the tarmac with only the slightest of bumps. By this time Annika was on her second call and Jack had come to the glum conclusion that for the moment he was alone in hostile territory with the First Daughter and a Russian Security Service agent he scarcely knew, and both FSB assassins and *grupperovka* liable to play Whac-A-Mole with them if their faces popped up in the wrong place.

THE MAN who came on board with a slim-hipped swagger provided by his position was named Igor Kissin. He was not, as Jack had expected, Annika's contact, but the contact's emissary, a younger facsimile, who was authorized to take Jack's money for the service Annika had been promised.

He glanced at Alli, and for a split instant Jack was terrified he had recognized her from photos in the press directly following the inauguration but then his lidded eyes moved on, tracking past Jack, who he didn't look directly at, not even when he accepted payment. His burning black eyes were only for Annika, who he appeared to devour with his gaze. His high cheekbones and vaguely almond eyes hinted of his Asian ancestry. His skin was dark, glossy as satin, his mouth and jaw cruel and barbarous. Jack had no difficulty imagining him as a Cossack, bearing down on fleeing peasants as he set fire to their crops and houses.

"We should go now," Annika said, after the money had changed hands.

Alli was slipping into her coat when Igor said, "Wait." He had a deep, abrasive voice that rumbled through the cabin like mountain thunder.

They all turned to look at him.

"There are still matters to be resolved."

"What matters?" Jack said.

Igor was still staring at Annika, and when he spoke it was clear he was addressing her: "Administrative matters."

"Dmitri and I have an understanding," Annika said calmly but firmly. "The transaction has been consummated."

"With him," Igor said, "not with me."

"I'm not giving you more money." Jack would have said more but Annika's raised hand stopped him.

"It isn't money Igor wants," she said. "Is it?"

Igor continued his obscene scrutiny of her. "There is the matter of consummation."

Taking a step between them, Jack said, "I won't allow—"

"Stop it!" Annika was looking at him. "Stop it now!" Her voice, though very soft, had about it the unmistakable steel of command.

"Annika—"

She smiled ruefully and, on her way past him, placed her hand briefly against the side of his face, so that he felt burned or marked in some mysterious way. "You're really quite sweet." When she took Igor's hand she was still looking at Jack. "Stay here now, yes? Stay here with the girl. When we return, all will be well."

Then she led Igor back down the aisle to the rear of the aircraft, where they vanished into the restroom.

Alli came up beside him. She looked disheveled, smaller than usual, as if her unhappiness had altered her, or had diminished her presence. Her eyes were red-rimmed from crying, and dark circles had already risen like bruised half-moons beneath them. She glanced up at him. "Jack, you're not actually going to let her bang this sleaze-bucket."

"This is Russia; I can't interfere."

"Jesus," Alli said, "do you believe this psycho-bitch?"

SEVEN

THEIR FIRST view of Kiev in the flickering gold-and-blue dawn light was of wide boulevards, vast circular plazas, monumental buildings guarded by Doric columns or crowned with blue and green cupolas. Golden domes, burning in the first rays of dawn, rose above the rest of this city that straddled the banks of the wide, periwinkle blue Dnieper River. The streetlights were still on. A tepid rain had recently ceased falling, the cobbles of the streets sleek and shining as snakeskin.

Their taxi from the airport dropped them at the Metrograd shopping complex in Bessarabskaya Square, where Annika directed them toward the modern facade of a branch of a restaurant chain. On the way into the city, Annika had assured them that it would be open for breakfast at this early hour. Stretching their legs, Jack and Alli had been surprised and pleased to find the weather here far milder, though more humid, than it had been in Moscow. Alli unzipped her coat and already had it off before they entered the restaurant. She looked different now, with her hair cut short. Not wanting to take chances after the scare with Igor, Jack had insisted she cut her hair before they left the aircraft. In the taxi, he'd told Annika that they needed to find hair dye for her before the day was out.

In the cheerful interior, amid brightly colored balloons and car-toonlike paintings of *dva gusya*, the two geese of the popular folk song that gave the restaurant its name, they sat on café chairs at a blond-wood table and ordered the first food any of them had had in twelve hours.

"We must wait several hours for the documents—the passports—that Gustav is preparing for us."

"Can I sleep here?" Alli said.

Outside the plate-glass windows, the sky was clearing, revealing a cerulean sky as the city stretched, yawned, and came to life around them. The rumble of traffic rose and fell like a drowsing giant peri-odically clearing his throat.

Annika ordered more coffee, drinking it black this time. It steamed like a stoked engine. "Stop looking at me that way," she said.

"What way?" Jack's voice held the rueful tone of voice of a child caught at the cookie jar.

"Like I'm an exhibit at the zoo, or the sex museum."

"Was I doing that? I'm sorry."

"No, you're not."

She was partially right. "I don't—I don't know how you could have done it."

"It's not for you to know."

"That's not an answer."

"It is, but you don't want to acknowledge it." She sipped her coffee as if it weren't scalding. "In any event, we're safely here, just as I promised."

"But the price—"

She put down her half-empty cup. "You want me to be just

the way you imagine, and when I'm not you're disappointed in me."

"In my country women don't do what you just did with Igor."

"Yes, they do, you just don't know about it."

Jack looked down at the smeared remnants of his breakfast. He could hear Alli's calm, even breaths as she slept, and he thought of what he'd told her about the past, that you only knew what happened to you, not to others around you, and even then wasn't everything distorted by the unreliable lens of memory?

"Would you like me to tell you something about this city?" Annika said this in an altogether different tone, as if the last contentious exchange had never happened, or had happened to two other people.

"Yes," he said, grateful to be brought out of his thoughts. "I know nothing about Ukraine besides its difficult history with Russia and the secret naval base in Odessa."

"War," Annika observed, "that's all you men know." She fished a cigarette out of her purse and lit it with a metal lighter, took a first, long inhalation, and let it out slowly and luxuriously.

She regarded him for a moment through the veil of smoke. Then she said, "Kiev, the mother of Slavic cities, was founded by nomads, fifteen centuries ago, if you can believe it. The name is derived from a man, Kyi, a *knyaz*, a prince of the Polans, a tribe of eastern Slavs who, along with his two brothers and a sister, felt this place on the western bank of the Dnieper was an ideal point on the transcontinental trade route, and he was right. Now, of course, the city spans both banks, but the left bank only came into being in the twentieth century." She blew out another languid cloud of smoke. "That this story is shrouded in myth only makes the current inhabitants all the more certain of their beloved city's origin."

Just then, a pair of police officers entered the restaurant. Annika's hand froze halfway to her mouth, the glowing end of her cigarette releasing its curl of smoke, rising toward the ceiling. Jack didn't think they should stop talking, but just as he was about to open his mouth he realized that his accent was something he should keep to himself right about now. He could see Annika tracking the cops' movements as they crossed to a table and sat down facing each other. They took off their hats, stroked the greasy hair off their low foreheads as if one were the mirror image of the other, and settled themselves to look at menus.

As a waiter arrived at the cops' table to take their order, Jack was acutely aware of how vulnerable he and the women were without identity papers, of how fragile was the line between freedom and incarceration. All it would take was for one or both of the officers to saunter over and ask for their passports, and they would be undone. He felt a cold sweat creep out from under his arms, slide down his spine to rest like a serpent at the small of his back.

Annika had unfrozen and was now sipping at her coffee again. "Don't look over there," she said, smiling. "Stare into my eyes as if you love me. We're a family, remember?"

He did as she asked, but the serpent, restless in its anxiety, kept coiling and uncoiling, creeping him out.

As if sensing this, Annika said, "I have the keys to a nice flat not far from here. An apartment, you Americans say." Her smile broadened as if to help ensure that he would not look away. "From Igor. You see, he isn't all bad."

Jack was aware that he was still judging her decision on the plane. He didn't like that in himself, especially under the current circumstances, but he couldn't seem to help himself.

"It has two bedrooms," she continued, "so the girl can have her privacy."

"That leaves the other bedroom for us."

"Yes," she said, "it does."

A dirty joke told by one of the cops to the other caused both to laugh raucously, and their voices never lowered, reverberating around the restaurant. They rose; they'd come in for coffee and pastry only, it seemed, and had wolfed both down in record time. As they passed through the open door, their voices faded slowly, as if reluctant to relinquish the vigilance of their masters.

"Wake the girl," Annika said, "we should leave."

"The police are still outside, smoking cigarettes and ogling female legs."

"All the better," she said, putting money on the table, "they can ogle my legs."

"I wish you wouldn't call her 'the girl.' She has a name."

Annika gave him a level stare in which he could discern no irony. Nevertheless, she said in a light tone, "So do I, but she feels 'psycho-bitch' fits so much better."

THE COPS, slouched against the wall, did, indeed, ogle Annika's legs as she, Jack, and Alli walked away from them, and she even turned her face to them, presenting them with a warm smile.

"Was that so smart?" Jack muttered.

"Flirting with the police is not a suspicious action." Annika kept their pace up in the face of a brisk wind. "In fact, just the opposite."

Since Jack had no experience in the matter, he made no comment. She took them into a department store, where they all bought a change of clothes, as well as a package of hair dye for Alli. The entire time the women were shopping Jack kept a keen eye out for police officers, but all he saw were glum, overweight shoppers who paid them not the slightest attention.

Twenty minutes on Kiev's crowded streets brought them to a yellow brick building with a trio of cupolas rising from its copper roof like doffed hats.

Annika rang a bell, one of many in four long ranks next to the locked doors. A moment later, they were buzzed into an antechamber, where she was obliged to repeat the process. The dim, cathedral-like vestibule smelled of wet wool and old shoe leather. Their footsteps set up echoes, like protestations for old inequities perpetrated on the souls the building had once harbored.

The agonized groans of the tiny elevator caused Jack to say, "We'll walk down on the way out."

"This way," Annika said, as they went down the dusty fourth-floor corridor, which in better times or at night would be lit by the bare bulbs screwed into cheap plastic sockets bolted into semicircular niches in the walls.

At the far end, they stopped in front of a door on which she rapped twice, then three times, then twice again. Afterward, nothing. The bellicose sounds of a TV show rolled along the hallway like a damp fog.

At length, Jack heard a scratching on the other side of the door, as of a dog or a cat. The door jerked inward and a pair of eyes magnified by wire-rimmed spectacles peered out at them from a long, sallow, emaciated face.

"Hello, Dyadya Gourdjiev."

At the sight of Annika, the old man's face lit up like a neon sign. "My child!" he cried as she flew into his arms. "Too long, my little one, too long!"

"What's going on?" Alli asked. "Lazarus is too old to be her father."

"She called him 'uncle,'" Jack said. "Anyway, I think you mean Methuselah. Lazarus was the beggar Christ supposedly raised from the dead."

"He ought to do it with this guy before he turns to dust," Alli whispered conspiratorially.

Annika made the introductions and asked Dyadya Gourdjiev to speak English because the girl didn't understand Russian.

"Who does?" Dyadya Gourdjiev said with a grave laugh as he welcomed them into his apartment.

Jack supposed he was expecting a broken-down musty mess, typical of old people who live on their own and, with eyesight and attention to detail failing, continue to exist in squalor without ever being aware of it. The apartment smelled of lemon oil and applewood. It held none of the sickly-sweet scent caused by the imminence of death.

True, the apartment itself was old, as was the furniture, which had been built in another age. But all the exposed wood shone, the brass and copper lamps glittered, and the floor gleamed with a new coat of wax. Not a mote of dust emerged from the deep pillows of the sofa as they sat while Dyadya Gourdjiev went into the kitchen to brew tea and set out an enormous tin of homemade cookies, "baked by my girlfriend, who happens to live next door."

He must have been eighty if he was a day, Jack judged, but apart from the peculiar thinness of the old man and a slight stoop to his shoulders, which might just as well have stemmed from his profession rather than time, he exhibited none of the unsteadiness of body or vagueness of mind normally associated with old age.

His voice was still strong and sonorous, and his eyes—easy to examine, enlarged as they were through the twin lenses of his spectacles—twinkled and sparked like the man he must have been fifty years ago. But his skin was so thin that it appeared blue from the ropy veins that were now so close to the surface.

He made a great fuss over Alli, believing, as most people did, that she was much younger than she was. Jack thought it interesting that Alli didn't disabuse him of his mistake. Possibly, he thought, it was out of deference to Dyadya Gourdjiev's extreme age, but it seemed just as likely that she was in need of the coddling the old man provided without hesitation or wanting anything in return. She was not immune to his obvious pleasure in her.

When the tea had been served in glasses set in metal holders with handles, and the cookies nibbled on, at least by Alli, Dyadya

Gourdjiev finally sat in a large leather chair that exuded like perfume the odors of sweet tobacco and lanolin.

"I must say, Annika, you always arrive with fascinating people in tow and under—well, what would one say—remarkable circum-stances." Dyadya Gourdjiev chuckled like a Dutch uncle. "I imagine that's one of the reasons I so look forward to your visits." He leaned forward and patted her hand affectionately. "Which, despite being exhausting, are too few and far between for this old man."

"You're not old," Annika said. "You'll never be old."

"Ah, youth," said Dyadya Gourdjiev, addressing everyone in the room now, "forever flirting with the concept of immortality!" He chuckled again, as if signaling that he forgave Annika her delusion. "The truth is when you get to be my age living becomes a deliberate act of will. Nothing works quite right, the mechanics, the mecha-nisms of the body and the mind so interconnected begin to erode, and yet we go on." He squeezed the hand he'd just caressed. "Because of those who love us and those we love most fiercely. In the end, there's nothing else to life, is there?"

"No, Dyadya Gourdjiev," Annika said with tears in her eyes, "there isn't."

The old man took out a linen handkerchief, newly washed, pressed, and meticulously folded. Like an opthalmologist, he used one corner to soak up each tear before it slid down her cheeks. "Now, little one, tell me what mischief you've got up to this time."

Annika flicked a quick complicit glance Jack's way, possibly to warn him to keep quiet before addressing the old man. "This is one time I think saying nothing is the best option."

For a moment Dyadya Gourdjiev said nothing. While they had chatted, sipping their tea and nibbling on sugar cookies, the light from outside was caught in the sheer lace curtains on either side of the windows, honing their outlines, lending them a substance they oth-erwise would never have. Now that weight gathered in the room so densely time itself seemed to slow to a crawl. Everyone—even Alli, whose attention was apt to wander—was watching Dyadya Gourdjiev for a reaction, as if they were scientists drawn to a volcano they feared would erupt after decades of uninterrupted slumber.

"I don't like the sound of that, little one," he said after a time during which he appeared to be struggling with his response. He pulled out a thick manila packet, which he opened. Tipping it, he slid out three passports. "Now that you're an American, little one, you no longer need a visa to enter Ukraine, but I've provided one in the event you choose to be Russian once again."

"Thank you, Dyadya Gourdjiev."

She leaned forward, gathering up the documents, but as she moved to stuff them back into their manila envelope, the old man put a hand over hers, stopping her.

"You must answer me this, little one: Do you think I'm too old to be of help beyond what I've already provided?"

Annika appeared alarmed. "No, not at all, Dyadya Gourdjiev, it's just that I . . ."

Jack immediately saw his opportunity and took it. "What Annika is trying to say is that I need some help finding someone here and she wasn't sure she should ask you."

Dyadya Gourdjiev took his hand away from Annika's and sat back in his chair. He eyed Jack with a keen appraiser's eye, honed through decades of experience. Slowly, a smile spread across his face and he lifted a forefinger, moving it back and forth through the air in mock admonishment.

"I see what you do, young man, don't think I don't, but—" he poked the air with the finger "—if you're serious, let me hear what you have to say, because, after all, I'm quite certain my Annika wishes only to protect me, though the truth is I've never required her protection before."

"Today is a different day, Dyadya Gourdjiev," she said.

"Hush, child. Let the young man speak his piece and then we'll see if he's come to the right place in Kiev, hmm?"

Jack put his hands together, trying to block out everyone but the old man. He wondered whether what he was about to say was a breach of security, in light of who Annika was and who she had worked for. But that couldn't be helped now; for the moment, all he could do was forge ahead into the dark and see what happened next.

"Six days ago, a man named Lloyd Berns was killed on the island of Capri, off Naples."

"I know where Capri is," Dyadya Gourdjiev said. "I may be a forger but, by God, I'm not a philistine. In fact, it might surprise you to learn that in my youth I was something of a Roman scholar. I spent two weeks on that magnificent island, tracing the latter part of the life of Augustus Caesar." He waved a hand for Jack to continue.

"What's important is that Berns should not have been in Capri at all. He was scheduled to be here in Kiev. In fact, he was here in Kiev until about ten days ago, when he took off unannounced."

"And just who was this Lloyd Berns, young man?"

"He was a senior United States senator."

There ensued the suffocating silence one normally finds only in the deepest recesses of forgotten libraries or long-buried reliquaries.

Dyadya Gourdjiev was staring up at the ceiling in contemplation. "So one would assume that you also are in politics, Mr. McClure."

It was the first time the old man had addressed him by name. "In a manner of speaking," Jack said.

Dyadya Gourdjiev's head came down and his eyes snapped into focus on Jack's expression. "If that is the case," he said slowly and evenly, "why are you here? Why aren't you in Capri?"

"I want to speak to the last person Senator Berns was with before he left Kiev."

"And you need my assistance for this?"

"All I have is a name. Actually, it's only an initial and a surname: K. Rochev."

"Rochev, Rochev." The old man closed his eyes, sat repeating the name as if needing to taste it on his tongue. Then his eyes opened slowly, marking him with a sly, reptilian look. "I knew a Karl Rochev, but I haven't seen him for a very long time."

"He's here in Kiev?" Jack said.

"He may still be." Dyadya Gourdjiev shrugged. "But I have no doubt there are many K. Rochevs in Kiev. It's not, after all, such an uncommon name. Besides, this man may not have been a Kiev resident at all."

There was an intimidating darkness about him now, a gathering of energies, like glue or ink, a hint of what he must have been like in his prime, when his frame was filled out with muscle and he sparked with power. Something about him had changed the moment Jack had mentioned Rochev. The avuncular cheeriness had vanished, replaced by a professional wariness, even though Jack had been brought here by Annika, or possibly even because of that very fact. What was clear, however, was that he knew far more about Karl Rochev than he was letting on. Why was he holding back, Jack asked himself, and if he'd decided on that tack, why hadn't he simply lied outright and said the name was unfamiliar to him?

A possible answer was not long in coming.

"You can trust Mr. McClure, Dyadya Gourdjiev," Annika said. "He saved my life last night and, in doing so, put his own in jeopardy. If you know something about this man Rochev that could help Mr. McClure, please tell us."

Jack noted with interest that she used the plural, *please tell us.*

The old man interlaced his fingers and a frown further creased his forehead. The darkness he had summoned still held about his summit, guardians from a time far distant in every way save in memory.

No one had been able to touch him in the old days and, Jack was certain, no one was going to touch him now. He might be old, but the accretion of power could not be scraped off him even with a jack-hammer.

"I must tell you that I find it most disturbing that a member of the United States Senate was with Karl Rochev."

"If Karl Rochev is the man I'm looking for, which I very much doubt," Jack said. "Besides the fact that there might be dozens of men in Kiev, perhaps as many as a hundred, with that name. I'd find it too much of a coincidence that the first man Annika takes me to in Kiev can identify this K. Rochev."

"I see your point, young man." Dyadya Gourdjiev shook his head slowly. "In fact, I have no doubt that the more you ponder it, the more likely it seems that Karl is the wrong K. Rochev."

"That's right," Jack said.

"There's no reason to disagree with your analysis of the situation, except that in a few moments' time you may change your mind."

Jack shrugged. "I don't see how."

"Of course you don't. Nevertheless, grant me a moment more of your time." Dyadya Gourdjiev's expression had become grave. "Karl Rochev and I grew up together in the same rotting slums of Kiev. We were both beaten many times by the Russian occupiers and, because of those beatings, we made a pact to revenge ourselves. I became a forger, creating identity papers for the underground. Karl was always the man of action. When we were boys, it would be he who led us on forays against Russian soldiers. Even his pranks—before we were old enough to arm ourselves and to shoot to kill—had a sadistic bent to them. In those days, he was not a man who thought hard and long, he was too impatient, too restless. Not surprisingly, he became an assassin in the guerilla war against the Russians. He accepted all the assignments believed to be suicidal, that no one else would willingly take. It wasn't that he was reckless, mind you, I don't believe he had a death wish. The worst you could accuse him of was being myopic. He didn't think about anything beyond the present moment. In other words, possible consequences were of no interest to him. He was assigned to murder a Russian colonel or general, he knew it was right, and he did it. He never failed. Never."

"He was never wounded?" Jack asked.

"That depends," Dyadya Gourdjiev said, "on how you define wounded." He paused to pour himself more tea, though by this time it was room temperature. He appeared not to notice or mind as he sipped it. "Those who didn't know him well, which was almost everyone he worked with, claimed that no, he had never been wounded. And in a sense that was so. Not a scratch, not a drop of blood marred his assassination record. But I, who knew him like a brother, knew that his work had wounded him grievously. One does not become an assassin without serious consequence. You are killed, either in the midst of a mission or in the bathtub having a relaxing soak in the treacherous aftermath. What does it matter, you may ask, either way you're dead. Well, yes, but in the first example you're lying in a foul ditch somewhere far from home, food for the worms. In the second example, you're home safe and sound—at least your body is. It's your mind or, rather, your heart, that has died."

Dyadya Gourdjiev put down his glass, which was now empty, save for the dregs of tea leaves, dark as dried blood. "My old friend Karl Rochev belongs to the second example. It is said, or written about, that every time one murders a human being part of you dies. This is said or written by artists or journeymen who have not killed, and so don't know the truth."

The old man was silent for a time; his eyes slipped slightly out of focus. Sounds rose up from the street and entered the room like sunlight, coagulating on the carpet at their feet.

At last, Dyadya Gourdjiev expelled a deep sigh. "The truth. There is a millipede, I'm told, somewhere in Asia, the Mekong region perhaps, that manufactures cyanide. The truth is this act of killing another human implants just such a creature. With each death, the insect releases more of its poison, until the heart of the assassin withers and dies. In just this way, Karl Rochev became a man without conscience, without a moral compass. Without his heart, he lost interest in distinguishing good from evil."

"So when there was no more need for an underground, when Ukraine freed itself from the Soviets, he became a criminal," Jack said.

"A politician," Dyadya Gourdjiev said. "But then, as we all know, the two are indistinguishable."

EIGHT

"THIS IS why I know Karl is the man you seek." Dyadya Gourdjiev snared a cookie between two fingers free of the crooks and unnatural bends of arthritis. As he contemplated it, he turned it, revealing first the top, then the bottom. "Politicians," he said. "Your senator and Karl, two sides of the same coin, pulled inexorably together even from opposite sides of the world."

The old man gave the cookie to Alli then, taking another, popped it into his mouth whole, crunching on it happily. When he'd swallowed the last crumbs, he continued, "Your senator—what was his name again?"

"Lloyd Berns," Jack offered.

"Yes, your Senator Berns would have had to meet with Karl if he wanted to get anything accomplished in Ukraine." He cocked his head. "Have you any idea why the senator was in Kiev?"

"So far as anyone knows, he was here on a Senate fact-finding mission, but his very last appointment was with K. Rochev," Jack said, "and it wasn't official, which is what caught my attention."

The old man eyed him carefully, listening perhaps for a misstep on Jack's part—if, for instance, Jack had said "what caught our attention," which would have given him the opening to ask who, precisely, Jack worked for. As a lifetime forger, he was not in the habit of asking such questions outright.

"Then it's Karl you want to speak with." He stood and walked across to a hand-rubbed rosewood table with cabriole legs as delicate as a fawn's. For a moment, he rummaged through some papers until he found a much earmarked address book. He didn't look like the kind of man to rely on Outlook. He made two quick phone calls, then turned back to his guests.

"As I suspected, you won't find him at the Verkhovna Rada of Ukraine, our parliament. Likewise, it would avail you nothing to seek him out at home; you'd find only his wife and his mother, though, in truth, there's little to distinguish them." He shook his head. "No, if history is prelude to the present, today being Friday, Karl will be with his current mistress. He will be with her all weekend."

"Do you know her name or where he might be keeping her?" Jack asked.

"As I said, Karl and I haven't been in touch for years. It's a curious thing with longtime compatriots in their old age, they sometimes have a falling out. Ours was quite bitter. He's dead to me. However, all is not lost, Mr. McClure, *if* I can find a certain number." He paged through the book, moistening his forefinger every so often to ease the process. "Ah, here it is. Milla Tamirova." Reaching for a pencil, he wrote a few lines on a scratch pad, ripped off the top sheet and, turning back, handed it to Jack. "Milla Tamirova was Karl's mistress at the time he and I parted ways. I very much doubt that she still is, since he changes girls like other people rotate the tires on their cars. But she might know who his current one is."

"Why would she know that?" Jack asked.

"All of Karl's mistresses came from one stable."

"Why bother paying?" Alli asked. "So far as I can see there seem to be a hundred willing girls for every man in Moscow and I imagine the same's true here."

The old man smiled as he wagged a finger at her. "A clever one here. Of course, there's a reason. The stable mistress trains all the girls in different, er, disciplines."

"Your friend's into fetishes," Alli said without blinking an eye.

"Well, well." For a moment, Dyadya Gourdjiev seemed at a loss for words, or perhaps he was busy reassessing the young woman he'd mistaken for a childlike adolescent. "And what do you know of fetishes, young lady?"

"That there's at least one to satisfy every possible psychological itch."

"Indeed." Dyadya Gourdjiev stood with his hands clasped behind his back. "Karl's into bondage, serious stuff, very unpleasant."

"Not for everyone," Alli said so dryly she drew a sharp look from Annika.

"Clearly not," Jack said, already troubled by Alli's interjections, which illuminated a topic she'd never brought up with him. "If you'll allow me to use the phone, I'll call her right now."

"I don't think that's the best idea," Annika said.

Dyadya Gourdjiev nodded. "I agree. A woman like that is highly likely to be suspicious of a man like you."

"Let me do it," Alli said.

Jack snorted. "Yeah, right." He waved a hand. "Forget that. It's bad enough you're here altogether." He held out the paper the old man had given him. "Annika, you make the call."

Alli snatched the paper before Annika could take it. She stood in front of Jack with her legs planted firmly on the carpet. "Listen to me. This woman will get suspicious of anyone wanting to know where her former lover is now. I mean she might not respond at all or if she does she might give us a bum address or if she gives us the right one she could call him the minute we leave."

"Alli, stop this nonsense right now—"

Dyadya Gourdjiev took a step toward her. "Mr. McClure, what harm is there in allowing Alli to finish her thought?"

"I don't want her involved in this."

The old man shrugged. "It appears to me that she's already involved."

Alli grabbed the ensuing shocked silence by the horns. "Look," she said, excited now, "I call Milla Tamirova—"

"And say what?" Jack asked. "You don't even speak Russian."

"No matter," Dyadya Gourdjiev said. "Milla speaks perfect English." He rubbed two fingers against his thumb. "And why not? English is the language of money."

"I'm going to tell her that I'm his daughter and I need protection." Alli went over to where Dyadya Gourdjiev stood, as if seeking protection from Jack's further protests. "*That's* why I need to find him."

She picked up the phone.

"I'VE SLAVED your cell phone to mine," Jack said. "So just press the Two button if you get into trouble."

"I'm not going to get into trouble," Alli said. "I can take care of myself."

He knew that wasn't an idle threat. One of the things he'd been doing with her was training her in physical combat. She was a quick learner, which was no surprise to him, since she'd been athletic in college. Emma had taken him to see her in several track meets. He'd also taught her how to shoot a pistol; they'd spend an hour twice a week at the ATF firing range in Virginia.

"If you get into trouble," he repeated, "I'm only a floor away." He tapped the butt of the Mauser Dyadya Gourdjiev had given him, along with a box of bullets.

They were on the second floor of Milla Tamirova's building on Andrivyivsky Spusk, a beautiful street filled with markets, steepled churches, and tiered wedding-cake buildings that wound its way up from the lower part of the city, known as Podil, to the upper city. Rochev's former mistress occupied a corner apartment on the third floor. She refused to speak over the phone. In fact, it appeared that she was about to hang up, but once Alli broke down in tears, her voice quavering pathetically, she had agreed to see Alli. When did Alli learn to cry on cue, Jack asked himself as he watched her work over Tamirova like a champion boxer.

"And don't get cocky, okay?"

She stared at him steadily now. "Okay."

As she turned away to sprint up the iron fire stairs, Jack took her elbow and gently turned her back to him. "Alli, are you sure you want to do this? We can find another way—"

"I'm so sure, Jack." Her gaze met his without guile. "Besides, it's already set up."

Then she gave him a quick grin. "You don't want to queer the pooch."

This response caught Jack flat-footed. For the first time since Emma's death, the spark of life had returned to Alli. She was visibly excited about using her skills, being part of something other than the hurt and pain that soaked through her insides. It was at this moment that Jack understood something about her that her entire battery of doctors had missed: What she needed more than anything else was to be drawn outside herself, to be engaged by the world, to be given a challenge, to feel once again her own expertise. Morgan Herr had taken away her sense of control. Jack saw that from the moment she had formed this plan she had set herself on the road to regaining what had been snatched from her, what now mattered most to her.

He nodded to her and smiled. Kissing her cheek, he let her go, watching her scamper up the steps with a newfound energy.

"I hope to God you know what you're doing," Annika said.

Jack's gaze was fixed on the place on the stairs where Alli had vanished. "That makes two of us."

MILLA TAMIROVA opened the door the instant Alli knocked. She must have been waiting at the door. She was another in a long line of Slavic blondes with magnificent bone structure, porcelain skin, cornflower blue eyes, and breasts with no need of being inflated with silicon. She had the kind of feral, predatory face men found irresistible, at least around the bedroom, which meant that she wore her sexuality outside her skin. Alli despised her on sight.

Nevertheless, she smiled winningly as she stood on the threshold, aware that the older woman was scrutinizing her as if she were a frog pinned to a board, its insides exposed for study.

"*Pajalyste chawdeetzye*," Tamirova said, taking an abrupt step back. "Oh, forgive me, I forget that you don't speak Russian. Please come in."

She continued to peer at Alli as she shut the door and led her guest into a tastefully furnished room full of chintz and striped satin fabrics. Heavy drapes half covered the windows, the furniture was large and looked deep enough to get lost in, which, Alli thought, was probably the point.

Tamirova, her painted lips moving softly, said, "I find it odd that a child of Karl's wouldn't speak Russian."

"I was brought up in America," Alli said with an ease that amused her almost as much as lying to her doctors. "It's only recently that I found out my origins—a photo, a name, a date, and a street name. I Googled it and came up with Kiev."

The scrutiny clearly over, Tamirova raised her arm. "Sit down. Please." She spoke English almost as well as Annika, one of many languages, she said, part of her training to be all things to all clients. She wore a long sea green robe of some material that both clung to her slim curves and seemed to foam around her ankles, which were strapped into high-heeled shoes. Who wears high-heeled shoes when they're home, Alli asked herself.

When they were comfortably settled, Milla Tamirova said, "Have you any idea who your mother is?"

"Not a clue," Alli lied without hesitation. She cocked an eyebrow. "You're not my mother, are you?"

"Heavens, no!" Milla Tamirova chuckled deep in her throat. "I've never been pregnant—well, except one time and then, you know . . ."

"Don't you ever think of what that baby would have been like?"

"I wouldn't have been a good mother, I don't have—what do you call it in English—?"

"A conscience?"

"A maternal instinct." A small smile played around her full lips. "Perhaps someday you'll understand."

"I hope to Christ I never do."

"Is that what they teach you in America? Religion?" She lifted a hand. Her nails were longer than Annika's. "You can't be more than fifteen or sixteen."

"I'm twenty-two."

"Good lord!" Milla Tamirova stared at her without seeming comprehension.

"I need to use the bathroom," Alli said.

"Down the hall, second door on the left," the older woman said as if still in a trance or plunged deep in thought.

Alli made use of the bathroom, flushed the toilet, ran water over her hands and dried them. Then she did a bit of reconnoitering. She saw Milla Tamirova's bedroom directly across the hall, lushly feminine and inviting, except to Alli, who was revolted. Further down, where a second bedroom might logically be, was a closed door. Alli stood in front of it for a moment then, reaching out, turned the faceted glass doorknob. And came upon the dungeon.

Along the left wall was an array of whips and crops of all kinds, made of different materials. Below it, an assortment of manacles linked by chains. In front of this display was a Western saddle, complete with stirrups and cinch, thrown over a custom-made sawhorse. In the center of the right wall was a floor-to-ceiling mirror, on either side three tiers of dummy heads on each of which was a full-head mask of either leather or black latex. Below each one, lined up like little red soldiers, were what she knew were gag balls. The one small window had been blacked out and was covered with thick metal grillwork straight out of *The Count of Monte Cristo*.

This regimental exhibit was unsettling enough, but it was the object in the center of the room that riveted her attention: a massive wooden armchair bolted to the floorboards. On each arm and on each of the front legs was a leather restraint with metal buckle. The sight of the chair, so similar to the one Morgan Herr had tied her into for the better part of a week, gave her a sick feeling in the pit of her stomach.

"Do the tools of my trade interest you?" Milla Tamirova leaned against the open doorway. She had lit a cigarette while Alli was in the bathroom, and now she exhaled a cloud of pale smoke toward the high ceiling.

Alli couldn't take her eyes off the chair, which both repelled and fascinated her. The atmosphere seemed saturated with sweat and sexual musk. "I want you to tell me about this."

"The mechanics of bondage are simplicity itself."

"Forget the mechanics." Alli circled the chair as if in a death spiral. "I want to know about the psychology of it."

Milla Tamirova, smoking slowly, studied her for some time. "It's not about sex, you know."

"It's about power, right?"

"No," the older woman said, "it's about control, gathering it to you and letting it go."

Alli turned to look at her. "Control." She said this as if it were a word that Milla Tamirova had invented, one that was as potentially fascinating as it was inscrutable.

Tamirova nodded. "That's right."

"Give me an example."

Milla Tamirova seemed to flow, rather than walk, into the dungeon. "Take this chair, for instance. The client is strapped in. He begs to be released, I ignore him. He says he'll do whatever I want and I say, 'Anything? Anything at all?' and he nods his head, eager, avid, greedy, even, for the punishment I will mete out."

A loathsome shiver crawled down Alli's spine. She felt as if she were witnessing the beginning of an accident, a car crash, perhaps, the two vehicles heading toward each other at high speed.

"Why?" she said in a whisper. "Why do they do it?"

"Why does anyone do anything? Because it feels good." Milla Tamirova exhaled noisily, like a horse or a dragon. "But that isn't what you're asking, is it?"

"No."

"Mmm." The older woman circled the chair, or perhaps it was Alli she was circling, as if drawn by a desire to see all sides. "These men are very powerful. They spend their days at the top of a pyramid of power, barking out orders to those groveling around them. Strange to say, they find this state of affairs enervating—all these people asking them what to do, waiting to be given orders, drains them of energy. They come to me to be rejuvenated. To them, being in a position where they not only don't have to give orders, but are forced to obey them is sweet release."

She stopped, curled her fingers around the back of the chair. "You understand, don't you, that this is all theater. There's nothing real about it, except as it exists in their minds."

"You hold no malice toward them."

"Quite the opposite, I . . ." Milla Tamirova broke off and, relinquishing her position, walked to where Alli still stood in front of the chair. "What happened to you, child?"

Without taking her eyes from the chair, Alli clamped her lips together.

The older woman took Alli's hand in hers, but as she began to move it toward the chair, Alli jerked it away. Milla Tamirova then reached out and put her own hand on the chair arm.

"Can you do that?"

Alli shook her head.

Milla Tamirova sat in the chair, her hands lying along the arms. "Touch my hand, child. Just my hand."

Alli hesitated.

"Please."

Taking a deep breath, Alli placed her hand over Milla Tamirova's. She began to have trouble breathing.

"I'm going to take my hand away," the older woman said. "Do you understand?"

Alli, her eyes wide with terror, nodded.

Slowly and gently Milla Tamirova slid her hand out from under Alli's. For a moment, Alli's hand remained hovering above the gleaming wood and leather. Then, closing her eyes, shuddering with fear, she let her hand drop. With the touch of the cool wood came a terrifying vision of Morgan Herr's repulsively handsome face, the evil words whispered in her ear.

"Open your eyes. Now look at me." Milla Tamirova smiled. "It's all right, yes? You're here with me. Everything is fine, isn't it?"

Alli barely found the strength to nod.

"Now—" Milla Tamirova rose. "Why don't you sit where I was sitting?"

Alli felt her gorge rising, she was gripped by a kind of panic that throbbed behind her eyes, that threatened to take over her entire be-ing.

"It's important for you to sit in the chair."

"I . . . I can't."

Milla Tamirova engaged Alli's eyes. "As of this moment, you're ruled by your fear. Unless you face it, unless you conquer it, you'll live in fear the rest of your life."

Alli felt paralyzed, completely powerless. It was as if she had once again been stripped of conscious volition.

"And then," the older woman continued, "whoever did this to you, whoever abused you will have won." She smiled. "We can't have that, child, can we?"

"It's too much," Alli said, breathless. "I can't."

"Can't, or won't?" Milla Tamirova surveyed Alli's pale, sweating face. "In here, you're in full control. You're the one who decides whether or not to sit in the chair."

"I want to leave."

Milla Tamirova lifted an arm. "Leave, then." Her smile was rue-ful. "No one can make you do what you don't want to do." Alli was in the doorway when she added, "Without knowing it, you've made the memory sacred, you must understand that."

Alli looked at her without seeing, her eyes watching something that had already happened, someone who was dead now. "The mem-ory is profane."

"And that is precisely where religion fails us." Milla Tamirova's hand seemed to caress the thick arm of the vile chair. "Memory can-not distinguish between the sacred and the profane, because it an-nihilates time. What was profane in the past memory makes sacred in the present." The fingers—long, stark, bloodred at their ends—seemed, like memory itself, to have a life of their own. "This is the only possible explanation for why you hold on to your fear, why you cannot let it go."

"Control," Alli whispered. "That's what I want."

"It's what we all want, child." She paused for a moment, then walked toward Alli.

At that precise moment, as if they were two cars heading toward one another, Alli passed by her so closely she could smell Milla Tamirova's pleasant, earthy scent.

Alli lowered herself into the chair, her arms placed where the older woman's had been moments before. Her heart beat so hard it was almost painful, and she felt as if she were on fire, as if at any moment she would spontaneously combust. But gradually she became aware that what she felt was a seething energy that coincided or perhaps was the aftermath of the cresting of her terror. She felt the chair beneath her buttocks and thighs, her elbows and wrists. She looked at the restraints and they were just pieces of leather and metal, they weren't talismans of voodoo or black magic that forced her back into that week of despair and fear. At least for the time being, that memory became manageable instead of overwhelming. Still, she couldn't look at it for long without feeling blinded or perhaps plunged into a darkness beyond all comprehension.

She got up from the chair because she wanted to, because she could. She still felt her flesh tingling where it had made contact with the wood through her clothes.

"Would you like some tea?" Milla Tamirova asked. Her face held an expression that might have been tenderness or even solace, that Alli couldn't quite digest. "Or perhaps something stronger to celebrate your small victory."

"Where's my father?" Alli said.

"You said you need his protection. From what—or should I say, from whom?"

"Nothing," Alli said. "I lied because I was afraid you wouldn't see me otherwise."

Milla Tamirova frowned. "You were probably right. Not that it matters, I don't think it would be a good idea for you—"

"I want to see him."

"I understand." Milla Tamirova shook her head. "But your father is a very dangerous man, there's no telling how he'll react to the news that he has an illegitimate daughter. Better for you to stay away."

"Okay, you've done your duty, consider me warned."

Milla Tamirova closed the door to the dungeon behind them as they walked out into the hallway. "You just took a first step, that's all it was. Don't mistake it for a silver bullet. You have a long, dark journey ahead of you."

Alli would not meet her penetrating gaze. She wished she understood; she'd rather bite her tongue than admit she didn't.

"I wish you'd take my advice, even though you don't like me."

"That's not true," Alli said, "or, at least, it isn't now."

"I appreciate your candor." Once again, the rueful smile played across Milla Tamirova's lips. "You still won't take my advice, will you?"

Alli shook her head. "Where is he holed up?"

"Excellent choice of words." Milla Tamirova swept them both across the living room to the front door. "That would be his brand-new dacha, just outside the city. Here's the address." She pulled the door open. "Go to him, then. Perhaps you'll be in time for the christening."

NINE

WHY DOES memory persist, Jack asked himself, long after the details of an event or a person become frayed or indistinct? The core of memory remains like a dream or a stain on a photo that is rapidly growing blank.

Karl Rochev's dacha, deep in the thick woodlands past the far boundaries of Kiev's eastern suburbs, blighted with hideous Soviet-era apartment complexes marching to nowhere like the undead, bore the dimensions and hallmarks of an old farmhouse. The wooden frame had been augmented and, in some places, replaced by massive fieldstones, lending it at once a more stolid and more militaristic aspect.

Jack, sitting with Annika and Alli in the car he had rented, could easily imagine the structure the dacha must once have been, because it was eerily similar to his own house. He felt a shiver run through him as the image in memory overlaid the image he stared at now.

The dacha sat at the end of a winding driveway, newly planted with evergreens yet to reach a height sufficient to completely screen the house from the road. It was ablaze with light, every window emitting a cheery butter yellow that held at bay the gloom of the failing afternoon. A cool wind ruffled the feathery tops of the pines, creating a dreamy sound not unlike the surf. Otherwise, the stillness was absolute. Clouds had rolled in with the twilight, obliterating both shadow and birdsong.

Jack rolled the car off the road and into the low overhang of hemlock branches. Rooting around, he found an old toothpick in the glove compartment, which he leaned up against the gearshift. As they got out, he made certain that the vehicle could not be spotted by someone driving by. He had already taken the precaution of switching license plates on the car with one they'd found parked on a suburban side street, so he felt that he'd done all he could to protect them. Then he looked around in all directions. Nothing but close-knit stands of evergreens greeted him. There was not another house in sight, the only vehicle theirs.

As they were about to start down the driveway, Annika said, "This man is dangerous. Maybe we leave the girl with the car."

"Stop calling me 'the girl,'" Alli said sharply.

"Stop calling me 'psycho-bitch,'" Annika responded.

The two women glared at each other for a moment, then Alli turned away and snorted in disgust.

"I'm not leaving Alli alone out here," Jack said. "She comes with us."

Annika shrugged, as if to say, *It's her funeral*, and they went down the driveway, following Jack, who, as much as possible, kept to the lightless areas nearest the line of six-foot evergreens.

Jack signaled them to halt when they were more or less three-quarters of the way to the dacha. Again, he looked around. Apart from a large black crow high up, guarding his nest, the edge of which Jack could just make out, the view was scarcely different than it had been at the driveway's head. The sense of isolation or desolation was acute, the atmosphere as far from the bustle of Kiev as you could get, which, Jack supposed, was the point, especially if you planned to use the dacha as a trysting spot.

It wasn't until they were on the broad veranda that Jack saw that the window on the far left was wide open. He tried the knob of the front door, but found the door locked. Motioning the two women to stay put, he moved along the veranda until he was beside the open window. Deep red curtains rippled like sails, and from inside he heard the sound of a stereo or radio playing Sergey Rachmaninoff's sumptuous *Rhapsody on a Theme of Paganini*, which conjured up images of Karl Rochev and his new mistress on an oversized bed covered with satin sheets.

For a time, he listened for other sounds: voices, footsteps, the clink of crystal and cutlery, but apart from the silky music, there was nothing. Ducking his head, he climbed over the sill. Inside, he drew the Mauser, the thick curtains still concealing him from whoever might be in the room. The scents of wood smoke and a perfume sweet and sharp came to him. With the Mauser slightly raised, he parted the curtain and like a magician appearing on stage found himself in a living room dominated by the kind of massive stone fireplace one found in old hunting lodges. A fire was crackling along merrily, providing a warm glow. Twin sofas faced each other, a low table between. The room was deserted, as was the adjacent dining room. He checked the rather large kitchen with its simple trestle table around which were grouped four ladder-back chairs. To the left was the back door. No one lurked in the small, windowed pantry on the right. In the entryway, a huge spray of dried flowers, garlanded with pinecones, filled a globular ceramic vase on a narrow wooden side table. He walked to the front door, unlocked and opened it for the two women. Then he headed for the stairs to the second floor.

Putting his back against the wall, he ascended without a sound.

The second floor consisted of three rooms and a bath. The first room was set up as an office, the second as a library, wood-paneled, redolent of the two snifters of cognac and a half-smoked Cuban Cohiba in a heavy cut-glass ashtray. Jack stepped into the room, picked up the cigar, and smelled its tip. It had only recently gone out. Back in the hallway, he saw Annika and Alli making their cautious way up the stairs. They looked at him inquiringly and he shook his head, indicated that he was heading toward the third and last room, doubtless the master bedroom suite.

The door was ajar. Rachmaninoff's *Rhapsody* was nearing its end. While he still had the music for sound cover, he crouched down and opened the door with the barrel of the handgun. It swung open on a room almost as large as the living room, but carpeted and somehow cozy. To one side stood a delicate-looking escritoire on which was a photo of a man past middle age, still handsome in a rough-hewn Russian manner, dressed in a hunting jacket, standing in front of the dacha—Karl Rochev. A sitting area with a love seat faced a pair of windows that overlooked the deep forest and the fall of night. Porcelain lamps in the shape of graceful women were lit on either side of the bed, which was even larger than the one Jack had imagined. Not that it mattered.

The sheets were rucked back like foamy surf to reveal the lower sheet, rumpled and stained, on which lay a woman's naked body in an angle of repose so relaxed that, apart from the arrow or spear sticking up straight from her left breast, she might have been asleep.

Behind him, Jack heard the women enter the room. The nude girl was very pretty, angelic, even. With her golden hair and blue eyes she might have been Annika's sister.

"Take Alli out of here," he said to Annika.

"Too late," Annika replied. She went into the en suite bathroom and when she returned said, "No one's in there. Where the hell is Rochev?"

"Maybe he fled after he killed her," Alli said. And when the others turned to look at her, she added, "Isn't that what killers do?"

"Assuming the murder was premeditated," Annika said.

Alli turned ashen, and ran into the bathroom where they heard her retching and vomiting.

"She's right about one thing, Rochev isn't here," Jack said. "The faster we get out of here the better."

"In a moment." Annika knelt on the bed.

"What the hell are you doing?"

She was peering at the murder weapon, which had a slender shaft perhaps three feet or a little more in length. "There's something odd about this thing."

Jack heard the sound of running water, then Alli appeared, looking whey-faced and red-eyed. He held out a sheltering arm and she came to him, putting her arms around him and hugging him tight. Her face was averted from the mess on the bed and she was trembling violently.

"Can we leave?" she said in a small, lost voice.

"Absolutely," Jack said. "Annika, what's odd about that thing, it's an arrow, right?"

"No," she said, touching the end. "See here, there's no fletching." Then, quite shockingly, she grabbed the shaft in both her hands and, with a grunt, pulled it so violently from the victim's chest that for a moment the corpse rose up, its white back arched, until Annika could tear the murderous tip from the flesh.

Backing off the bed, Annika brought the weapon over to him and held aloft its business end, steeped in blood and viscera. "You see, the tip is diamond-shaped. Very unusual, very distinctive."

Alli caught a glimpse of it and began to whimper.

"Let's go," Jack said, heading to the bedroom door.

He heard Annika following him down the stairs. In utter silence, they crossed the entryway. The Rachmaninoff was done, and a vis-

cous, choking silence pervaded the dacha. Alli had begun to hyper-
ventilate, and Jack urged her to take slow, deep breaths. He pulled
open the door and they stepped out onto the veranda. The gathering
wind had brushed away the late-afternoon clouds and now, in the
aftermath of sunset, the sky was a deep pellucid blue. He looked up
into the evergreen, searching for the vigilant crow, but it was gone
from its perch, leaving the nest unprotected.

"Back!" he said. "Back inside the house!"

Floodlights snapped on from the tree line on either side of the
driveway, blinding them. Then came the furious shouts, followed by
gunfire.

TEN

"SBU," ANNIKA shouted over the hail of gunfire as they retreated into the dacha. Ukrainian Security Service. "Shoot first, ask questions afterward. This is their method of operation."

"They were waiting for someone to show up," Jack said, "and we obliged them."

Annika slammed the door shut and locked it. Jack was holding on to Alli, shielding her from the possibility of a bullet that might find its way through the wooden door. Handing a reluctant Alli off to Annika, he ran to the hearth. Grabbing fire tongs, he picked a burning log off the fire, brought it back to the entryway, where he kicked over the side table. The ceramic vase crashed to the floor, spilling its contents. The hail of bullets had ceased, but the shouts of the SBU operatives were growing louder as they ventured nearer the veranda. Jack kicked the dried flowers up against the front door, making sure the pinecones were visible.

Jack dropped the burning log onto the highly flammable pile.

With a whoosh, the pine pitch in the cones ignited and flames exploded. Almost immediately, the paint started to peel off the door, smoldering, catching fire itself. Soon enough, the wood was starting to burn. Jack ripped the curtains off the nearest window and threw them onto the pyre.

"Annika, your lighter," he said. "The fluid."

She nodded, fished in her handbag, and drew out the lighter. Unscrewing a knob on the bottom, she emptied the lighter fluid onto the curtains, then stepped back as the flames roared upward so intensely they began to lick the ceiling. The heat was fierce; paint was peeling and melting everywhere. The side table was afire.

"Let's go!" he said, grabbing Alli's hand and, with Annika on his heels, ran through the house. In the darkened kitchen, he said to Annika, "Take Alli into the pantry and open the window. The high hedge will protect you."

Annika nodded in understanding. "What about you?"

"I'll follow you," he said. He gave Alli a smile of encouragement. "Get going. Now!"

He waited, watching through the open pantry door as Annika opened the window and climbed through, then turned back, helping Alli over the sill. Then he went through the drawers until he found a flashlight and a roll of black electrician's tape. The flashlight was military issue, large and heavy, with a thick waterproof coating. He attached it to the end of a broom handle with a length of the tape. Then he positioned two chairs in front of the door and rested his makeshift contraption on the top slat of the chair backs at a height that he estimated was the one at which he would hold the flashlight if he were coming through the door. He unplugged the toaster, then carefully crept to the door and tied the end of the toaster's cord to the knob, then unlocked and unlatched the door. He crept back to the flashlight, paying out the cord as he went.

He could hear crashes from the front of the dacha. Either the

SBU men were attempting to knock down the fiery front door or trying to gain entrance through the same open window he'd used. Either way, he'd run out of time.

He pulled on the cord attached to the knob. The door opened inward, and as he switched on the flashlight, the beam shot out into the night. Immediately, shots were fired by the men who, as he surmised, were stationed at the rear of the dacha.

He dropped the cord and, scuttling across the kitchen into the pantry, climbed through the open window to the area behind the hedge where Annika and Alli waited, crouched over. Even from behind this screening they could smell the fire and, if they craned their necks, see the lick of flames shooting up into the darkened sky.

Jack led them out through the side of the hedge furthest from the back of the dacha and the men who must already be rushing, guns blazing, through the back door. On this side of the house, there was only a narrow expanse until the tree line rose up, black and solid-seeming as a stone wall. Jack took Alli against his shoulder, ran crouched over across the open space and into the evergreens. Behind him, Annika kept pace.

She was almost into the first pines when a black shape shot across the open space and slammed her to the ground. In the lurid, inconstant light of the growing blaze Jack saw the man claw his way on top of her. He had a handgun out, but Annika batted it away with the edge of one hand. He was bent low over her, panting like a bloodhound. The firelight illuminated his long, lupine face, lips pulled back from teeth clamped tight in his effort to subdue her.

Annika kicked upward, managing to upend his balance for just a moment, but she was unable to overcome his superior weight, and he struck her a hard blow on her cheek. Jack saw droplets of blood, black as tar in the light.

"Stay put," he whispered to Alli.

Her eyes were wide and staring. "Jack!"

He squeezed her shoulder briefly. "No matter what happens, don't leave the protection of the trees."

The SBU goon had drawn his fist back to deliver another heavy blow and Jack was already outside the tree line, moving toward him, when Annika drove the arrow or spear or whatever it was that Karl Rochev had used to murder his mistress deep into the man's chest. His eyes opened wide in shock and pain, his cocked fist went slack. Then Jack was on him, pulling him off Annika, giving her a hand up.

"Come on," he urged as she bent over the body. He saw her pocket his pistol and then her hands were busy with another task. "What the hell are you doing?"

She had one shoe on the man's chest, her hand gripping the shaft of the weapon.

"For God's sake, leave it!"

"No," she said. "We have to take it with us." With a great heave, she ripped the diamond-shaped point out of the flesh and fabric.

Then, regaining the dense shadows of the forest, they were off and running from the burning dacha and its complement of Security Service agents.

IT WAS Jack's dyslexia that allowed him to lead them unerringly through the maze. As they had walked down the driveway on the way in, his mind had formed a three-dimensional map of the area surrounding the dacha. Their car lay just as they had left it, hidden beneath the screen of intertwined hemlock branches. He motioned them down and they sat on their hams while he listened and looked for anything out of the ordinary. It had been the crow's absence that had warned him of people in the area. The bird would never have abandoned guarding its nest had it not been scared away by the surreptitious creep of huge creatures on the ground.

Still, he had them hang back while he moved cautiously forward, crouched and tense, his Mauser at the ready. Moving against the car, he pulled open the rear door, stuck the muzzle of the Mauser inside, but there was nothing to see. Climbing in, he stuck it over the driver's seat back. The car was deserted. Checking the gearshift, he found the toothpick just as he'd left it. He let out a breath. No one had been in the car. Still, he checked the trunk before he signaled Alli and Annika that it was safe to approach.

Gathering Alli to him, he put her into the car. He turned, scanning the woods again as Annika rose and ran toward them. He saw a dim glint in the trees at the same instant a shot spun Annika around. She fell, and Jack, pumping off three shots on the run, grabbed her, hauled her to her feet and, one arm wrapped around her slim waist, brought her back to the car. As he maneuvered her into the backseat he could see the wound, which by its size looked like it had been made by a rifle bullet. He slid behind the wheel as floodlights began to appear through the narrow gaps in the hemlocks and pines.

He turned the ignition, put the car in gear, and sped out onto the road without turning on his headlights. In the rearview mirror he could see figures rapidly receding as he floored the accelerator. Several shots rang out but they either went wide or the car was already out of the range of their guns. He wondered briefly why the sharpshooter who had shot Annika wasn't firing his rifle. Surely, they were still in his range.

"Alli," he said as he drove over a rise, "see how badly Annika is hurt."

Without a word, she climbed over the seat back into the rear, crouching beside Annika, who was lying on the seat.

"It's her arm," Alli said.

Jack risked a glance in the mirror. She hadn't flinched or needed to turn away. Over the rise, he turned on his headlights, looking for a turnoff or a crossroads. The road reared up ahead, devoid of traffic. That wouldn't last long, he knew. At this moment, the SBU was probably radioing their coordinates. Therefore, it was imperative they get off this road and change directions as soon as possible.

"Annika," Jack said, "how are you doing?"

"Nothing broken, I think." Her voice sounded faint or thin, as if she were far from him. "Just a flesh wound."

"Nevertheless, we've got to get the bleeding to stop."

"I know a doctor," she said, "back in Kiev." She gave him the address and the area of the city.

Jack signaled Alli and she scrambled back to the front seat. "The map I got from the rental office is in the glove compartment," he said.

It took her a few minutes to locate the street Annika had named, then she traced a route in reverse to where they were now. Since she'd been the navigator on the way out of the city, she had no difficulty planning out a route.

"There should be a turnoff somewhere in the next quarter mile," she said. "A left turn, then straight for three miles. At the light make a left again and we'll be headed back to the city."

THE KHARKIVSKYI neighborhood of Kiev lay on the south end of the left bank of the Dnieper River. It was a fairly new neighborhood, harking back only to the 1980s. It was filled with lakes and beaches; because of its sandy soil few trees lined the blocks of modern high-rise buildings. Dr. Sosymenko lived in one of these Western-style apartment complexes, virtually indistinguishable from the neighbors with which it stood shoulder to shoulder.

Sosymenko had a ground-floor apartment, which was lucky since Annika was as bloody as a stuck pig. Alli had ripped a sleeve from her shirt to tie off the arm just above the wound, so now it was barely oozing blood, but the left side of Annika's clothes was soaked through.

The doctor opened the door to the sound of the bell. His eyes opened wide at the sight of Annika leaning on Jack's arm. He must have seen her like this before, because after his initial reaction he nodded them in, not wasting time with introductions or asking her what had happened—actually, it was obvious that he was looking at a gunshot wound.

"Let me get her into the surgery," he said in Russian. He was a small, round man, dapperly dressed in a suit and tie despite the late hour. He had a knot of a nose, ruddy cheeks, and a small mouth almost as red. Apart from a fringe of ginger-colored hair above his ears he was bald. He took Annika across a carpeted living room and into a hallway leading to the rear of the apartment. "Make yourselves comfortable," he said over his shoulder. "You understand?"

"I speak Russian," Jack said.

"Good. There's food and drink in the kitchen. Please feel free to help yourselves."

With that, he disappeared with Annika through the door to the surgery, which he closed behind them.

Jack turned to Alli. "Are you okay?"

"I could use a drink."

"What, exactly?" Jack said, heading for the kitchen, which was through an arched doorway off the living room.

"I don't care, vodka, anything," Alli said.

She went off to the bathroom to clean herself up, and when she returned, he had two glasses of iced vodka on the coffee table beside the worn brown tweed sofa in the living room. Shelves on two walls were filled with groups of thick textbooks interspersed with a wide variety of antique clocks, porcelain vases, and copper teakettles. There were paintings on the wall, portraits of an imperious-looking woman who might have been the doctor's late wife, and a young man who was either his son or possibly himself at an earlier age. The heavy curtains were closed against the night and the heat was at sauna level. Jack took off his coat, already sweating, and Alli plopped herself down on the sofa.

"Aren't you hungry?" he asked as he watched her sip the liquor.

"First things first," she said in her best hard-boiled voice.

He came across the carpet, crouched down in front of her, and set her glass on the table. "How are you?"

Her eyes searched his face.

"Doesn't matter, really."

"Why do you say that?"

She shrugged, took a long pull of her vodka, made a face. "God, this is awful, why do they drink this stuff?"

"To take away the pain."

She turned her head for a moment, as if remembering something important. "'I must create my own system, or be enslaved by another man's.'" She recited the lines from a William Blake poem that was Emma's favorite. "'I will not reason and compare; my business is to create.' When I say that, I know she's still here with us, that for some reason she hasn't left both of us. Why is that, Jack? Is it because we still have something to learn from her or that she has something to learn from us?"

"Maybe it's both," he said.

"Have you seen or heard her? You promised you'd tell me if you had."

Jack bit his lip, recalling the sound of his daughter's voice in his head when he was falling into unconsciousness.

Alli, growing anxious at his hesitation, said, "You have, haven't you? Why don't you want to tell me?"

Jack took a long swig of the vodka, feeling the liquid fire all the way down to his stomach, where it began to burn like a furnace. "It's part of the reason Annika's here with us. Two people were trying to kill her. I intervened and was almost knocked out." He wasn't going to tell her that he'd shot Ivan to death. "I heard Emma then, she was calling to me. I felt so close to her, closer than I'd ever been." He took a ragged breath. "I think I was close to dying. Her voice led me back." To that blood-spattered alley behind Bushfire, but he didn't finish the thought.

"Oh, Jack! So she *is* here with us."

"Yes, but in some way I can't pretend to understand."

She let out a long sigh. "She's looking out for us, protecting us."

The vodka fumes were rising up into his esophagus. "I don't think it's wise to count on that."

Alli shook her head as if shaking off his words. "I told you once that growing up I felt like I was in a cage—so many rules and regulations, so many things I, as a fast-rising politician's daughter, was forbidden to do. All I could do was look longingly through the bars and try to imagine what the real world might be like. And then you came along and I began to see what it was, I began to understand that quote from Blake and why it was Emma's favorite."

The door at the end of the hall was opening. Annika emerged with Dr. Sosymenko.

"Jack," Alli said with some urgency because their time alone was coming to an end, "I like it here, outside the cage."

"Even when you're puking your guts up?"

She nodded. "Or when I'm crouched in a forest or tying a tourniquet around what's-her-name's arm. Especially then, because I can breathe without feeling a pain in my chest. I know I'm alive."

Jack, noting that it was the first time she'd referred to Annika as anything other than "the psycho-bitch," rose to welcome Annika back and to thank Dr. Sosymenko. *One step at a time*, he thought.

"The wound was clean," the doctor said as soon as he and his patient entered the living room, "and because of the tourniquet the loss of blood was acceptable. I've cleaned everything, bandaged the wound, and given Annika a shot of antibiotics. She also has some painkillers and a vial of antibiotic tablets she needs to take twice a day for the next ten days, not a day less." He turned to Annika, whose left arm was in a sling. "You understand me?"

She nodded, smiled, and kissed him on the cheek. "Thank you."

He clucked his tongue and, addressing Jack, said, "Please take care of her; she does such a poor job of it herself." .

"I'll do my best," Jack said.

"All right then." Dr. Sosymenko rubbed his hands together briskly.

Annika adjusted her arm in the sling. "There's one other thing."

Dr. Sosymenko produced a wistful smile and said to Jack, "With my dear Annika there is always one more thing. She's like that American detective, what's his name, Columbo. That detective makes me laugh—and he's so clever!"

Annika, unperturbed, said, "I wonder if you'd mind giving us the name and address of your antiques dealer."

"Not at all." The doctor went into the kitchen and rummaged through several drawers, returning with a small notepad. "Are you thinking of becoming a collector of teapots?"

"I found what might be an old Russian weapon. I'd like it identified."

He nodded. "A weapon, of course, what else would appeal to you, my dear?" He chuckled. "In that event you want Bogdan Boyer, a Turk, but his first language is English, which makes things easier. He's a specialist in many things, weapons included." He neatly wrote several lines on the pad with a ballpoint pen. Tearing off the top sheet, he handed it to Annika.

Annika thanked him as she folded away the slip of paper.

"He opens at ten A.M., not a moment before. Tell him you're friends of mine and he won't try to overcharge you."

Annika seemed shocked. "You associate with a dealer who's dishonest?"

"Bogdan isn't dishonest," Dr. Sosymenko corrected punctiliously. "He overcharges when he thinks he can get away with it. That's being a businessman."

———

THE APARTMENT to which Igor had provided the key was in the Vinohrader, an older district, but because of its beautiful park, it had a softer and therefore more welcoming atmosphere than many of the newer districts. The apartment itself had the advantage of being high up, and the windows in the living room overlooked the park. The rooms were not large, but they were adequate for the trio's needs, which at the moment consisted largely of showering and sleeping.

The floorboards creaked beneath his feet, not eerily, as if he were in a haunted house, but in a comforting way, the sound of a fire in a grate, cozily cracking through burning logs. This apartment, furnished comfortably, painted in warm shades of biscuit and toast, felt lived in by a benign presence, as if it belonged to Dyadya Gourdjiev. There were drawings on the wall of sinuous nudes and young faces incongruously filled with wisdom, and a depiction of a Tibetan mandala over one end of a sofa, which stood against the wall opposite the windows. Thick curtains hung to either side of the windows, which were concealed by blinds, directing the street light upward onto the plaster ceiling with its molding of twined acanthus leaves. There didn't seem to be a speck of dust anywhere.

By mutual consent, Alli went into the bathroom first. She had just stepped out of the shower, winding a towel around her small body, wondering dispiritedly if she'd ever look any older than she did now, when Annika walked in.

"I hope I'm not intruding," Annika said.

Alli turned away to wipe the condensation off the mirror over the sink. "Too late for that."

"I feel like I have fifty layers of sweat, dirt, and blood on me. I'm dying for a shower, but Dr. Sosymenko said I can't get the dressing wet."

"Why don't you ask Jack? I'm sure you'd love to get him in the shower with you."

Annika closed the door behind her. "I was wondering if you would help me."

"Me?"

"Yes, Alli. You." Annika kicked off her shoes and started to fumble behind her, trying to find the zipper on her ruined dress. "But first I have to get undressed, which I see is damnably difficult with one hand." She turned around.

Making sure her towel was tucked in tight, Alli unzipped the dress and helped Annika off with it. They had to maneuver the sling off before it was possible, and Alli saw the tears spring into Annika's eyes.

"Are you all right?"

Annika nodded, but a flash of pain had compressed her lips into a thin line.

Alli reached into the shower, turned on the water, then unhooked the other woman's bra. Annika stepped out of her thong and, leaning against the sink, rolled down her ripped and filthy stockings.

She stepped awkwardly over the tub rim while extending her left arm outside the shower curtain. Alli ripped the other sleeve off her ruined shirt, wrapped it around the bandage to help keep it perfectly dry.

Alli tilted the mirror until Annika's reflection appeared, the side of her neck slick and shining, trisected wisps of hair plastered to the porcelain skin. There was something intensely intimate about watching someone soaping their naked body, possibly because they were unaware of your presence, their expression at once relaxed and engrossed, as if in meditation. Even the most well-armored personality seemed vulnerable to scrutiny. The tip of Annika's tongue appeared between her lips, moving slightly as she concentrated on soaping herself with one hand while not slipping.

"So what's your story?" Annika asked so suddenly that Alli startled, as if she'd been caught smoking in bed.

"I don't have a story."

It was an automatic defense that Annika saw through at once. "Bullshit, everyone has a story. Why do you look seven years younger than you are?"

"Graves' disease," Alli said, thinking she'd gotten off easy. "It screws around with growth and development."

"So you'll be stuck looking fifteen all your life?"

Alli was startled again because the question echoed her own thought. "Hell, no. At least I hope not."

"Why not? I think it would be kind of cool. Everyone's aging around you." She laughed. "Just think, when your daughter is fifteen everyone will think you're twins."

For some reason, Alli didn't think that was funny, and said so quite emphatically.

"So now we're back to my original question: What's your story?" Annika turned slightly, putting a further strain on the arm Alli was keeping dry. "It sure as hell isn't your Graves' disease, you got over that years ago."

"How would you know that?"

"You talked about it without hesitation. But there's something else, isn't there? A kind of shadow hanging over you."

"You don't know what you're talking about."

Alli saw Annika's reflection shrug.

"It's always possible, but I doubt it." She tried to rotate her arm. "Hey, you know, I can't wash my back."

Alli cursed, unwound her towel and, drawing aside the curtain, put one foot into the shower. She took the soap Annika offered and used quick, circular motions to lather her back. Annika moved the shower-head up a bit and bent her head forward so some of the spray reached her back. There were a series of vertical scars down her back.

"What're these?" Alli asked.

"Just what they look like," was Annika's laconic answer.

"You're done." Alli put the soap back in its dish and, maintaining the angle of Annika's left arm, stepped out onto the tiles.

A moment later, Annika turned the shower off. The silence in the small room seemed deafening. Alli let go and Annika stepped out. *Wow, she is smokin' hot*, Alli thought a moment before she handed the other woman a towel.

As Alli rewrapped herself, Annika said, "You have a beautiful body."

"I don't."

"Who told you that?"

"I only have to look in the mirror."

"Tell me, have you ever been with a boy?"

"Been with? You mean in the biblical sense? You mean have I been fucked." Alli shook her head. "Christ, no."

"Why Christ? What does Christ have to do with it?"

"It's just an expression."

Annika shook her head. "Americans and their religion." She began to dry her hair. "You know, with your hair short you remind me of Natalie Portman."

Alli scrutinized herself in the mirror. "Come on, what bullshit."

"Why would I lie to you?"

"I can think of several reasons."

"All of them leading to Jack, I suppose."

Alli couldn't help laughing, and then Annika was laughing, too. She saw that Annika was having difficulty drying her back. Without being asked she took part of the other woman's towel and began to soak up the droplets of water.

"Don't worry, they don't hurt anymore."

Nevertheless, Alli continued carefully patting dry Annika's back. The scars set her thinking about cruelty, pain, dissolution, loss, and, inevitably, death. "I had a friend." The words came out almost before she realized it. "Emma. She was Jack's daughter. We were best friends at college. She was killed late last year. She drove her car into a tree."

"That's terrible. You weren't with her?"

Alli shook her head. "I would have been killed, too." She took a breath. "Or maybe if I'd been there I could've saved her."

Annika turned around to face her. "So that's it. You have survivor's guilt."

"I don't know what the fuck I have," Alli said in despair.

"Two days shy of my seventeenth birthday I was out partying with my boyfriend and my best friend. I drove us from party to party, we got drunker and drunker. And then on the way out to the car to go to yet another party I'd suddenly had enough. To this day, I don't know what happened, it was like a switch had been thrown, as if I was seeing us from another perspective, as if I was floating above myself, dispassionately observing. All at once, I realized how stupid it all was, the partying, the drunkenness, vomiting and then drinking again. What was it all for? So I called it a night. My boyfriend agreed, no doubt because he didn't want to miss an opportunity to climb all over me, but my best friend—Yuriy—he was always up for more, always, a real party animal, that's the right phrase, yes?"

Alli felt a terrible foreboding in the pit of her stomach, a dreadful upwelling of dark and dangerous thoughts that contained the poisonous seeds of suicide. "Yes."

"I had the only car, so Yuriy said he'd walk to the next party. I begged him not to but he insisted—it wasn't far and, anyway, he said, the night air would sober him up enough to enjoy getting drunk all over again."

Annika stood in front of the mirror as Alli had done moments before. "That was the last time I saw Yuriy alive. He was hit by a truck running at high speed. They said he was thrown twenty feet in the air. You can imagine what was left of him when he landed." She shook her head. "What would have happened, I have asked myself endlessly, if I hadn't gone back home, if I'd driven us to the next party? Wouldn't Yuriy still be alive?"

"Or your car could have been struck by the truck and all of you killed."

Annika stared hard at herself in the mirror. Then she nodded. When she turned around she saw that Alli was weeping openly, uncontrollably. After a time Alli regained her composure. When she moved to unwrap her shirt sleeve from around the bandage Annika stopped her.

"Don't," she said. "I want to wear it."

ELEVEN

WHY ARE emotions—some of them, the deepest, most important ones—inarticulate or muddy, as if filtered through a fishing net or a sieve? This was the question that Jack asked himself as he sat on the lid of the toilet and, while the shower was running, punched in Sharon's cell number. Midnight in Kiev, which meant it was five P.M. back home in D.C. No answer, which could mean anything, including her looking at his number coming up on her screen and deciding not to answer. That would be like Sharon, the Sharon that once was, the Sharon who over the past weeks had started to reemerge.

He tried the home number with the same result, didn't leave a message. What was there to say? Already the sense of her was fading, as if she were made of celluloid exposed to sunlight. Emma, dead for five months, was clearer to him, so clear, in fact, they seemed to be on either side of a thin pane of glass, transparent but unbreakable.

He turned the phone off, put it on the edge of the sink, and stepped into the shower. He almost groaned aloud. The hot water felt so good on his aching muscles, the soap sluicing off the layers of sweat and grime. There was blood, dark as ink, under his fingernails. Prying out each crescent was like reliving each incident that had happened to him since leaving his hotel in Moscow on his crazy, quixotic mission to save Annika. Since then, he'd been nearly killed, had shot two men, come close to being picked up by the police, found a naked girl murdered in a truly bizarre fashion, been saved by a crow, and narrowly escaped from an SBU stakeout.

He put his face up to the spray, feeling the soft battering like a masseuse's hands. There were a growing number of questions to be answered, such as why were the SBU on stakeout at Karl Rochev's dacha? Had they already been inside and seen the murdered woman? Probably not, otherwise the house would have been crawling with crime scene investigators. So why were they there? Who were they waiting for? Rochev, a confederate, or, chillingly, Jack and Annika? But, if so, how had they known they'd be coming there—the only other person who knew where they were going was Dyadya Gourdjiev. It seemed absurd to suspect him; nevertheless, Jack filed the possibility away. And then there was the mystery of the SBU sharpshooter who had winged Annika: Why hadn't he shot at them as they were driving away?

It wasn't any one of these questions that nagged at him, but all of them, and all the while his unique brain was working on the whole picture as if it were a Rubik's Cube, moving incidents around in order to see them in three dimensions and thus find their proper place in the puzzle he'd been presented.

He turned off the water. Pulling back the curtain, he reached for a towel and saw Emma sitting in the precise same spot where he had sat moments before, trying to call Sharon. Jack pulled the towel around him as if his daughter were still alive.

"*Hi, Dad.*" Emma's voice was soft, almost like the sound the spray of water made shooting out of the showerhead. "*Mom's not home.*"

"Emma." He felt his knees weaken and he lowered himself onto the edge of the tub. "Emma, is it you or are you in my head?" Was this image of Emma merely a manifestation, a more concrete expression of that thought?

Emma, or the image of Emma, crossed one leg over the other. *"You're in a dark place, Dad, so dark I can't see. I don't know whether I can help you here."*

"That's all right, honey." Tears glittered in Jack's eyes. "That's not your job. It's time for you to rest."

"I'll rest," Emma said, *"when I'm dead."*

There was a knock on the door, shifting his attention.

"Jack, I have to pee," Alli said from the other side of the door.

He stood up. "I'll be right out." But when he looked at where his daughter had been sitting a moment before, she was gone like a will-o'-the-wisp.

HE AND Annika hadn't discussed their sleeping arrangements, but crossing the living room he saw no linens or pillows piled on one end of the sofa, so he pushed open the door to the larger of the two bedrooms, which was already half open like a question or an invitation. The room was roughly a square, with windows on two walls, both covered with old-fashioned Venetian blinds. Street light shone through the slats, painting tiers of parallel bars across one upholstered chair, across a faded hook rug, up one side of the bed and across approximately a third of it. The overhead light was off, but one lamp threw a scimitar of light on the empty side of the bed, which was actually two double beds pushed together.

The bedspread and blanket had been rucked back to the foot of the bed. Annika lay beneath the top sheet, turned away from him. She hadn't bothered redoing her hair, which as a consequence lay rather wildly along one cheek, snaking down her neck to cover one shoulder and the shallow indentation between her scapulae. Her injured arm lay on her hip outside the sheet. He couldn't be sure in the dimness but it looked like it was still wrapped with Alli's shirt.

Jack unwound the towel, found some of his new clothes, put on a T-shirt and underpants. The moment he sat on the bed he was overcome with exhaustion. Every muscle in his body, it seemed, was crying out for rest. He climbed under the covers gingerly so as not to wake Annika and, switching off the lamp, put his head on the pillow. The bars of street light seeping through the blind were thrown into prominence, looking like a staircase or a bridge to Emma's world, whatever or wherever that might be.

Slowly he stilled his breathing, but as sometimes happens when one is exhausted, sleep did not immediately come. While his body longed for surcease his brain was on fire problem-solving. He knew from experience not to interfere with this fiendish engine when it was on a roll.

Annika stirred. "Jack?"

"Sorry I woke you," he said softly.

"You sighed."

"I did?"

"Yes, you did," she said. "Why did you sigh?"

"I don't know."

She turned onto her back and he saw her face, freshly washed without a scrap of makeup, illuminated only by the bars of light, and it struck him how utterly desirable she was. She was also beautiful, but that he had seen the first time they'd met at the hotel bar. But what was beauty? Large eyes, full, half-parted lips to be ensnared by, deep cleavage and powerful thighs to catch the breath, but all of these were surface considerations, delicate and ephemeral enough to be invalidated by a nasty comment, a violent temper, or a lack of understanding. Desirability took into account all those things, and more.

"Did you take your antibiotic?" he asked.

"Yes."

"How's your arm?"

"It hurts."

"Time for one of Dr. Sosymenko's magic pills."

She tossed her head. "I don't want a painkiller."

Jack reached for the twist of paper that held the pills. "Stop being a stoic."

"That's not it. I don't want my mind impaired." She stared up at the ceiling.

They lay side by side for some time steeped in a silence that seemed to crackle with silent electricity or a confused magnetism to which he was both attracted and repelled. But perhaps repelled was the wrong word. What was it called when you wanted something you knew or at least suspected was forbidden? It wasn't just Sharon he was thinking of, because even without Emma's doom-laden pronouncement the ship that had been carrying them back to land had hit a violent squall where all hands were in the process of becoming lost. It was also that Annika was a member of an undercover unit of the Russian Federal Police—or had been, at any rate. You could call her a spy without fear of contradiction. Not for the first time since Emma's death, since his marriage had fallen apart, since, especially, Emma had appeared to him, he wondered whether he'd become unhinged, whether he was in the grip of some long-form mental illness in which he was slowly spiraling down toward insanity. How else to explain the situation he now found himself—and Alli!—in? But deep down he also knew that his inability to help his daughter when she needed him the most would color everything he did for the rest of his life. Saving Alli from Morgan Herr had been an attempt to atone for his mortal sin; so, too, his compulsion to save Annika from Ivan and Milan.

"What are you thinking?"

Annika had drawn closer while he'd been plunged into his black thoughts. Her scent was like the beach, slightly salty, redolent of freshly washed dark places. Her heat made the hair on his arms stand on end.

He hesitated only moments. "To be honest, I was thinking about my daughter."

"Emma, yes, Alli told me. I'm sorry for your loss."

Those words, so often repeated by cops all over the world in whatever language, including himself, took on an altogether different aspect when Annika spoke them because there was genuine emotion behind them.

"Thanks."

"Alli seems to miss her almost as much as you do."

"They were very close," Jack said. "In fact, at school they were everything to one another."

"What a tragedy." It was unclear from her tone whether she was talking about the two friends or about herself. Possibly it was both, coming together at the junction of present life and memory. "Jack, let me ask you a question. What if you see a truth no one around you sees? What if everyone, including teachers, friends—former friends!— think you're a liar and a freak?"

"I think that's what happened to Emma," Jack said. "I know it happened to me."

"You're not sure?"

"I'm ashamed to say that was another thing about her I don't know."

"Don't be ashamed. You loved your daughter, there's nothing more important, is there?"

"No, I don't believe there is."

He heard a rustle of the bedsheets, then felt her hand take his. It was cool and slim and dry, and yet it created an electric shock that ran all the way through him.

"Did you feel that?" she whispered. "I felt it."

He turned his head to find that she was looking at him.

"I can't see the color of your eyes," he said. "It's an amber that glows as if with a light inside it."

She moved her head off her pillow and onto his. "Better?"

"Yes."

"Tell me more about Emma."

Jack thought a moment, considered whether he should answer such an intimate question. "She loved music," he said at length, "blues and rock. And she loved the philosopher-poets like Blake."

Annika looked at him questioningly. "And?"

"My knowledge of her only goes so far."

"All this is in your memory." Annika said this with a curious intensity. "You remember her."

"Yes, but more as a dream, really, the way you dream when you're at war, to take yourself away from painful reality."

"Yes, a war," she said, as if she understood him completely. "In war you do what you have to do." But her voice carried a note of insincerity or self-delusion, as if this were a sentence she told herself over and over until, for her, it became the truth. Then, unaccountably, her voice softened. "Nothing is ever what it was, do you recognize this? Every moment immediately dissolves into the next one, seconds and minutes are diluted until your past becomes what you want it to be, as if memory and dreams become so intertwined you can't tell them apart."

"The terrible moments become less so as the present dissolves the past into memory."

"Yes, that's it exactly." She moved even closer to him, her smooth, aromatic skin brushing against his. "This is how we survive. The terror dissolves like dreams when we wake up and go about our daily routine."

"I wish Alli felt that way, but I know she doesn't."

Another silence consumed them. Apart from the hiss of an occasional vehicle passing by outside, there were no street sounds, not even a dog's querulous bark.

After a time, she sighed. "I'm tired."

"Go to sleep, Annika."

"Put your hand on me. I want to feel you, I want to be connected . . ."

Reaching out, he cupped his hand over the tender ridge of her hip, soft as silk. She stirred languorously, and his hand slid to the top of her thigh, hard-muscled and powerful. He could feel his heart beating slowly. It felt good to be near her, their warmth mingling. The soughing of her breath came to him like wind in the trees or distant birds calling to one another.

"There's no time for us now," she whispered, but she might already have been asleep.

TWELVE

"IT's CALLED a *sulitsa* or, less commonly, *dzheridom*," Bogdan Boyer said. He was the antiques dealer Dr. Sosymenko had recommended. His shop was in Gorodetskogo, near the Maidan Metro stop, though they had driven from the apartment, after dying Alli's hair dirty blond and wolfing down a hasty breakfast, because it wasn't conveniently located near the Metro.

Boyer, a small man with the pinched, avid face and busy hands of an inveterate collector, turned the murder weapon over and over under a large magnifying glass with an illuminated fluorescent ring. He sat scrunched on a high stool, much as Bob Cratchit must have sat hunched over his ink-stained desk in his dismal little cell, as Charles Dickens described his tanklike workspace.

"The *sulitsa* is one of what's known collectively as splitting weapons, because—see here, how the point is diamond-shaped, beautifully functional—they were forged to pierce armor," Boyer said, warming to the task Annika had given him.

"This is a missile spear, though it was also used for close-to stabbing, hence it's nickname, 'the lunger.' Weapons like this one and the much larger boar-spear, which had a spade-shaped point, were used by Russian soldiers as far back as 1378 in a fierce battle in Ryazansk along the Vozhe. The Russian Cossacks, the mounted regiments, used these splitting weapons to defeat the invading Tatar army."

He looked up at Annika. "It's interesting, but I can't give you much for it. Apart from a collector here or there and possibly a museum, there's no market for these things. Besides, it's incomplete."

"Incomplete?" Jack said. He was keeping an eye on Alli, who was rummaging through the bowels of the overcrowded, overheated shop. "What do you mean?"

"Typically, *sulitsa* came in threes, packed in an *elaeagnus*, a small cured leather quiver that sat against the left hip." He shook his head. "Without its brothers—or sisters—" He grinned at Annika "—it's worth next to nothing."

"I'm not interested in selling it," Annika said. "I want to know who its owner is."

Boyer frowned. "That might be difficult."

He picked up his phone and made several calls. While he did so, Jack went to find Alli, who had disappeared behind a glass case filled with copper teapots and kettles. He found her examining a sheet of paper—no computer printouts here. The sheet was a written list of shipments that had either gone out over the past several days or were about to be packed and shipped. Beside each item was a name. She pointed wordlessly to the name "M. Magnussen," and his address written just below an item labeled, "Three *sulitsa* (a set) in original *elaeagnus*, ca. 1885, prov. J. Lach." FOR IMMEDIATE DELIVERY was noted in red.

Seeing that he was having difficulty reading the list, Alli beckoned him to bend down so that she could whisper the notation as well as the name and address of the intended recipient in his ear.

Jack had her put the paper back where she'd found it, then he took her hand and led her back to the front of the store.

Boyer was just putting down the receiver. He smiled insincerely. "I'm afraid I've had no luck."

"No matter," Jack said. "Thank you for your time." He took the murder weapon and turned to Annika. "In any event, we're late for your appointment. Dr. Sosymenko has to change your dressing."

Annika played along smoothly, though she must have been as taken by surprise as was Boyer. "Oh, yes, I got so engrossed here I forgot all about it. Come along, darling," she said and, taking Alli's hand, walked out the door with Jack right behind her.

"What was that all about?" she said when they were out on the street.

"In the car," Jack said. "Now!"

He flipped Annika the keys and she slid behind the wheel while he got in beside her and Alli climbed into the backseat.

As she started up and pulled out into traffic, she said, "Do we have a destination or should I drive in circles for a while?"

"Drive in circles," Jack said, staring intently at the off-side mirror.

"That was a joke, Jack."

"I know, but I want to make sure we're not being followed."

"Okay," she said, turning right at the first stoplight, "I give up."

"Alli found a bill of lading in the back of the shop for a set of those *sulitsa* complete in their quiver about to be delivered to a client by the name of M. Magnussen."

Annika nodded. "Which means Boyer was lying to us."

"So who the hell was he calling?" Jack said.

"The SBU or the cops?" Annika ventured.

"Or maybe this Magnussen, who asked him to be on the lookout for anyone coming around with a spare lung sticker."

"You're thinking he's the killer," Alli said, hunched forward, her face between them.

"That's right, you heard Boyer, a single *sulitsa* is worthless. Magnussen ordered a new set of *sulitsa* because he used one from his original set to kill Rochev's mistress."

"But why would anyone use one of those things to commit murder?" Alli asked.

"D'you think the police would know what they're looking at?" Annika made another right. "It would simply confuse them."

"Except," Jack said, "if someone else other than the police found the body. Someone smart enough—"

"—or interested enough," Annika cut in.

"Yes," Jack continued, "to pursue the investigation."

"Which is why," Alli said, "he gave Boyer instructions to call him if anyone came in inquiring about it."

"By the way," Jack interrupted, "see that dark sedan two cars back? We *are* being followed."

Annika proved herself as adept as Jack at flushing tails and getting rid of them, which was, he thought, one advantage of her being trained by the FSB. On the other hand, he couldn't bring to mind another.

She spent the next ten minutes lulling them into thinking they hadn't been made before she tore through a red light, leaving an angry chorus of blaring horns and squealing brakes. She made a right, then an almost immediate left, rolling down an alleyway so narrow the brick walls sheared off their side mirrors. A third of the way along, she turned off the engine, and they sat waiting. Forty seconds later the black sedan sped by the alleyway, and Annika immediately fired up the ignition, and they rolled to the far end of the alley, where she turned left.

"Where are we going?" she asked.

Jack gave her the address. "The collector's named M. Magnussen."

"Doesn't sound Ukrainian," Alli said.

"Or Russian, for that matter," Annika added, as she navigated through Kiev's crowded streets.

"Whatever his nationality," Jack said, "there seems to be a clear line back to my starting point. Senator Berns is killed by a hit-and-run on Capri after having flown from here. The last person he met with was Karl Rochev, whose mistress has been murdered in bizarre fashion with an antique Cossack weapon, and Rochev himself is nowhere to be found. Now it seems clear that the murder weapon belonged to this M. Magnussen."

"Whoever he is," Alli said.

WHOEVER MAGNUSSEN was, he was wealthy. He lived outside the city, in one of the areas so high-priced that not a high-rise or even a block of cement was to be seen. Instead, rolling farmland not unlike that of rural Virginia protected his domicile from the ravages of the modern-day city. The driveway to his estate was a half mile long, snaking through dense stands of pine forest that would have completely obscured the house from the road even if it were only a hundred yards from it. The structure, which stood on a shallow knoll, was modeled after an English manor house with two wings attached to either end of a long central section that faced the visitor with both the square shoulders of a soldier and the chilly contempt of a high-court magistrate.

"This place looks like any minute Keira Knightley is going to draw up to it in a gilded horse-drawn carriage," Alli said.

She wasn't far off the mark, Jack thought. The place was fit for a nineteenth-century baron or viscount, but a dead one. The place was lightless and, as they soon discovered, locked up tighter than a duck's behind.

"Not making sense," Alli said.

Which was also true, Jack thought, unless Magnussen, having gotten the warning call from Boyer, packed up and flew the coop in the hour or so it had taken them to drive out here. It would have taken them far less time if they hadn't been slowed down by the dark-colored sedan tailing them. And then, of course, he understood.

"Magnussen's gone," he said. "The purpose of the tail was not to see where we were going, but to slow us down. Boyer must have gone to the back of his shop the moment we left and seen the bill of lading out of place."

"Nevertheless," Annika said, "it couldn't hurt to take a look around the grounds."

They set off in a more or less northeasterly direction, making a full circle of the property. The dull, clammy morning had been swept away by a freshening wind out of the west, but high up the remnants of the morning's clouds drifted across the sun. They came first to an apple orchard, the orderly rows of gnarled trees looking abandoned and forlorn. Next came a fenced-in section that in the summer would be bursting with rows of pole beans, cabbage, cucumbers, and lettuce, but now lay fallow.

By this time they were behind the manor house, approximately at a forty-five degree angle to its right-hand wing, moving in a counter-clockwise direction. Coming over a rise they spotted a finger of water that turned out to be a small lake or perhaps a large pond, it was difficult to tell from their present position. But what surprised them was a small family cemetery set in the adjoining lowland planted with mature weeping willows, which so craved water. Here were the headstones of perhaps four or five members, Magnussen's forebears all, from what Jack could glean as he scanned them. The letters *M* and *S* were for some reason the easiest for his brain to interpret immediately.

"Father, mother—and a brother, I think," Alli said as she came up beside him. "Each stone has the places they died, along with the dates." She squinted through the watery sunlight. "The father was ten years older, but curiously, though they both died during the same week it wasn't in the same place.

"Who's the smart one?" Alli said. "Daddy could have made the money."

At that moment, they heard Annika calling them. They turned, saw her standing on the opposite rise, waving them on. Jack, wondering what she'd found, strode up the gentle incline, Alli scrambling after him.

"Look." Annika pointed to their left, as soon they gained the modest crest.

Now Jack could confirm what he'd suspected, that Magnussen, spending like a drunken sailor, had had the pond or lake built, because on a spit of land that perfectly bisected the body of limpid water was a stone pergola, a folly in the classic Roman style. But the pergola, per se, wasn't what had caught Annika's attention; rather it was a seated figure drenched in the shadows beneath the pergola's dome. From their viewpoint they could see that the figure, bent slightly forward, forearms on knees, had the aspect of a person deep in contemplation.

They descended the far side of the rise, walked on the damp, mossy ground around the skeletal willows whose branches arched overhead in a tangle of rheumatic fingers. Skirting the edge of the lake they walked out onto the small peninsula. From this angle it was impossible to tell anything about the figure other than it was male.

"Magnussen?" Jack called out. But if Magnussen had flown the coop as Jack had surmised this man wouldn't respond to that name. He didn't, remaining in the same position, plunged deep in thought.

They approached ever more cautiously until Jack, his spine tingling, moved around in front of the figure. He looked hard at the man for a moment, then very quietly said, "Alli, stay where you are, please."

Her curiosity piqued, she felt the urge to take a step forward, but something in Jack's voice stayed her. "Why? What's going on?"

By this time Annika had joined Jack in front of the figure, whose eyes were fixed on the horizon. The man was sitting on a gaily painted wooden Adirondack-style chair. It was difficult to see at first for all the blood and the gaping hole in his chest, but the top of each thigh where it creased with his abdomen was punctured by a *sulitsa*—seemingly identical to the one that had killed the young woman—which some force, terrible in its rage, had driven all the way through muscle and fat so that the points had buried themselves in the wood beneath, pinning the victim in place.

"It's the man in the photo at the dacha,"Annika said. "This is Karl Rochev."

Jack knelt in front of yet another example of man's barbarity. "Which means that our prime suspect in his mistress's murder has himself become a murder victim."

"Not that it matters, we're at a dead end." Annika sighed. "This murder tells us very little."

"On the contrary," Jack said, rising to his feet. "It's proof that Senator Berns's death wasn't accidental. He was murdered because of something Rochev told him, something the senator was about to tell someone else." He reached out to touch one of the shafts, then thought better of it, stuffed his hands in his pockets instead. "This leak is being sealed one hole at a time."

PART TWO

Sleep after toil, port after stormy seas, ease after war,
death after life does greatly please.
—EDMUND SPENSER, 1590

THIRTEEN

RHON FYODOVICH Kirilenko used one thin, reddened hand to shake out a cigarette and put it to his mouth. He slid open the slender box of wooden matches he always carried and lit the match. For an instant the sharp scent of sulfur sucked the oxygen out of his nostrils, causing a little gasp, an involuntary exhalation. Slowly and deliberately, as he did all things large and small, he put the flame to the tip of the cigarette, then took a deep pull on the harsh, black Turkish tobacco and held the smoke in his lungs until his mind ceased its hurrying. A hurrying mind was a disorganized mind, and a disorganized mind made mistakes. Ever since he had become a homicide detective in the FSB, that had been his philosophy; it was so simple, so succinct, so true that in his twenty-odd years running down murderers and serial rapists he'd never had cause to change it even one iota. This was precisely the sort of man Kirilenko was: practical, stolid—his few detractors accused him of being plodding, dull, even pedantic. On the other hand, his benefactors understood that this persona—bland

and gray as the federal building in which they all toiled—was a carefully constructed facade. They saw him as being smart enough to follow orders to the letter, possessed of a quiet rectitude that ruffled no feathers and that allowed him to run his investigations as he saw fit. Everyone knew him as relentless; once he sank his teeth into an investigation he never let go until he'd reached a satisfactory conclusion, which meant a conviction of the perpetrator, or his death, whichever came first. That was about the only thing Kirilenko wasn't fussy about. Incarceration or death, it was all the same to him because these death-wielding perps infuriated him. He looked on them as something other—other than human, less than human, a subspecies inferior even to animals.

Having gotten what he needed from it, Kirilenko blew out the Turkish smoke in a rush, then inhaled slowly and deeply. Behind him he could hear the small, familiar sounds of his men sifting through the charred remains of Karl Rochev's dacha, but he paid them as much mind as he would the noises coming from the seats around him in a sports stadium, inconsequential until proven otherwise.

His attention was focused on the mattress his men had salvaged from the upper floor bedroom just before the staircase collapsed. It lay now among the trees, brushed by dead leaves and blades of unmowed grass. On the bed was the twenty-two-year-old body of Ilenya Makova, Rochev's current mistress or, he corrected himself, his late mistress. She was lying on the charred and smoldering mattress, a ragged hole opened up clear through her. On close inspection he could see that the wound had been inflicted by neither a bullet nor a knife. It looked malevolent, ugly, ancient, as if whatever had killed her had been used to rip her insides out. But whatever that weapon might be, it was nowhere to be found.

His gaze moved now to the digital photo on the screen of the cell phone in his hand. One of the men assigned to this detail by the FSB had had the presence of mind to snap a photo of the three people as they emerged from the front door before the fire started: Ilenya Makova's killers. Sadly for him that man was Mondan Limonev, the one member of the division he worked out of who he despised more than any other. Worse still, he instilled both a sense of fear and distrust in Kirilenko. Limonev, a dead-eyed killer if Kirilenko ever saw one, was just the sort of animal Kirilenko had spent his entire adult life hunting down and bringing to justice. It offended him no end that this creature should be employed by the FSB. In his fantasies he'd discovered many novel ways to exterminate Limonev, none of which, sadly, he was at liberty to put into action.

The photo on Limonev's cell was grainy, slightly blurred. Three figures. By narrowing his eyes slightly, he could recognize a male and two females. This, in itself, was a mystery. Why would Rochev hire three people to kill his mistress? Why would he want her dead in the first place? Kirilenko knew him as a serial fucker—he cheated on his wife with a roster of women as professional as they were beautiful. He'd never seen fit to kill one before so why start now? And, anyway, where was he? Disappeared from work, from his home, and not in a tryst at his own private love hotel.

But first things first. Back to the killers: Not only were there three of them, but it seemed that one was either an adolescent or a midget. Neither fit the usual profile of a professional hit man who, so far as Kirilenko's extensive experience decreed, worked solo. But, actually, that meant little, since his experience also confirmed that professional hit men would use any tactic they could think of to throw him off the scent. As of this moment, none of them had succeeded; he'd run each of them into the ground. One of the reasons he always tracked down the perp, the murderer, strangler, shooter, knifer, was due to his orderly mind, which allowed him to know more about each situation than anyone around him. He absorbed a crime scene with all his five senses, then allowed his mind to look for patterns. A crime scene, steeped in death, in anger, violence, fear, even disinterest, was the very definition of chaos. Death disordered life. Many of the killers he was after were, in their way, as detached as he was. The difference was outrage. Murder outraged him, whether it be premeditated or accidental, professional or amateurish. To him, the taking of a life—any life—was unthinkable, a sin worthy of full retribution, lawful or otherwise. The taking of a life was a violation. It created a state of affairs unto itself, one that had nothing to do with society, that existed, throbbing painfully, outside the boundaries of civilization. Let the punishment fit the crime. Nevertheless, he lived with these acts of cruelty, with the most heinous of insults, as if they were lodgers who had overstayed their welcome in his mind and who would not now relinquish their place in his life for love or money.

He tried zooming in on the faces of the perps, but the man appeared to have his arm raised in front of his eyes, the woman was in the process of turning away, and the face of the adolescent or midget was lost behind the woman's body. He was about to try zooming in on her face when he saw that she was gripping something in her hand: an arrow or a short spear, something with a wicked tip, meant to tear the insides out of its victim: the murder weapon. Now he moved up the image to the woman's face. By zooming in, though not too much, he could discern her features. With a sickening lurch of his stomach he recognized Annika Dementieva.

"There is no trace of the marksman, the man in the woods who fired his weapon."

The thin man with the saturnine face had emerged from the wreckage of the dacha to stand beside Kirilenko's car. Kirilenko, becoming aware of his approach, had quite sensibly pocketed Limonev's phone with its incriminating photo. He'd be damned if he'd share inside information with this man. As for Limonev, he had made a mental note to have the Ukrainians get him a replacement cell immediately.

"He wasn't one of mine," Kirilenko said, "so he must have been one of yours."

"He wasn't," the man said. "Anyway, I wasn't supplied with a marksman, you know that."

"When it comes to you people," Kirilenko said without rancor, "I know nothing."

"Well, take my word for it." The thin man glanced back over his shoulder. "Perhaps one of the SBU men, you know how undisciplined these Ukrainians are."

Kirilenko regarded the man impassively through the smoke passing out of his half-open lips. "Do you judge Russians as harshly as you do the Ukrainians?"

"We have high regard for you," the thin man said with some asperity. "I thought we'd made that perfectly clear."

Kirilenko continued his study of the man. He had golden hair and the ruddy cheeks of an athlete. Unconsciously, Kirilenko rubbed the backs of his hands, reddened and stiff with a rheumy ache. "It wasn't one of the Ukrainians," he said. "They know not to make a move without checking with me first."

"They despise you," the thin man said.

"But they fear me more."

"And whom do you fear, Kirilenko?"

Kirilenko took his time drawing on his cigarette, holding the smoke deep so his lungs could absorb the nicotine. Releasing the smoke, he said, just before he turned away, "Not you, American, if that's what you think. Certainly not you."

"MAGNUSSEN OR one of his people was at it a long time," Jack said after some deliberation. "Rochev must have had something or known something Magnussen wanted very badly."

"What did they do to him?" Alli said.

"It's bad enough to give you nightmares." Jack rose, and Annika was left to inspect the corpse on her own.

"The people who did this," she said, "are professionals—experts, I must say, in torture and the application of pain."

"Spoken like a professional yourself," he said.

She looked up at him. "What an odd thing to say. Do you take me for a torturer?"

He deliberately ignored her comment. "Whoever they are, they must have a strong international connection to plan and execute a hit-and-run murder on Capri. It's a small island with extremely limited vehicular traffic."

Alli was staring out at the flat expanse of the water. "But Annika's right. We've hit a dead end. There's nothing left for us here and we have no way of finding out where Magnussen went."

"Not necessarily."

Jack led them back over the shallow crest and into the lowland of the cemetery. The afternoon was waning; the sun, exhausted from its misty journey, was sinking as if weighted down by the earth or by sorrow. The lengthening shadows seemed to thrust the headstones across the grass like accusing fingers.

"Alli, didn't you say that Magnussen's parents died on the same day?"

She nodded. "But in different places."

Jack examined the headstones, one by one. Using his fingertips to trace the outlines of the chiseled letters allowed him to read what had been written more easily and quickly. "They died on August first, seventeen years ago. Magnussen's father passed away here, on these grounds, but his mother died in Alushta."

"Alushta is on the east coast of the Crimea," Annika said. "It's filled with expensive villas that overlook the Black Sea."

"Bingo! That's where Magnussen's gone," Jack said.

Annika frowned. "What? How could you possibly know that?"

"His mother was buried there."

"I don't see the connection." Annika shook her head. "Maybe she was on vacation, maybe she was visiting friends."

"In that event she would have been brought back here to be buried," Jack said with such perfect logic that Annika was unable to contradict him.

"But a villa—"

Jack's mind was working faster than the others could match or even imagine. "Look at this spread here. This family was wedded to money and prestige, they wouldn't have remained here all year long. The summers are hot and unpleasant, aren't they?"

Annika nodded, still dubious.

"Where would the Magnussens go in the summer? I'm willing to bet they own a villa in Alushta."

"This is ridiculous, you're not the Delphic oracle."

"In a way he is," Alli interjected. "Jack's mind works differently than yours or mine, he can see things we can't, make connections we can't until much, much later."

Annika stared at Alli as if she'd grown wings or had been struck by lightning. "Is this a vaudeville act between the two of you, or some idiotic sleight of hand trick?"

"Why would it be a trick?" Alli said so fiercely that Annika seemed stopped in her tracks.

"If you've got a better idea," Jack said to Annika, "now would be the time to tell me."

Annika looked away for a moment, her gaze roaming over the back of the manor house in the distance. "Seriously?" she said as she turned back to him. "You think Magnussen has gone to ground in Alushta?"

"SO WHO was he then," the golden-haired American said, "the marksman who took a shot in the woods?"

He was not a tall man, nevertheless he was imposing, like all the American agents Kirilenko had met or had seen in surveillance photos. He was possessed of a confidence that bordered on arrogance. Kirilenko envied him or, at least, was jealous of his sense of entitlement. The world was his oyster, he moved about in it as he pleased, with an ease Kirilenko imagined only in his dreams. Kirilenko, the good *silovik*, who was tied to Russia as if by a chain-link leash. And he thought: *I am faithful, like a dog, and the American is my master. He holds my fate in his hands—hands that do not ache in the cold, are not reddened and chapped, aged before their time. He has not seen what I've seen.* And then with the briefest flash of contempt like heat lightning that comes and goes in one breath: *What does he know of life, anyway? What can he know, he's American.*

Was it contempt Kirilenko felt for the golden-haired American or was it pity? His name was Martin, like the bird. Harry Martin. But what was his real name? Likely Kirilenko would never know.

"Harry Martin," the American had introduced himself when they first met, "from Latrobe, Pennsylvania." And when Kirilenko had looked at him blankly, he'd added, "You know, the home of Arnold Palmer, surely you've heard of the legendary golfer."

Kirilenko just barely stopped himself from laughing in Harry Martin's face. God in heaven! While Russians were struggling to survive, Americans were playing golf.

The two men sat side by side now in the backseat of Kirilenko's car, drinking hot coffee from a thermos one of Kirilenko's men had fetched.

"So who was he then?" Harry Martin repeated. "Any theories?"

They appeared to be two old friends chatting about something inconsequential, a sports match, perhaps, or the prospects of a favorite soccer team.

"I don't deal in speculation, only facts," Kirilenko said with a good deal less irritation than he felt. It wouldn't do to rub the American the wrong way, he had too many powerful friends who, with one phone call, could seriously impact Kirilenko's career, not to say his life. Just knowing this caused him a level of stress he found intolerable. Harry Martin was like an itch he couldn't scratch, and it was driving him to distraction.

All at once he threw open the car door and stepped out into the waning day. The air smelled of smoke, charred fabric, and burnt plastic. While he was facing away from Martin he took out the cell phone and sent the photo of Annika Dementieva emerging from Rochev's dacha to his assistant with specific instructions. A moment later Martin clambered out and without a glance at Kirilenko strode into the woods beyond what had once been the front porch of the house.

"All your men out of here?" he asked.

Kirilenko pocketed the phone as he followed the American into the woods. "The SBU also. It's just us here now."

"I need theories," Martin said as they wound through the thick stand of hemlocks. He switched on the flashlight Kirilenko had given him. "I need *something*."

Swallowing his emotions, Kirilenko said in his best fatalistic tone, "Someone has taken Karl Rochev, by force I would guess, judging by the corpse impaled to the mattress back there. It wasn't us and I guarantee it wasn't the SBU. Which means that there's another faction in this mysterious, unnamed pursuit of yours."

"Another faction." Martin turned this phrase over as if it were alien to him or an idea to which he needed to adjust. He trained the flashlight's beam on the forest floor as they picked their way across the soft earth. "Then we'll have to find them, whoever they are. And we'll have to eliminate them."

Kirilenko made a noise deep in his throat. It was a kind of warning, as primitive as it was inarticulate, not that Harry Martin would notice, or even care. "And how do you propose we do that?"

Dying light, red and yellow, seeped through the evergreen boughs.

Martin knelt, running his fingertips lightly over the nest of evergreen needles, pointing out to Kirilenko a muddle of fresh footprints, none of them made by the boots of his men. "A man, a woman—and these." One set was significantly smaller than the other two. He stood. They were very close to the road. "We pick up the perpetrators' trail and follow them back to the source."

He seems so sure of himself, Kirilenko thought bitterly, *even though he's in a land foreign to him, among people who don't even speak his language. Such an American trait.*

They walked to the edge of the trees.

"This road goes in only two directions," Kirilenko said. "Several miles away is a turning that takes you back to Kiev, otherwise it goes straight to the city of Brovary."

"What's there?" Martin asked.

Kirilenko shrugged. "It's the shoe-making capital of Ukraine."

"We split up. You go on to Brovary, see if you pick up their trail. I'll take my man and two of yours and head back to Kiev and try to do the same. At least it's a city I know."

Kirilenko felt a wave of relief flood him. It was a minor miracle to have this gorilla off his back.

Martin nodded at the twilit road that unspooled before them, a tar-black ribbon, vanishing into the darkness of the evening. "Wherever Rochev is you can be sure of one thing: These three people will take us there."

FOURTEEN

"DAD—"

There were people, Jack knew, who confused the word "haunt" with memory. Since Emma had appeared to him, spoken to him, answered his questions and asked some herself, there were people—Sharon among them—who were absolutely certain that he had confused haunted with memory, that what he had mistaken for an encounter with his dead child was nothing more than his memories of her resurfacing, asserting themselves in order to ensure that she wouldn't be completely lost to him, that she would remain with him until his own dissolution, whenever that might come, years from now, or tomorrow.

"Dad—"

Jack knew they were wrong. Emma remained, some essential part of her that death could not touch or even alter. She remained because their relationship was, in some essential way, incomplete, their time together, though cut short, had not ended. Her will survived the car crash that had stolen her life away in brutal fashion, before she could feel the joy and pain of adulthood.

"*Dad*—"

Jack heard Emma as they returned to Igor Kissin's apartment.

"*Dad, I'm here.*"

The door swung open and he stepped into the apartment. While the others went about their business, he looked for his daughter—his dead daughter.

"*No, Dad, over here.*"

At that moment, his cell phone rang. It was Sharon, and he took the call.

"Hello, Jack," she said in a cool, preternaturally calm voice, "do you know yet when you're coming home?"

He closed his eyes. "I don't, Sharon, I told you—"

"Then I'll leave the key under the doormat."

His eyes flew open. "What?"

"I'm leaving, Jack. I've had enough of you not being here."

And all at once he understood that they had returned to square one, to the point they'd been at immediately following Emma's death, when she'd blamed him for not taking Emma's call, for not somehow intuiting that their daughter was in mortal peril, that her car was about to veer off the road into a tree. Months later, Sharon had sworn to him that she'd put her anger and bitterness behind her, but he saw now that she hadn't. Perhaps she'd been telling him the truth, or the truth as she understood it at the moment, but then she'd been fooling herself or, more accurately, hiding from herself, which every human being did from time to time.

He didn't blame her for that failing, how could he? But he blamed her for not telling him the truth now, because she knew the truth. It wasn't his job or the fact that he was overseas, far from her at the moment, it wasn't that he couldn't tell her when he'd be home again. What she meant was, *I can't forgive you for not being* there when Emma needed you, I can't forgive you for not preventing her death.

He said nothing into the phone because there was nothing to say. She'd had a revelation or maybe her mother had forced the revelation on her. But for the first time he realized that it didn't matter. The truth was the truth; it did no good to fight it.

"Good-bye, Jack."

He said nothing, not even then, he merely folded the phone away, and looked around the apartment as if trying to find his bearings, or an answer for what had just happened, though he knew perfectly well where he was and that he was now alone.

At the far end of the sofa, directly below the painting of the Tibetan mandala, was a shadow of a deeper substance, curled like a cat. Curious, because Jack could remember reading something about the mandala in the writings of Carl Jung. What was it? Jung believed the mandala, which in Sanskrit meant both completion and essence, to be the perfect manifestation of the human unconscious.

As he walked to the sofa and sat down near the curled shadow, he wondered whether this was what he was looking at now: a manifestation of his unconscious.

"Hello, Dad."

That was what everyone else but Alli believed, that this manifestation of Emma came from deep inside himself, but he knew that she was something more. He knew it as surely as he knew he was sitting here on a brown velvet sofa in this unexpectedly homey fourth-floor apartment in Kiev.

"Hi, honey." He squinted into the shadows. "I can't really see you."

"Don't worry, that's normal."

He laughed under his breath. "There's nothing normal about this, Emma."

"We're both Outsiders, Dad, so for us it is normal."

He shook his head helplessly. The truth was he'd been an Outsider for so long that he didn't know what the word "normal" meant, if he ever had.

"Your mother—"

"*I know. Don't be sad, it was inevitable.*"

"You sound so grown-up."

"*You and Mom, it never worked, not really.*"

"There certainly was heat."

"*Heat isn't enough. There was nothing solid, ever.*"

Jack put his head back. "No, I suppose not." Tears leaked out of his eyes.

Then he felt a stirring beside him, as if someone had opened a window. A cool breeze kissed his cheek.

"*You've got to stop dwelling on it, Dad.*"

"Your mother? No, I—"

"*The car crash.*"

She was right about that, too. He supposed death might give you a unique perspective on what had gone before, a form of omniscience not unlike that of an immortal.

"*You remember 'The Beginning Is the End Is the Beginning'?*"

He nodded. "Sure. That Smashing Pumpkins song is five-starred on your iPod."

"'*There's no more need to pretend cause now I can begin again.*'" Her voice, lost in time and space, was a haunting soprano as she sang the lines from the song.

"What are you saying?"

"*What if my death was only the end of the beginning?*"

Jack, his heartbeat quickening, turned more toward her, or the darkness where she now dwelled. "Can that be true?"

"*I'm saying that your guilt is still eating you alive. I'm saying that the thing you're fixated on is over and done with.*"

"That moment I lost you and for months afterward the terrible past seemed interminable, repeating itself like a virus, but then later it's as if it happened in a millisecond, so quickly that I never had the chance to take action or even make the right choices."

"*I don't think about that, and neither should you.*"

He shook his head. "I wish I could understand."

"*I know it's confusing, Dad, but think of it this way: Maybe I'm here now because I'm still disobedient, even in death.*" Her laughter rolled over him like gentle surf. "*I don't know, I have as little experience with this as you do. I know you want answers, but I don't have them. I have no idea where I am or what I've become—although it seems likely I'm what I've always been, right? I do know there's no point in trying to figure it out. What it boils down to is faith and acceptance. Faith that I'm really here, acceptance that for some things there is simply no answer.*"

"I don't want you to fade away, like everything else. Emma—" and he gave a little cry, aching with despair and, yes, she was right, guilt.

"Jack?"

He turned his head sharply at the sound of Alli's voice.

"What are you doing?"

And then, as he looked at her blankly, she sat down beside him. "She's here, isn't she?" Her breath seemed to catch in her throat. "Emma's here!"

He was about to answer her when he saw Annika standing in the doorway to one of the bedrooms, observing them. How long had she been there? Had she overheard his conversation with Emma—at least his side of it, which would have sounded absurd to her?

"Let's talk about this another time," he told Alli. "We're all exhausted."

"But—"

"Questions later." He pulled her up with him as he rose to his feet. "Right now it's time to rest."

———

AT THE doorway to the master bedroom, Jack paused, watching Alli pad into her room and softly close the door. Then he turned to Annika, but before he could say anything she beat him to it.

"Come in," she said. Her smile widened. "I didn't bite last night, did I?"

He smiled. "I think Alli is right about you."

"Me being a psycho-bitch or wanting to get you into bed?"

He laughed, but the truth was that in these surroundings and this close to her he felt a frisson, an erotic charge that made him momentarily short of breath.

On his way to the bed he passed close enough for his hip to brush against her, where she sat, her legs crossed at the knee. Her wrists, which perched on her knee, were delicate, so thin they looked eminently breakable. He knew better. His gaze inevitably dropped to her legs, long, powerful, and gleaming in the illumination from the bedside lamps she must have put on when she'd entered the bedroom.

"You know you have this obsession to protect everyone," she said.

He came and sat down on the bed next to her. "Is that such a bad thing?"

"I didn't say it was bad."

"Why did you ask me in here?"

"Really?"

"Really."

"Last night . . . our connection . . ." She looked away for a moment. "I don't want to be alone. I'm tired of being alone."

"What about Ivan?"

She snapped back into focus. "Are you trying to insult me? Ivan was an assignment."

He nodded. "I won't sleep with you, if that's what you're angling for."

"I'm not angling for any damn thing. My arm hurts and I need some rest. We all do."

"All right then." He slapped his thighs and, rising, went to the doorway. "I'll be right outside on the sofa."

As he was about to cross the threshold, she said: "I know who the girl is."

Her timing was impeccable. He turned and stared at her.

"I know she's the American president's daughter." She cocked her head. "Do you take me for a fool?"

"You told me you knew nothing about affairs outside your line of work."

She shrugged. "I didn't know you then, I didn't know whether I could trust you, so I thought it better to lie. The truth is, I can't bear to be the victim of ignorance. Besides, it seemed important for you to keep your secret, changing her hair, her appearance, whatever, and since then I've wanted to help you keep that secret. I would keep it now, even if we were captured, even if the FSB hurt me."

"I don't believe you," he said flatly.

She shrugged again.

"Why would you do it—protect Alli—if it came to that?"

"You know why. When I look in her eyes, when I listen to her voice, I see myself."

"Even when she calls you the psycho-bitch?"

"Especially then, because her high emotion betrays her."

Jack took a step back into the bedroom. "How do you mean?"

"That look in her eyes, the sound of her voice when the anger engorges her throat, when it seems as if she's strangling on emotion, I know that look; I saw it every day when I looked at myself in the mirror. And that sound . . ." She shuddered. "The news stories were vague, even the so-called in-depth articles, but something very bad happened to her."

"Yes," he said as he sat beside her, "it did."

"You saved her from whoever abused her. I can see that, too, in her eyes when she looks at you."

Now it was his turn to look away. "She was abducted, bound to a chair and brainwashed, perhaps more, I don't know. She won't talk about it to anyone."

"She'll tell you." Annika's voice was as soft as a caress as she laid a hand over his. "She needs time, that's all."

Jack turned to look at her face. "How can you be sure?"

"Because she wants to tell you, she needs to tell you. I think she's coming to grips with the realization that she can't move on until she does. I believe that's why she wanted so badly to be the one to talk to Milla Tamirova."

Jack frowned. "What do you mean?"

"Milla Tamirova has certain . . . equipment, shall we say, that I think drew Alli."

Jack was growing alarmed. "What kind of equipment? What the hell are you talking about?"

"Milla Tamirova is a professional mistress—that is to say she has a dungeon in her apartment."

A chill sped through his system and he shivered. "Why in the world would she want to revisit—"

"To relieve herself of the terror, to conquer it. The only way to exorcize it is to demythologize it, to see it in the light of day, to understand that once she overcomes her terror she'll no longer be its victim."

Jack sat bent over, elbows on knees, hands clasped loosely in front of him as if in rumination or, maybe, prayer. Then he looked up. "I had no idea. I should be with her."

Annika's hand clasped his and he felt her steely strength. "Leave her alone for the moment. Allow her to regain her innate power. She needs to think about what Milla Tamirova must have shown her. If you interfere now, she'll move away from both you and the hard work that lies ahead of her."

Sighing deeply, Jack covered his face with his hands and lay back

on the bed. Annika, turning, regarded him with empathy and perhaps a bit of pity.

"She's yours, Jack, for better or for worse."

"It's all for the better," he said, "believe me."

"I do." She hitched herself fully onto the bed, keeping off her left
arm as she did and, before he had a chance to say another word, lay
down on top of him. "There, that isn't so bad, is it?"

ALLI, FULLY clothed, lay on the bed. She was staring at the ceiling,
but in fact she was seeing the restraint chair in the center of Milla
Tamirova's dungeon. In her mind's eye she sat in that chair, felt the
restraints, hard, twisted, and nasty, against the insides of her wrists.
She felt little electric shocks go through her, as if sparks launched
from a nearby fire were singeing her, burning off the pale, almost
transparent hair on her arms.

The demonically handsome face of Morgan Herr, whose pseudo-
nyms Ronnie Kray, Charles Whitman, Ian Brady were all notori-
ous serial killers, hovered over her, whispering in her ear. He told her
things about herself—intimate things that she was certain only she
could know, including private conversations she'd had with Emma,
everything they'd discussed in their dorm room at school—as if he'd
crawled inside her head and insidiously appropriated the details of her
life.

She shuddered so deeply that her torso came off the bed as if
through a bolt of electricity. She felt the familiar, horrific nausea rising in her, and she fought to stay where she was, held at bay the urge
to flee to the bathroom and kneel beside the porcelain bowl to puke
up her guts.

No, she told herself in a remarkably steady voice, *you no longer need
to do that. Morgan Herr is dead, there's nothing more he can do to you. Whatever is happening, you're doing it to yourself.*

And yet, once again, as she'd felt in Milla Tamirova's dungeon, she was paralyzed, completely powerless, as if she had once again been stripped of conscious volition.

"*Whoever did this to you, whoever abused you will have won.*" Milla Tamirova had smiled. "*We can't have that, child, can we?*"

But Milla Tamirova didn't know, because Alli didn't dare tell her, the other reason for her feeling powerless. The urge to cut herself open, to have the secret spill out with her guts, left her shaking and drenched in cold sweat. She could feel the bed vibrating beneath her, or was it her own body that was making the bed quiver?

"*You're a coward,*" Morgan Herr's voice echoed in her head. "*You're a little, sniveling bitch, and who paid for your cowardice? Tell me, who paid?*"

Racked with sobs, she lay back down on the bed and, turning on her side, pulled the coverlet over her. Sometime later she was plunged into a sleep where, in dreams, she strode across the leafy campus of Langley Fields. Emma, whispering beside her, had the sun on her face, so her eyes, usually as transparent as lake water, were hidden in the glare. Then Alli passed into the cloud of shade thrown by a pear tree, and as she turned to Emma, she screamed and screamed, and could not stop screaming.

JACK PUSHED Annika off him, not roughly but firmly, so that there would be no question of his intent.

Part of him felt as if he should be thinking of Sharon, but Sharon was far away in every manner imaginable; she was lost to him in the way he'd been afraid he'd lost Emma. He realized now that from the moment he'd first met Sharon, from the instant of their first incandescent coupling, they were headed toward dissolution, like a body that sinks beneath the waves and, in a split instant, becomes nothing more than a reflection, a reminder of what was or, possibly, what might have been. But, in any event, it was losing its coherence, if it had any to begin with, as it plunged headlong into oblivion.

Emma had been their only chance to stay together, but, really, that was a false hope. For a moment he forced himself to imagine his life had Emma not died, and the inescapable conclusion was that as far as he and Sharon were concerned nothing would be different. From the moment Emma was born, they disagreed on everything concerning their daughter, a dangerously scattershot method of child-rearing, but they were both blinded by their immaturity. It was the wrong moment for them to become parents, and they didn't handle it well, taking their fundamental differences into a more public arena.

The other part of him was both hard and on fire. Though he fought against it, his breath came in short, hot pants, as if he were nearing the end of a long, grueling race. He knew the thoughts of Sharon and dissolution were meant as a distraction from his current situation, but his mind refused to stay thrust back in time, returning again and again to the seductive stimuli his five senses brought in.

He drank in Annika's scent, felt the warmth of her body, heard the soft soughing of her breath, like wind through the treetops. He could not help but savor the taste her lips had left on his, the first bite into a fresh peach.

He turned his head to see her lying on her right side, facing away from him. Her body was curled up slightly, lending her a more vulnerable appearance, as if she were already asleep, but he could tell by her breathing that she was still awake.

Her blouse, or what was left of it, had ridden up, revealing her bare back. The sight of the scars took his breath away. They must be from the eighteen months she had been incarcerated. The abuse she had suffered had been extreme, or one manifestation of it had been extreme. How extreme had Alli's abuse been, how profound her terror and her suffering? How deeply was Morgan Herr embedded in her psyche? *"The terror dissolves like dreams when we wake up and go about our daily routine,"* she had said, which set him wondering. At the moment when Annika's scars lay revealed to him, when it crossed his mind to touch them, to ask her how she had come by them, it occurred to him that there was something voyeuristic, even obscene about poking around in a person's sordid past. That's what people did these days, however, and the more sordid the deeper the urge to pry, to learn why, when logically the opposite should apply. But there was nothing logical about the reflex to stare at a car wreck, to watch, spellbound, as bodies were pulled from the wreckage, to think: How badly hurt are they? Are they alive or dead? Thank God I'm here, safe and sound, passing by this disaster, but, hang on, slow down, I want to see more, blood and all.

Without a clear understanding of what he was doing or the consequences that might ensue he reached out. As he curled his hand over her hip she emitted a sound that was neither a sigh nor a moan, but contained the essence of both. That sound acted like a trigger, releasing him from whatever safety mechanism that had short-circuited what he had been feeling ever since he'd crossed the threshold of the bedroom.

"Forget it," she said in a voice partially muffled by the pillow or perhaps her arm. "I don't want you now."

Laughing softly he removed his hand and turned off the second lamp, enveloping them in twilight. And yet it seemed to him that he'd been plunged into darkness so absolute it was possible to lose his bearings, as if he were at sea beyond sight of all land. He wondered whether he should go or remain on the opposite side of the bed, trying to find a place comfortable for himself, at which point she turned around as lithely as a gymnast, folded her arms around him, and pressed her soft, half-open lips to his. He could feel her panting breath as his mouth closed over hers.

Their bodies moved in concert, in a back-and-forth rhythm not unlike the tide that rules the seas. They were like engines revving up, yearning to be released, longing for the fury that only a vehicle at speed and slightly out of control could generate, summoned like a genie or a djinn from shadows where no one looked.

Lost inside her he became unmoored from a sense of either place or time, dimly aware that in plummeting toward oblivion he sought an end to the dissolution of his life.

FIFTEEN

"LLOYD BERNS'S death was almost certainly the work of Benson and Thomson." Dennis Paull, the head of the Department of Homeland Security, leaned forward tensely, seeking to keep his voice low. He was speaking of two prominent members of the previous administration, Miles Benson, the war vet and former director of the CIA, and Morgan Thomson, the former national security advisor, the last of the neocons who had managed to maintain his power, due mainly to his ties to companies manufacturing war materiel.

On one of those dank District days when winter and spring, for a short time evenly matched, fought one another to a standstill, five of the most powerful men in the capital, and therefore in America, clustered beside the newly turned grave of Senator Lloyd Berns, following the mournful pomp and circumstance of his funeral and burial among the fallen heroes of the country at Arlington National Cemetery.

Paull was huddled with President Carson; Vice President Arlen Crawford, the big, rangy, sun-scarred former Texas senator; Kinkaid Marshall, the new head of NSA; G. Robert Kroftt, director of Central Intelligence; Bill Rogers, the national security advisor; and General Atcheson Brandt, who had handled the delicate arrangements with Russian president Yukin for Carson's historic U.S.-Russian security accord. This meeting had convened following the services, after Berns's family—his wife, sister, two sons, daughter, various in-laws, and grandchildren—had stood stiffly, wept, and thrown handfuls of dirt on the coffin. Around the six men, at a discreet distance, was a constellation of Secret Service operatives, all staring outward across the sea of headstones, bouquets of flowers, mourners, miniature American flags, and the occasional eternal flame.

"You've given us no proof, Denny," Marshall said, "but even if you had, what have they accomplished with Lloyd's death?"

"I've already appointed Ben Hearth as the new whip," President Carson said, "and he's tougher with the opposition than Lloyd ever was. I'm not suggesting that Benson and Thomson aren't still formidable enemies, but that particular motive's a no-go." He spread his hands. "What else do we have?" He briefly considered bringing up Jack's mission, then almost at once dismissed the notion.

"Setting aside the matter of Senator Berns's demise, I'm still of the opinion that our most pressing business concerns the changes taking place inside the Kremlin even as we speak." This from CIA Director Kroftt, who was understandably alarmed by the recent developments in Russia.

Vice President Crawford nodded emphatically. "The severe downturn in Russia's energy-based economy has made those inside the Kremlin—especially President Yukin—nervous about the longevity of the country's influence."

"The fact is," Kroftt continued, "Russia as a power has been in retreat ever since the end of the Cold War. The West's decision to formally recognize Kosevo as an independent Serbian state marked the nadir of Russia's sphere of influence. Ever since then, the Kremlin has been spinning its webs at light-speed, manufacturing a plan that would bring the country back into prominence."

"Pardon me, but if I may interject an observation and some pertinent facts," General Brandt said, "the Baltics, the Balkans, the Caucasus, all of Central Asia and Central Europe, in fact, are experiencing the same fate as Russia's."

Carson, watching Lloyd's family marching slowly toward the limousines that had brought them here, saw a small boy turn and stare back toward his grandfather's grave. Carson recognized him because he was the only one of the grandchildren who had remained completely dry-eyed during the burial. But now, with his back to his family, free to vent his terror and his sadness, he wept openly. Perhaps he was remembering how his grandfather had taken him to the zoo, or to a movie, letting him stuff his face with chocolate and ice cream. Certainly he had no inkling that his beloved grandfather had left behind a mistress, a mysterious younger woman who might herself be mourning his passing, wherever she was. And seeing the sadness leak out of this child reminded him of his own daughter so far away in every manner imaginable. The thought pierced his heart, made him want to run to the child, pick him up in his arms, and tell him that everything would be all right.

"However," Brandt continued, "Russia maintains a distinct advantage over its surrounding neighbors in that, owing to its rich stores of oil and natural gas, it maintains an enormous amount of reserves, both in funds and in currency, more than all the other countries combined. Moreover, it owns and controls the natural gas that supplies virtually all of Western Europe."

"True enough," Kroftt affirmed, "as far as it goes." He cleared his throat as he handed around Xeroxed dossiers. "However, my Russia desk has prepared a white paper, the major thrust of which is this: Based on the successful military incursion Russia recently made into Georgia we envision an imminent reemergence of Russian power using a three-pronged strategy through military, intelligence, and energy means. What this, in effect, means is that the era of Russian retrenchment is over. Yukin intends to extend its sphere of influence outward once again, to encompass Georgia and Ukraine, to name only the first two strategic expansions."

"This is all purely conjecture, and in fact has been put forward in other forms by other members of the intelligence community." Closing the dossier, which he had skimmed with a practiced eye, General Brandt turned to Carson. "Sir, as you know, I've had many one-on-one meetings with President Yukin over the past eight years and in all that time I've never once caught a glimpse of this bellicose scenario."

"I beg your pardon, General," Crawford drawled, "but I can't think how it would benefit Yukin to let you in on what he's planning. On the contrary, as you can see by the previous administration's hostile response to Russia's war with Georgia, he would take great pains to keep you from knowing anything at all."

"It's the previous administration's grievous errors vis-à-vis Russia I'm trying like hell to amend," General Brandt said. "What we don't need is a return to our old adversarial position, which resulted in the bitterest of exchanges between the White House and the Kremlin."

"The Kremlin's time has come and gone, which is why it's flailing away at anyone or anything it believes is antagonistic to it." The CIA chief thumbed through the dossier. "As you all can see from the exhibits on page five we are most concerned with Ukraine because strategically it's the cornerstone of any Russian expansion. Ukraine's location gives Russia access to the Black Sea and, from there, the Mediterranean. Without an integrated Ukraine, Russia is vulnerable to the south and the west. Furthermore, the preponderance of a Russian-speaking population, along with the fact that Ukrainian transport is already entwined with Russia's agricultural, industrial, and energy businesses, make it an absolutely vital acquisition."

Kroftt let the pages of the dossier flutter closed. "All that being said, there's yet another aspect to Russia's designs on Ukraine that make us the most uncomfortable. As he's done with Gazprom, Yukin has nationalized Russia's uranium industry. Like China, Russia sees no viable future without atomic energy to take the place of coal, oil and, yes, even natural gas. The trouble is that Russia itself has fewer uranium resources than its geologists had forecasted even three years ago. That means Yukin *must* venture outside Russia's current borders in order to build up its reserves."

General Brandt cocked his head. "Have you heard something I haven't, Bob? Because there's been no indication that Ukraine is or even could be a significant source of uranium."

For the first time, the CIA chief looked less than confident. "That, of course, is the conundrum we're wrestling with. The General is correct. As of this moment there has been no major uranium strike in Ukraine."

General Brandt looked vindicated. "Sir, I'm not trying to dismiss the hard work the CIA has put into this white paper, but the fact is that during the past eight years so much damage has been done to our relationship with the Kremlin that just to get President Yukin to agree to the summit with you took untold hours of blood, sweat, and tears. I respectfully submit that now is not the time for rash action, saber rattling, or even accusations. Sir, together we've made significant progress. We've forged a diplomatic détente with Russia. Now you're about to sign an accord that will solve the worldwide deadlock on the Iranian nuclear weapons threat and bring a renewed level of security to the American people." He looked around at each grim face in turn. "Do we really want to jeopardize what will turn out to be your presidential legacy on the basis of one intelligence report? Besides, as we are all painfully aware, our military capability abroad is already stretched to the breaking point."

"Edward," the vice president said in his deceptively soft Texan drawl, "you can't deviate from our position now. The press will excoriate you; your own party will accuse you of flip-flopping on an issue you made a cornerstone of your first one hundred days in office."

There was silence for a moment as everyone looked to President Carson for an answer. He'd staked much of his reputation on this rapprochement with Russia. He'd expended a great deal of political capital on the two bills the Congress had failed to pass. If he failed with the accord with Yukin he risked being dead in the water for the rest of his term—and forget about a second one. No matter his private thoughts on the subject, everyone present knew the president had no choice.

Carson looked over for the young boy, but he was gone now, bundled into the back of one of the anonymous-looking limos. Was he crying still, or had he put his stoic face back on in front of his family? *It's going to be all right*, Carson thought. Then, his attention returned to the matter at hand, he sighed. "The General is right. For the moment we bury this intel; what we have spoken of here today goes no further." He turned to his CIA chief. "Bob, in the meantime have your people follow up on this intel. I want specifics. If and when your boys unearth a smoking gun, we'll move on it, but not a moment before. And Dennis, continue to pursue all avenues regarding the investigation into Lloyd's death. If there's something to it I want to know about it pronto. Okay?" He nodded. "Good. Thank you, gentlemen, for your valued input and opinions. Now it's time to return to Moscow. General, you have just under two hours to get your kit together and hustle on over to Andrews. I want you with me when I meet with President Yukin again. Dennis, you're with me."

As SOON as they were in the presidential limousine and on their way to Andrews Air Force Base, Carson turned to Dennis Paull, his longtime confidant, and, slapping the CIA white paper against his thigh, said, "To be honest, Denny, this report concerns me, especially Yukin's designs on Ukraine. The incursion into Georgia was bad enough, but if he decides to make a move against Ukraine how can we stand idly by?"

"The report is intel, and like all intel it shouldn't be taken as gospel," Paull said as he settled back in the plush bench seat. "Besides, after six years of constant battles, our military is in need of withdrawal from the field, the men need time to stand down. But even if the intel is correct it wouldn't change a thing, would it? Your intent is on record, your position clear." Pulling a cigar from his vest pocket he stuck it between his teeth and went searching for a match or a lighter. "It doesn't matter what action Yukin takes or is planning, it doesn't matter if you like the sonuvabitch or if you hate him. The accord has got to be signed and with all due haste."

"I agree, but Brandt has been urging me to rush past minor points in the negotiations."

"Ignore him, get what you want out of Yukin," Paull said firmly. "But I must point out with the security accord signed Yukin's hands will be tied, he won't be able to follow the scenario Bob has outlined, not with us as allies. No, the best way to stave off Russian expansion is to follow through on your promise as quickly as possible."

Carson threw the dossier aside. "In office less than ninety days and already my hands are dirty."

"The nature of politics is to have dirty hands," Paull astutely pointed out as he lit the cigar. "The trick is to govern without being concerned with your dirty hands."

"No, the trick is to wash them constantly."

Paull puffed away contentedly. "Lady Macbeth tried that without success."

"Lady Macbeth was mad."

"It seems to me that madness is inherent in politics, or at least a preternatural ability to rationalize, which can be a kind of madness."

"The ability to rationalize is a trait common to all humans," Carson observed.

"Maybe so," Paull said from within a cloud of aromatic smoke, "but surely not on such a massive scale."

Carson grunted. "Anyway, it's not the first time I've gotten my hands dirty."

"And we both know it won't be the last."

Reaching over, Paull pressed a button and the privacy glass slid into place, ensuring that their conversation couldn't be overheard even by the driver or the Secret Service escort riding shotgun.

"Speaking of which," he said in a soft voice, "I want to run an investigation on everyone in the cabinet."

The president sat up straight. "You suspect someone? Of what?"

"Of nothing, of everything." Paull took the cigar from between his teeth. "Here's how the situation looks from my particular vantage point, Edward. Frankly, I don't trust anyone in your inner circle. It's my opinion that Benson and Thomson have taken steps to ensure they know what your moves will be before you implement them."

"Denny, what you're saying—"

"Please let me finish, sir. Consider: Your first two initiatives have been shot down in Congress, embarrassing defeats for a newly elected president. Recall that Lloyd Berns had assured you that he'd have the votes from the other side of the aisle to ensure the bills' passage, but unaccountably he was wrong. It was as if someone had spoken to the right congressmen before Berns, which could only have happened if the opposition had knowledge of the decisions of the inner cabinet."

The president blew out a little puff of anxious air. "Come on, Denny. I've known you a long time, but this sounds preposterous. What you're intimating is that a member of my cabinet is leaking information to my enemies."

"I'm not intimating it, sir, I'm stating it straight out."

"On the basis of what? Circumstantial evidence, a series of setbacks that are normal—"

"With all due respect, Edward, the string of setbacks we've suffered are anything but normal."

The president made an exasperated sound. "But there could be any number of explanations, all of which might be perfectly innocent."

"Innocence doesn't belong in politics, you know that. And, if I may say, in the position you're in you don't have the luxury of kicking suspicions into the gutter. If I'm right, your enemies have already started to poison your presidency. We've got to short-circuit your enemies, and I mean right now."

Carson considered for some time. At length, he nodded. "All right, Denny. Begin as soon as you get back to the office. Pick your team and—"

"No. All the work is going to be done by me alone, unofficially, outside the office. I don't want to leave a trail of any kind."

The president rubbed his temples. "You know this is the sort of assignment Jack ought to be handling."

"Naturally, but you and I have sent him on what I trust is a parallel course."

"I detested lying to him."

"You didn't lie, you withheld knowledge, and for a damn good reason."

"Jack is a friend, Denny. He brought my daughter back to me. I owe him more than I can ever repay."

"Then trust in his abilities." Paull stubbed out his cigar. "For the moment, that's all we can do."

ENTWINED, CRADLED by the softly breathing night, Jack and Annika spoke in the secretive tones of ghosts:

"What do you think is happening beyond these walls," Annika said, "in the hallway, the other apartments in this building, out on the street, in other sections of the city? It's impossible to know, just like it's impossible to know who's thinking about us, thinking about following us, extracting the secrets we keep so close to us, who harbors thoughts of murder and mayhem." She turned in his arms. "What are your secrets, Jack, the ones you keep closest to you?"

"My wife left me—twice," Jack said with a vehemence that was almost like menace. "Who the hell knows what secrets are held inside the human heart."

Annika waited a moment, possibly to allow his anger to subside, before she said, "What happened on the sofa beneath the Tibetan mandala?"

Jack closed his eyes for a moment as he felt his heart beating hard. "Nothing happened."

"So you were talking to a ghost, is that it?"

"I was talking to a secret."

"A secret Alli knows."

"She and I, yes."

"This just underscores what I said. We know so little, less than what seems apparent, less even than we believe." She placed her hand on his arm, moved it down to the back of his hand, tracing the veins. "So you won't tell me your secret, but I'll bet it has nothing to do with your wife, or ex-wife, because she's just a word now and words fade with incredible quickness. It has to do with your daughter, with Emma." Her fingers twined with his. "Was she out there on the sofa? Is she there now?"

"Emma is dead. I told you that."

"Mmm. Is she one of the things we don't know about?"

"What do you mean?" He knew exactly what she meant, but Emma was too intimate, too precious to share.

"I've killed a man, as you know, but still I know nothing about death. Do you?"

"How could I?"

"Yes, how could you. I have asked myself that very question many times since I saw you on the sofa, and the answer I've come up with is this: I think you know more about it than I do. I think you were talking to death, or something like death, under the Tibetan mandala."

"What an insane notion."

He halfheartedly sought to disentangle himself, but she climbed on top of him, reached down for him, her fingers encircling. "We all have insane notions, now and again." She squeezed gently, bringing him to readiness. "It's the human condition."

DYADYA GOURDJIEV was in the midst of making coffee, strong enough to keep him up for the rest of what remained of the night, when a pounding on the front door set his heart to racing. Setting down the plastic dipper full of freshly ground coffee he stepped out of the kitchen, padded on slippered feet across the living room. The pounding came again, more insistent this time, if that were possible.

"Who is it?" he asked with his cheek nearly against the door.

"Open up," came the voice from the other side, "or I'll have the damn knob blown off!"

Figuratively girding his loins for what was to come, Dyadya Gourdjiev flipped open the lock. No sooner had he begun to turn the knob than the door fairly exploded inward. Had he not stepped nimbly aside the edge of the door would have cracked the bone above his eye socket.

Two men rushed inside, one of them slammed the door shut behind them. He was the muscle, the one with the Makarov pistol. The other man was Kaolin Arsov, the head of the Izmaylovskaya *grup-perovka* family in Moscow. Dyadya Gourdjiev had been expecting him more or less from the moment Annika and her new friends had left his apartment.

Arsov had the eyes of a predator and the complexion of a dead fish, as if he preferred darkness to sunlight. Perhaps he was allergic or in some perverse fashion averse to natural light of any sort. He looked like the kind of man you wouldn't want to cross, a man whose strong arm you'd want with you in, say, a knife fight or a street brawl, even if his judgement was suspect. He'd sell his brother to the highest bidder—Dyadya Gourdjiev knew that he had, in fact, done just that—in order to gain territory and prestige, but once given he'd never renege on his word, which was, in his neck of the world, the only true and lasting measure of a man.

"Gospodin Gourdjiev, what a pleasure it is to see you again." His lips were smiling, but his eyes remained as cold and calculating as any predator.

"I'm afraid I can't say the same." Dyadya Gourdjiev held his ground, which was the only way to play this situation. Arsov could smell fear and indecision from a mile away. Weakness of any kind or to any degree was what he sniffed out, using it like a cudgel against his prey, because for him the world was strength and weakness, nothing existed in between. Not that Dyadya Gourdjiev thought that Arsov considered him prey, but in the end the difference was negligible. Gourdjiev was someone to intimidate, knock around a little, someone from whom he could get information. That was how Arsov would play it, anyway; there were no surprises with men like him, who were akin to steel girders, neither bending nor breaking, thinking themselves invincible.

Arsov shrugged as he swaggered around the living room, picking up a statuette here, a framed photo there, studying them with blank eyes. He returned them in deliberately haphazard fashion, a silent warning to Dyadya Gourdjiev that Arsov had the power to turn his world upside down. "No matter. I've come for Annika. Where is she?"

"In the back of beyond," Dyadya Gourdjiev said. "Far away from your clutches, I expect."

"And of course you helped send her there." Arsov paused in his perambulation and grinned with teeth that were preternaturally long, wicked as a wolf's. "Wherever *there* is."

"I don't know where she is."

Arsov leered. His breath was sour from vodka, cheap cigarettes, and a stomach that could tolerate neither. "I don't believe you."

"I can't help that."

Arsov's head flicked only slightly, but his muscle cocked the hammer on the Makarov.

"That's not a good idea." Dyadya Gourdjiev held his ground like the front line against a putsch.

Arsov beckoned his man with a wave of his hand that was almost perfunctory, or negligent, as if the life or death of Dyadya Gourdjiev was of little moment. "I'll decide whether it's a good idea or not, old man."

"He's right, Arsov, it's not a good idea." The man who spoke had emerged from the kitchen as silently as an angel, or a demon. He was wide shouldered and slim hipped. With his wire-rimmed glasses he looked like a professor, or perhaps an accountant. And yet there was something in him that made the observer wary, set him back on his heels, as if struck by a sudden fistful of air. A discernable chill invaded the room, as if the man had sucked the oxygen out of it.

Arsov's eyebrows arched in hateful surprise. "I had no idea you might be here."

Oriel Jovovich Batchuk spread his hands. "And yet, here I am." His basilisk gaze alighted on the muscle. "Put that idiotic thing away before you hurt yourself."

The man, mumbling something, looked to his boss for guidance. "What's that?" Batchuk said.

"I said I don't take orders from you."

Everything happened at once then. The muscle lifted the Makarov, Arsov started to speak, and Batchuk raised his left arm as if he were about to direct traffic, or hail a friend on the street. Something small launched out of the space between his sleeve and his wrist, blurred through the air, and buried itself in the center of the muscle's throat. The man dropped the pistol, clutching at his throat with his trembling fingers. He gasped, his lips took on a distinctly bluish tint. A white froth foamed out his half-open mouth as he collapsed in a heap.

"Who do you take orders from now?" Batchuk said with contempt rather than irony. Then he turned his attention back to Arsov, smiling without revealing a single iota of emotion. "Now, Arsov, what were you saying?"

"I have a legitimate grievance," Arsov said, his gaze magnetized by his own man, now nothing more than flesh poisoned by a dart coated with hydrocyanic acid. "Annika Dementieva must pay for the murder she committed."

"You leave Annika to me."

Arsov's eyes at last engaged Batchuk's. "You yourself guaranteed me complete noninterference."

"I said I will deal with the matter." The deputy prime minister cleared his throat. "There will be no more interference in Izmaylovskaya business."

Arsov nodded. As he was about to step over his fallen bodyguard, Batchuk said, "You brought it in, you take it out."

Grunting, the mob boss dragged the corpse to the front door and opened it. As he was about to drag him over the threshold, Batchuk added, "A grievance doesn't excuse vulgarity. You're in society now, Arsov, you'd do well to remember that."

The door slammed behind the two men and, in three strides, Batchuk crossed the room, locked the door, and turned back to his host.

"The vermin that comes in off the street these days." He clucked his tongue and shook his head. "Perhaps I should send an exterminator over for a week or so."

"I'm sure that won't be necessary, Oriel Jovovich." Dyadya Gourdjiev returned to the kitchen to continue preparing the coffee.

"Still," the deputy prime minister said as he leaned against the doorway, "it might be prudent."

"I'd really prefer not." Dyadya Gourdjiev set the coffeepot on the fire ring, took down two glasses as large as beer steins. "You'll do what you want, in any event."

"It's a deputy prime minister's prerogative."

"I'm talking about long before you rose to that position." Dyadya Gourdjiev turned to face Batchuk. "I'm talking about the young man I knew, the young man who—"

"Stop! Not another word!" Batchuk raised a hand, a singularly violent gesture that might have been directed as much at himself as at the older man.

Dyadya Gourdjiev smiled, much as a father might at a mischievous child. "It does my heart good to know that all the feelings haven't been squeezed out of you by Yukin and his murderous kind."

Batchuk waited until the steaming glass of coffee was in his hand and he had sipped it graciously. "You knew these people were going to come, didn't you?"

"I knew it was a possibility, yes." Dyadya Gourdjiev took his coffee, padded back into the living room, and made himself comfortable in his favorite chair.

After spooning in sugar, Batchuk followed him, stirring the coffee with a tiny silver spoon. He remained standing for some time, as if to remind Dyadya Gourdjiev of his superior status. Apparently he thought better of the stance, because he did not continue the conversation until he had settled on the sofa obliquely across from the older man.

"Do you know why Arsov is interested in your daughter?"

For just an instant Dyadya Gourdjiev looked startled, fearful even. Then he gathered himself. "No, and I'm not interested."

"You trust her too much."

Dyadya Gourdjiev did not respond. He wondered whether this statement was an admonition or an admission of envy. It could be either, or both, he decided. Batchuk was impossible to read, he'd proved that many times over. Dyadya Gourdjiev was reminded of a video he'd seen of an elephant safari in Rajasthan, in northwest India. Nothing but a sea of tall grass could be seen in front of the people on the elephant, until, with the quickness of a heartbeat, a tiger appeared. It ran directly toward the elephant and, in an astonishing attack, leapt onto the head of the elephant and severely mauled the mahout. Tigers aren't supposed to attack elephants, but unlike other big cats tigers are as unpredictable as they are deadly. In Dyadya Gourdjiev's mind Batchuk was aligned with this tiger.

"Oriel Jovovich, please. Trust is an absolute, either you trust someone or you don't. There's no halfway position."

Batchuk, sipping his coffee, appeared to mull this over. "I don't trust anyone, why should I? People make an industry out of lying to me. Sometimes I feel as if there's a cash prize awarded to anyone who can put something over on me."

Dyadya Gourdjiev knew this was absurd, but he also knew that this was the only place for Batchuk to safely blow off steam while someone listened. This spoke directly to the matter of trust, which, in Russia these days, was uppermost on every *silovik*'s mind.

"Every day, it seems, there are new people joining the applicant's pool for the cash prize." Batchuk made a face. "And, you know, it's impossible to kill them all, or at the very least, put their balls to the fire."

"Yet another industry underwritten by the Kremlin."

At this, Batchuk laughed. Actually he smiled, which, for him, was more or less the same thing. "Time hasn't dulled the edge of your sword. Your daughter doubtless gets her smart mouth from you."

"I was happy to give her whatever I could."

On the face of it, this was a simple, declarative statement, and yet with these two men nothing was simple, everything possessed layers of meaning that struck at the very core of their friendship, if their relationship could be called friendship. It was at once less and much more; there was, perhaps, no word adequate for what they meant to one another, or how entwined their pasts were. Several months ago, Annika had used a word, perhaps it was American slang, or possibly English, that had stuck in Dyadya Gourdjiev's mind. In speaking about an associate of hers she had said, "what we really are is frenemies." She'd supplied the explanation when he'd asked for it: The word was a contraction of the phrase "friendly enemies," though she admitted that the actual relationship was far more complex than that, that this was the norm for frenemies.

Were he and Batchuk frenemies? He shrugged mentally. What did it matter? Why was there always a human desire to put a name to everything, to neatly sort, catalogue, pigeonhole even things like relationships that by their very nature were so complex they defied classification? They liked one other, admired one other, even trusted one another, but there would always be friction between them, always a bitterness and, on Dyadya Gourdjiev's part, a profound disappointment whose origin could not be erased or forgiven. And yet here they were like two old friends who confided secrets to one another they'd never reveal to anyone else. It was their shared secrets, their shame, envy, and dispassion, that bound them tighter than father and son, than brothers. There was bad blood between them, but there was also love—curious, mystifying, impossible in any creature other than a human being.

"There you can't be faulted," Batchuk said with a tone that implied that there were other matters for which he still held Dyadya Gourdjiev liable.

Finishing off his coffee, Dyadya Gourdjiev smiled as if with secret knowledge, an expression that infuriated Batchuk and also put him in his place. "Now you must tell me why you've come here. I need some facts to offset the armada of innuendo you've been launching."

Setting aside his cup, Batchuk rose and walked to stand in the entryway. He stood for a moment, hands in his pockets, frowning as he stared down at the smear of blood Arsov had left behind.

"Kaolin Arsov is no one to count as an enemy," he said, as if speaking to the polished tips of his expensive English shoes. "To have the Izmaylovskaya *grupperovka* aligned against you is to court disaster."

"This is *Trinadtsat*-speak." Dyadya Gourdjiev shook his woolly head. "To think it comes to this. Warnings of this nature would never have been necessary even two years ago."

"This is a new world, it's being remade every day," Batchuk said. "If you don't have a spade in your hand then get out of the way."

Dyadya Gourdjiev turned to confront the younger man. "*Trinadtsat* is your doing, I warned you that it would be your undoing. Crawling into bed with the *grupperovka* was a grave mistake—"

"It couldn't be helped," Batchuk interjected.

"—and now, as you yourself have discovered, it can't be undone. You'd have to exterminate the Izmaylovskaya, and even Yukin doesn't have the stomach for that."

"Circumstances had come to a head, they demanded to be dealt with by the harshest possible measures."

"And now you have your wish."

Batchuk sighed and looked back at Dyadya Gourdjiev as he covered the smear of blood with the heel of one shoe. "The truth is I face reality every minute of every day. The truth is the *grupperovka*—most notably the Izmaylovskaya—have both the power and the access to avenues crucial to the success of *Trinadtsat*." He lifted a finger. "And make no mistake, Yukin needs *Trinadtsat* to succeed. His entire vision for Russia's future rides on it."

Dyadya Gourdjiev scrutinized him now because he knew they were coming to the crux of the visit. Oriel Jovovich Batchuk was a long way from the Kremlin; he hadn't come all this way to simply vent his frustrations, or to seek advice. Not this time, anyway.

Batchuk took a step forward and put his hand on the doorknob. Looking back over his broad shoulder he said, "It's your daughter."

"Yes, of course, it always comes back to Annika, doesn't it? And do you know why? People want to see what's best for them, not what actually exists. You do nothing but pretend, to yourself as well as to me. You try to reshape events in the past to suit yourself when we both know very well that what happened—the terrible events that must never be mentioned—is immutable, it can't be changed and, therefore, expunged, no matter how hard or in which ways you try."

Batchuk's eyes glittered; no one else on earth would dare speak to him that way. When he was certain Dyadya Gourdjiev was finished, he continued his own thought to prove to the old man how little he thought of what he'd said. "She's like a spanner in the works. I don't know what she's been up to—I suspect you don't, either, not that it matters, I know you wouldn't tell me even if you did. But I know she's not stupid enough to tell you."

"She's not stupid at all," Dyadya Gourdjiev felt compelled to say. "On the contrary."

"Yes, on the contrary." Batchuk opened the door, the empty hallway looming in front of him. There was a smear of blood there, too,

too large for him to cover with his heel, or even his entire shoe. "And that, essentially, is the problem. She's too smart for your own good."

"*My* own good?" Dyadya Gourdjiev said, reacting to the warning.

"Yes," Batchuk acknowledged as he stepped into the echoey hallway. "And hers."

SIXTEEN

JACK AWOKE with the scent of Annika on him, and it was as if he were in another world, as if he'd eaten a bowl of peaches last night and now smelled of them. Nevertheless, opening his eyes, he immediately felt a kind of remorse. Not that he hadn't enjoyed himself, because he had, immensely; what occurred to him were the consequences, because experience had taught him that there were always consequences from having sex with another human being, no matter what your partner claimed at the time. If you had any emotions they were bound to be stirred by intimacy of any sort. He'd known plenty of guys who hadn't cared who they'd slept with—to a man they were either in loveless marriages or divorced. In any case, they still inhabited the same bars where, back in the day, they'd always scored. Now, however, they felt old, isolated from the feverish pace of a dating scene they no longer belonged to, or even understood.

Next to him, Annika was still asleep, her cruel scars rising and

falling with her slow breathing. She turned, then, her head still bur-
rowed in the pillow, facing him. For a moment, he did nothing but
watch her, as if, in her sleep, she would tell him something about
herself. But she remained resolutely a mystery, as, in fact, all women
were mysteries, and he wondered now whether he knew her any better than he knew Sharon. On the face of it, an absurd notion, equat-
ing a woman he'd just met with the woman he had lived with for
twenty-three years. But the truth was staring at him with Annika's
quiescent face, which held no expression, or perhaps just the hint of a
smile, as if her dream were more real to her than the world around
her, than Jack himself. It made him wonder whether it was possible
for one person to know another. Weren't there always surprises, like
layers of an onion being peeled away only to reveal another person,
one we scarcely knew, or had for years tried our best not to understand,
preferring a manufactured reality that reflected the things we required?

This was what he'd done with Sharon, and now that the reality
he'd manufactured had cracked and crumbled away he knew Emma
was right: they'd never had a chance. And yet, in retrospect it was
heartbreaking to see how one misstep had led to another, and another, and so on, small accretions of mistakes that had become a life
less lived. It seemed odd to him, even ludicrous that he had once held
her in his arms, that they had whispered intimacies to one another,
that they could have said "I love you," in any conceivable setting. That
time had collapsed in on itself; it was the opposite of when you walked
into a house you used to live in or a room you'd once known like the
back of your hand and nothing had changed. Now that house, that
room, that woman were all changed, unfamiliar to him, as if observed in another man's life. He closed his eyes for a moment, wanting to completely uproot all the acrid memories and stark revelations
cropping up in his mind like weeds after a soaking rain.

Lifting the covers, he rolled out of bed carefully enough not to wake her. Slipping into clothes, he opened the door and padded into the living room, where Alli, already awake, sat curled on the end of the chocolate velvet sofa directly beneath the mandala. She held a mug half filled with hot tea, which she handed to him as he sat down beside her.

"Have fun?" she said as he took a sip.

Jack tried to assess her tone. Was she disapproving, pissed, being ironic, or trying for casually adult? He came to the conclusion that it didn't matter. Sitting beside her made him realize how foolish his brief stab of fear had been; he'd never be like those former acquaintances of his, not as long as he had Alli. "*She's yours, Jack, for better or for worse,*" Annika had said last night.

"Did you?" he said at length.

She took back the mug of tea he offered her. "I didn't even have to put my ear to the wall." When he looked over at her, she added mischievously, "I heard everything."

His face drained of blood. "I'm sorry you heard anything."

"I didn't." She laughed. "But now I know what the two of you did." Leaning over, she sniffed him. "Besides, you smell like a rutting animal."

"Charming."

She shrugged, utterly unconcerned. "Hey, we're all animals when you come right down to it."

"So you don't disapprove?"

"Would you care?"

He considered for only an instant. "Yes, I think I would."

She looked surprised, or perhaps a better word would be amused. "Thank you."

Jack took the tea back from her. He was feeling both the warmth and the caffeine.

Watching him sip what was left of the tea, she said, "Now I want to hear all about the visit from Emma."

Alli was the only one who believed that Emma had returned, or hadn't actually gone away, he'd given up trying to figure out which. It was a relief being able to confide this aspect of his life, which was both eerie and joyous.

"And then you'll tell me everything, right?"

Her face screwed up in a quizzical look. "About what?"

"You know about what, about what happened to you when you were with Morgan Herr."

With the mention of her abductor's name her expression changed subtly. Perhaps he was the only one who would have noticed, and a wave of regret washed over him, because the last thing he wanted was to alienate her. But he was trusting Annika now, trusting what she had said to him last night: *She wants to tell you.*

Alli cocked her head to one side, a bad sign, he knew. "Are you proposing a quid pro quo?"

"I'm asking—"

"Like a politician? Is that what you are now?"

"Forget it." He closed his eyes. "I don't want to know."

"Why not?" Her voice changed suddenly, grown deeper and darker, as if with an adult's disappointments and loss. "Why wouldn't you?"

"It's too late, it's over, there's nothing in the past except tears."

The little sound she made caused him to look over, to see that she was crying, the tears overflowing her lids and rolling down her cheeks.

"Don't take her away from me, I already miss her too much."

"I'm not taking anything away from you," he said as he gathered her into his arms, "least of all Emma."

But it wasn't just Emma she meant, he was certain of that, she was also saying, Don't take away my chance to tell you. And now he knew for a certainty that Annika had been right. So he recounted word for word—a quirk of his dyslexic brain—his conversation with Emma last night, and when he was finished, she said: "Is it true what she said about you and Sharon?"

He nodded. "We were just fooling ourselves. There's nothing left, because there was nothing to begin with, nothing but sex."

"'Things fall apart; the center cannot hold,'" Alli said, quoting Yeats, one of the poets she'd learned to love from Emma. "Emma always said everything that's born holds the seeds of its own destruction."

And Jack thought again of dissolution, of how being an Outsider, of hiding in the shadows, observing without yourself being observed, was its own form of dissolution long before the advent of death.

"Did Emma say that or did Morgan Herr?"

"I know you don't want to hear this," Alli said, pulling away, "but they both did."

Jack felt a shiver run through him, as if Herr had somehow managed to walk over his grave. "Did Emma get her philosophy from him?"

Alli shook her head. "No, but on some level they were both nihilists. I don't think Emma ever saw the point in life, and I know he didn't."

"He said that to you?"

"Not in so many words." Her eyes could not meet his. "He didn't have to."

"I'll make us more tea," he said gently.

"No. Stay here, don't leave me."

He settled back into the sofa cushions. It was getting toward nine; he knew they needed to get moving because the longer they stayed in Kiev the colder Magnussen's trail would become. On the other hand, he was reluctant to make a move that would break the tenuous strand to Alli's past she had begun to spin. Besides, with her wounded arm, Annika could use all the sleep she could get.

"I'm not going anywhere," he said, as much to himself as to her.

She smiled at him, but it was thin and brittle enough to put him on edge. What could be coming? he wondered. What had she been bottling up inside her since her abduction?

"Emma knew him way before I did."

Jack knew this, just as he knew she was speaking of Morgan Herr, whose name she couldn't bear to say.

"Emma saw something in him—she never told me what—but I imagine they sat around and talked about how things were falling apart, how the center couldn't hold, how chaos ruled everyone and everything."

Jack wanted to interject a comment, but he bit his lip instead, trying to warm his abruptly chilled extremities.

"He was charismatic, girls especially were drawn to him—as you know. But with Emma it was different. She wasn't sucked into his orbit, she never adored him or was fooled by his charming exterior. She knew what he was; in fact, I'm convinced now that was why she spent time with him. He was an Outsider on a level it would never occur to her to go. Emma would never harm another human being, but I think she wanted to know why *he* would."

Jack was listening very carefully, even though Alli was talking about his daughter and not about herself. Or was she? He knew that whatever had happened to her during the week she had been under Morgan Herr's control had had a profound effect on her, possibly even changed her, perhaps forever. Whatever this thing was she had been struggling with it for months, trying to understand it, or to see it for what it really was.

"I . . . I never told you the truth, during that time before the inauguration." Alli stared at her hands. "He told me not to."

Jack couldn't help himself now. "Of course he told you not to, that was part of the brainwashing."

She shook her head, slowly but firmly. "It wasn't only the brainwashing—I mean I don't remember that part. I *wanted* to do what he

told me to do. I *wanted* to carry the anthrax, I *wanted* to hurt all those people. I hated my parents so much for all the years they didn't—"

She broke down abruptly and Jack took her to him again, feeling her body wracked with sobs.

"I was weak. Emma would never have been so stupid to do what he wanted—she knew that beneath the charismatic exterior he was the worst kind of monster. I knew nothing, he hooked me when he got inside my head, he knew all the strings to pull, all the buttons to push. He knew where I was weak, which was easy, because, unlike Emma, I had no strength anywhere inside me, and he knew that, too." Her sobbing had taken on epic proportions. "How do you fight someone who knows you better than you know yourself?"

"I don't know," Jack said gently. "I don't think anyone—"

"Oh, but Emma could, and that's the point. I'm a product of privilege, there isn't anything I wanted that my parents didn't get me—every piece of crap, no matter how expensive. And what did that do? It made me soft—that's what he said to me, 'You're soft as the underbelly of a sow, you wallow in money, prestige, privilege, and what have you to show for it? You make me sick to my stomach, but you can change that, you can become tough as nails, hard as a rock if you set your mind to it. Like your best friend, like Emma.'"

She clutched at him as if he were a lifeline, as if he were the only resource she had to keep her from drowning in the deep sea of her emotions. "And I wanted to be like Emma so, so much. He knew that, just like he knew everything else about me. He knew how much I envied Emma, he knew that even though I loved her I was jealous of what she had—not money, not prestige, not privilege, those were all as phony, as ineffectual as I was. She was tough, she was hard, she could be anything she wanted to be, and it all came from inside herself. She was everything I ever dreamed of being, and I was nothing, nothing at all."

"What's going on here?"

Jack held Alli tighter as if needing to protect her from Annika's question. "Nothing," he said. "She's out here in the back of beyond, she's just homesick, that's all."

"That's all?"

He heard the skepticism in her voice and he said more harshly than he had perhaps intended, "That's enough—more than enough."

"Of course it is."

Annika turned and went down the hall into the bathroom. Through the closed door he could just barely hear the sound of running water over Alli's slowly weakening sobs.

"It's all right," he said. "Everything is going to be all right."

"That's what I want. You don't know . . ."

But he did know, because it was what he wanted, too. Emma's death had been a nightmare, and then Alli's abduction, a nightmare for everyone. Where was it going to end, when was it going to end? If everything was moving toward dissolution why wasn't it ending, why were both he and Alli still suffering so?

With a conscious effort, he pushed her away from him, held her at arm's length until he willed her to look at him. "You've got to stop torturing yourself, that's only your guilt talking. You're brave and smart and resourceful. Maybe Emma was the catalyst, but those things came from inside you, they're nobody else's, they're yours."

Alli's eyes, still enlarged with tears, locked onto his, and a wan smile crossed her face. "Guilt isn't all that binds us, is it, Jack? I'd hate to think—"

"It's not," he said. "Of course it's not."

"That's what Annika thinks, I'm sure of it."

"Does that bother you?"

She tried to laugh, wiping away the tracks of her tears. "I wish it didn't."

"She's the psycho-bitch, remember?"

Now Alli did laugh. "She isn't, you know she isn't."

Jack was somewhat surprised. "What changed your mind?"

"I don't know, I—"

"Enough crying, for pity's sake!" For the second time, Annika interrupted them. She had emerged from the bathroom, her head to one side, drying her hair with a towel. "With that flood of misery anyone would think you're Russian. Come on, what are we waiting for?"

Both Jack and Alli jumped up as if they were stung. As Alli passed Annika on the way to the bathroom, Jack said, "We need to get to Alushta. Driving will be the safest way."

"Also the slowest." She threw her damp towel onto the sofa cushion where Alli had been sitting and, before her, Emma. She watched to see if he would protest, or even comment. When he didn't, she continued. "It will take us too long to get to the coast by car. Besides, there are regular roadblocks between here and the Crimean peninsula to catch contraband. Thankfully we have your private jet."

"It's not my private jet," Jack said, "but I take your point."

While Alli padded by him to get dressed he pulled out his cell phone and punched in the pilot's number.

"Give me forty minutes and we'll be ready to go," the pilot said, "but I need to log a flight plan. Where are we going?"

"To the airport nearest Alushta," Jack told him, "in the Crimea, on the Black Sea coast."

"I'll get right on it," the pilot said, and disconnected.

Forty minutes later the three of them arrived at Zhulyany Airport.

"SIMFEROPOL NORTH Airport."

"Where?" Kirilenko pressed the cell phone to his ear so hard the cartilage ached. "Where the hell is that?"

"Crimea." His assistant's voice came through the ether hard, abrupt, and ominous, like a nail punched through a tin can. "She showed up on the Zhulyany Airport CCTV as she passed through into the VIP terminal."

"The VIP terminal?" Kirilenko, driving back to Kiev from the wild-goose chase in Brovary, was trying to process information that was coming at him too quickly. "First, tell me, was Annika Dementieva alone?"

"She was with a man and girl," his assistant said.

Kirilenko pulled out Limonev's cell phone and looked again at the low-resolution photo of the people caught emerging from Rochev's dacha. In his mind's eye he saw again the three sets of footprints in the woods: the man's, the woman's—and the girl's. Yes, yes, he thought excitedly, he was onto something here. "Did you get photos of them from the CCTV images?"

"Of course. They're on your desk."

"Tell me you discovered why Annika Dementieva and her friends were in the VIP terminal."

"I have the information right here." There came the sound of shuffling papers. "They boarded a private jet that's on its way to, as I said, Simferopol."

Kirilenko scowled. Something was not adding up here. "Since when does a fugitive have access to a private jet?"

"I don't know."

"Well, dammit, bloody well find out!"

"I already tried," his assistant said. "But the jet is American, under full diplomatic protection. I can't find out a thing about it, except its next destination, which, if you have the right contacts, is public knowledge."

His assistant was of course trying to recoup points he'd lost with his boss, but Kirilenko scarcely noticed. He'd broken out into a cold sweat. *This must be Harry Martin's doing,* he thought, panic-stricken. *That sonuvabitch has been playing me, he's known all along about Annika's ties to Karl Rochev, or at least suspected them. As soon as I brought him to*

Rochev's dacha he must have known. That was why he sent me to that absurd town, Brovary, while he returned at once to Kiev. It was a ruse to keep me occupied while he reeled Annika in like a fish. He wiped the sweat out of his eyes. *Christ,* he thought, *what are the Americans up to?*

Such was the turmoil of his mind that he almost missed what his assistant said next: "As I said, Simferopol North Airport is in the Crimea, approximately midway between Balaklava and Alushta."

His initial panic turned to outrage at being manipulated by the Americans—of all people!—and then to rage at Henry Martin in particular. In so doing he managed to gather himself. If that was how Martin was going to play it, he told himself grimly, then that's how it would be played all around.

"I'm only twenty minutes away from Kiev," Kirilenko said, heading directly for the airport. "I want to be on the next flight out from Zhulyany to Simferopol North."

"Two seats, I assume, one for you and one for Harry Martin," his assistant said.

"One seat." Kirilenko put on speed. "If Martin asks, I'm still in Brovary, my nose to the grindstone. And if word of where I've gone should leak to the Americans I will personally shoot you in the back of the head."

SEVENTEEN

HARRY MARTIN, hanging on the phone in the middle of a bustling Kiev street, didn't like his job—in point of fact he loathed it with a seething, poisonous intent. The truth was he was sick to death of all the double-dealing, disinformation, obfuscation, and outright lies that came so easily to him. And that, of course, was what he despised most of all—that all the artifice was second nature to him now, ingrained like the whorls of his fingerprints or the pattern of his DNA. He simply did not know any other way to live, if this was living at all, which he'd begun to seriously doubt. And therein lay the rub, as the good Bard wrote, he thought, because the only thing to fear was doubt. He knew from his mentors that the moment you allowed doubt to creep into your thinking—doubt about your ability, about the people around you, about the dark and gravelike profession you were in—you were as good as dead. It was time to get out while you were still on your own two legs, rather than lying in a coffin stiff as a log. Doubt made you hesitate, doubt clouded your judgement and, worse, dulled your instincts, because, really, when you came down to it, your instincts were all that kept you alive. Instincts and, to an extent, experience.

Feeling as apart from those around him as the shadows on the building facades, he listened while the electronic connections were made, one by one, like the tumblers of a lock or a safe falling into place. He knew his call was being routed and rerouted through a complex network. This was how his boss liked his security; this was how it was done, no questions were ever asked by anyone within the system, least of all Martin himself.

Doubt felled few of his kind, however. More often, if it wasn't a bullet or old age, years of stress delivered the knockout blow via a dyspeptic stomach, ulcers, or worst of all, irritable bowel syndrome. Nothing, he thought, would take you out of the field faster than having to hug the porcelain horse unexpectedly and in debilitating succession. Martin had developed none of these symptoms. Not that he didn't feel the stress; it worked its corrosive magic on even the most inhuman of agents. But he relieved the stress by being angry; the more stress he felt the angrier he got. Anger kept him sharp, kept him close to his instincts. Even more important, it kept doubt at bay.

"Yes?"

At last his master's voice entered his ear via his cell phone. "Can you talk?"

"What do you have for me?" General Atcheson Brandt, said.

"There's another faction in the field," Martin said.

"What, precisely, do you mean?"

Martin could feel in those words the General coming to full attention, as if he were a pointer who'd smelled blood. "Someone else was at Rochev's dacha—someone who belongs neither to Kirilenko nor to the SBU."

"I trust you can be more specific," Brandt said with all the considerable asperity at his disposal.

Martin began walking, more to dispel nervous energy than toward any specific destination. His lack of success in finding Annika Dementieva was going to be last on his discussion list with the General.

"There was a sharpshooter hidden in the woods," Martin said. "He took a shot at one of the people who were in the dacha—" He stopped right there, knowing he'd made a mistake.

"You let them get away?" Brandt's voice was like a rumble of thunder heading Martin's way at tremendous speed. "How did that happen?"

At this very instant Martin hated his job with a malevolence that set his heart palpitating. "There was a fire, confusion, everything collapsed into chaos, and when we—"

"Most convenient, that fire, wouldn't you say? Most clever."

Martin, leaning wearily against the plate-glass window of a men's clothing store, found himself staring at an Italian cashmere sweater he yearned for but couldn't afford. He needed to slow his heart rate, to learn not to hate so much, but it was too late, the venom was in his blood, in the very marrow of his bones.

"Yes, sir. They used the fire to escape."

"They, you keep saying 'they.'" Brandt's voice buzzed in his ear like a trapped wasp. "Who, precisely, are 'they'? Besides Annika Dementieva, of course."

That was the crux of the issue, Martin thought sourly—he didn't know and, worse, he couldn't tell the General that he didn't know. It was clear that he had to change the subject, go on the offensive, take the pressure off himself, deflect the General's questions by raising others the General needed to answer.

"I hope to God you haven't been keeping anything from me—"

"Keeping what?" the General said. "What are you talking about?"

"—because out here in the field where tough decisions, terrible decisions, life-and-death decisions have to be made in an instant, not knowing the complete playing field could prove fatal."

"Listen—"

"If you know anything—anything at all—about this other faction, who, it must be assumed, are after the same thing you are, then I need to know about it now, not tomorrow, not later."

"I don't cotton to being interrupted."

The General's voice was like a fistful of fury, and Martin knew it was fortunate that he wasn't in the same room with his boss. There was a story about Brandt: As a senior in the Academy he threw a rival out a second-floor window, breaking his leg. Anyone else would have been summarily expelled, but Brandt was so brilliant, his family so well connected, that no disciplinary action was taken nor was there a civil suit filed. Though the story might very well be apocryphal it nevertheless served the General well, having lent him a mythical sheen all through his career.

"It goes without saying that if I knew anything about a rival faction in the field I'd let you know," the General said, filling the awful void that had sprung up between them. "I don't know what the hell is going on, but I'll tell you one thing: I sure as hell am going to find out."

While staring at the cashmere sweater with its V-neck, double stitching, and magnificent silky texture, he discovered that he didn't believe the General, not for a minute. On the contrary, he knew in his bones, in their very venom-riddled marrow, that the General was lying through his teeth. Of course he knew about "another faction," he'd known from the beginning of this wretched assignment. And at that precise moment Martin suspected this mission would be the death of him. Worse—far worse, as far as he was concerned—he finally understood, with a godforsaken clarity, the underlying reason why he loathed his job with a seething, poisonous intent. The General was like Harry Martin's father, so much so, in fact, that he now couldn't for the life of him understand why he hadn't seen it before.

"In that regard," the General carried on, "your instructions vis-

à-vis Annika Dementieva are hereby changed. Finding her and taking her into custody will no longer suffice. I want her terminated
ASAP."

Leaning with his forehead against the cool plate-glass window,
he closed the phone and at the same time thought, *It's that damn cashmere sweater.* It reminded him so much of the one his father used to
wear around the house, swapping his suit jacket for the sweater, but
never taking off his tie, not at dinner, not afterward. Martin remembered wondering whether his father slept in his tie, except the next
morning he'd emerge from the marital bedroom in a crisp white or
blue shirt with a different tie knotted perfectly at his Adam's apple.

I want that cashmere sweater because it was my father's, Martin thought
now. He turned away from the shop window display, lurched over to
the gutter and, bending over the gap between two parked cars, vom-
ited up his breakfast. He hadn't done that since he was fifteen and,
sneaking home after curfew, had encountered his father in the lightless foyer, who had struck him so hard across the face his outsized
knuckles had drawn blood from his son's nose and cheek. Turning on
his heel, the old man had climbed the stairs and closed the door to his
bedroom without uttering a single word.

Martin had raised himself to his knees and, without thinking,
spent the next twenty minutes wiping his blood and vomit off the
wooden floor, scrubbing and polishing the boards until they shined
even through the darkness. With each tread he climbed, his dread at
encountering his father again mounted until, as he reached the second-
floor landing, his hands were shaking and his knees refused to carry
him any further. He collapsed there, rolling onto his side, curled up
like an injured caterpillar, and eventually fell into a sleep made fitful
by images of himself running from a pack of grinning dog-faced boys
in military uniforms.

Standing abruptly erect Martin staggered away from the scene of
his unspeakable humiliation and sought refuge in a tea shop down the

block, where he slid onto a chair by the window and stared bleakly at the hurrying masses of bundled, red-faced Ukrainians. What his mind saw, though, was the General, or rather his father—now they were murderously interchangeable. He thought when he'd buried his father that would be the end of his misery, his suffering, his neediness, but no, he had chosen a job, or perhaps it had chosen him, that mimicked the relationship he had found both intolerable and indispensable. What was he now in middle age, he asked himself, but the same adolescent whom he'd despised for so desperately needing the approval of a man he loathed. *How does the human mind do it?* he wondered. *How can it thrive on antithetical, antagonistic, diametrically opposed absolutes?*

And then, his mind still unable to let go of that cashmere sweater, he began to think of Sherrie because—and this was the really strange part—in the wintertime she had liked to walk around the apartment in an oversized man's V-neck cashmere sweater. Just the sweater and nothing else, her long, pale legs emerging from the bottom, and when she turned around, a glimpse of the bottom of her lush buttocks. She liked to tease him that way, a behavior that must have been a form of revenge, because one evening when he returned from overseas—Munich or perhaps Istanbul, he couldn't remember which—she was gone: Sherrie, her suitcase, and her cashmere sweater; the drawers in the bedroom, the shelf in the bathroom, the half of his closet he'd ceded to her empty. The smell of her lingered like a last cigarette, but only for a day or so. By that time he'd called her more than a dozen times, had gone by her apartment at night, like a stalker, looking for lights, for her silhouette against the drawn Roman shades. Nothing moved, nothing remained, and eventually he forgot her.

But he hadn't forgotten her, because here she was now, or at least the memory of her, as he stared bleakly out into the crowded Kiev street, haunting him as if she had just left him moments before, or yesterday, instead of three years ago. He wished she were here now, though what he'd say to her he had no idea. Not that it mattered; he was alone. There was no Sherrie, or any of the girls before or after her, whose faces folded into each other along with their names. They were all gone, they'd never actually been there, he hadn't let them.

The waitress took his order, returning almost immediately with a small pitcher of cream and miniature bowls of sugar and honey. She smiled at him but he didn't return it.

His eyes were red-rimmed with bloodlust, his heart a blackened cinder beyond any hope of repair or remediation. He wanted neither; he wanted only to kill someone, to steep his hands in blood, Annika Dementieva's blood.

"YUKIN IS going to want tangible concessions," General Brandt said as he and President Carson landed in Sheremetyevo airport. "That's how it works here, they're Russians, talk means nothing—less than nothing. People say things here—Yukin among them—they don't mean. The air needs to be filled with buzzing, any form of buzzing will do, in fact, the less truthful the better."

"I know all this," Edward Carson said. "Lies obfuscate, and as far as the Russians are concerned, the more obfuscation the better." He wore a neat charcoal suit with a red tie and an enamel pin of the American flag affixed to his lapel. Brandt, on the other hand, had decided to come to Russia in his military uniform, complete with his chestful of medals. Uniforms impressed the Russians, they always had. They were like the worst bullies on the block, lashing out with strained aggression to compensate for their insecurities. They knew better than anyone that the Western powers viewed them as semicivilized, as if they were apes pretending to be human beings.

Having slowed to nominal ground speed, Air Force One turned off the runway and began the long slow taxiing to the VIP terminal.

"We have prioritized the concessions we've put into the final draft of the accord," Carson continued, "chief among them the revision of our missile defense deployments around Russia."

"The conservatives are going to scream about that one," the General said.

"They forfeited the right to complain when they fucked things six ways from Sunday when they were in power," the president said. "Besides, General, you and I both know the technology for the missile defense system is still not in place. If we had to implement it today or next week or even six months from now it would be a joke."

"It's real enough to President Yukin."

"Because it surrounds Russia like a noose."

The General nodded. "I've gone on record on both ABC and CNN that our proposed MDS is the main reason for Yukin's recent aggression into Georgia."

Carson lifted a finger. "One thing I need to make clear. Yukin can't expect unilateral support from us, I'm not coming to him on bended knee."

"Absolutely not. That would give him an advantage he'd never relinquish. But that can't happen now, because he wants something from us only we can give him."

"I hope to God you're right, General. Everything depends on this security accord being signed."

Brandt sat back, never more sure of the plan he'd outlined to the president days after his taking over the Oval Office. It was crucial, he'd argued, to enlist Russia in the crusade to keep nuclear weapons out of Iranian hands. They knew through intelligence and back-channel diplomatic sources precisely what missile parts Russia was selling to Iran. Nothing the previous administration had done had had any effect on Yukin's business dealings with Iran, a result Brandt had predicted with unerring accuracy. Carson was different, however; he'd listened to reason, had agreed when Brandt had outlined an alternative method of weaning Yukin away from the dangerous Iranian teat.

If the diplomatic rapprochement was the foundation method,

then the security accord was the cornerstone to its success. Which was why Brandt was replaying in his mind the disturbing phone call from Harry Martin. Of course he knew about the other faction in the field—that was the whole point of Martin's mission to intercept Annika Dementieva. Annika was the key to everything. That Martin had not yet been able to find her was unsettling enough, but the fact that he had now gotten wind of the other faction meant that it was far more advanced in its plans than he knew about or had been led to believe. One of two conclusions could be drawn from this: Either the other faction had suddenly gained in power or the sources he'd been relying on had underestimated it. Neither possibility was a happy thought, especially with the accord signing imminent.

"Excuse me, sir," he said, unbuckling his seat belt and standing up. "I need to make a call."

Going forward down the wide aisle, he punched in a number that was too secret to keep either on his speed dial or in the cell's phone book. It was a number he'd committed to memory the moment it had been given to him.

As the connection was going through he reflected on just how much he hated dealing with the Russians. To a man, they were a treacherous lot, the long shadow of Josef Stalin stretching into the present. They were all Stalin's students, the General thought, whether or not they were aware of it. His viperous double- and triple-dealing became the political template—not to mention the KGB's modus operandi—set in the kind of monumental stone it was impossible to undermine, let alone destroy.

Brandt himself had become a secret student of Stalin's, of his history of blood, broken bones, and broken promises, in order to prepare himself for taking on the Soviet Bear. The dissolution of the USSR hadn't fooled him the way it had others. Russia's power might have been broken, but he knew it to be temporary; its flinty spine, fortified by Uncle Joe's vampiric shadow, was still very much intact.

"I have three minutes."

The voice in Brandt's ear caused him to bristle inwardly, but he swallowed his outrage because he knew that, in fact, he only had three minutes. "My man in the field has just informed me that the opposition is gaining ground."

"Even if that's the case," Oriel Jovovich Batchuk said, "these people are no match for *Trinadtsat*. They have neither the manpower nor the resources to take advantage of the situation."

Batchuk wasn't denying it! Brandt massaged his forehead with his fingertips while shielding his eyes with the palm of his hand, dispelling the possibility that anyone on board Air Force One might inadvertently see the expression of consternation on his face. "It seems to me that we have to entertain the possibility that the situation on the ground is being rewritten even as we stand here talking to one another."

"A hiccup, that's all," the deputy prime minister said. "We still hold the high ground, that's all that matters."

Batchuk had power in spades, that was indisputable, but what they were aiming for was so complex that no one man could guarantee its success. Acknowledging this reality was, after all, the prime reason he and Batchuk had forged this risky alliance and even riskier plan, why each of them was wagering their power and their influence—everything they possessed—with their respective presidents. For Brandt, however, there was another matter: money. He'd never had it, had been forced by his expertise at political maneuvering to be around those who did, and he burned with envy. He wanted his share of the gravy train and God help anyone who stood in his way.

"To ensure our success," he said now, putting stress on every word, "I've put out an immediate sanction on Annika Dementieva." He expected a response, possibly an irate one, from Batchuk, but his words were met only by silence. "I'm convinced she's causing this hiccup, as you call it. A cure is needed, even for a hiccup."

"I would find it difficult to disagree with you," Batchuk said. "Who has been given the assignment?"

"Harry Martin. He's the assassin-in-place."

"Where is he at the moment? At Zhulyany, I assume."

"If he was at the Kiev airport," the General said, growing annoyed at the note of condescension in Batchuk's voice, "I'm sure he would have told me."

"Hmm, interesting."

Now the General really was annoyed. "How so?"

"Rhon Fyodovich Kirilenko, the FSB officer your man Martin is supposed to be shadowing—"

"I know who the hell Kirilenko is," the General said, beginning to lose his temper despite himself.

"Kirilenko's name has just shown up on a flight manifest departing Zhulyany in forty-three minutes, bound for Simferopol North Airport in the Crimea." Batchuk cleared his throat, the better to emphasize what he said next: "Either your man Martin is an incompetent or he's decided to play both ends against the middle."

"I know Harry," the General said, "and he's neither."

"Then figure out your own explanation," Batchuk said.

The General immediately phoned Martin and informed him of Kirilenko's whereabouts. The moment he heard the surprise in Martin's voice he resolved to put another man in the field ASAP. This he did the moment his call to Martin was over.

He shifted from one leg to another, his body creaky and diminished inside the perfectly pressed uniform with its splendid show of medals and commendations.

"General, it's time."

The president's voice, strong and firm as always, caused him to return down the aisle at his usual crisp pace to where Carson was now standing, waiting for the door to open while the contingent of Secret Service operatives buzzed around him like horseflies.

"You look gray-faced, Archie," the president said under his breath. "Is there anything wrong, anything I need to know?"

"No, sir," Brandt said, struggling to regain his composure, "of course not."

"Because we're on the firing line now, about to go into battle and, to paraphrase Sonny Corleone, I don't want to come out of this aircraft with only my dick in my hand."

The General nodded. "Understood, sir. I have your back, your guns are loaded, and all your ammunition is dry and awaiting your orders."

"That's the spirit," Carson said with a tight smile.

The flight attendant spun the door wheel and it opened inward. The first of the president's agents took command of the rolling stairs, then others checked out the immediate vicinity. For a moment, they spoke with their opposite numbers in the Russian secret service, then one of them turned, gave a brief, reassuring nod to his commander in chief.

"Okay, General," the president said. "Here we go."

THESE DAYS Dennis Paull never slept; he never stayed in one place for very long, either. It was as if he needed to keep one step ahead of the banshee that was on his trail. That banshee—or demon or ghost, whatever you wanted to call it—had a name: Nina, the woman he'd had an affair with who had almost killed Edward Carson at his inauguration. Only Jack McClure's timely intervention had saved the president. For that Paull would be eternally grateful. If only Jack could exorcize the demon or ghost or banshee that haunted Paull's waking life, but Jack was just a man, not a sorcerer.

Paull, who had set up a temporary office in a Residence Inn on the outskirts of the District, planned to spend his nights unearthing all there was to know about the members of Edward Carson's inner circle. He sat at a drab desk in front of his souped-up laptop, scanning a screen full of information from yet another government database he'd hacked into. Factoids from the public and private lives of Vice President Crawford, Kinkaid Marshall, G. Robert Kroftt, and William Rogers floated across his screen like messages from a phosphorescent universe. He was particularly interested in Crawford. Like John Kennedy and Lyndon Johnson before him, Carson had been drawn into a shotgun wedding with the old-line and conservative Crawford in order to carry Texas and the other swing states in the old South. The two men never got along. Though their public face was all smiles, behind closed doors their politics was fraught with friction and, at times, animosity. Though Crawford wasn't nearly as bad as some of the intransigent members of the party, Paull didn't like him; he certainly didn't trust his style of backroom wheeling and dealing. Who knew what insidious pols Crawford was in bed with.

This was the work Paull had been doing since he arrived at just after six in the evening. It was now half past eleven. To one side was an open cardboard box with the remaining two slices of pepperoncini pizza from Papa John's. He rose, went to the bathroom, and washed the olive oil off his hands. Then he crossed to the window, peering through the slatted blinds at the smeared headlights on the highway. The traffic's constant drone made him feel as if he were inside a beehive, an appropriate sound track for his working environment.

All at once he shivered and, focusing on the reflection of the room in the glass, thought he saw Nina, or more accurately her shadow, passing from right to left. Whirling, he confronted the half-dark room, lit only by the lamp that shed a pool of light over the desk, his work area, one corner of the stained pizza box, bloody with tomato sauce.

He wanted to laugh at the empty space, at his own foolish fears, but something stopped him, a sense of foreboding, perhaps, that he couldn't shake. There was, for him, a sense of things ending, instead of beginning as they should have with the installation of the new administration. The world appeared to be sliding away from him, as if it were falling off the edge of a table into darkness.

Of course he was furious for allowing himself to be deceived by Nina, but that was in the past and it belonged there. Nevertheless, he was still furious, possibly more so, because he couldn't forget her, because he missed her. She hadn't been just another fuck, she hadn't been just another sexy woman. When she betrayed him she'd devoured a piece of him he now knew he'd never get back. In the wake of her betrayal he felt diminished, not simply foolish or abashed. She'd stolen something vital.

Turning back to the window he stared out at a world hustling by, indifferent to his pain. He was alone, as he would be in the moment before death took him, and this made him think of his father, who was alone when he died because Paull was busy studying for his graduate school finals. He wished his father were here now, because he was the only person Paull had ever been able to confide in. Even Edward Carson, arguably his best friend, didn't know everything Paull's father had. The man had been compassionate enough to forgive Paull his sins and mistakes no matter their severity. "Why wouldn't I forgive you," he said once, "you're my son." And then, continuing, said, "Your mother's gone and forgotten. You're all I've got, I have to forgive you." And yet he died alone, Paull thought, as we all do, whether we forgive or not, whether we hold people close to us or push them away, as Paull had his own wife, who was in the final, horrifying stages of Alzheimer's, locked away in a facility. He went to see her less and less these days; she didn't know him, but what did that matter, he had an obligation, didn't he, he'd taken an oath: in sickness and in health. But he'd distanced himself from her, both physically and emotionally. She was like a painting, or someone perpetually asleep, dreaming a life he could never understand. Did a radish dream, or a head of cabbage? She never responded in the slightest

way to the music he put on during his visits—Al Hibbler singing
"After the Lights Go Down Low," for instance, or the Everly Brothers singing "All I Have to Do Is Dream," songs they had loved and, in
their youth, had danced to. He'd thought of this, a calming consolation, when six months ago he'd taken up one of the spare pillows and
prepared to lower it over her face that, in her infirmity, had grown
round and shiny as a metal globe. She wouldn't know what was happening, what he was doing to her, and if she did, he was certain she'd
be grateful. What kind of life was this she led? Even cows had it better, but not, perhaps, radishes. He was seconds away from doing it, his
fingers gripping the sides of the pillow, his mind already made up, set
on its path, when the music came on: Roy Hamilton's "Don't Let
Go." It seemed somehow sacrilegious to commit murder—even compassionate murder—while that song was playing ("I'm so happy I got
you here/Don't let go, don't let go"), and something inside him shifted,
everything changed and, turning, he put the pillow back where he'd
found it. Then, without a backward glance at his wife or the radish, he
left and hadn't been back since.

He turned back into the hotel room, away from the glare of the
headlights, and sat back down at the dingy desk and the endless lines
of information scrolling across his laptop's screen.

Why wouldn't he forgive Nina, she was all he had.

But Nina was beyond his forgiveness, Jack had shot her through
the heart before she'd had a chance to poison everyone at the inauguration with the vial of anthrax given to her by Morgan Herr. This,
then, was Dennis Paull's dilemma as he sat scrolling through the so-
far innocuous mountain of electronic data: He was indebted to Jack
McClure for saving Edward Carson, but he hated Jack for killing
Nina.

RHON FYODOVICH Kirilenko had just enough time to swing by
his office and pick up the photos his assistant had pulled off the CCTV

cameras at Zhulyany Airport before transferring to a waiting FSB vehicle that took him, at reckless speed, to board his scheduled flight to Simferopol.

While his driver was weaving through the clogged arteries of Kiev he studied each of the three photos. The first was of the three people: Annika Dementieva he could see clearly enough. Behind her, his face partially obscured, was a man who looked vaguely familiar. Kirilenko spent several fruitless minutes trying to place the visible features before moving on. The second photo was of the young girl, who bore no resemblance to anyone in Kirilenko's memory bank. He studied this photo in a rather abstract manner; for the life of him he couldn't figure out what she was doing with the two adults. To his knowledge, which was extensive to the point of encyclopedic, Annika Dementieva had no sisters, and the girl was too old to be her daughter. So who on earth was she? Sighing in frustration he turned to the third and last photo, which was a full-face shot of the man. Almost immediately a galvanic shock rode up his spine. He knew this man, he worked for the President of the United States. What the hell was he doing with Annika Dementieva?

Kirilenko stared out the window, seeing nothing but his own muddled thoughts. He knew his duty was to inform his superior of this shocking development, but something—a stubbornness, resentment, a feeling of being at once played and betrayed—stayed his hand. He was tired of being manipulated. Bad enough to be fucked over by the Americans, that kind of treatment was a given, but to be fucked by his own people, who had to know they were throwing him into an international arena filled with land mines, was more than he could tolerate. But there was something else—something deeper—at work in his mind. He was finally in possession of information not available to his superiors; now, fate had given him a modicum of power, and he was not willing to part with it so quickly. Shoving the photos away, he resolved to keep his own counsel until he could determine just what was going on.

IT WAS too bad for Kirilenko that he wasn't carrying the only copies of the photos his assistant had taken off the airport CCTV. Twenty minutes before he'd arrived, Oriel Jovovich Batchuk, standing in front of Kirilenko's desk, confronted his assistant. He received the latest oral report from a young man he'd found it ridiculously easy to suborn, with half his mind still chewing over his disturbing conversation with Gourdjiev.

When it came to the subject of Annika there could be no equivocating, no ending, no exit for either of them. No matter how hard either of them tried to fight it their roles were set in stone, there was no reversing position, no going back. But the knowledge of what had happened, of what could never be changed, was a hateful thing, a spider spinning its malevolent web in his mind. And this was because of one simple fact he'd never uttered to anyone, but which he suspected Gourdjiev knew: Even if he possessed the impossible power to change the past, he wouldn't. He did what he had to do, something a man like Gourdjiev could never understand, let alone condone. Batchuk was a man who could not afford to second-guess himself; rather, he preyed on others' not wanting to know, not wanting to see the truth about themselves or those whose acquaintance was politically or financially important to their careers; preyed on people afraid of conviction, of being wrong, who would rather close their eyes and listen to his guidance. Gourdjiev had done that once—only once—to his unending sorrow, a situation Batchuk could read on his face every time they met.

A certain silence made it clear that Kirilenko's assistant had finished his oral report. Nodding, Batchuk ordered him to make copies of the photos. He took them without comment and, turning on his heel, left.

He was already on his cell phone as he descended in the elevator and exited the huge, intimidating lobby of the FSB building, striding through the slush of Red Square.

GENERAL BRANDT, seated next to President Carson and across a gleaming marble table from President Yukin, received Batchuk's call at a most inconvenient time. Nevertheless, seeing who was calling, he excused himself, went out of the room and partway down the corridor, out of earshot of the various Secret Service personnel from both sides who were flanking the door like sphinxes.

"There's been a new development," Batchuk said without preamble. "Annika Dementieva isn't moving on her own. I'm looking at a photo of her from one of the closed-circuit cameras at Zhulyany Airport. She's with two other people, one of whom is the American Jack McClure."

"President Carson's Jack McClure?" the General said, and almost immediately regretted the stupidity of the question. Of course it was Edward's Jack McClure. "I don't understand."

"Carson is playing you," Batchuk said tersely. "He's got an agenda he's keeping from you, which means he no longer trusts you."

The General gave an involuntary glance over his shoulder, toward the silent bodyguards and closed door that led to the negotiating room, where Carson was even now locking horns with Yukin. "But that's impossible."

"Nothing's impossible," Batchuk said with unconcealed fury. "Clearly. This is on you, General. McClure is your mess, I suggest you clean it up with all the haste you can muster."

"I can't imagine what Carson is playing at, putting McClure into the field, and with Annika Dementieva, no less."

"It doesn't matter what either of them are up to. McClure needs to be extinguished, expunged, immolated. Do I make myself clear?"

"Perfectly." The General was too taken aback to be offended by

Batchuk's taking control. They were facing a mess, he'd trusted Carson, and in doing so had allowed matters to get out of control. They were all finished if McClure remained alive, of that he was absolutely certain.

"Don't worry," he said, gathering himself. "McClure won't live to see another sunrise, that I promise you."

EIGHTEEN

"WHO'S HUNGRY?" Jack said as they entered the echoing Arrivals hall at Simferopol North Airport.

"I am," Alli said immediately. "I'm starved."

"Good, so am I." Jack led them over to a crowded cafeteria-style coffee shop with food that looked as if it had been prepared last week. Nevertheless, they loaded up their plates, paid for the food and drinks, and took their trays to the lone empty table near the check-out, a location lousy for a peaceful meal but ideal for watching passengers as they stumbled off their flights.

They dug into leathery pirogi, cabbage rolls, and pungent *kovbasa*, washed down with glasses of cherry-red Crimean wine. While he ate Jack kept one eye on the waxing and waning stream of humanity. From the other side of the table Annika watched him. He knew what she was thinking: If they were hungry why not just go into Alushta, where they'd have their choice of restaurants with food better than what they were eating now? She said nothing, however, doubtless waiting for him to provide an explanation.

"Karl Rochev, the last person Berns visited before he left Kiev for Capri, was tortured and killed on the grounds of Magnussen's estate," Jack said.

Annika shrugged. "The evidence seems straightforward. Both Rochev and his mistress were killed with *sulitsa*, the antique Cossack splitting weapon. Magnussen is a collector of antique Russian weaponry, including *sulitsa*. Magnussen just ordered replacements for his *sulitsa*. Ergo, he killed Rochev and his mistress. It couldn't be simpler."

"It isn't simple at all," Jack corrected her. "Did whoever killed Rochev and his mistress also kill Senator Berns in Capri, or order his death? If so, then we're dealing with a conspiracy of international proportions and unknown dimensions. Some of what we know is fact and some of it is supposition or deduction, however you want to look at it. Either way, at this point, before our investigation goes any further, we have to ascertain what is fact and what could turn out to not be supposition at all, but rather the product of imagination and invention and, therefore, a dead end or, worse, an erroneous conclusion."

Annika stared at him with a baleful look. "And how do you propose to find out? Ask Magnussen himself?" She gave a short, derogatory laugh.

It was now just over an hour after they had sat down, and the next flight from Kiev had arrived, spilling its passengers out onto the concourse. Jack's eye was drawn to a well-built man with reddened hands who had stopped to light a cigarette with the haste of an addict. He wore his hair in the same rumpled way he wore his cheap, shiny suit. Everything about him shouted Russian bureaucracy, but without the accompanying dullness. Instead, he emanated something toxic—the odors of fear and death congealed into a gluey substance that lodged in the folds of his neck and made his cheeks shiny as a wax effigy.

Jack, who absorbed and analyzed all these intangibles in less than a second, answered her in what at first appeared to be an enigmatic manner: "Who do you think that is?"

Annika shifted her gaze while she admonished Alli. "Don't stare, for the love of God."

Alli obeyed, albeit with a pout.

"There's a man who just came in from Kiev," Jack explained in a low voice. "It looks as if he's trying to find someone by showing what might be photos or sketches to airport personnel."

"Christ, I know him." Annika, worrying her lower lip, had turned back. "That's Rhon Fyodovich Kirilenko. He's an FSB homicide detective. The man's a fucking bloodhound. What's he doing here?"

"I think he's after us," Jack said.

"But how? It's the Izmaylovskaya who is after us. We killed Ivan Gurov and Milan Spiakov, two members of the *grupperovka* family."

"Unless Kirilenko is *Trinadtsat*." Jack turned to her. "You told me *Trinadtsat* was composed of members of the Izmaylovskaya and the FSB."

"Not FSB, per se," Annika corrected. "Batchuk's people, who could be FSB, but are also likely to be Kremlin apparatchiks, interior ministers, secret services, who the hell knows who he's recruited."

"That certainly doesn't rule out your friend Kirilenko."

"He's not my friend," Annika said sharply. "I hate his guts."

"Part of a long line, I gather." Jack nodded. "Look, he's heading toward the airport facilities."

"I wonder what he's up to?" Annika said.

"Let's find out."

Jack rose, and the others with him. Staying within the clots of people, they followed Kirilenko as he entered a corridor with doors on either side. Hanging back, they saw him open a door on the left, halfway down the corridor, and as he went inside, they hurried along toward it.

"He's gone into the CCTV control room," Annika said.

"What does that mean?" Alli asked.

"He's going to look at the closed-circuit video tapes of arrivals and departures," Annika said.

"I'm willing to bet he has photos of us." Jack rubbed his jaw meditatively. "We must have been picked up on the cameras at Zhul-yany Airport in Kiev."

Annika took an involuntary step back. "Which means he's recognized me and has photos of the two of you."

"Alli's disguised," Jack said, "but do you think he knows who I am?"

"Doubtful," Annika said. "But even so it won't take long for him to discover who you are."

Jack eyed the closed door. "Then we'll have to stop him from finding out."

DENNIS PAULL had been staring at his computer for nine hours straight, scrolling through one restricted database after another in search of a chink in the cabinet members' red, white, and blue armor. His bladder was full and he felt as if all the low-grade mozzarella he'd consumed had congealed in the pit of his stomach like a bocce ball. Pushing himself away from the screen, he rose and stumbled into the bathroom to relieve himself.

When he returned to his battle station he saw that a new piece of information had popped onto his screen. He'd just used his cursor to copy it when it vanished. Switching windows, he brought up a new Word document into which he deposited—he hoped, he prayed—what he'd snagged off the database. An instant later two lines of enciphered words appeared on a field of pristine white, followed by an echelon code Paull knew belonged to General Atcheson Brandt.

For a moment he stared at the gibberish, trying to place the cipher pattern, which seemed familiar to him. Then he had it: It was a particular NSA cipher used exclusively for Eyes-Only interdepartmental communications on its cell phones.

Switching to another Firefox tab, he logged on to the Department of Homeland Security site, then, using his proprietary ID code, accessed his department's algorithm database. Once there, he fed the two lines of enciphered text into the algorithm engine, hit the Enter key, and sat back, waiting for the database to find the algorithm that would decipher the message Brandt had just sent.

While he waited he thought about the choices he'd made in his life, the people he had had to befriend, rely on, depend on, even though he knew that at some point, if the opportunity arose, they would betray him or denounce him in order to advance their own career path. With the possible exception of Edward Carson he was surrounded by a pack of sharks all too eager to take a chunk out of him the moment they smelled blood in the water, or even before, in some cases. And yet he'd gone ahead and forged these alliances, even, when the occasion demanded it, putting himself in these people's debt. He forced himself not to see what he didn't want to see, what would otherwise stop him from doing what had to be done in order to rise to his position of power within the current administration.

Was there nothing people like General Brandt wouldn't do to gain power, he asked himself rhetorically. Was there really no line that these people—he among them—wouldn't cross to keep accumulating power?

A moment later he had his answer. The two lines of gibberish were replaced by the deciphered text: XEX ANNIKA DEMENTIEVA AND JACK MCCLURE.

Jesus, he thought as he ran a trembling hand through his hair. *Jesus Christ.* At first he thought it must be a mistake, perhaps he inputted the encrypted text incorrectly, so he sent it back through the department's algorithm engine, careful to get each letter right. The same message came back at him like a punch in the solar plexus.

It couldn't be, but there it was in front of him in black and white. "EX" meant that General Brandt had put out a sanction—an immediate death sentence—on the subjects. The "X" prefix meant "use all available methods at your disposal."

"KIRILENKO MUST have been with the team that surrounded us at Rochev's dacha," Annika said.

"What a joke," Alli said. "He must think we killed Rochev's mistress. That's why he's coming after us."

Jack and Annika stared at her. "It's no joke," they both said, more or less at once.

They were still in the mouth of the corridor leading to Airport Services. Jack was looking around for security personnel who were sure to be patrolling the area, while Annika kept an eye on the door to the CCTV control room through which Kirilenko had disappeared not five minutes ago.

"There's no doubt he's looking for us," Annika said. "And, as Alli pointed out, now we're suspects in three murders." She shook her head. "There's no help for it, we're going to have to terminate him."

"What?" Jack spun around. "Are you crazy? We can't attack an FSB officer."

"I didn't say attack." Annika's carnelian eyes never looked harder. "I said terminate."

"As in kill?" Alli said.

"Yes, dear. We have to kill him in order to save ourselves."

"I won't hear of it," Jack said.

"Then we're doomed." Annika indicated the door with her chin.

"Unless we put him six feet under, I promise you this sonuvabitch won't stop until he's either killed us or dragged us back to Moscow in manacles."

A look of pure terror distorted Alli's face. "Jack—"

"If not for us, then for the safety of the girl," Annika pressed her point. "For so many reasons, we can't allow anything to happen to her."

Jack shook his head. He knew she was right, but he wasn't willing to give in just yet. "There's got to be another way."

"I'm telling you there isn't, we've got to do it now while we have the chance," Annika said urgently.

As if to underscore her anxiety, the door to the CCTV control room opened. They shrank back into the shadows as Kirilenko emerged, his face marred by a smug look that told Annika everything she needed to know.

Without another word to either of her companions, she sprinted from the shadows and, while he drew out his cell phone, she delivered a vicious blow to his kidneys, wrapped her crooked arm across his throat, and with astonishing power, jerked him backward off his feet.

GENERAL ATCHESON Brandt was the last person Dennis Paull had suspected of treachery—so much so, in fact, that in nine hours of eye-watering work he hadn't yet gotten around to shining his investigatory spotlight on Brandt or his life.

Paull had finally quit his room, reeking of human sweat and the peculiar odor of heated electronics. It was two thirty in the morning and he was walking down the hallway of the Residence Inn, looking for the cigarette vending machine he'd noticed when he'd checked in. In these days of universal smoking bans, cigarettes were hard to find, never mind an old-fashioned vending machine that sold them. Nevertheless, there was one here, crouching on a brown carpet whose pattern failed to hide stains even steam cleaning couldn't get out.

He hadn't smoked in twenty years, but the pressurized developments of the last half hour had caused his old craving to reassert itself. He'd tried to fight it, but it was no use. Like most vices, once it lodged in your mind it couldn't be denied.

Slitting open the pack, he tore the filter head off a cigarette, then lit it with a match from a pack thoughtfully provided with his purchase. He used the key card to his room to open the side door to the parking lot, went out into the chilly night. It had rained sometime while he'd been working and the concrete walkway was slick and wet; cars gleamed in the security lights. The hum of traffic from the highway was reduced to the inconstant hiss of occasionally passing cars on their way to or from mysterious errands. What were people doing up at this hour, he wondered. Whatever it was he doubted they had the weight of the world on their shoulders as he did.

The smoke, deep in his lungs, calmed him, or at least gave him the illusion that he had time to make a decision. The night was quiet, not another soul stirring in all of the Residence Inn, though as he looked up at the facade he could see lights on in several rooms, a reminder that insomnia lurked like a ghost here as everywhere.

He smoked the cigarette down to the end without coming to a decision. His mouth felt dry and stale, but he ripped off the filter on another cigarette, stuck it between his chapped lips, and lit up. With the information he had on General Brandt the road before him forked in several directions. He could inform the president, but that would surely distract him, in the process derailing the delicate negotiation process with President Yukin. He could call Jack and warn him, which again would expose his knowledge of the General's treachery. McClure was a good friend of Edward Carson's—they knew each other long before Paull himself met Carson. Therefore,

Jack could be counted on to inform the president ASAP even if Paull begged him not to disturb Carson until the crucial accord was signed.

As Paull walked up and down the walkway, growing colder and colder, he realized that he was on the horns of a serious moral dilemma. How could he allow Jack to remain uninformed about the sanction? How could he allow the U.S.-Russia accord to be disrupted? He had no doubt that General Brandt was insane. He had determined that his own self-interest was paramount, anyone who threatened it was to be terminated. He could call Edward and tell him what he'd discovered, but he had no solid proof and the call would only serve to muddy waters that were already fouled.

Grinding the second butt beneath his heel, he scrabbled in the pack. He was going through cigarettes as if they were Tic Tacs. Well, why not, considering the behemoth he was confronting. The fact that Jack had somehow become a clear and immediate danger to Brandt was of less concern to Paull than why Jack was threatening the General's self-interest.

What the hell was the General up to? And then he remembered a bit of the conversation he'd had with Edward Carson in the presidential limo following Lloyd Berns's interment. The president had complained that Brandt had been pushing to sign the accord. Why would he do that, Paull asked himself. Of course the General was one of the primary supporters of the current rapprochement with Russia. In fact, Carson had leaned heavily on the General's advice for why to engage Russia and how. But Brandt was smarter than to advise the president to elide over minor details Carson wasn't comfortable with, especially with the Russians.

However, his restless mind was turning over the question of paramount importance at the moment because there was a clear-cut decision to be made: To warn Jack or not to warn Jack, that was the question. And the answer hinged on morality and self-interest, one of which was clear-cut while the other was nebulous, open to interpre-

tation of every kind. He wasn't like Edward, whose enduring senti-
mental feelings for family and friends was both a weakness and a
blinder to the harsher aspects of reality. Paull understood the truth
that the president refused to acknowledge: The notion of morality
was a squishy subject, never more so than nowadays when there were
mountains of information, factoids, and electronic data to sift through
that provided a multitude of reasons for making or not making a decision. There were always extenuating circumstances, hidden explanations coming to light like corpses in a river appearing at the first
spring thaw. Nowadays there were any number of ways to make a
decision understandable, credible, acceptable, convincing.

All of which led him to one inescapable conclusion: He needed
to pursue the inquiry into General Brandt's sanction without informing anyone, not the president, not Jack. His own self-interest was and
must remain paramount. He had no other recourse now, none at
all.

"WE DIDN'T kill Rochev's mistress," Jack said, waving the CCTV
photos he'd found. "She was dead when we found her."

Kirilenko, disarmed and bound to a chair with lengths of electrical flex Annika had found in a nearby utility closet, said nothing.
They were in a spare office Jack had discovered, reluctantly but need-
fully, because they had an unconscious body that required a quiet
place to rest and come around, which Kirilenko did when Annika
slapped him sharply across the face. Now there was a red blotch there
like a congenital wine stain. The space was a standard office with a
desk, table, several wooden chairs. A filing cabinet stood against a
wall. Old-fashioned venetian blinds obscured the single window.

"We went to the dacha looking for Karl Rochev," Jack continued. "We wanted to talk with him, that's all."

Kirilenko, maintaining his silence, ignored Jack and Alli completely, his baleful gaze fixed on Annika leaning nonchalantly against

a wall, her arms crossed over her chest, watching him like a hawk inspecting a snake.

"When we didn't find him there we decided to leave, and that's when we ran into your people."

Kirilenko continued to glare at Annika, but with a smirk that made Jack think he was privy to information vital to them.

Apparently Annika thought the same thing because she came off the wall and smashed her fist into Kirilenko's jaw. Blood spattered onto his suit lapels and his lap.

"That's enough," Jack said, grabbing hold of her right arm, which she'd already cocked for another blow.

"Someone had to knock that smirk off his ugly face."

"And you'd be just the one to do it, eh?" Kirilenko said as he spat a thick wad of pink spittle onto the bare concrete floor. "Wild, short-tempered, out of control—in sum, a classic rageaholic—all the reports were right about you."

Annika, pulling away from Jack, lunged at him with her head. "If by that you mean I'm impossible to control then you're damn right."

Alli interposed herself between the two, forcing Annika to look at her, not Kirilenko, and so throttling down on her anger level. After a moment of cooling Annika put a hand on her cheek and nodded her thanks.

For the first time Kirilenko looked at Jack. "What I can't work out is why you're with this very dangerous creature. She's a murderer."

"We're all murderers here, Kirilenko," Annika said.

"What about the girl?"

Jack leaned in beside Annika. "Leave her out of it."

"Too late," Kirilenko said. "From my point of view she's as culpable as either of you." He jerked his head away from Annika's bared teeth. "She'll pay the same ultimate price you two will, that's a promise."

Annika stood back, hands on hips. "You see, what did I tell you? There's only one way to deal with a man like him."

"Yes, by all means kill me," Kirilenko said. "It's the only way to stop me from taking you in, or killing you for your crimes."

"We've committed no crimes," Jack said.

"That's what they all say." Kirilenko shook his head. "Once, just once, I'd like to be surprised, but, no, you murderers are as sadly alike as crows."

"There has to be another way," Jack said, ignoring him. "It's simply a matter of finding it."

"Good luck with that," Annika said. "I don't know about you but I don't plan to be here when security comes around to check all the vacant rooms."

Jack took her by the waist and half dragged her into the far corner.

"Let's stop this insanity," Kirilenko said softly, conspiratorially to Alli. "Untie me and I'll make sure you won't be arrested or incarcerated."

"You're the one who's incarcerated," Alli said, "and it's you who's trying to bargain."

She took a step toward Kirilenko, who was grinning at her like a monkey. He seemed sure he had taken the proper measure of her.

"I won't be incarcerated forever and when I—"

"You think I'm the weak link, that you can somehow terrify me, but I'm not afraid of you."

"Alli," Jack said sharply, "please put your ear to the door. If you hear anyone coming let us know."

"You should be." Kirilenko clacked his teeth together like a chimpanzee or a crocodile. "If you don't listen to me I swear I'll bite your head off."

"Alli . . . ," Jack warned.

Alli, staring down Kirilenko, spat into his face, then she turned and, crossing the small room, obediently put her ear to the door.

"You asked for it," Jack said to the Russian in a mocking voice, before turning back to speak in low tones with Annika. "You're not going to kill him, that's out of the question. Besides, he knows something."

"What if he's simply pretending he knows something?"

"What if he's not?"

But Jack's attention was now divided. He was watching Alli, who had come away from the door in the wake of their conversation. She had begun to walk back toward Kirilenko.

Annika, becoming aware of Jack's growing agitation, turned to watch. "What the hell is she doing?" she said under her breath.

"Alli, get away from him," Jack said sharply as he strode toward her.

But before he could get to her, she waggled in front of Kirilenko's face the cell phone she'd scooped up from the corridor floor as the others were dragging his body in here.

"It's you who should be frightened," she said. "I have your life in my hand."

Jack pulled her back. "What do you think you're doing?"

"You missed this," she said to Jack as she proffered the phone in the palm of her hand.

"This girl has balls," Annika said with a laugh, "you have to give her that."

Jack, noting the sour look on Kirilenko's face, wondered whether Alli was onto something. He was about to pluck up the cell, when he changed his mind. "Check it out yourself," he said. "You earned the right."

Alli hesitated, looking as if she didn't quite believe him. Then, seeing no contradiction in his expression, she flipped it open. She spent a few minutes scrolling through different menus before she apparently came upon something of interest. Reversing the screen, she showed Jack and Annika the grainy photo of the three of them as they emerged from Rochev's dacha.

"Mine is the only face identifiable," Annika said, peering closely at the image.

Alli zoomed in on a portion of the photo. "Look at what you're holding."

"The *sulitsa*," Annika breathed.

"What the hell is a *sulitsa*?" Kirilenko still had the remains of his own blood and Alli's spittle on his cheek. "What did you use to kill Ilenya Makova?"

"At last we know her name," Jack said, taking the phone from Alli.

"I didn't kill her, none of us did," Annika said. "As Jack said, we found her with this thing—this antique Cossack splitting weapon—sticking out of her—"

"I don't believe you, Annika Dementieva."

"—so deeply she was impaled to the mattress."

Kirilenko moved his head from side to side. "I know you."

"The fuck you do."

"I know people just like you, I know you killed her."

Jack pushed his way past a seething Annika and said to the Russian, "Listen to me because I'm only going to say this once. Annika is intent on killing you and I'm now inclined to agree with her." He adjusted Kirilenko's ugly tie so that the knot bit into his Adam's apple. "Against my better instincts I'm going to give you this chance. Tell us what you know."

"And then what?" Kirilenko said. "She'll kill me anyway, I see the look in her eyes."

"She won't kill you if you answer my questions."

Kirilenko laughed. "You think you can stop her?"

"Yes," Jack said softly and slowly. "I do."

The Russian peered into Jack's face with his weary gaze. "Fuck you, Americanski. Fuck you and your entire decadent fucking country."

FOLLOWING HIS numerous night visits Dyadya Gourdjiev had slept uneasily until noon. He dreamt that it had been raining for days, possibly weeks, and his apartment was developing cracks in the poorly constructed ceiling, around the cheap aluminum window frames. As a result water was leaking in from so many places it was impossible to caulk or patch them all. As soon as he dammed one up, two appeared in its place.

He awoke entirely unrefreshed. As he lay staring up at the ceiling, spider-webbed with cracks, he knew what must be done. Hauling himself out of bed he padded to the bathroom and with some difficulty relieved himself. Then he shaved his cheeks pink with a straight razor, carefully brushed his hair, dressed in a neat suit and tie in the best Western style, and ate his usual breakfast of black coffee, toast, butter, and Seville orange marmalade. He chewed slowly and thoughtfully. He felt like the root of a tree, the years fallen on him like the rusty leaves of autumn. He washed the dishes and cutlery, stacked them neatly in the drainboard, dried his hands on a dish towel.

In the closet next to the front door he extracted the things he needed, including his lambswool overcoat and soft cashmere scarf in the signature Burberry plaid, which he wrapped around his neck, making certain his throat was well protected against the strong April wind. Shrugging on his coat, he opened the door, went out into the corridor, noting that the bloodstain, now a dark, almost purple brown, had not yet been cleaned up. Everything continues to slide downhill, he thought, to erode, to sicken, wither, and die.

He met no one in the elevator, but as he saw the charming widow Tanova coming in from the street with an armful of groceries, he smiled, holding the elevator door open for her. She returned his smile, thanked him, and asked him over for tea and her homemade stollen later in the afternoon, an invitation he accepted with genuine pleasure. The widow Tanova had lived almost as long as he had, she understood the nature of life, what was important and what must be let go. She was someone he could talk with, confide in, commiserate with, mourning the losses they had suffered. Also, she had great legs—stems, as they said in the old black-and-white American films he still adored.

Waiting until the elevator and its comely occupant were on their way up, he crossed the now deserted lobby and, pulling open the heavy front door, stepped out onto the yellow-brick stoop. He drew a breath of the chilly air deep into his lungs as he glanced both ways along the street. There were no pedestrians and few moving vehicles. But there was the car, just as he'd expected. He saw it immediately, a gleaming black Mercedes—in their supreme arrogance these people felt no need for discretion, vigilance, foresight, or even tact: last night being a perfect case in point. There were two men sitting in the front seat, flamboyant as every member of the Izmaylovskaya learned to be. Like a fucking cult, Dyadya Gourdjiev thought.

Having looked this way and that he strolled away from the car on the opposite side of the street, then crossed the street and turned back. When he was abreast of the vehicle he stopped and tapped on the driver's window. The driver, startled, slid down his window in reflex. Even before the window was fully down Dyadya Gourdjiev had his Glock out. He pumped two bullets into the man on the passenger's side as he was reaching for his pistol, then shot the driver between the eyes.

At once, sliding the Glock into the deep pocket of his overcoat, he sauntered away with jaunty insouciance. It was as if with each step several years had melted off him until, at the corner, he had been resurrected into the strong young man he'd once been.

As he turned the corner he began to whistle "Dva Gusya," the old folk tune his mother used to sing to him when he was a child.

ANNIKA PRODUCED Kirilenko's gun, which, as a member of the FSB, he was allowed to carry on all modes of public transportation. Aiming it at him, she cocked the hammer back. At that moment, the cell phone in Jack's hand began to burr.

"Whoever's calling you, will have to wait," Jack said, "possibly forever."

"It's not his phone," Alli said. "I checked."

"Whose phone is it?" Jack said, staring at it.

Alli took the phone out of his hand, manipulated several keys to access the SIM card information. "A man named Limonev."

Annika took a step forward. "Mondan Limonev?"

Alli looked up at her. "You know him?"

She nodded. "I know of him. He's said to be a contract killer for the FSB."

"A despicable lie put about by anarchist enemies of the FSB," Kirilenko said sourly.

But Jack, studying his face, saw a different answer the Russian was afraid to voice, or possibly in the course of plying his profession he had come to believe the lies he uttered every day.

Annika came to stand beside Jack. "Limonev is also rumored to be a member of *Trinadtsat*."

Kirilenko's upper lip curled in a sneer. "Now that's simply laughable, especially since I very much doubt this *Trinadtsat* exists."

Limonev's cell had received a text message, not a call. "Well, now," Jack said, concentrating hard on reading the two words in Cyrillic, "this is an interesting development."

He showed it to Annika, who laughed and said, "Jesus, these people eat their own."

"I'd like to show it to you," Jack said to Kirilenko.

The Russian remained stone-faced. "I'm not interested."

"No? But you should be. It proves everything Annika has said."

Jack held the screen in front of Kirilenko, who managed to hold down his curiosity for all of thirty seconds before his eyes slid back. They fastened on the text message, which consisted of two words:

TERMINATE KIRILENKO.

NINETEEN

HAVING TRACKED Kirilenko, Mondan Limonev arrived in the Crimea. He'd spent four years here, a time when he'd been happy— almost carefree, or what might pass for carefree in a man of his dark calling. Six commissions, all assassinations of Russian oligarchs who had fled their country after the tide had turned against them. Limonev was unique among FSB assassins inasmuch as he was paid per commission. His fees were exceptionally high, but Yukin and Batchuk were more than happy to cough up state money for the exclusive privilege of his services. They knew that the moment he was handed a commission the target was as good as dead.

Kirilenko had been no exception. Using his FSB elite-level credentials Limonev quickly canvassed the airport personnel in the Arrivals hall, one of whom had seen Kirilenko enter the CCTV monitoring station. Kirilenko had left by the time Limonev reached it, but with his usual thoroughness, Limonev made a complete circuit of the hallway. Further down he saw something lying against the wall. Reaching down he retrieved a slim box of wooden matches. He'd seen Kirilenko strike matches from this very box numerous times. Drawing a handgun, he put one foot silently in front of the other. At each door he paused to place his ear against it. Such industriousness paid off when he heard Kirilenko's voice seep through the fifth door. He had his hand on the doorknob and was about to turn it when he heard other voices he could not identify. Listening carefully, he determined that these people, whoever they were, had managed to capture Kirilenko, something of a feat in its own right. However, it was Kirilenko alone who interested him.

THE MOMENT Kirilenko's brain registered the text message he broke out into a cold sweat.

"I don't fucking believe this," he said. "There's no way, no way at all." He looked up at Jack. "This is a trick."

"How could it be a trick?" Jack asked in a pleasant, almost friendly voice.

Kirilenko indicated Alli with his chin. "The girl. She must have done something when she had the phone, manufactured that message."

"Don't be idiotic." Jack shook his head. "How could she—or any of us, for that matter—know about Mondan Limonev, who he was, or that he was a member of your team at the dacha?"

Kirilenko stared at Alli as if he was seeing her for the first time. Then his eyes went out of focus as the bleakness of his current situation began to sink in. At length he nodded. "Fuck it," he said to Jack, "what d'you want to know?"

"What can you tell me about *Trinadtsat?*"

"What?"

"You heard me. Are you a member of Thirteen?"

Kirilenko reared back as much as his bonds would let him. "I don't know a thing about it. I keep my head down and my nose

clean. I'm a detective, not an apparatchik. I'm a field man, small po-
tatoes."

Unsure whether the Russian was telling the truth, Jack tried
another tack. "I could understand why the Izmaylovskaya might be
after Annika, but what were you and your people doing lying in wait
for us at Rochev's dacha?"

"My people. You mean *your* people." Kirilenko nodded. "That's
right, Americans. The Americans are after Annika Dementieva."

"You're full of shit," Jack said. "What Americans?"

"I'm dying for a cigarette," Kirilenko said. "There's a pack—"

"I know where the pack is," Alli said, fishing it out of his pocket.

Jack put a cigarette between Kirilenko's lips and Annika lit it
with her lighter.

Kirilenko took a deep drag and slowly let out the smoke. "Harry
Martin, you know him?"

"Harry Martin sounds like a made-up name."

Kirilenko nodded. "That would be my guess. In any event, the
man—whatever his real name is—is no fiction. He's a spook, of that
you can be sure. I was assigned to be his support."

"Why? What's he here for?"

"I don't actually know because he didn't tell me. I took him to
Rochev's dacha because that's where he wanted to go. You know the
rest."

"Pretend I don't know a thing," Jack said. "What else do you
know about Harry Martin?"

"Only bits and pieces, what I picked up overhearing parts of his
cell phone conversations, presumably with his handler." Kirilenko
took another drag deep into his lungs. When he spoke again the
smoke drifted out of his mouth and nostrils as if he were a dragon. "I
overheard a word—Aura. I have no idea what it means, but I'm fairly
certain that whatever else he's after he needs to talk with that one."
He indicated Annika with a lift of his chin.

Jack turned briefly to Annika but she shook her head. "I never heard of Aura."

Jack returned his attention to Kirilenko. "If you were assigned to Harry Martin, where is he?"

"I ditched him after I saw that photo and identified Annika Dementieva." The acrid smoke drifting upward caused his left eye to half close. "I'm tired of being pushed around by everyone, my superiors included."

"Is that why they want you dead?"

Kirilenko blew out smoke and shuddered. "I have no fucking idea why a sanction was put out on me, nor who authorized it. Like I said, I've kept my head down and my nose clean."

"Not clean enough, apparently; you've picked up some serious shit on the way to the office," Annika said dryly.

"Maybe it's because you ditched Harry Martin," Jack said.

"Everything went into the shitter when I was assigned to him," Kirilenko said morosely.

"Who did you get the assignment from?" Jack said. "Who do you report to?"

"It wasn't him, or at least it didn't begin with him, though my boss is the division head. When he called me into his office he said he'd been given the directive. He didn't seem happy about it."

"Who?" Annika said. "Who would give him his marching orders?"

Kirilenko shrugged, then winced at the pain the gesture caused him. "You know the FSB, it's a fucking mare's nest of bureaucracy above division level. There are so many competing *siloviks* vying for power it's difficult to know where anyone stands."

Annika took out her cell phone. "What's the name of your boss?" When Kirilenko told her, she punched a number on her speed dial and began to speak into the phone.

"I think we should untie him," Alli said.

RETRACING HIS steps down the hall Limonev hurried though the Arrivals hall and out the glass doors. He ignored the taxi lineup, and went swiftly around to the side of the building. From the layout of the Arrivals hall, he determined the window that led to the room where Kirilenko was being held. Looking for the most likely escape route, his gaze passed over the westernmost runway, the drop-off and subsequent field that led up to the parking lot. It was to the lot he went, stationing himself on the top of a car that overlooked the route. Then, using the replacement cell phone the SBU had given him, he called airport security and reported a disturbance in one of the airport facilities offices. Immediately following, he opened the case he'd been carrying and assembled the Dragunov, slamming home the ten-round magazine. Then, stretched out on his small but perfect patch of high ground, he put his right eye to the 4X PSO-1 telescope sight and waited for events to unfold.

JACK, LISTENING to what Annika was saying, at first missed her comment. People spoke to other people in varying ways. His brain was a repository of those different intonations. That was how he knew Annika was talking to Dyadya Gourdjiev, asking him about Kirilenko's boss.

Alli was already behind the chair to which Kirilenko was bound by the time he'd diverted his attention back to her.

"What are you doing?"

"Untying him," she said. "I think that's what we should do."

"You're the one who spat in his face."

"I didn't like what he said to me, that doesn't mean I hate his guts."

Annika folded away her cell. "I'll know who assigned you to the American spy in a couple of hours," she promised. Then, seeing Alli unwinding the electrical flex from Kirilenko's crossed wrists, said, "That's a mistake we'll all regret."

"I don't think so," Kirilenko said.

"There's a surprise!" Annika still held his pistol in her hand, though it was no longer pointed at him.

"Listen, in light of everything that's happened here I have a proposal to make."

Annika snorted. "This from a supposedly incorruptible FSB homicide investigator?"

"Let's hear what he has to say." Alli threw the unwound flex into a corner.

Jack was about to answer her, but into his mind came the image of Alli bound to a chair, which was immediately supplanted by the memory of Annika explaining why Alli had wanted to go to Milla Tamirova's apartment, or, as Annika put it, to her dungeon. Kirilenko sat in the chair into which up to a moment ago they'd bound him. Jack knew Alli couldn't help but equate his position to hers, and who was to say she was wrong.

Kirilenko made no aggressive move, or even an attempt to rise from the chair. He did nothing but massage his wrists in order to return circulation to his terribly chapped hands.

Lifting his head, he addressed Annika frankly, "My proposal is this: You kill Mondan Limonev and I'll take care of the American Harry Martin who's been sent to find you."

"Wait a minute," Jack said, "I think I've seen this film."

"*Strangers on a Train*, yes, I'm familiar with it." Kirilenko stopped his massage to gratefully put another cigarette between his lips. He leaned forward as Annika lit it. "But I'm not joking."

"Aren't you the great detective who relentlessly runs down murderers?" Annika said with understandable skepticism.

"Yes, yes, of course you would say that. I would, too, in your position." Kirilenko expelled smoke in a deep sigh. "In the last half hour it's occurred to me that you and I have been cleverly set up. I may not know what's going on, but I'm convinced that you didn't kill Ilenya Makova."

"We've been trying to find out who did," Jack said. "The trail has led us here."

"I believe that, as well."

Annika was obviously still a skeptic. "What could possibly have changed your mind so quickly? You're known as the great crusader against murder and rape; your convictions, your sense of right and wrong must be immutable."

"It's true I hate criminals and that my outrage at the taking of a life is absolute, but my hatred of mistakes trumps them all. This is why in my twenty-two years as a manhunter I've never brought down the wrong perpetrator. When it comes to my employers I may be deaf and dumb, but I'm not blind. I'm aware that a percentage of their activities is criminal. Head down, nose clean, that's what's needed to survive in their system." He peeled a bit of tobacco off his lip, eyed it for a moment before flicking it away. "But I suppose that's true of any system, the larger the system the greater the need to ignore the illegalities going on around you, the more vital it is to keep your mouth shut."

"Illegalities!" He'd clearly hit a nerve, and Annika was outraged.

"Look, I'm not in the directorate that spends its days and nights trumping up charges against the officers of legitimate companies and the oligarch owners on Yukin's and Batchuk's orders. I'm not throwing innocent people in prison to rot for the rest of their lives. I'm not terrorizing their wives and mistresses, I'm not putting my gun to the back of their heads and pulling the trigger."

"But you won't do anything to stop it."

"My God, be realistic, what could I do?"

"Then explain to me why *they* do it."

"Like everyone else you want answers, you want to know why people do evil things. But evil can't be parsed, because, in fact, it's too simple, too stupid. And, anyway, why would you want to understand it, why the desire to dissect it? Don't you understand that devoting your energies to the subject gives it a power, a rationale, a legitimacy it doesn't warrant?" He smoked for some time, seemingly deep in thought, then he looked up. "As for me, self-interest is the best rationalizer, isn't it, and, let's face it, these days you can't live your life without employing some form of rationalization." He looked at them all in turn. "So the long and the short of it is I'm different from my coworkers because I've learned to adapt when I discover that I've been wrong. Considering the sewer in which I work, I couldn't live with myself otherwise."

Now, having explained himself, he looked at Annika. "My proposal?"

Jack said to her, "You're not seriously considering—"

"The idea has a logic," Annika said. "A symmetry I find immensely appealing."

"Annika, really—"

"Can you think of another way we're going to stay alive long enough to find out who killed Rochev?"

"Wait." Now Kirilenko stood, but there was nothing threatening in his body language. "Karl Rochev is dead?"

Jack explained how they had been led to Magnussen's estate by the odd murder weapon, how they had found Rochev, who bore the clear signs of torture before he'd been killed by the two sister *sulitsa*.

Kirilenko was about to reply when they heard a sharp scraping from the corridor. Then the door opened inward.

HARRY MARTIN arrived at Simferopol North Airport one pissed-off human being. During the flight from Kiev he'd done nothing but seethe inwardly, feeding a rage that felt overwhelming by the time he emerged in the Arrivals hall. All he could think of was putting a bullet into the back of Kirilenko's head. It had been Kirilenko who had misdirected him, ditched him, humiliated him with General Brandt. Now he understood why Kirilenko had so easily agreed to separate when he himself had suggested it, thinking that by heading back to Kiev while sending the Russian off on a wild-goose chase he'd be able to find Annika Dementieva on his own.

He scrutinized the passengers milling around the Arrivals hall as he would examine his past, looking for the one person on which his laserlike attention was currently fixated, so he could expunge the memory of what had happened.

So many things in Martin's past needed extermination or exorcism, depending on whether your bent was practical or metaphysical; he'd concluded long ago that it all amounted to the same thing. The past was a vast swamp, reeking of mistakes, betrayals, lies, and delusions. If he'd had any say in it he'd obliterate his past and everyone in it. Wouldn't that be sweet, he thought as his eyes swept the concourse, searching for Kirilenko.

Perhaps they'd both disappeared—Kirilenko and Annika Dementieva—and he'd never be able to find either of them. Then he could walk away and never come back. But he doubted that would happen because he knew all there was to know about disappearing. Harry Martin was a legend—in spook terminology, a fiction, like a short story or a novella. And what an exacting effort it took to maintain him! Creating him had been a snap, a conjuror's trick backed up by documents the Legends Department had manufactured like the air in a plane or a refrigerator, canned, artificial, recirculated, hermetically sealed. He was a ghost built up like a Frankenstein's monster from the pasts of people long dead. That's where the legends wonks got their ideas, God knows they had none of their own. But with every lie he told Harry Martin became more difficult to sustain. The short story became a novella with a crisscrossing of fabrications that took immense care to keep from contradicting each other.

By this time he had circumnavigated the Arrivals hall, cataloguing each person, but without seeing Kirilenko. He took another visual sweep of the hall. As he glanced down the corridor leading to Airport Services he saw a security guard stepping across the threshold of a doorway on the left perhaps two-thirds of the way down the corridor. Something in the man's expression—surprise, shock, even—warned Martin even before the man collapsed. As he was dragged inside, Martin was sprinting down the corridor. He pulled his ceramic pistol from its hard leather holster at the small of his back, thumbing the safety off. He reached the door just as it was being shut. Throwing the bulk of his leading shoulder between the door and its frame he kicked the door backward, so that it slammed wide open.

He just had time to register Kirilenko's presence, other people on the periphery of his vision, when he fired blindly. He was fixated on Kirilenko, who had thrown himself behind a table. He aimed and was in the process of pulling the trigger when he heard a deafening noise.

Blown violently backward by the bullet that entered his skull, Harry Martin was dead before he hit the floor.

TWENTY

"I HOPE you rot in hell," Kirilenko said, spitting on Harry Martin's corpse.

Jack wasted no time riffling through Martin's suit. He found his cell phone, a wad of cash, passport, two credit cards, an international driver's license, and little else.

"There's nothing here to indicate this man was anyone other than Harry Martin," he said.

"No surprise there." Annika was busy going through the security guard's uniform. "Ah, but look what I found," she said, holding up a set of car keys.

At that moment there came a hammering on the door, along with querulous voices raised in mounting fear. Jack grabbed the chair on which Kirilenko had been sitting, wedged the back under the doorknob at an angle so the back legs were braced against the floor. At the same time Annika raised the blinds on the window, only to find that the glass was reinforced with wire mesh. The hammering became more insistent, they could hear someone calling for help or backup, they couldn't distinguish which. Annika took a second chair and smashed it into the windowpane, then she repeatedly slammed it against the wall until one of the legs came loose. She gripped this, hacking away at the wire mesh to make a hole large enough for them to get through.

They heard a shot from behind them and the door lock exploded inward. Now the only thing between them and the officials in the corridor was the angled chair, which was already shuddering from the pressure being exerted on it from the other side of the door.

"Let's go!" Annika said, helping Alli through the aperture she'd made.

Jack went next, then Kirilenko. Finally Annika herself climbed out. Without any other choice, they began to run away from the building, a route that took them directly onto one of the runways. A jet was just on the turn from the taxiway onto the head of the runway. They could hear its engine winding up to launch it along the runway and into its glide path up and away from the airport.

Behind them the office they had vacated was swarming with people, screaming and shouting. A shot was fired at them, and they broke into a ragged zigzag as they reached the runway itself. By this time the jet was already rolling along the tarmac, picking up speed with the firing of its four massive engines.

Over the mounting roar they could just make out the high-low sound of a police car siren, and then, as Jack threw a glance behind them, the car itself careened into view. They were so close to the on-coming jet they began to choke on the fumes, and Jack pulled Alli close to him, away from the nearest engine on the outside of the jet's left wing. They bent over double as they ran awkwardly across the vibrating tarmac, the foreshortened sight of the oncoming plane making it look as large as an apartment building.

The careening police car, putting on speed, was heading directly for them, and Jack, realizing their only hope was to maneuver so the plane was between them and their pursuers, led the way. The vectors formed their three-dimensional patterns in his mind, changing as their position changed in relation to the jet. He could see the one path that would keep them safe. Holding Alli's hand, he continued on across the tarmac even as the jet threatened to intersect their path. It was so close now it blotted out most of the sky, like the onward rush of a hurricane or a tornado, the sky black and shiny and so close above their heads its windswept underside turned into a scythe.

Heads down, huddled on their knees like refugees, they clung to one another as the storm came upon them, the huge belly of the aircraft rushing by above them, the two sets of enormous wheels hemming them in on either side before they sped by at teeth-rattling speed. Then the four of them were freed, up and running again toward the far side of the tarmac, choking on the fumes pluming off the engines, their eyes tearing, the lining of their noses inflamed, the backs of their mouths aching and dry.

The jet had taken off from the western runway. Just beyond a wide verge, a steep slope led down to a grassy field on the far side of which was the parking lot, including the separate area for employee vehicles. They crossed over the verge and scrambled down the slope as the jet was lifting off the tarmac. The police vehicle, which had stopped to allow it to pass, had reached the runway.

The incline was too steep for the police car, which stopped on the verge to allow three uniformed cops to disembark and sprint toward the slope. They half slid, half skidded down the incline. One of them tripped, lost his gun, and had to make a detour to retrieve it. Then he was up and running, but because he was ashamed that he had lost ground to his two fellow officers, he stopped, planted his feet at shoulder width, and, cradling the butt of his Makarov in one hand, aimed at the fleeing figures and fired round after round until the pistol was empty.

DYADYA GOURDJIEV was in a box. Just five minutes after receiving the call from Annika and making one of his own he discovered that he was being shadowed by two men, one behind him, the other in front of him. This was the nature of the box, a method of surveillance employed when you were sure of the target's superior skills at countering surveillance.

He was perhaps six or seven blocks from the street outside his apartment where he'd shot to death the two Izmaylovskaya hit men. Arsov would not be pleased, but the last thing on Gourdjiev's mind was Arsov's displeasure. These two men who had him in a box could not be handled the same way because they weren't *grupperovka* goons, they were government men, Kremlin men, *Trinadtsat*, and therefore under Batchuk's direct command. He knew they must be *Trinadtsat* because they wore the signature black leather trench coats. The moment Batchuk had asked about Annika, having come all the way from Moscow, Dyadya Gourdjiev knew that she had gotten herself into terrible trouble. It wasn't often Batchuk asked him about her—he knew better—it had been several years, in fact. Perhaps his interest stemmed from her two companions, but Gourdjiev doubted it. Batchuk's interest was in her, no one else.

As he strolled along Kiev's windswept streets, dragging his surveillance box with him, he wished he knew what she was up to, but Batchuk had been right about one thing: She was far too canny to tell him about her plans. She would never expose him to the risks she herself was taking. He wished, too, that he could talk her out of taking such risks, but he knew it would be a fool's errand. Annika was an extremist; he'd seen it in her almost from birth. This was who she was and no one, no circumstance or experience, could change that. But there was another reason why he'd never tried to talk her out of the life she'd chosen: He was secretly proud of her, proud that she was fearless, tough, and clever. He'd taught her, true enough, but she brought a great deal to the table: You couldn't teach someone to be clever, just how to be cleverer still, and as for being fearless, he was convinced that was a genetic trait.

As he moved at a normal gait he continued to check the box he was in, using any reflective surface he came upon: shop and car windows, the side mirrors of parked vehicles. The two shadows varied their distance, occasionally allowing people to get between them and their assignment in order to remain as inconspicuous as possible.

At this point there was no possibility of losing them; he hadn't the time. Besides, he had no problem with them knowing where he was going, it might even give them a laugh.

The brothel was on the west bank, in the Pechersk district, in a beautifully restored postwar building with a splendid view of the river that more or less bisected the city. He could have ascended in the tiny elevator, but he preferred to take the stairs, which were wide, curving, and ornamented with a polished, hand-turned wooden railing that felt good and solid beneath his fingers. By the time he reached the third floor he was only slightly winded, but his legs felt terrific. He hadn't been this exhilarated in years.

The young girl took his coat and scarf into her booth just inside the vestibule. Ekaterina, in one of her more provocative ensembles that showed off her long legs and her ample breasts, came bustling out, and kissed him on both cheeks. Linking her arm through his, she asked him what he was in the mood for, the usual or something a bit different. She spoke in French, because it lent her establishment a degree of upscale romance.

"*Mon habituelle.*" My usual.

"*Toujours la même fille,*" she said with a heartfelt sigh. Always the same girl.

"*Mais une tellement belle fille,*" he replied. But such a beautiful girl.

She led him through a door she unlocked with both an eight-digit combination and a key that hung around her neck.

"Beauty is in the eye of the beholder," she said, switching to English because it was an idiom with no analog in either French or Russian. They stopped in front of one of the many closed doors lining both sides of a wide, imaginatively lit hallway. "Just remember," she whispered, rolling one impressive breast against his arm, "if at any time you change your mind, you've only to ask."

He thanked her in his charming, rather formal old-school manner. Waiting until she had disappeared behind the locked door at the end of the hallway, he knocked on the door twice, waited five seconds, then knocked three times.

Without waiting for a reply he opened the door, stepped through, shut and locked the door behind him. He found himself in a square, dimly lighted room with furniture covered in yellow and pink chintz. The one window overlooked a steep green bank down to the somnambulant Dnieper River. Young children, overseen by their mothers, rolled down the embankment, laughing and shrieking, while two lovers lost in themselves stood arm in arm staring out across the gunmetal water.

"Did she try to get you into bed?" Riet Boronyov said.

Gourdjiev nodded. "Again."

"She wouldn't charge you, you know." Boronyov jackknifed his small but very fit frame off the bed on which he'd been reclining, almost as if he had been daydreaming. "She's hot for you."

Dyadya Gourdjiev thought of the widow Tanova, her tea and fresh-baked stollen, and laughed. "She's just rising to a challenge."

"Don't tell me you think you're too old," Boronyov clucked his tongue against the roof of his mouth, "because I wouldn't believe it."

"I'm not here to speak about Ekaterina or my sex life."

"No, of course not." Boronyov gripped the older man's hand in friendship. "But it would make her happy, and a happy employee is a productive employee."

"I don't see how Ekaterina could be more productive than she already is. You take a great deal of money out of this business."

"Indeed."

Boronyov looked more like a bug-eyed wizard than an oligarch. When you were a billionaire, Gourdjiev thought, you could afford to be strange-looking without fear of anyone commenting on it. Everyone wanted to be your friend, unless they were too terrified to approach you, and those people were of no use to you anyway. "But because of that shitbag Yukin this is the only one of my businesses that's currently making money. He and that cocksucker Batchuk are appropriating every last vestige of capitalism I acquired in the nineties. It's all illegal, of course, but the judges have their heads stuck so far up Yukin's ass they can't hear the complaints."

Gourdjiev had heard this rant many times before, of course, but like Batchuk, Boronyov needed to find some temporary release from his resentment and outrage. He was a capitalist, after all, and anyone who interfered with the free market system was anathema. Besides, his companies and much of his fortune had been stolen by a rigged system, rife with legal nihilism. Had he not fled Moscow just ahead of the armed commandos Batchuk had sent to take him into custody, he would be in a Siberian prison now, stripped of both freedom and money.

It had been Gourdjiev who had warned him of his imminent arrest, not because he held any particular love for the oligarch, but his business model was sadly preferable to that of Yukin and Batchuk, whose level of corruption was staggering both in its scope and its abuses. He had needed Boronyov's brains and contacts.

Unlike Yukin and, no doubt, Batchuk, Gourdjiev viewed the reign of the oligarchs as a necessary evil, a bridge between Soviet Communism, which had proved to be an abject failure, and a free-market economy. But the oligarchs' hubris had sealed their own doom. High on the enormous wealth they had amassed in just a few years, they began to shoulder their way into the political arena. Yukin, whose instincts for self-preservation were acute, moved against them as soon as he detected a threat to his absolute power. He brought down the monarch of the oligarchs, Mikhail Khodorkovsky, then the head of Yukos, the largest oil company in Russia. With Khodorkovsky's fall the other oligarchs turned into Yukin's fawning toadies. All save a precious few. To Gourdjiev's way of thinking Yukin's steps to renationalize the largest companies in Russia smacked not of socialism, but of a twenty-first-century fascism that was far more pernicious.

"I need to know who gave the FSB orders to assist an American spy who went by the legend 'Harry Martin,'" Dyadya Gourdjiev said. "And I need to know the name of Harry Martin's handler."

Boronyov sat down in one of the chintz chairs and crossed his legs. Surrounded by yellow and pink he looked healthy and robust. Perhaps he was, perhaps life outside Russia agreed with him, or maybe it was his new clandestine life in which he was reveling, his life as a dissident.

Steepling his fingers he said with a Mona Lisa smile, "These are strange days, indeed. I sometimes feel as if I've become a seer." His smile deepened. "Odd to say, but exile can sometimes do that. Wrenched away from the nexus, you become an Outsider, and in order to not merely survive but to be resurrected you're forced to change your point of view, forced from the subjective to the objective. It's like putting on a pair of contact lenses, or recovering from cataract surgery, everything becomes clear, sharply delineated. Motives reach the surface at last, and all becomes transparent."

"So you know the aim of *Trinadtsat*."

"I know it as well as I know the aim of AURA." He rose, and with that the color seemed to drain from his face. "But far more importantly, I know your role in both."

———

AFTER THE first shot, Jack put himself between Alli and the gunman, but they had already made significant progress through the field and the bullets lacked the range, falling harmless behind them. Still, there were two cops running full tilt at them, steel truncheons gripped in their hands like batons in a relay race. Unlike their compatriot, they hadn't bothered to draw their sidearms, having decided to concentrate on closing the gap between them and their quarry.

"We're never going to make it," Annika said. "They'll be in pistol range any minute now."

"What do you suggest?" Jack said.

Before he had a chance to react, she slowed and, turning, drew her gun. "Keep going!" she shouted. "Don't slow down!"

Jack had to drag Alli along with him as she started to drop back. "Come on!" he said urgently. "She's right."

"We can't just leave her," Alli cried.

"If we stop we'll all be killed." He nodded at the figure sprinting ahead of them. "In this instance Kirilenko has the right idea."

Behind them, Annika knelt and, cupping one hand beneath the butt to steady the gun, aimed at the leading cop. Her left arm felt as if it were on fire. She took long, deep, slow breaths to manage the pain. The cops saw that she'd stopped and began a peppering fire in order to distract her, but she ignored the bullets whistling by her, squeezed off one shot, missed. The second shot caught the lead cop in the right side of his chest, spinning him around before he collapsed. The second cop started to zigzag, stutter-stepping in order to make himself a more difficult target. He fired as he came, forcing Annika to roll, come up on one knee, squeeze off a shot, then roll again.

Looking back, Alli broke away from Jack's grip and ran back toward Annika. She ignored Jack's yell, closed her ears to the pounding of his feet behind her. Neither Annika nor the cop were as yet aware of her, and she dropped her gaze to the field across which she ran. At last finding what she was searching for she slowed and scooped up a rock. Planting her feet with her left leg forward, she threw it with unerring accuracy. It struck the cop on the forehead, just a glancing blow, but it was enough to stop him in his tracks, enough time for Annika to come up on one knee, aim, and shoot him twice in the chest.

"MY GOOD Riet Medanovich," Dyadya Gourdjiev said, "you should know there are two members of *Trinadtsat* downstairs even as we speak."

"So after all this time you were playing us." Boronyov drew a small-caliber pistol from his vest pocket. "You've betrayed us and everything we stand for."

"Don't be idiotic, I've done nothing of the sort," Gourdjiev said dismissively. "Do you actually think you know what *Trinadtsat* is all about?"

"I know they're after the same prize we desperately need if we're to align ourselves with AURA and rise again as a dissident force Yukin can't stamp out or bully."

"Then you don't know anything. Do us both a favor and keep your mind on what you're meant to do. AURA needs your expertise and your contacts." Gourdjiev put his back against the window and leaned on the broad sill. "Now please tell me what I want to know about who gave the FSB orders to assist Harry Martin and who Martin's handler was."

Boronyov said, "Let's go down and talk to Batchuk's ambassadors of pain."

Gourdjiev was genuinely alarmed. "And announce to them that you're still alive after all the trouble we went through to 'kill' you? That's the last thing we're going to do." He came off the windowsill. "Where is this sudden aggression coming from?"

"Your relationship with Oriel Jovovich Batchuk. You two go way back, you grew up together, had each other's back for years."

A whiff of a revelation came to Gourdjiev. "This suspicion isn't your style, Riet Medanovich."

"No? Whose style is it?"

"Kharkishvili."

Boronyov stared at him, silent as a sphinx.

"You understand what he's doing."

"He's questioning the special relationship you have with Batchuk."

As a gesture of frustration Gourdjiev jammed his hands into his coat pockets. "I've explained that."

"No, you've explained nothing, or at least not to anyone's satisfaction."

"Be truthful, Riet Medanovich—"

"Have you been truthful with us?"

"I set you all up," Gourdjiev said. "You, Kharkishvili, Malenko, the others. And now you think—"

"Kharkishvili says it's all a con—a long con you cooked up with your good friend Batchuk."

"That's insane," Gourdjiev said. "And furthermore don't tell me you believe it, because I'll laugh in your face."

"At this delicate stage, when everything is at stake, it really doesn't matter what I think or believe."

"I see. All that matters is what Kharkishvili believes."

"Think what you will."

"Oh, I know what he's done, Riet Medanovich, I've known it for some time," Gourdjiev said. "Ever since I brought him on board he's sowed the seeds of distrust in order to gain power, in order to displace me. It's a ploy as old as time, but what it will do is rend us asunder, in civil war we will all fail."

"He has a better plan."

"That's what all would-be tyrants and usurpers say."

Boronyov appeared unmoved, or at least unconvinced. "We can

end the speculation, distrust, and suspicion right now. All we have to do is go downstairs and talk to the ambassadors of pain."

"Who was Harry Martin and who was his handler?"

Boronyov stared at him unblinkingly for a moment. "You know who I'm going to have to call to get the answers."

Gourdjiev waved his hand in the air, Boronyov punched in a number on his cell phone, and spoke briefly to Kharkishvili. "All right," he said finishing up. "Five minutes," he said to Gourdjiev, who turned to stare out the window.

The kids and their mothers were gone but the lovers were still there, holding hands, talking perhaps about wedding plans. Their whole lives were ahead of them, Gourdjiev thought. His legs had begun to ache.

He did not turn around even when Boronyov's cell burred. A moment later Boronyov said, "Harry Martin is a deep-cover assassin out of the American National Security Agency. His handler is General Atcheson Brandt."

Good God, Gourdjiev thought in mounting agitation, *now I know why he was after Annika.* However, when he turned back to Boronyov his face was serene and untroubled.

"Now let's forget all about you going downstairs. Yukin and Batchuk think you're dead. You've got to remain in the shadows."

Boronyov lifted the gun. "That assumes we're going to allow these men to walk away."

Gourdjiev's mind was working overtime. "You want us to kill the deputy prime minister's men?"

"No," Boronyov said, unlocking the door, "I want to watch while you kill them."

JACK GRABBED Alli around the waist, swung her off her feet, and ran with her toward the far side of the field where, on a rise, a chain-link fence separated it from the parking lots. No one followed them. Annika was up and running after them. As she came abreast of them she gave Alli a fierce grin. Fifty yards still separated them from the fence. Kirilenko was scrambling up the slope toward it. Gaining the crest, he hooked his fingers through the links and began to climb. There was no razor wire at the top so he had little difficulty reaching it.

They were close to him, having reached the slope themselves. They were scrambling up it when they heard the sharp crack. Kirilenko's body arched backward as he lost his grip. The second bullet took part of his skull off, and he tumbled backward toward them. His trousers caught on a link, and he hung there, upside down, his rageful eyes glaring at them fixedly as blood turned his hair black and shiny as oil.

MONDAN LIMONEV folded the butt of the SVD-S Dragunov sniper rifle. He spent precisely twenty seconds admiring what he'd done to Rhon Fyodovich Kirilenko, whose corpse hung like a plastic sack of garbage from the chain-link fence. Without conscious thought he broke down the lightweight Dragunov with its polymer furniture. It was gas-operated, quieter yet more deadly than other rifles, and it fit in a case small enough to carry beneath one arm, like a baseball bat or a pool cue. The 7.62x54R steel-core rounds he'd fired into Kirilenko had done a satisfying amount of damage.

For precisely ten seconds he listened to the rushing of blood in his inner ears, the tympani of his heart within his ribs, and he felt the familiar exhilaration. There was nothing like the proximity to death to make him feel alive, vibrant, potent. What was life but mastery over others? He inhabited a universe of gods, who could snuff out mortal life with the slow pull of a trigger or the flick of a shining blade. What was Kirilenko now, nothing his mother would recognize, that was for certain.

He rose from his position on the top of a parked car and, clambering down, walked through the lot at a measured pace.

"CHRIST, IS he dead?" Annika said.

"As a doorpost," Jack, who was in a better position to see, answered.

"We're pinned down here," Annika said.

It was Jack who saw the figure rise from the top of a car in the parking lot and, with a small case under one arm, leap down and begin to walk away.

He led Alli and Annika to a spot along the fence far enough away from Kirilenko so Alli wouldn't have a clear look at the aftermath of the murder. "I don't think he's interested in us."

Peering through the fence he waited until he could no longer see the figure, then he said to Annika, "Okay, it's safe. Up you go."

She scaled the chain-link fence without question and, as soon as she was on the other side, Jack boosted Alli up. Climbing and scrambling, she rolled her body over the top and descended until she was met with Annika's outstretched hands. Jack followed, ascending and descending as quickly as he could.

Once in the parking lot Annika took them to the area cordoned off for airport personnel. Fortunately, there weren't that many cars, as a majority of the workers used public transportation to and from the airport. With less than twenty-four cars to check, they found the one they were looking for within five or six minutes, a beaten-up Zil. By that time, however, more sirens were tearing through the afternoon, pitched louder as the police cars approached the airport from the city of Simferopol.

Annika slid behind the wheel with Alli beside her. Jack took possession of the backseat, armed with the pistol they'd taken from Kirilenko. Annika started the car without difficulty, eased out of the parking space, and drove to the exit as the convoy of police cars careened by. Jack noted that her hands were perfectly still on the wheel, not even the hint of a tremor visible.

After the police cars had passed, she waited, breathing deeply and slowly. The tension mounted to almost unbeatable levels, Alli squirming in her seat, but it was imperative they avoid the danger of calling attention to themselves by appearing to flee the scene. In this way, three minutes crawled by while their hearts beat furiously and their pulses pounded in their temples.

At last, Annika put the Zil in gear, took a left turn out of the lot, and drove south toward Simferopol and, eventually, the coast around Alushta. Jack, with his back to them, kept an eye out behind them for any sign of a police vehicle. He counted six civilian cars on the road behind them, but nothing official. With a sigh of relief he swiveled around, watching, as Annika and Alli did, the unlovely countryside that would, at length, lead them to Magnussen's villa on the Black Sea coast, where, he hoped, many questions would be answered.

THREE CARS and a hundred yards behind them a man known only as Mr. Lovejoy drummed his blunt steel-worker's fingers on the steering wheel of his rented car. Though it might be something of a conceit to think of himself as a steel worker, his blue-collar Detroit background dictated his way of thinking. Uncomfortable with the suits he'd been obliged to rub shoulders with when he'd come to D.C. as a very young man, he had transferred out of the office and into field work with what some around him had deemed unseemly haste. But he was happy now and never looked back.

He'd asked for and by the grace of God had received a rental with a cassette player, an old but serviceable Toyota. The first thing he did after starting up the car was to slide in a cassette, turn the volume up to maximum, and when the first few bars of Breaking Benjamin's "Evil Angel" ripped and roared through the interior, his lips drew back from his teeth in a contented grin.

His gaze fixed on the Zil, he saw himself as a winged creature who, having caught sight of its prey, rides the thermals high above, following, following in twists and turns, dips and rises, waiting for the perfect moment to strike.

RIET BORONYOV accompanied Dyadya Gourdjiev out of the brothel. In the elevator Gourdjiev pulled out his gun and replaced the three bullets he'd fired earlier. Boronyov looked on with a mixture of superiority and tacit approval. Downstairs, the lobby seemed as chill as a meat locker, colder certainly than the outside temperature, which had moderated as the afternoon wore on.

The two *Trinadtsat* agents, stalwart and intimidating, were cooling their heels on the corner, smoking indolently, speaking very little, and generally acting as if they owned the block of buildings. They saw Gourdjiev approaching at the same time and their hands went to the pockets of their ominous black trench coats. Gourdjiev already had his gun aimed at them, and he shook his head, causing them to freeze for a moment, then slowly remove their hands, presenting them in what in other people could have been interpreted as a sign of surrender or placation. Not in these two, of this Dyadya Gourdjiev was certain.

It was at this moment that Boronyov, walking behind the older man, chose to show himself. The *Trinadtsat* agents, even as well trained as they were, could not keep the expression of consternation off their faces. Their bewilderment served as entertainment for Boronyov, and he laughed, reveling in their dire predicament.

That was when Gourdjiev turned the weapon on him and shot him point-blank in the side of the head. Boronyov's laughter turned to a burbling gurgle and then to stunned silence as he pitched to the pavement.

The *Trinadtsat* agents scarcely had time to register what had happened when Gourdjiev said, "Bring this traitor to Oriel Jovovich Batchuk. Tell him Boronyov is a gift from me. Tell him he can stop looking for Annika Dementieva. He now has the answer to what she is doing here in Ukraine."

TWENTY-ONE

AFTER HOURS of wildly pumping adrenaline a stunning fatigue had set in. Jack lay back against the seat, closed his eyes, and allowed the vibration of the car to lull him to a kind of shallow sleep.

"*Dad. Dad, tell me that story again.*"

He opened his eyes, turned his head slightly, and there was Emma sitting beside him. So it wasn't a dream, or perhaps it was, perhaps he was still sleeping.

"Which story?" His voice was so soft it barely registered over the road noise. Besides, Alli and Annika were talking to each other in low tones.

She was turned partway toward him, her right leg drawn up beneath her, the other one hanging down, the heel of her shoe tap-tap-tapping against the seat. "*The one about the scorpion and the turtle.*"

"I told you that so many times."

"*Dad, please tell it again.*"

There was a tension in her voice, an intensity he found disquieting, so he told her about the scorpion and the turtle who meet on the bank of a river. The scorpion asks the turtle to ferry him across on his back. "Why would I do that?" the turtle says. "You'll sting me and I'll die." "I can't swim," the scorpion says. "If I sting you I'll die, too." The turtle, a logical creature, is swayed by the scorpion's reply, so he allows the scorpion to climb on his back and out they go into the river. Midway across, the scorpion stings the turtle. "Why?" the turtle cries. "Why did you lie to me?" "It's my nature," the scorpion says, just before they both drown.

Jack looked into Emma's dark eyes, as if trying to peer beyond the veil of life. "Why did you want me to tell you that story again?"

"*I wanted to make sure you remembered it,*" she said.

"How could I forget it?"

"*That's what I thought, but I guess you need a reminder.*"

"I don't understand, honey."

"*Dad, everyone is lying to you.*"

He was suddenly tense. There was a knot in his stomach. "What do you mean everyone is lying to me?"

"*You know what I mean, Dad.*"

"I don't. Everyone, like Edward?"

"*The president,*" she said.

"And, what? Alli?"

"*Alli, as well.*"

"Why would Alli lie to me? Come on, Emma. What is this?"

"*Dad, I'm not telling you anything you don't already know.*"

"You always tell me things I don't know," he said.

"*About us, yes. The two of us. That's why I'm still here. But about everything else, no, I can't.*"

"The way you say it . . . as if it's some kind of law."

"*I suppose you could look at it that way.*"

"A universal law, like physics or quantum mechanics?"

He rubbed his eyes with his knuckles just in case he really was sleeping. But when he opened them, whether in fact he was asleep or awake, he found himself alone in the backseat. There was no one to answer his question.

"NOTHING IS inherently good or evil," Annika was saying to Alli as Jack looked around for his daughter, "it's just disappointing."

"Give me an example," Alli said.

Annika, her eyes on the road, thought for a moment. "All right. In ancient Rome, there was a man, Marcus Manlius, who had masterminded the plan to save the Capitol from destruction when Rome had been overrun by the Gauls. This was in, oh, three ninety, B.C. Anyway, in the aftermath of the war that drove the invaders out, as in all wars, the soldiers who had so bravely defended their homeland were now out of a job, and soon so deep in debt they were thrown in prison, an injustice Marcus Manlius would not tolerate. He used much of his great fortune to buy these heroes their freedom, an act of altruism that pissed off the patricians of the city, so much so that they accused him of building his own private army in order to force his way into power. The plebs, incited by the patricians' charges, sentenced Marcus Manlius to death. They threw him off the Tarpeian Rock."

Alli remembered that the Tarpeian Rock had fascinated Emma because it was the spot where criminals were hurled to their death. It was named after the traitor who opened the gates of Rome to the Sabines for the promise of gold bracelets. Instead, when she let them in, they crushed her with their shields, which they wore on the same arm as the bracelets so coveted by Tarpeia—a vestal virgin, no less! How ironic. She was buried at the base of the rock that came to bear her name, which rose from the summit of a steep cliff on the southern face of Capitoline Hill, overlooking the Forum.

Rome had been founded by thieves, outlaws, murderers, and slaves who'd been clever enough to escape their masters. The only trouble was there were no women, which is why these early Romans, as they called themselves, decided to steal females from the neighboring Sabines. It was this infamous rape—the Latin *raptio*, meaning kidnapping—of the women that led to the Sabines' revenge, using Tarpeia as their cat's-paw.

This dark side of Romans—of Rome itself—had caught and held Alli's attention, because in addition to being responsible for the invention of roads, the aqueduct, and numerous other innovations, it was the Romans who, infamously, had created the homicidal system of election. Those leaders they didn't like, learned to dislike, feared, found fault with, or about whom they invented transgressions (out of envy or greed) were murdered forthwith. Alli, having been born to and brought up in the incubator of politics, felt the tension, the unspoken fear of assassination that swirled around her father in ever thicker layers the higher on the political ladder he climbed. And when she'd come to Moscow she almost immediately had intuited how similar it was to ancient Rome, how much the modern-day political system had been infected by that of the Romans: institutionalized murder as a means to an end.

"So," Alli said after her moment's thought, "what you're saying is that even the best intentions turn to shit."

"I'm saying that all of us are doomed to disappointment. I'm saying I embrace that disappointment because it's the ultimate leveler, it doesn't care about class or money or power. It's the great reaper."

"You mean the *grim* reaper," Alli said. "That's death."

Annika shrugged. "Take your pick."

THE CALL came in to Dennis Paull's cell phone at three thirty in the morning. He was in the middle of a labyrinth of data he'd finally been able to pull off of General Brandt's cell phone records, as well as a definitive report on his comings and goings over the last year. In fact, Paull was busy reading the item that interested him the most:

two unofficial round-trip flights to Moscow, both in the last six months, both over weekends, that were neither recorded or expensed by any government agency. That wouldn't have necessarily set off an alarm bell in Paull's mind, but there were a number of oddities. For one thing, General Brandt paid cash for first-class tickets. For another, both flights had been on Aeroflot, not Delta, an American airline, which by all rights he should have taken. Where in the world did the General get ten thousand in cash for two trips to Moscow? He hacked into the General's bank account at District National. A day before the withdrawal, ten thousand was wired into the account from Alizarin Global, an entity Paull had never heard of.

His cell buzzed. He was plunged so deep in thought he almost didn't answer it.

A local number not recognized by caller ID. "Hello?"

"Mr. Paull?"

"Yes?"

"This is Nancy Lettiere, we've met several times. I run the Alzheimer's wing at Petworth Manor. I'm sorry to report that Mrs. Paull expired at three eleven this morning."

For a long time after that Paull sat very still. His eyes still ran over the lines of information on his laptop just as they had during the long hours before the call, but now nothing registered in his brain, which was suddenly filled with a dreadful little refrain repeated over and over—"You weren't there, you weren't there, you weren't there when she died"—as if it were a ridiculous children's song coming out of a ghostly radio in her room. All at once he was suffocating in the sickly-sweet odor of her, of . . . good God, he couldn't even say her name, she'd been a vegetable for so long. And yet now he was choking on what was left of her, of Louise, as if he'd inhaled the ashes of her funeral pyre.

He pushed back his chair, rose, and left the room without retrieving his coat. The fire stairs echoed harshly with his hurried footfalls.

Outside, he lit a cigarette, but almost immediately the night manager appeared behind the glass door, pointed to the cigarette, and shook his head vigorously. Paull took a deep drag and blew the smoke against the glass.

The night manager frowned, slid his key card into the slot, and opened the door. "I'm sorry, sir, but federal regulations prohibit any smoking within twenty feet of the building."

Paull said nothing, stood looking at him while he continued to smoke.

"Sir, did you not hear me? If you persist I'm going to have to call the authorities—"

He gave a startled yelp as Paull grabbed him by the lapels and slammed him up against the wall, then struck the man in the stomach. As he doubled over, Paull hit him in the side of the head, then flush on his nose, which immediately gushed blood.

For a moment Paull drew smoke into his lungs and let it out in a luxurious plume. He was dizzy with the onrush of adrenaline. At length, he knelt down and showed the night manager his credentials.

"I *am* the fucking authority, buddy." He hauled the man to his feet and pushed him roughly through the door. "So fuck off before I turn you in as a suspected terrorist."

Alone again, Paull stamped out his ruined cigarette and lit another. He stepped out onto the asphalt lot. Shouldn't it be raining, he thought, gloomy weather to match his mood? Instead, a brilliant butter-colored moon rode in the sky, and all at once he was thrust back twenty-eight years, when he used to read Claire *Goodnight Moon*. He read it so often that she had soon memorized it and then she recited it aloud with him as he read.

He took another long drag and let the smoke drift out on its own. Seven years ago Claire had visited for a long weekend with her then boyfriend, one of those young men full of entitlement based on an inflated assessment of their own self-worth. She was nothing but smiles and laughs, even when they had gone together to visit Louise, who, at that time, might on occasion still recognize her daughter.

Following dinner on Saturday night, in an awkward attempt at male bonding, the boyfriend had invited Paull out onto the back porch. Producing a pair of cigars, he boasted that they were Cubans. Not a good way to get into Paull's good graces. Nevertheless they smoked together companionably for a time while the boyfriend spoke about his important job on Wall Street, his conservative views on politics, religion, and morality, his plans for the future, which appeared to include Paull's daughter.

It wasn't until late in the day on Sunday that Claire told him she was pregnant, that she wanted to marry the boyfriend as soon as possible, which, Paull intuited, was the underlying reason for the visit. He did not argue with her, he said scarcely anything at all. She no doubt thought he took the news quite well, but then he'd done an excellent job of making her think he liked the boyfriend who, Claire made clear, as yet knew nothing of her changed physical state. In fact, she was excited about telling him, having picked out the time and the place that to her seemed the most romantic. "It'll be just like a scene from the movies," she gushed, her eyes shining.

For his part, Paull chose his own time and place to tell the boyfriend, watched in satisfaction as the young man choked on an inhalation of Cuban cigar smoke when he delivered the news.

"I expect you to do the right thing and marry Claire," he said, which was a risk he'd carefully calculated. Instead, as he'd suspected, the boyfriend cleared out, wanting nothing to do with a child conceived out of wedlock. What a hypocrite, Paull thought. He had no trouble taking my daughter to bed before their wedding night but his moral righteousness kicked in the moment the consequences of his reckless fornication reared their ugly head. He was enraged and had been since the cigar-smoking incident of the night before when the boyfriend had stupidly revealed himself, telling Paull how important he was, how much he made, talking about the house he had his eye on in Connecticut, giving his bona fides for buying Claire at any price, as if she were an expensive cut of meat, or a racehorse, he rode her well enough.

The only problem was Claire. Instead of being grateful to him for saving her from such a shallow hypocrite, she railed against him endlessly, screams and tears bursting forth in equal measure before she slammed out of the house. Certain that her hysterics would pass he allowed several days to go by before he phoned her. She wouldn't take his calls, and to this day never again spoke to him. He had a grandson, this much he knew, but whether or not his daughter had married, or married the hypocrite, or whether she was a single mother he had no idea. Once, he'd hired a private detective to find out, but paid him off a day later, sick of the whole sorry issue. The only thing he was grateful for was that Louise was too far gone to understand the unpleasant mess that without warning had been dropped into his lap.

As for Claire, he rarely thought about her now, except at odd times like these, and then he recalled her not with a twinge of nostalgia, but with a pang of disappointment. He did miss knowing about his grandson, even if he was the offspring of entitlement and hypocrisy, but only because someone would have to wean the boy off those tendencies before they poisoned his system. He found it sad, tragic even, that it wouldn't be him.

The thought of his anonymous grandson living an unknown life burned his skin as if he had thrust his arm into the furnace that would soon enough consume the sadly wasted remains of Louise. He stared down at his open hand, pulsing with blood, and for the first time came face-to-face with what it meant to be alive, to look back and see nothing but loss, a diminution of self, of his soul. He backed up against the cold wall that still held a smear of the night manager's blood, slid slowly down it. The moon was hidden from him now. Goodnight Claire, goodnight nameless little boy of seven, goodnight moon.

UPSTAIRS IN his darkened room, which sudden and unwanted sentiment had caused him to vacate, a brief but telling hacker's probe scanned General Brandt's private data over which Paull had been poring like the devil's advocate, then it captured the ISP address of Paull's computer. Within fifteen minutes of the probe being withdrawn an anonymous car hit the road, driven by a man who looked like an accountant, or possibly a schoolteacher, but who, having received his orders, was fully weaponized and ready to destroy life.

MR. LOVEJOY KNEW this road like the back of his hand. The Crimea had been his theater of operations for five years now. Not that he'd ever gotten used to it. The food still lay like a leaden ball in his stomach, his skin always itched from some fungus or other, and he hadn't slept in the same bed for more than three straight nights. The saving grace was the women, who were young, tall, blond, and plentiful. They loved foreigners, particularly Americans, who they hoped to rope into marriage in order to get them out of the hellhole into which they had been born. Once you knew that about them you could entice anything out of them. Mr. Lovejoy was looking forward to this evening's festivities, which he'd already set in motion, anticipating a quick resolution to this commission.

The road had risen up as it reached the cliff face. Already he could see the aquamarine sparkle of the Black Sea as the road began its long sweep around the coastline. Checking his odometer he saw there was less than a kilometer to the apex of the curve where the commission would be, as he put it, realized. It was time and, pressing down on the accelerator, he moved the Toyota into position.

The great sweep of the Black Sea, now darkly bruised by low-hanging clouds on the horizon, was rapidly opening up as he approached the apex. The Zil had already entered the first part of it. Swinging out into the oncoming traffic lane, he put on a sudden burst of speed. A moment more and he'd slam his off-side front fender into the left rear quarter of the Zil, launching it into a death spiral that, by his calculations, would send it over the cliff during its second rotation.

"MORE SPEED!" Jack shouted from the backseat.

"Hang on!" Annika called back to him.

As he saw the Toyota pull out into the left-hand lane, he added, "Jesus, he wants to send us over the cliff."

"This damn auto." Annika's hands gripped the wheel as firmly as possible, but it had begun to vibrate alarmingly as the Zil started to shimmy. "If I go any faster we'll go over the damn cliff without his help."

"Here he comes!" Jack said. "Alli, curl yourself into a ball and stay that way."

He rolled down the window and began firing at the oncoming Toyota, but their own car was behaving badly, shaking as if at any moment it would fly apart from the excessive stress it was under. Jack was thrown back and forth, making it impossible to get off a clean shot.

"Annika, for God's sake, put on more speed!"

She did as he asked, and for a moment it appeared as if the maneuver would work. They began to pull ahead of the Toyota, but then something lurched, forcing Annika to flutter the brake to stop them from flying off the road into thin air.

In that moment, the Toyota hit them and they slewed badly, beginning their spin. Jack, thrown against the open window, caught a glimpse of the Toyota before they spun around in a circle.

Annika threw the Zil into neutral and turned off the ignition.

The car continued to spin, coming perilously close to the edge before she was able to regain a semblance of control. Not that it mattered, Jack thought, because the Toyota would hit them again, the driver finishing what he had started. But as he caught a second glimpse behind them, something slammed so violently into the Toyota it rose into the air. An instant later, it exploded, hurtling down the cliff face, and the choking smell of burning gasoline engulfed them.

By this time, Annika had brought the Zil to a shuddering stop on the right verge of the road.

"Alli," Jack said, scrambling across the backseat, "are you all right?"

She came slowly out of her defensive position and, slightly dazed, nodded. It was then that Jack saw the movement out of the corner of his eye and, turning, watched a figure walking down off the high embankment on the landward side of the road. In one hand he carried an M72 LAW, an antitank weapon, the lightweight successor to the World War II bazooka, but he held it loosely, pointed at the ground. His size made it look like a child's toy. The man continued to walk heavily across the road toward the Zil. Jack's mind was working on the appearance of this man in the same way it had calculated the vectors of their run toward the oncoming jet, trying to find explanations in the extraordinary, working backward from the moment the Toyota exploded to the filthy back alley in Moscow. He came up with various explanations, possibilities, conflicting judgments, and fantastic speculation, but, unfortunately, no definitive conclusions. He had come to one of those moments when assumptions are derailed by a reality you could not have imagined, like turning a Rubik's Cube and finding a fourth dimension you hadn't calculated into your reasoning. In fact, for the moment the rational had been obliterated, logic was of no use whatsoever. Death and life had merged, or changed places, and everything else had come to a standstill.

"Stay inside the car," he told Alli.

She turned and, peering out the driver's side window, saw the man coming across the road. "Who is he? Jack, what's going on?"

"Please, Alli, just do as I say."

As if in a trance he opened the door and got out. The large, bear-like man came on, his slicked-back hair shining in the sunlight, and Jack experienced an eerie chill that went clear through him. The fourth dimension of the far side of the Rubik's Cube was almost upon him. In an attempt to make sense of the present his mind flashed back to the hotel bar in Moscow, where the man facing him had been arguing with Annika and her friend; the back alley where the bearlike man and his partner had lain in wait to kill Annika; the pitched battle that had followed, at the end of which the bearlike man lay in a pool of his own blood.

In self-protective reflex Jack pointed the gun at him, but Annika, having emerged from the collapsing automobile, strode quickly up to him and pushed down the barrel.

"This isn't possible," Jack said as the hulking figure stopped in front of him. "I shot you dead in the alley behind the Bushfire club."

"Aren't you going to thank me? No?" Ivan Gurov waggled the M72 slightly. "Don't be rude. Without me you would have gone over the cliff instead of the American agent sent to kill you."

PART THREE

Portia:
"Think you I am no stronger than my sex,
Being so father'd and so husbanded?"
—WILLIAM SHAKESPEARE,
   Julius Caesar

TWENTY-TWO

"*DAD, EVERYONE is lying to you.*"

With the echo of Emma's voice in his head Jack turned on Annika. "What the hell is going on?" He was so filled with fury his voice had turned guttural. "What are you playing at?"

"There's an explanation—," Annika began.

"Of course there's a fucking explanation." His voice rose even more. "You and Gurov were in on this from the beginning. Do you think I need an explanation from either of you now? I used Gurov's gun to shoot him, but it couldn't have been loaded with live ammo. That scene in the alley was a con." He turned on Gurov. "The other man, your pal . . ."

"Spiakov."

"Yes, Spiakov, where is he?"

Gurov shrugged. "Six feet under, I imagine. We required verisimilitude."

"*Verisimilitude.*" Jack turned back to Annika. "You murdered a man for verisimilitude?"

"It had to be real," Annika said. "At least part of it."

Jack was only dimly aware of Alli getting out of the car and approaching them, precisely what he told her not to do. "What I want to know is why you lied to me. Why are you offering an explanation now, at this late date?"

"Because now we've gotten you here," Annika said simply. "Because, dammit, it's time."

"You told me you hated Gurov, that he was an assignment."

"He *is* part of my assignment." Annika was getting worked up herself. "I only lied to you when it was absolutely necessary."

"And that makes it okay? That's a forgivable offense?"

"Don't confuse me with your ex-wife, who lied to you constantly," Annika said hotly. "Believe me, I haven't confused you with anyone else. You've made that quite impossible."

"What is that, your idea of a fucking compliment?"

Jack took a threatening step toward her, and the confrontation might have degenerated into physical violence if Alli hadn't stepped between them before Gurov could make a move.

"Stop it, the two of you!" she cried.

"If you'll only give me a chance to explain," Annika said, taking her cue from Alli.

"Jack, don't you want an explanation?" Alli chimed in.

"I already have an explanation." It was clear he was furious. "She's been lying to me from the moment I met her."

"Maybe she had a good reason."

"There's no good reason for lying," he said.

"You know that's not true."

"Why are you taking her side?"

"I'm not taking anyone's side," Alli said. "Anyway, even if you don't want to know what's really going on, I do."

That slowed him down a bit, at least enough for Annika to say, "I'm sorry, Jack, really and truly sorry."

He saw a change in her, perhaps because she was asking for forgiveness, but, probing beneath the surface, more possibly because of her proximity to Alli, or Alli's palliative words, as if being near Alli or even hearing her voice changed her subtly, brought her back to herself, whatever lay under her mask, in her unknown and unknowable heart Jack had talked about last night.

"If this could have been done another way," Annika continued, "I promise you it would have been. But we had no choice."

"We?" he said, more calmly in response to his probing. "Who is 'we'?"

"AURA," Annika said.

But immediately his anger fired up. "The entity or business or whatever you claimed to know nothing about."

Alli put a hand on his arm. "Let's not go there again," she said.

"It may be necessary." Jack's eyes were on Annika.

"We'll deal with that then," Alli said as if she were the smartest person in the group. Certainly she was the calmest.

He looked over at her, and taking in her tentative smile, nodded his assent. "All right," he said to Annika, "who or what is Aura?"

She said, "It's an acronym for the Association of Uranium Refining Allies. It's made up of—"

All at once, Ivan Gurov stepped forward. "Annika, no. This is a very bad idea."

She shook her head. "He has a right to know, Ivan."

"This could lead to dire consequences."

"Your job is done. Stay out of it."

Addressing Jack again, she continued: "AURA is made up of a group of Ukrainian businessmen, certain international energy interests in the Ukraine, and a small circle of dissident Russian oligarchs."

The moment Ivan Gurov had returned from the dead Jack had

seen the nature of the universe into which he had plunged. Now, at last, he saw its structure, as clearly as if he were looking at a scale model of Earth's solar system.

"So we have AURA on one side," Jack said, "and Yukin, Batchuk, and their creation, *Trinadtsat*, on the other."

"Observe, Ivan, this is a man who sees more than you or I," Annika said. "A man who—how shall we put it?—sees around corners. How much he has gleaned from only the stray bits and pieces he's picked up along the way, he's a chess master who sees the endgame forming the moment his opponent makes the first move."

The sound of an approaching car brought them all into awareness of their surroundings.

"I think," Gurov said, glancing dubiously at the wreck of the Zil, "I'd best get the car."

THE CAR in question turned out to be a clunky cab, decrepit but, because of that, absolutely anonymous.

"Where are we going?" Alli said.

"The Magnussen estate," Ivan Gurov said.

"You knew this all along," Jack said to Annika. His anger was still smoldering.

She shook her head. "I swear I didn't know where we needed to go. It was protocol. In the event we got picked up I couldn't tell our interrogators our destination."

"Interrogators," Jack said. "Charming." And Alli shuddered.

"Mikal Magnussen's father purchased fifty-five acres perched on a cliff overlooking the Black Sea," Gurov said as he drove, "high up so he could look down on his neighbors, all of whom consider themselves rich."

It was five thirty on an evening marked by towering clouds building along the horizon. Not a breath of wind stirred the trees. It was just over thirty-one miles from the airport to the thickly forested area

above Alushta where Magnussen's father had built his summer compound. They had already come seven-tenths of the way, so in less
than twenty minutes they turned off the road and came to a stop before stainless-steel gates, modern and as impregnable-looking as a
castle's portcullis. The gates were attached to a pair of fluted twelve-
foot-tall granite columns.

Gurov rolled down his window in order to press a red button
and recite something, perhaps a code phrase, into the grill of a small
speaker. A moment later, the gates swung soundlessly open and they
rolled through, tires crunching on a wide, looping bed of crushed
shells.

The Magnussen estate was something out of a storybook, or a
gothic novel, possibly *Wuthering Heights*, because its high stone walls,
turreted garrets, and dizzying spires were more appropriate for the
English or Scottish moors than for a seaside playground. Nonetheless
it was impressive and, furthermore, gave an excellent window onto
the elder Magnussen's predilections.

As the taxi approached the house a pair of black-and-white Russian wolfhounds came bounding out of the front door, their eyes
bright and curious, their pink tongues lolling.

"Boris and Sasha," Gurov said helpfully.

"Don't look at me, I've never been here," Annika said, in response to Jack's silent query. "I'm surprised that Ivan has, but then I
shouldn't be, our sliver of the world is so compartmentalized—
watertight, as we say. That's how superior security is built brick by
brick from the foundation up."

The wolfhounds—thick, shining coats; small, spear-point heads—
pounced on the people as they piled out of the car. Initially they went
right to Gurov, but gradually they became interested in Alli who,
alone among all of them, knelt on the gravel, engaging them at their
own level.

As Jack watched her distractedly a man appeared, came down the wide front steps, and approached them with the easy gait of someone born to money or power, possibly both. *So this is Mikal Magnussen*, he thought, making his first appraisal of the man he took to be the leader, or one of the leaders, of AURA.

He was a sturdy, even stolid man with startling platinum hair and even more startling blue eyes. His nose, like the prow of a wrecked ship, and ruddy, almost feminine lips, advertised an unsettling dissidence that set off in those who met him a sense of impending disaster. He wore a casual outfit that made Jack think he'd spent the afternoon hunting grouse. The wolfhounds circled him like moons, their tails wagging unrelentingly, licking his polished knee-length leather boots. Those boots, the color of burnt sulfur, were another curious contradiction: hunting boots, clearly handmade of glove-soft leather, without a scratch on their gleaming surface.

His bowlike mouth broke into a smile as he held out his hand. "Jack McClure, at last you've found us." His hand enclosed Jack's in a firm, dry grip, but he spoke to the others. "Ms. Dementieva, thank you for bringing him, and Ivan, thank you for ensuring they got here safely."

He had not yet let go of Jack's hand, and now he returned his attention to him. "It is a pleasure to meet you, Mr. McClure. May I introduce myself? My name is Grigor Silinovich Kharkishvili."

DENNIS PAULL did not see it coming, but then you never do, not this kind of ferocious death, or at least deadly intent. There are people out there in the world who mean you harm, who think of your ending, plot your demise as meticulously as a military campaign. These people don't matter in the end, the ones who wish you harm, who conspire at arm's length, studying methods of destruction in small, windowless rooms, swept daily for electronic listening devices, only to return home at the dwindling of the day to their wives and families, their potent cocktails and robust meals. It is their agents, the ones who you come face-to-face with, who matter, because they're the ones who carry your destruction in the palms of their hands or on their fingertips as if it were a bottle of champagne to pour over you, or a bouquet of flowers to lay on your grave.

Having been up all night, neither wanting nor needing sleep, Paull prepared to go to his day job as Secretary of Homeland Security. He showered in very hot, then very cold water, shaved and dressed. Uncharacteristically, he spent five minutes aligning the dimple in his tie so that it was in the exact center of the knot. His fingers worked both tirelessly and unconsciously as his mind ticked off the items on his agenda today. The first was stopping off to make arrangements at the funeral home where he'd instructed Nancy Lettiere to send Louise's body, then the office for six meetings that would take him through two o'clock, possibly three. At four, he was scheduled to hammer out interagency protocol with Bill Rogers, the national security advisor. At five thirty he had a phone appointment with Edward Carson who, he was certain, would be anxious for an update on what he had discovered about the activities of the president's inner circle. There might be some time to wolf down a bite of food somewhere in there, but he doubted it, so he resolved to stop at a McDonald's or a Denny's, whichever popped up first, for a breakfast on the run.

Slipping his laptop into its case, he went out of the room, down the echoing concrete stairs, and out the side door to the parking lot. He stood for a moment, checking the immediate vicinity for anomalies, an action now habitual, so ingrained he couldn't move from place to place without this specific scrutiny.

Having visually cleared the area he walked to his car, pressed the button on his key ring that popped the trunk. Bending slightly, he placed the laptop inside. He was just beginning to straighten up when he felt the sting in the side of his neck. His hand shot up in reflex. He just had time to register the tiny dart protruding from his flesh when he collapsed, unconscious, his head and torso inside the trunk.

A moment later a man strolled up, nonchalantly rolled Paull's hips and legs into the trunk with the rest of him, picked up the car key, closed the trunk and, sliding in behind the wheel, drove Paull's car sedately out of the Residence Inn parking lot.

"PLEASE. CALL me Grigor."

"You'll forgive me if I get right to the point," Jack said, as Annika walked back outside to take a call on her cell phone. "Where is Mikal Magnussen, the man who murdered, or ordered the murders of, Karl Rochev and Ilenya Makova?"

Kharkishvili raised his eyebrows. "You know Ilenya's name, you are unusually well informed." He led Jack and Alli into a solarium at the rear of the mansion. He turned, smiling at Alli. "And this lovely young lady is . . ."

"My daughter," Jack said.

Kharkishvili's brows knit together. "I have a daughter more or less your age. She's in school in Kiev, where her mother looks after her."

"My mother is dead." Alli stared unblinkingly up at his face. "My father is all I have."

Kharkishvili cleared his throat, obviously taken aback. "Would you like to sit here while your father and I take a stroll? There's a fine view of the surrounding hills and forests—"

"Hell, no."

He glanced at Jack, who gave him no help at all. "As you wish." He seemed to say this to both of them, his tone one of disapproval rather than of concession. He cleared his throat again, clearly uncomfortable discussing matters in front of Alli, whom he took to be a teenager. "Rochev had to be eliminated—he had ordered Lloyd Berns's death. Why? Because Berns, having learned about us, about AURA, was going to leak the information to General Brandt, and

Brandt would have told Yukin, who would have informed Batchuk, and then a *Trinadtsat* extermination squad would have been dispatched to kill us all."

"And Ilenya Makova?"

"Ah, well, killing Rochev's mistress was collateral damage. He was there with her in the dacha, but managed to escape the property."

"Not that it mattered," Jack said with controlled vehemence. "He was captured, brought to Magnussen's estate outside Kiev, and tortured before he was killed."

"That, I'm afraid, was an instance of, how best to put it, unbridled enthusiasm."

"What a clever way to put it," Alli said, but then, seeing Jack's admonishing look, at once shut her mouth.

"You can use any clever phrase that comes to mind, but the outcome is the same: Rochev was tortured. Why? Because your killer—Magnussen or whoever he was—couldn't control himself."

Kharkishvili, aware that Jack had thrown his phraseology back into his face, said, "I don't want a fight with you, Mr. McClure."

"You may have no choice," Jack said.

Kharkishvili hesitated, then laughed. "I like you, sir." He wagged a finger. "I see where your daughter gets her sharp tongue."

"Do you think this is a joke?" Jack said. "Torture, collateral damage, murder—none of them are what I'd call a laughing matter."

"Of course they aren't." Kharkishvili spread his hands. "What I mean to say is that none of us has complete control over events. I assure you that the perpetrator of these unfortunate atrocities has been punished."

"Meaning?"

Kharkishvili pointed out the window. "You see that large blue spruce up on the rise there?" He crossed to a glass door that led out to a flagstone terrace, beyond which appeared to be an apple orchard. He opened it and gestured. "Shall we walk across his unmarked grave together?"

"Your dog could be buried there," Jack said, "or your ex-wife, or nothing at all."

"You don't believe me."

"Where is Mikal Magnussen? I want to ask him some questions."

At that moment Annika appeared. Catching Jack's eye, she motioned for him to join her on the other side of the solarium. Jack walked over without excusing himself.

"Harry Martin was an NSA hit man," she said in a low whisper, "under the control of General Atcheson Brandt."

"I don't understand," Jack said. "Why was he sent after you?"

Her expression of concern deepened. "The NSA must have found out about us. Your president is determined to sign this treaty with the Kremlin."

Jack shook his head. "Even so, he would never authorize the NSA to do Yukin's dirty work."

"I want to take your word for it," Annika said, "but then what's the explanation?"

Jack thought a moment. "General Brandt is the joker in this particular deck."

"What?"

"I have no idea what Brandt is doing handling an NSA assassin, that doesn't track."

"Mr. McClure." Kharkishvili was beckoning. "If you'll come with me . . ."

Jack stepped outside and together they walked through the apple orchard to the rise beneath the blue spruce.

"So then?"

Jack rubbed the toe of his shoe over the freshly turned earth, dug deeper. "Nothing is buried here," he said, "or at least no one."

Kharkishvili was eyeing him closely. "Are you saying that I lied to you?"

"Without hesitation."

Kharkishvili stood with his hands clasped behind his back, breathing deeply. "This sense, or ability, is why you're here now, Mr. McClure." His eyes met Jack's. "You see, we need you."

"I don't know what ability you're talking about."

"We're inside a puzzle now, Mr. McClure. A Gordian knot, if you will. You have a special gift—a way of seeing around barriers that keep other people paralyzed."

"I think you have me confused with someone else," Jack said. "I uncovered your lie, but Annika fooled me."

Kharkishvili nodded. "But there came a time when you began to have doubts about her, wasn't there?"

"Yes, as a matter of fact there was, when we came out of Rochev's dacha into the ambush."

A vague smile played across Kharkishvili's mouth. "Yes, we anticipated that probability."

Sixteen diverse bits of information formed a pattern on the Rubik's Cube in his mind. "Wait a minute, it was Gurov who shot her in the woods. He aimed for the fleshy part of her arm, a minor wound, it's true, but my doubts vanished when she was hit."

"You see what I'm driving at, Mr. McClure. It takes so little information for you to grasp the big picture, to determine how vectors intersect. You were the one who found your way here; Annika had no idea where we were, we couldn't allow that. Compartmentalization is our watchword." He brought one hand from behind his back, gesturing for them to walk to the cliff face. As they came down off the small rise the wolfhounds appeared, racing each other to Kharkishvili's side.

"If you have any doubts about how Annika fooled you, I would counsel you to keep in mind that people don't simply lie, because lying is never simple. Lying leads to complications—the more one lies the greater the complications. I think that's clear enough, but for our purposes we must take these thoughts a step further, a mental exercise people rarely bother with because they're essentially lazy."

They were nearing the rocky promontory; the mansion rose on their left, a guardian of titanic proportions. The water looked as dark as its name. The dogs were excited either by the height or the sight of the seashore where, perhaps, Kharkishvili or Mikal Magnussen ran them on occasion.

"People lie for a reason, or for a cause, something, at any rate, larger than themselves," Kharkishvili continued. "The causes—the things that are larger than any individual, larger, even, than a group of like-minded individuals such as AURA. Which is where you come in, because now everything that surrounds AURA seems a threat, at least to us who are on the inside. We have been blinded, made paranoid by our growing peril, so we cannot be trusted. How can we, when we cannot even see past point A to see whether point B will connect with it or destroy it. You have found the land of the blind because you can see for miles. You're the one with the ability to make sense out of the chaos of life. You see, interpret, understand the disparate elements, you can sense if they connect or not. This is why we need you, Mr. McClure, why no one else will suffice."

"So this was all a test," Jack said. "The clues, the bits and pieces, like breadcrumbs in a labyrinth."

"Oh, nothing we devised was so easy as that, Mr. McClure, but I take your point." Kharkishvili nodded. "A practical test, yes. Why? Because we had only read about your abilities, and personally I find written reports unreliable. However, an eyewitness account, now that's an entirely different matter."

Jack felt the sea breeze against his cheek, saw the wolfhounds chasing their own tails. "You know what? I think you're all nuts. If you needed me so badly why didn't you just ask me?"

"Because you wouldn't have come, and even if you'd had a mind to your president wouldn't have allowed it."

"Why?"

"Because our meeting, should it have become a matter of public record, would have jeopardized his precious accord with the shit Yukin. Because as far as the shit Yukin is concerned, as far as his ass-wiper Batchuk is concerned, we're dead, this group of dissident Russian oligarchs: me, Boronyov, Malenko, Konarev, Glazkov, Andreyev—hunted down and killed by the FSB's crack assassin, Mondan Limonev. Except that Limonev works for us. All these secrets I lay in your care, Mr. McClure." He spread his arms wide. "I trust you."

"You don't know me. Why would you trust me?"

"Because Annika says I should. Because she trusts you."

"That's of no interest to me," Jack said, though it was impossible to be immune to what Kharkishvili had said. "Edward Carson is my friend as well as my employer. I won't betray him under any circumstances, so it seems you do have the wrong man, after all."

Kharkishvili sighed. "Your President Carson is being betrayed even as we stand here. I think you'd better hear the whole story before you make a decision that could have dire consequences not just for AURA but also for the United States."

"YOU MUST hate my guts," Annika said when she and Alli were alone in the solarium.

"Not really." Alli was watching Jack and Kharkishvili walking between the martial lines of apple trees. "But I am disappointed."

Annika produced a rueful laugh. "Yeah, I definitely deserved that."

"Why did you do it?" Alli asked. "Why did you lie?"

Leaning over, Annika pushed a lock of newly shorn hair off Alli's forehead. "I had no choice."

Alli moved away. "Don't change the subject. That's what my father and all his friends do when a question is too difficult or embarrassing. It's a politician's trick, and I hate it."

Annika went and sat down in a teak chair, sinking back into the patterned cushions. "I explained to Jack as best I know how." She gave Alli a rueful smile. "But I know that some actions can't be explained away, some actions stay with you, like a stigma. I was prepared for that with him, but not with you."

"Oh, please, don't bullshit me." Alli crossed the room, leaned against the glass windows, staring out at the now deserted apple orchard with its sharp, twisted branches seeming to scrape the mottled gray and blue sky.

Annika watched her as she moved, as she crossed her arms over her breasts, as she looked longingly out onto the empty grounds. "The truth is fixed, immutable," she said, "because if it contains even a grain of a lie, it's no longer the truth." By examining the girl's face she could work out just how much Alli missed Jack when he wasn't with her, but also a terrible sadness. There was a strong cord between them, no doubt, she thought, but there was also something dark there, a lie of some measure, or perhaps something unspoken, an omission, a truth deliberately unsaid. "But a lie comes in infinite gradations, it can be judged on a scale, whereas truth cannot, you see, because a lie can contain a grain of the truth, or even a great deal of truth and still remain a lie. But of what sort, on what level?

"You can tell a, what, a white lie, I think it's called in English, isn't it?" When Alli didn't answer, didn't even move from her blank contemplation, she continued undeterred. "You're not punished for telling a white lie, are you? You needn't feel remorse or guilt, or wish you could take back your words."

"Why do you say it as if it's about me," Alli said. "It isn't about me."

"I was just using a figure of speech," Annika replied, a deliberate lie. "How would I know if you had lied, or to whom?" She paused, as if expecting an answer, then went on. "Anyway, a lie can be useful when the truth won't do, when it's too sad, for example, or too shocking." Alli twitched, one shoulder rising involuntarily as she sought to protect herself from the assault of Annika's words.

"The point is you make a choice when you tell a lie, or even when you withhold the truth—"

"Stop it!" Alli said sharply. Her face, when she turned it toward Annika, was very pale.

"—even in instances when you must tell a lie in order to protect a person you're close to or love, or in order to serve a higher end. This is what happened to me."

The two women eyed each other, almost, it seemed to Annika, as if they were gladiators in the Forum, overlooked by the Tarpeian Rock, the ancient burial place of betrayal. She felt energized by this electric charge, by the hope that the ongoing conflict between them would jolt the girl out of her traumatized shell.

"Every lie has its moment when it's believed," she said, with her teeth slightly bared, "even by those whose nature it is to doubt, or to be cynical. Lies are seductive in nature because they're what you want to believe, or contain an element, a seed of the distrust you yourself harbor, though you may not even be aware of it."

Alli gave a strangled little cry as she peeled herself from the glass. "Is this the way you think you can gain my trust?"

"I never even considered gaining your trust. The man who kidnapped you, who held you hostage, stole your trust, and you're incapable of getting it back."

Tears sprang to Alli's eyes as she tore out the door, stumbling across the flagstone terrace, around the side of the house, blindly following some strange, self-destructive instinct that took her toward the cliff face and the falloff to the churning water below.

TWENTY-THREE

DENNIS PAULL awoke in a room full of windows. Early morning light flooded the polished wood floor, by which he knew he wasn't in a hospital or institutional room. He wasn't bound, either. He was, however, disoriented. Where was he? What happened? The last thing he remembered . . . Christ, his head hurt.

"I have something for that headache."

He turned his head at the sound of a woman's voice and immediately experienced a tightness where the dart had sunk in. The woman was dressed in a conservatively tailored suit that was too stylish to have been bought on even a G-15 salary.

"Dr. Denise Nyland. I'm a neurologist." She smiled as she held out two pills in one hand and a glass of water in another. "Here, these will help." When he hesitated, she added, "They're just Tylenol, I assure you."

He took them from her and, when he had checked the logo imprinted on each tablet, he swallowed them with the entire glass of water.

"I know you must have a lot of questions, Mr. Secretary," she said. "All of them—and more—will be answered shortly. In the meantime, I suggest you rest while I tell you where you are." She glanced out one of the windows, where a marble fountain plumed water into the air. Beyond were lawns and carefully sculpted shrubbery, even perhaps a small maze, though from his present angle he couldn't be certain. He rose from the chair in which he'd been placed and at once felt a wave of dizziness, so that he was obliged to sit right back down.

"You're in Neverwood, an estate owned by the Alizarin Global Group. I'm employed by the firm."

Paull fought his way through the vertigo and the pounding in his head to pay strict attention. Alizarin Global was the entity that had paid for General Brandt's off-the-grid trips to Russia. He'd never gotten around to Googling it, his mind taken up by grief, remorse, self-pity, and rage following the news of Louise's death.

"Then you must be the one who concocted the chemical that was on the dart." Paull had trouble enunciating, as if his mouth had been shot up with novocaine.

"Neverwood is in Maryland, precisely ninety miles from the White House," Doctor Nyland said, pointedly ignoring his remark.

Paull frowned, which caused the pain in his head to eddy up. "Why was I brought here?"

"In a moment, Mr. Secretary, all will be made clear." That professional smile, clean and icy as a toothpaste ad, held no malice whatsoever. "For the moment let it suffice to say that no one means you any harm. As soon as you are briefed, you'll be handed the keys to your car. You'll be free to go without any strings attached."

"What is Alizarin Global?"

Doctor Nyland merely smiled. "Good-bye, Mr. Secretary. I wish you a pleasant day, wherever your journey leads you."

And then he was left alone for precisely six minutes. He timed it on his watch, which hadn't been taken from him. Using his time alone productively he went through his pockets and determined that, apart from his car keys, his possessions were present and accounted for.

At the six-minute mark the door opened and a young, pleasant-faced man entered the room. He was dressed in a dapper business suit, and he smelled vaguely of a cologne nearly as expensive as the clothes he wore. Clipped to the breast pocket of his jacket was a small laminated tag in the shape of a hexagon. It was orange, or perhaps a warm red. It bore no type or name; it must be, Paull intuited, Alizarin Global's logo.

"Good morning, Mr. Secretary," he said briskly, with the same slick smile that had animated Dr. Nyland's face. He clipped an identical logo tag to Paull's jacket. "I imagine you're hungry." Stepping back, he gestured to the open doorway. "There's coffee waiting, and freshly baked croissants with homemade strawberry jam. I understand strawberry is your favorite."

Without comment Paull followed him out into a hallway with hunter green walls, brass light sconces, and paintings of famous sailing ships of the 1900s. The man approached double pocket doors made of carved ebony, which he slid soundlessly open. He stood on the threshold, indicating that Paull should enter. As soon as Paull did, he slid the doors shut.

Paull found himself in an old-fashioned drawing room, complete with a marble fireplace, a baby grand piano, a pair of oversized chesterfield sofas, a wet bar along one wall opposite another filled floor to ceiling with books. An enormous bay window overlooked a pond elegantly spanned by a Japanese-style bridge. A brass ship's clock, crouched atop the mantel, chimed the time.

Two men sat in facing Queen Anne chairs, between which was a coffee table laden with a chased silver coffee service for three. To one side stood a hotel-style server's cart. The moment Paull walked in the two men rose as one. He recognized them immediately: Miles Benson, former director of the CIA, and Morgan Thomson, the national security advisor during the previous administration. Benson was one of those leather-necked battle vets for whom posters were invented. His face, though dented and deeply scored, was the more powerful and commanding for its battered mien. He had high cheekbones and a fierce Clint Eastwood squint. His manner was no-nonsense, even his glance was brusque, and yet Paull was willing to bet that he saw everything. Thomson was slender, ferret-faced, with a long, sharp-edged nose and hooded rodent eyes that looked out on the world with inveterate suspicion. He was virtually lipless, the better to show bright, white teeth, which were as sharp as his erudite tongue. His intellectual prowess was legendary in neocon circles, and even beyond, which made him the quintessential pundit on talking-head TV.

These two seemingly had nothing in common, and yet during the two terms in which they had been in power they had forged an unshakable alliance on which, until near the end, the former president had relied. These two had shaped his policy and were responsible for the shambles of his legacy. Unrepentant and every bit as arrogant as the day they had assumed their respective posts, they refused to believe that any decision they had made was wrong or misguided. The world, in other words, was their world, reality to the contrary. Complete control had been their aim as well as their hubris, because nothing so grandiose could be controlled by two men, a hundred, or even a hundred thousand.

All of this recent history flashed through Paull's mind in the three seconds it took for the two men—Edward Carson's archenemies, who plotted his destruction—to reach him and, with smiles a millimeter thin, pump his hand.

A moment later, Paull said, "Your behavior is outrageous, bordering on the criminal. I'll have my car keys now."

"Of course," Benson said, dropping them into his palm.

Without another word Paull turned to go. He was almost at the door when Thomson said in the plummy tones of his television voice, "Of course you're free to leave, Mr. Secretary, but it will be a pity if you don't get to see your daughter and grandson."

Paull stood frozen for the space of several thunderous heartbeats, after which he was compelled to turn back to face them. "I beg your pardon?"

"Your daughter, Claire, is in the room across the hall. Your grandson is with her."

Paull was virtually stupefied. "Why are they here?"

Thomson had clearly taken point. "They came to see you."

"Don't make me laugh. My daughter hasn't wanted to see me since before my grandson was born."

"She does now," Thomson assured him. "We told her that you were terminal."

"You people are insane." Turning away, Paull put his hands on the grips of the sliding doors and began to push the doors apart.

"Aaron," Thomson said in his richest tone. "Your grandson's name is Aaron."

Paull, filled with conflicting emotions, whirled on his tormenters. "None of this will mean a damn to me when you're taken into custody. Kidnapping a member of the United States government is a federal offense punishable by—"

"No one's being arrested," Benson said sharply. "No one's going to jail."

"He can't help himself, the military has marked him for life." Thomson said this in an equable, almost a kindly manner. He raised a hand. "Why don't we all sit down. Aren't you even the least bit curious as to why we want to talk with you?"

Turning, Thomson sat down on one of the chesterfields and poured coffee into the three cups. "I don't know about you, Mr. Secretary, but I'm famished." He looked up expectantly. "Is your opinion of us so set in stone that you won't give us a chance to explain the . . . unorthodox method by which you were brought here?"

"Unorthodox?" Paull echoed.

Thomson shot Benson a significant look. In response the ex-military man cleared his throat before saying, "I apologize for the extreme methodology that brought you here." He crossed to the chesterfield, accepting the cup Thomson offered. "However—and here I think you'll agree—I seriously doubt that we could have induced you to come here any other way."

Thomson nodded at his compatriot's conciliatory tone. Taking up another cup, he lifted it as a token offering to Paull. "Please believe us, Mr. Secretary, you're a guest here. An honored guest."

Paull, his best dubious face forward, slowly settled himself on the chesterfield across from the two men. He put three sugars in his coffee, a dollop of half-and-half, and stirred with a tiny spoon. While he did this Benson opened the warming cart and produced plates of croissants, eggs, bacon, and small, precise triangles of buttered toast. All very civilized, Paull thought, as he sipped his coffee, which was strong and rich, much better than the swill he would have bought at McDonald's or Denny's.

"If I may," Thomson said, "your mistake was in hacking into General Brandt's bank account. We monitor it twenty-four-seven."

"But, as it happens," Benson said, "your mistake was our good fortune, and I'll tell you why." He added Tabasco sauce to his eggs, took a bite, and nodded appreciatively before setting down his fork as if he were already full. "Brandt is our man on the inside."

"Brandt isn't a member of the cabinet," Paull said.

"He's in an even better position, he's an advisor who has Carson's ear, especially on all matters Russian." He shrugged. "Given what you've been up to the last several days I don't suppose that comes as much of a shock to you. However, we've become increasingly concerned with the General." He pursed his lips, as if he'd just bitten down on something acrid. "You remember Colonel Kurtz, I imagine."

"*Heart of Darkness*," Paull said. "Joseph Conrad, a great book."

"Thank God your frame of reference isn't *Apocalypse Now*," Thomson said. "Coppola made a mockery of that masterpiece."

"Back to Kurtz," Paull said. "Are you trying to say that General Brandt is insane?"

"Well, if not," Benson said sourly, "he's certainly in his own private heart of darkness."

For the first time Thomson looked disconcerted. He lifted a hand and scratched his eyebrow with the back of his thumb, a gesture that eerily mimicked the intelligence officer played by G. D. Spradlin, who briefs Captain Willard on his assignment to terminate Kurtz in a memorable scene near the beginning of the film.

Benson, who Paull could tell wasn't prepared to deliver what he intuited as bad news, cleared his throat again. "In point of fact, and despite what my esteemed colleague said, the allusion to *Apocalypse Now* isn't unwarranted." He paused for a moment as if unsure how to proceed. "You do know that the character of Kurtz was based on the much decorated Green Beret, Colonel Robert Rheault?"

"During the war in Vietnam," Paull said, digging back in his memory. "Wasn't Rheault relieved of his command?"

"That's right," Benson said, sitting ramrod straight. "He was accused of murder."

A small but terrible finger of ice seemed to pierce Paull's gut. "What does that have to do with General Brandt?"

Thomson, sitting stonily beside Benson, was positively white-faced.

Benson briefly glanced at him before he said heavily, "General Brandt has issued an immediate sanction on Jack McClure."

Paull knew this, of course, but he saw no advantage in letting them know it. In fact, quite the contrary. He was now sure that he had more information about Brandt's latest activities than they did, which meant that, like Kurtz, like Rheault, Brandt had lost touch with his superiors, or at least his coconspirators. As Benson had said, the General was now in his own private heart of darkness. What this meant for all of them he had no idea, but much to his own consternation, he became aware of a subtle shift in how he perceived these two men. Not that enemies had suddenly, recklessly morphed into friends, but the polar opposites of black and white seemed to be breaking down into shades of gray.

At length, he said, "How the devil does General Brandt think he can order a sanction?"

"That," Thomson said, at last unthawing, "is what we've brought you here to discuss."

EVER VIGILANT when it came to Alli, Jack saw a blurred shadow out of the corner of his eye and knew it was her. He turned away from Kharkishvili to see Alli racing across the rocky headland toward the cliff's edge. Without a second's thought he broke away and ran, calculating vectors as he did so, in order to ensure he would intercept her before she . . . did what? Was she going to hurl herself off the cliff? Was she suicidal? Had she exhibited any warning signs that he might have missed when he was paying attention to Annika?

The dogs, barking hysterically, followed him, loping uneasily, as if they had picked up on his mounting anxiety. She was still running full tilt toward the cliff's edge when he caught up with her. Her headlong momentum pulled him along for a pace or two, which brought both of them perilously close to the steep drop-off. The dogs growled, their haunches quivering, the hair at the back of their necks ruffled, until he had dragged her back from the brink.

They fell to the rocky ground, and the dogs moved in, licking their faces until Kharkishvili called them off, and the wolfhounds scampered back to where he was standing some distance away.

"Alli," Jack said, out of breath from both his sprint and the fright she had given him, "what on earth do you think you're doing?"

"Get off me!" She shoved him. "Get away from me!"

She was crying hysterically, and probably had been, judging by her tear-streaked cheeks, for some time.

"What happened?" he said, alarmed. "What's gotten into you?"

She turned her head away, into the grass, her body wracked by sobs.

"Alli, talk to me." Annika had said that Alli wanted to tell him what Morgan Herr did to her, that her need to tell someone about her week of terror would eventually override her reticence. "You can tell me anything, you know that, don't you?"

She struck him then, just a glancing blow to the side of his head, but he was shocked enough to lose his grip on her, and she scrambled away, first on all fours, like a wounded animal, and then, regaining her feet, making another jagged, confused run for the edge of the cliff.

Jack sprinted after her and, scooping her up, ran back in the direction of the manor house, but he stumbled over an outcropping of rock and had to put her down. For some reason he wasn't seeing clearly, and when he raised a hand to his eyes it came away wet with tears. He sat on the grass, panting and crying, while all three wolfhounds circled the two of them protectively as he had seen them do with Kharkishvili.

To his credit the Russian kept his distance. He had turned toward the mansion, where, Jack saw, Annika had emerged. Taking in the scene, she began to run toward him. Long before she got there Kharkishvili intercepted her, turning her away so that Jack and Alli could remain alone.

Jack felt the sea wind in his hair and on his cheeks. It was soft and moist with salt and phosphorus. The clouds overhead seemed unable to stir, as if some great hand had pinned them in place. He tried to listen for the crash of the waves, but he heard nothing. It was as if the world were holding its breath.

"Alli," he said softly, but made no move to touch her, or even to move nearer, "you don't want to kill yourself, I know you don't."

Trembling and shivering, she stared at him, red-eyed, and shouted, "I've had fucking enough of people climbing inside my head, telling me what to do!"

"Alli, please tell me—"

"I can't, I can't!" she cried. Her hands curled into fists, and then they began to beat against his chest, as if he were the physical manifestation of the terror that gripped her.

In the face of her mounting hysteria he knew he had to remain calm. He didn't stop her attack, but he didn't withdraw from it, either. "Why can't you?"

"Because . . ."

She seemed to want to hurt him, and perhaps through him, herself.

"Because—" Her voice was so thin and cracked he had to pull her close to hear her. "—you'll hate me, you'll hate me forever."

"Where did you get that idea? Why would I hate you?"

"Because I lied to you." A dreadful fear seemed to come over her. "I lied, I didn't tell you the whole truth."

He closed his arms around her and said in her ear, "I could never hate you. I love you unconditionally." Kissing her on her cheek, he said, "But I think you ought to tell me whatever it is that's causing you so much pain. It isn't healthy to sit with it."

She snorted in tearful derision. "You say you love me, but that'll all change the moment I tell you."

"Do it then." He held her at arm's length so he could look her in the eyes. Her fists had uncurled, the fingers trembling against his chest. "Let me decide instead of you deciding for me. Trust me. Trust *us*."

The light had gone out in her eyes, she stared at him as if without recognition, and he pulled her to him again, murmuring to her: "Don't go away, Alli. Stay here with me, you're safe, you're safe," just as he had when he'd rescued her from the black place where Morgan Herr had taken her.

Her head lay heavily against his chest, she seemed to be scarcely breathing.

"Alli, please, I won't hate you, no matter what, I promise."

He felt her sigh against him, a long exhalation that was as much resignation as it was a surrender. Her entire body seemed limp and frail, as if she needed to give up everything, even her physical presence, in order to make the terrifying leap he asked of her.

"I . . . I lied to you about what happened the morning Emma was killed."

"What?" He had expected some terrible revelation about what Morgan Herr had done to her, not this.

"I knew it." She squirmed in his arms, trying to pull away. "I knew I shouldn't've opened my big mouth."

"No, no," he said quickly. "Go on. What happened that morning?"

Her voice was muffled, as if she were talking into him rather than to him, as if she wanted to speak to something inside him with which she desperately needed to connect. "I . . . When you asked me I told you that I wasn't around, that I didn't know what Emma was up to."

"You told me in retrospect you thought she was going to see Herr."

"That was the lie. I knew where she was going because she told me." Alli's voice was further clouded by guilt and despair. "I was there. She asked me to drive her, she said she'd been up all night and was in no shape to drive." She was weeping again as she clung to him. "I told her I couldn't, I gave a totally bogus excuse because I was scared, I didn't want to get involved. And because I was so chicken-shit, she died. If I'd been driving nothing bad would have happened, she'd be alive now."

TWENTY-FOUR

"IRAN," PRESIDENT Yukin said, "is a topic of the utmost strategic importance." He shook his craggy head. He had eyes like nuggets of coal that had been burned deep into his face. The bulb of his nose was pocked and cratered, possibly from a childhood disease. "I have said this before, President Carson, but I see that I must say it again in order to underscore the weight the Kremlin reserves for such matters."

"You needn't bother," Edward Carson said. "I am well aware of the special status between Russia and Iran."

"Special status?" Yukin mashed his fleshy lips together, as if he wished to grind Carson's words to ash. "No, no, you misunderstand us. We have certain business dealings, yes, but as for—"

"Such as sending them nuclear reactor parts and refined uranium."

That statement hit the room, or more accurately, Yukin's ears, like a detonation. An awkward silence ensued. Carson, Yukin, General Brandt, and Panin, a high-level Kremlin apparatchik who had not been further identified, were sitting in a palatial room inside the Kremlin. The ceilings, twenty feet in height, perhaps more, were arched as in a cathedral, a comparison whose irony wasn't lost on Carson.

"Since the debacle in Iraq your fact-finding spies have been notoriously inaccurate," Yukin said at length. "This lie is but another example."

At Carson's gesture the General removed a dossier from his briefcase and handed it to his commander in chief. Without a word the president opened the dossier and spread half a dozen photographs on the table. One by one, he turned them so they faced Yukin.

"What's this?" Yukin said, not even bothering to look at them.

"Surveillance photos of enriched uranium being transferred from Russian transports to Iranian transports." Carson's forefinger tapped a photo. "Here you can clearly see the symbol indicating radioactive material."

Yukin shrugged. "Photoshopped." But something was caught in his eyes, a shadow mixing anger and embarrassment at being caught out.

"I have no intention of making these photos public." Carson gathered up the photos, shoved them back in dossier, and slid it across the table to Yukin. "But I must be clear: The position of the United States on the security accord will not change from where it was an hour ago, or yesterday. You cease your dealings with Iran and we dismantle the missile shield around Russia, we become security allies. We are done making changes; it's time for us to sign the accord that will prove to be invaluable to both of our countries."

Yukin sat very still for some time. The breathing of the four men seemed to come in concert, inhalations and exhalations caught on the tide of tension that had sprung up in the room moments before. Then the Russian president gave a brief nod. "You'll have my answer within the hour."

———

"THIS HAS become a perilous game," General Brandt said as he and Carson strode the frigid Kremlin corridors, the president's usual entourage strung out behind them. "If you had told me you were going to show Yukin those photos I would have cautioned you to find another way."

"There was no other way," Carson said shortly.

"Mr. President, may I point out that you're on the verge of signing the most historic accord with Russia in the history of the United States, one that will ensure the safety of the American—"

"I seem to be more concerned with the American people than you are," Carson snapped. "I won't sign the accord with the points that Yukin has insisted on." He didn't care for Brandt's admonishing tone, the inference that he, a neophyte when it came to the Russians, had acted rashly, that he should have deferred to the old Russian hand. "I get the feeling that Yukin is playing us to see how far he can push us, how many of his demands we'll accede to. I won't have it. I won't be pushed around, either by him or, quite frankly, by you, General."

"GENERAL BRANDT," Benson said.

"Where to begin with General Brandt?" Thomson said as if he hadn't been interrupted. He sighed, as if stymied by the enormity of the task before him.

"We recruited Brandt some time ago," Benson said helpfully.

"Three years, more or less," Thomson leapt back in. "Midway along in the second term. We saw the handwriting on the wall. The president and his other senior advisors were hell-bent on continuing down the same path we'd all started down when he was first elected."

"It wasn't working anymore," Benson said. "The commanders were telling us that privately, and the troops were worn down. The stop-loss program, though increasingly necessary, was, in practical terms, a disaster, plus it was a PR nightmare."

"Just the fact that we needed stop-loss should have sent a signal to the president's advisors, but they ignored it, just like they ignored every news event or incident that contradicted their vision."

Paull was familiar with stop-loss. It was a program instituted by the military, who, running short on recruits, abrogated the rights of its members to be rotated out of service. Stop-loss kept them in and fighting on the front lines in Felluja or Kabul, or wherever the power that be deigned to send them.

"How does this information tie in with General Brandt?" Paull said.

Again an expression of discomfort briefly crossed Thomson's face. "In the waning days of the administration we found ourselves without power, or nearly so. The fact is we'd been effectively blocked from the president."

"By whom?" Paull said, wondering if they'd divulge this secret, a yardstick by which he might judge both their sincerity and their veracity.

"Dick England," Thomson said at once. England had been the director of the White House Office of Strategic Initiatives, a unit set up by Carson's predecessor and now, happily, dismantled.

"England hated our guts," Benson said with some venom. "He was a power freak, he formed an alliance with the secretary of defense, on whom the president relied for much of his foreign policy."

"The war," Thomson said heavily, "was the secretary's idea and he pushed hard for it."

"I thought the war was your idea," Paull said, "and Benson's."

"Even to the point of fabricating evidence of WMDs," Benson said, with the stoic intonation of the seasoned warrior.

"He couldn't have done that without the connivance of the director of the CIA," Paull said.

Benson's smile was bleak and far from friendly. "He couldn't and he didn't."

"Though we tried hard, the three of them proved too much for us," Thomson said, "and we were shut out."

"It was time to abandon ship," Benson continued, picking up the thread of the original conversation, "so we decided to cast our net into the private sector. Eventually, we decided on Alizarin Global."

"Which is where General Brandt comes in." Thomson sighed as he poured more coffee for Paull and for himself. "We didn't particularly like him, but because of his ties with President Yukin we needed him to help us fast-track a deal with Gazprom, crucial to Alizarin, before a competitor could sew it up. Bottom line, we thought we could trust him."

"We were wrong." Benson stood up and walked to the piano, stood staring at it for some time, as if hearing an oft-played melody—possibly a martial air—in his head. Or perhaps he was fantasizing the methods by which he'd murder Brandt. He turned back abruptly, his face tense and grim. "And now he's left us hanging by the short hairs. This is something neither we nor President Carson can permit nor withstand."

Thomson put down his cup. "This is why we brought you here, Mr. Secretary. We had neither the time nor the means to engage you in any other way."

Paull found he had no more taste for coffee, or for any of the food, for that matter. "What is it you think I can do?"

"Wait," Thomson said. "You haven't heard the worst part."

EDWARD CARSON sat alone in temporary seclusion, as much as any American president can be alone. He sat in his suite at the hotel across Red Square from the Kremlin, a generous pour of single-malt scotch at his elbow. Peering out the window he could see that it had begun to snow again this late in the season, as if he were in Wyoming or

Montana. Astonishing, really. He watched with a kind of detached interest as the snowflakes swirled and spent themselves like moths against the windowpane.

Then he pulled out his cell phone and called Jack.

"Jack, where the hell are you?" Carson said. "More to the point, where the hell is my daughter? Lyn tells me that she bundled Alli off on you. I could be pissed off at her but, frankly, it's easier to yell at you. Did you think about what a security risk this poses?"

"It's never left my mind, Edward. I argued against taking her, but I don't have to tell you what Mrs. Carson is like when she makes her mind up about something."

"What was she thinking?"

"She was terrified that Alli would slip her handlers and take off for parts unknown in a city she scarcely knows, a city, I might add, that's far more dangerous than the aircraft she and I took to Kiev."

"I take it she's not still in the aircraft," the president said.

Jack's long relationship with Carson allowed him to shrug off the sarcasm. "It's a long story."

"Well, spill it. How's my daughter?"

"The Ukrainian air has done her a world of good, she's much improved."

This welcome news instantly deflated Carson's anger. "Well, dammit, it's about time. Lyn will be relieved, let me tell you." He grunted. "She's not getting in your way, is she?"

"On the contrary, she's proved extremely helpful."

"Well, that's a surprise. But look here, Jack, I don't want her put in harm's way. I think you should ship her back here."

"She's not a package, and anyway there's isn't a chance in hell that she'll come."

"She listens to you. If you insist—"

"Edward, listen to me, this may not be the safest place for her, but what is, the rehab facility she was in? You already know she won't talk to anyone there, but she's talking to me. Whatever she went through has to come out, it's eating her alive."

Carson was silent for a moment. "All right, dammit. If she's making progress to being normal again that's the important thing." Not knowing how else to respond, he tackled a topic he could handle: "Now, have you found out whether Lloyd Berns's death was accidental or premeditated murder?"

"I'm making significant headway, but I don't yet have the shape of the situation."

Jack's voice seemed thin and attenuated, as if it was coming from the dark side of the moon, but the president began to absorb the details of Jack's journey through Ukraine, and what he had uncovered to this point.

"You've made good progress, Jack," he said with a sigh. "Keep me informed. And, Jack, give Alli my love."

"Will do."

Carson disconnected and put away his cell. It was times like this, he reflected, weighed down by events, realizing that he was a constituency of one, when he fell back on his beloved Shakespeare. He'd always been drawn to the kings, even as a college student. And no Shakespearean monarch had captivated him more than Henry V, a humane ruler who understood what it meant to be isolated by his royal blood. But, cannily, he also knew that royalty was differentiated from the common man merely by pomp and circumstance, or, as Shakespeare put it, ceremony. This was never made more clear to the reader, or viewer, than when Henry disguised himself in a cloak and hood and sat among his troops on the eve of battle, talking with them, sharing stories, arguing with them as if he were one of them. Nothing would better prepare him for the coming deathly morning than trading barbs with his troops, treading the same ground, muddying his boots in the same muck, having them reach him with their lewd and tumultuous voices.

But who did he have? He felt alone and isolated, no longer trusting General Brandt, but having been given no valid excuse to dismiss him or to send him home. Denny was half a world away, immersed in his clandestine research. For every selfish reason he could name he bitterly regretted sending Jack away.

He stood up, sipping his scotch while he gazed at the Kremlin with a jaundiced eye. He was also beginning to regret staking the first ninety days of his presidency on this Russian accord. It had been General Brandt who had talked him into it, Brandt who had pointed out that what the American people wanted and needed most was a sense of heightened security, an outcome that shutting down the Iranian nuclear program would accomplish. Unfortunately, it couldn't be done without Yukin's help.

Brandt might be right about all that, he thought now, but the fact was he didn't trust Yukin, and now he didn't trust the General either, which was why he'd resolved to bring the surveillance photos into play now, rather than keep them in reserve.

Not that he himself was innocent—he had no illusions on that score. This was why he loved Shakespeare—because his kings were so self-aware. Not for them the delusions of lesser mortals; they were clear-eyed even in their madness. They knew their hands were covered in blood, that they had committed murder, that they had given difficult orders on which lives rose and fell, hung in the balance, and were ultimately plowed under the bloody fields of battle. Neither had they conveniently forgotten the plots and betrayals that had paved their way to the crown.

Into his wandering mind now came one of his favorite lines from *Henry V*: "What infinite heart's ease must kings neglect that private men enjoy!"

He lifted the glass to his lips, but he'd already finished the scotch. The remainder of the Talisker was in the bottle on the other side of the room, but instead of going for it, he put down the empty glass and headed for the connecting door.

A youngish, gangly individual who looked uncomfortable in his boxy suit looked up at the president's appearance, startled and pale beneath his African-American brown. He was already reaching for the portable defibrillator as he said, "Sir, are you feeling—?"

"Relax, I'm fine." Carson sat down in the chair opposite the person known colloquially as Defib Man, the doctor who trailed after him in case he had a heart attack. "Sit, sit."

The president looked over at the ultraportable computer Defib Man had set back on his lap. "Catching up on the news in the real world?"

"No, Mr. President, I'm e-mailing my daughter, Shona."

"What school is she in?"

"Well, it's a special school. She's crazy about horses."

"Does she ride English or Western? My daughter rides—"

"Neither, Mr. President. She's got Asperger's syndrome. She concentrates very well, especially on the things she likes, and in that sense she's something of a genius, but she has no emotions."

The president's brow furrowed. "I don't follow you. Surely she loves you and your wife."

"She doesn't, Mr. President, not in the normal sense, anyway. She doesn't feel anything—joy, sorrow, fear, love."

"And yet you said that she's crazy about horses."

"Yes, she's discovered a way to breed them that's some kind of breakthrough, though to be honest I don't get it. They fascinate her, but on a level neither my wife nor I can fathom. Maybe they operate on her level, who knows? Basically, she's in a world of her own making. It's as if there's a glass bell jar around her that nothing can get through. What makes it all the worse is that she's perfectly self-aware. She's a prisoner of her own mind, and she knows it."

With a pang the president thought of his own daughter who, in hindsight, had been lost to him a long time ago, there was no use pretending otherwise. He couldn't understand her the way Jack seemed to; worse, he was losing patience with her. Whatever she had gone through was over and done with, why couldn't she put it behind her like a normal human being? There was only so much time he could devote to her and her issues. He was used to solving problems, not having them continue to unwind like an endless ball of twine. How the devil had he and Lyn given life to a creature who seemed to feel nothing toward them except contempt? Of course that begged the question of what he felt about her. Of course he loved her, he had to love her, she was his daughter. As such he would protect her with his life, but that didn't mean he had to like her, or that he should accept who she was. What did she know of the real world, anyway? She exhibited only disdain at the compromises he had been forced to make in order to gain and retain his political power. These days his emotions tended to swing from praying she'd pull out of her depression or whatever the hell she was wallowing in to being fed up with her unacceptable and childishly narcissistic behavior. Lyn had always been in the habit of acceding to her whims and threats, never more so than now, but he was coming to the end of his tether.

Defib Man stirred uneasily causing Carson to think, *Heartache here, too. We're both unlucky fathers, there is no real difference between the two of us.* He said, "I'm truly sorry . . ."

He was groping around in his memory when Defib Man said, "Reginald White, sir. Reggie."

"Yes, of course. Reggie. Very good." He trusted his kilowatt smile to burn away his lapse. "I'm hungry, Reggie. Are you hungry? What say we get something to eat?" He reached for a phone, but one of his protectors got there first.

"What can I get you, sir?" the Secret Service agent said.

"How about a burger—no, a cheeseburger deluxe. How would you like that, Reggie?"

White seemed slightly terrified, as if his world had been turned upside down. "Surely, Mr. President, you have more important things to do than have a burger with me."

"As it happens, Reggie, I don't. And even if I did, this is what I want to do now." He turned to the agent. "A pair of cheeseburgers deluxe. And French fries. Do you like French fries, Reggie? Good, who doesn't. We'll share a large order then. And a couple of Cokes."

Then he turned back to Reginald White. "Now I want to hear all about Shona and her breakthrough. You have good reason to be proud of your daughter."

"IT GETS worse?" Paull said.

Thomson nodded. "I'm afraid so."

As if on cue Benson returned to the chesterfields, but now he sat beside Paull, rather than opposite him. "Now comes the chapter and verse on General Brandt."

"Not until I see my daughter and grandson," Paull said.

"We don't have time—"

"You're the one who brought my family into the mix, Benson." Paull stood. "I have enough to go to the president, which will save him, but not, unfortunately, the two of you."

Thomson, alarmed, rose as well. "If you let us explain fully—"

"Be my guest," Paull said, "*after* I see my family and after I tell them that I'm not dying."

"Consider," Benson said. "They might not then wish to see you."

Paull shook his head. "You really are a piece of work." He cocked his head. "Now I think about it I'm not going to make this easier for you. You're going to tell them I'm not terminal. It's your lie, you wriggle out of it."

Benson looked bleakly over at Thomson, who gave him an almost imperceptible nod. Then he got up heavily, straightened his jacket, brushed down his trousers, and sliding open the pocket doors, led the way across the hall to a somber study, devoid of sunlight.

Paull was at once terror-stricken. He hadn't seen his daughter in seven years, hadn't ever laid eyes on his grandson—Aaron, he had a name to which Paull was about to put a face. He realized that he could take Claire's rejection, she had become for him a shadow, an image in a photo, slightly faded from time and the slippage of memory. She had become, in a way, like Louise, shut away in her own private Petworth Manor, as if she, too, suffered from Alzheimer's, her forgetting him not of her own volition. It was easier, or at least less painful, to think of her as debilitated, ill, not in control of her mind or her emotions. In this way he had frozen her like a butterfly in amber, a small child he could still remember sitting on his knee while together they recited the words to *Goodnight Moon*.

But now here she was, rising from the floor where she had been sitting beside Aaron, smoothing down her skirt as Benson had smoothed his trousers, a small but telling gesture both of propriety and of nervousness. He both recognized her and didn't recognize her because the photo in his mind had become faded and fragile, thin as rice paper.

They stood looking at each another, silently assessing the damage and wear time had assessed on human flesh and the human heart. Claire was older, yes, but also more beautiful, as if when he'd last seen her the Great Sculptor hadn't quite finished his work.

"I'm sorry about Mom." She spoke first, her voice subtly deeper and richer than he remembered it, but also stiff and awkward, as if she wasn't sure who she was addressing.

"It's for the best. She's peaceful now, herself again." His voice was just as stiff and awkward, and he realized with astonishment that it was quite possible, likely, even, that he had faded from her consciousness as surely and inevitably as she had from his own.

"My grandson," Paull said, almost against his will, because it would be Aaron's rejection he could not bear. His throat felt tight and parched.

She looked down at the boy with a jerky little motion of her head, as if her mind and her body were not quite in synch. "Aaron, please stand up." Her voice changed, became clearer, declarative when she addressed her son.

The boy—Aaron—unfolded from his position on the floor, where he had been using an iPhone application and turned, stood facing Paull in ranked row with his mother.

"Aaron," Claire said, "this is your grandfather. His name is Dennis."

"Hello," Aaron said.

The boy was taller than Paull had imagined, but then he had no expertise with seven-year-old boys, no frame of reference except his memories of Claire at that age. Much to Paull's relief he didn't look like his father, or rather Paull's rancid memories of his father. Rather he looked like Paull himself, which made Paull's heart stop momentarily; it was as if he were looking into the face of immortality, another him just starting out along life's rough road.

"Hello, Aaron," he said, his heart in his mouth, and then despite what he'd said to Benson, he added eagerly, almost avidly, "Mom may have told you that I'm ill, but I'm not." He found that he could finally smile. "I'm perfectly fine."

"Dad," Claire said, "is that true?"

But Paull remained mute, entranced by his grandson. It was difficult to know whether he even heard her.

She turned to Benson, her face flushed with anger and resentment. "Is this true, Mr. Benson? You said my father was terminal."

"Yes, well, that was something of an untruth."

"Something of an untruth?" Claire echoed. "Good God, man!"

She was leaning forward at such an angle that she was forced to take a step toward him, an aggressive step, it seemed to Paull, who had come out of his near-trance, a threatening step, as if it were a prelude to an assault. Benson faced her like the ex-military man he was, ramrod straight, but his eyes were filled with battlefield humiliation.

"You lied to me and my son, added to our anguish and . . . My mother just died, you unspeakable toad!"

Benson held his ground, but made no reply because there was nothing he could say, no excuse he could fabricate in the face of her wrath—and wrath was the right word, Paull thought, because there was something old-fashioned, unfashionably traditional about her anger, and this made him proud of her. And it was precisely in that moment when the faded and fragile image he had of her collided with the Technicolor force of her actual presence and became concrete, past and present dissolving into each other and, by some mysterious alchemical process, leading him home.

He turned to Benson now and said, "My family and I would like some time alone."

Benson opened his mouth, possibly to reiterate that time was of the essence, but between the looks on both Paull and his daughter he ended up keeping his mouth shut.

After Benson departed, Paull was alone with the ghosts and demons that had bedeviled him even as he valiantly and vainly tried to push them far down into his subconscious.

"So," Claire said, her voice once again thin and terribly strained, "you're okay, you're well."

He nodded, suddenly unable to speak.

"But how is it that you're here, what do these people want?"

"I don't know yet." Paull felt safe talking about Benson and Thomson.

"These are important men."

"Well, they were," he acknowledged. "Perhaps they still are, who knows. They kidnapped me, more or less, and once I was here told me that I could see you and Aaron if I listened to them."

"I notice you didn't listen to them."

"I turned the tables on them, instead."

"That's so you, Dad."

He cleared his throat, wished he had a glass of water to hide his question behind. "Are you . . ." He felt a fresh rush of terror, as if he was entering a haunted house, or the lair of a dangerous animal. "Are you married?"

"No, I'm not." It was a simple, declarative statement, devoid of ruefulness or self-pity. "Lawrence never came back, he hasn't seen Aaron. I wouldn't want him to."

"I see." He had been right about that privileged bastard.

This flow of information was followed by a self-conscious silence during which Aaron looked from one to the other, his brow furrowed in a distinctly unchildlike manner, as if he were trying to parse the currents and undercurrents of emotions swirling around him.

"It must have been tough those last months with Mom," Claire said. "I'm sorry I wasn't able to get to see her more often."

"That's all right, I—" He stopped in mid-sentence. It would be so easy to keep, and even embellish on, the fantasy she had of him spending time with Louise when he hadn't. Guilt and remorse were powerful foundations on which to reunite, to ensure that she would love him again. Initially he'd had that impulse, the same selfish inclination that had kept him away from Louise. It was possible, he thought now, that Claire had succumbed to the same impulse. But he could not go through with it. This wasn't a time for selfishness or for lies. It occurred to him that, difficult though it might be, he could manage to bear Claire's and Aaron's rejection far better than he could a lie that brought them together under a false flag.

"Honey, the truth is I did what you did. I spent far less time with your mother than I should have. The truth is . . ." He looked away for a moment, at Aaron, who was watching him with a child's disconcertingly piercing gaze. And it was this gaze that gave him the courage to continue. He smiled in gratitude at Aaron before he got on with it. "The truth is I couldn't bear to see her in that state. She didn't know me, didn't respond to the songs we loved together. She didn't even know where she was. She was locked away in a place that had no key."

There were tears glittering in Claire's eyes. "I spent so much time hating you, shutting you out . . ." She paused long enough to catch her tears with a slender forefinger. "I put you in the same horrid room where Mom was. I couldn't bear to see either of you, I didn't want Aaron to see his grandmother like that, to remember her only as . . ." She took a hesitant step toward him. "Now she's gone and I realize that nothing can bring her back, nothing can bring back the days before . . ." She couldn't help but glance at her son. "But here you are, Dad." And then, rather defiantly, "Aaron is the best thing that ever happened to me."

"I can see that so clearly, so very clearly," Paull said, meaning every word.

TWENTY-FIVE

"JACK, I'M sorry." Alli turned her face into his shoulder. "I'm sorry, I'm sorry, I'm sorry."

"You have nothing to be sorry about, honey. You had no way of knowing what would happen. And what if the two of you had died, have you considered that possibility?"

She shook her head mutely.

Jack's heart constricted. He felt blindsided by Alli's revelation. He didn't blame her for her decision, he didn't see it as a betrayal of her deep and abiding friendship with Emma, only a deep and abiding ache in his heart that she had been carrying this anguish around in addition to her terror at what Herr had done to her.

"Jack, please say something," Alli said with a clear note of desperation.

It was no good wondering what would have happened if Alli had been behind the wheel the morning of Emma's death, Jack knew; no one would ever know what it was that caused Emma to swerve off the road at speed and into the tree. He could ask Emma, of course, the next time she appeared, but he suspected that she didn't know or couldn't remember. And, in any case, she had already urged him to move on from his own guilt, and this set his mind, expanding outward to absorb the different points of view, on the right track.

He saw Annika standing beside Kharkishvili, watching them, and he turned Alli away from her to face him. "Listen to me, we're both carrying guilt about the choices we made the morning of Emma's death, and maybe that wound will never fully heal, but I can assure you that we'll never know unless we let go of the guilt and stop punishing ourselves. That's what Emma wants for us now, more than anything."

Alli's eyes were glittering with held-back tears. "I don't know . . . I don't know if I can."

"You have to want to. Alli, so much has been taken away from you." A dark flicker passed across her face and it seemed as if she might crumble in front of him. He continued, still calm but with a subtle underlayer of urgency. "It's time you put things back inside yourself."

She shook her head. "What do you mean?"

"I think you know." He took a breath. "Did you think Herr was going to kill you, that you were going to die?"

"I want to go back inside."

"No one's stopping you." Jack was careful not to take hold of her.

Alli looked away, chewing on her lower lip, then nodded in a jerky motion. "At one point I was absolutely sure I wouldn't survive."

"That's when it happened," he said, "a little death, a partial death, your mind preparing itself for oblivion."

"What do you mean?"

"You're both alive and dead." Jack moved closer to her as he lowered his voice. "Something in you died, or at least grew critically ill, during that week with Herr."

"You're wrong, you're wrong!" she cried.

"If you can see yourself from this perspective, everything you say and do makes perfect sense. You're full of rage, contempt, spite, then you turn around and become the most warm and loving creature imaginable. You have trouble sleeping, and when you do sleep, you're beset by nightmares. You adore Emma but are also terrified of her, terrified Emma will somehow seek vengeance for what you see as your betrayal of her—walking away from her when, in hindsight, Emma needed you most."

Tears rolled down her cheeks. "I want to die now."

"Is it comforting to say that, because I don't think you really mean it."

Anger flashed in her teary eyes. "Don't tell me what I—"

"Alli, stop this." His voice was stern but not unkind. "You know, I was really pissed off at you when you showed up on the plane. I was going to send you back, but your mother more or less coerced me into taking you. But during the few days you've been with me I've seen something in you—a determination, as well as a fierce will to survive—so don't tell me that you want to die because I know it's only something you've gotten into the habit of saying or thinking. It isn't real, you know it isn't."

Alli seemed calmer now, or at least better able to listen to what he had to say. She was still in shock, so he understood that it would take her some time to digest their conversation, to allow her thoughts and emotions to find the equilibrium from which she could definitively move on.

"Are you all right?"

She nodded, put her head against his chest, leaning heavily against him as if she were exhausted.

Having walked slowly in their direction, Annika apparently decided it was now more or less safe to approach them. "Jack, Alli's violent reaction was my doing."

"You're going to have to explain that."

And Annika did. She told him about the conversation she'd had with Alli, how it had become more abrasive, more contentious, how she had been trying to force Alli out of her debilitating shell.

"What were you thinking?" He put his arm protectively around Alli's shoulders, holding her close.

"I forced her to look at herself," Annika said softly. "She had to get to this place, she had to sink so far down the only way to go was up."

"And what if she had jumped off the cliff?"

She put her hand tenderly on the back of Alli's head. "She's not suicidal, Jack. If she had been she'd have killed herself before this."

Jack looked at her and knew what she said was true. He looked around then as if suddenly aware of their surroundings and saw Kharkishvili standing at some remove, watching them with a mixture of pity and forbearance. The oligarch called his wolfhounds, who bounded toward him, and he turned with them at his heels, heading back to the estate at a quickened pace.

"We'd better follow him," Jack said, eyeing the rapidly darkening sky. The wind had picked up, gusting in off the water, and the sudden dampness foretold the coming rain.

DEPUTY PRIME minister Oriel Batchuk was waiting outside Dyadya Gourdjiev's building when Gourdjiev returned home. He lurked in the doorway like a wraith, wrapped in his leather trench coat, which was both sinister and absurd. He had a thirties-style fedora pulled low on his forehead. He looked like he was auditioning for *The Thin Man* or *Five Graves to Cairo*, and in another time and another place the sight might have tickled Gourdjiev's funny bone. As it was he felt only a deep sense of fate having its way with him.

As he approached, Batchuk stepped out of the doorway, but he brought his own shadows with him.

"I received your burnt offering," he said, referring to the sacrifice of Boronyov, whose still warm corpse Gourdjiev had laid at his agents' feet, "but this time I'm afraid it's insufficient."

Gourdjiev stood his ground, trying his best to appear unperturbed. "Meaning?"

"This time Annika has gotten in the shit too deep, beyond even my ability to cover for her."

Gourdjiev let go of a sudden spurt of anger, deep-seated and long-simmering. "Is that what you've done? I wasn't aware that you've ever done anything for her—"

"Contrary to your peculiar delusion of omniscience you don't know everything."

"Please. You've been too busy doing things *to* her."

The two men stood staring at each other with such malevolent intensity that it was possible to entertain the incredible notion that they were trying to destroy one another with their minds.

"I understand and sympathize with your frustration," Batchuk said at length. "Only Annika and I know what happened. She won't tell you and I certainly won't."

"She was only five, only a child!"

"She certainly didn't act like a child." Batchuk's smile was both smug and contemptuous. "You see, you never really knew her, you never suspected what she was capable of, you missed the point of her entirely."

"I'm the one she calls *dyadya*."

"Indeed you are." Batchuk's tone made it clear this statement was anything but a concession. "And you're the ignorant one, the scales have not yet dropped from your eyes. Unlike Saul of Tarsus you haven't yet had your road to Damascus moment, but then it seems you were untimely born."

"Untimely born?"

"'Last of all, as to one untimely born, he appeared also to me,'" Batchuk quoted. "Paul's first letter to the Corinthians."

"For a devout atheist you're quite the biblical scholar."

"I like to probe the weaknesses of my enemies," Batchuk said, with a meaning directed at Gourdjiev. The tenuous cord was broken, they were no longer frenemies. "In any event I came to warn you, or more accurately, to give you the opportunity to warn Annika. I'm coming for her—me, myself, not someone I've hired or ordered to do a piece of work. This I do personally, with my own hands."

Dyadya Gourdjiev fairly trembled in barely suppressed rage. "How can . . . This is monstrous. How can you do this?"

"Given the decisions she has made how can I not?"

"You know what this means."

Batchuk nodded. "I do."

"Nothing will ever be the same between us."

"My dear Dyadya Gourdjiev," Batchuk said, using Annika's nickname for him in a mocking manner, "nothing was ever the same between us from the moment I first saw Annika."

"I DID what I thought was right," Annika said, "but I know I don't always make the right choice."

Jack studied her at some length. They were standing in the entryway to the Magnussen mansion, just outside the bathroom where Alli had gone. Neither of them wanted to leave her alone at the moment, and as for Jack, the feeling of having been boxed in by both Alli's impetuosity and her mother's inability to control her had reasserted itself with a vengeance. And yet he knew quite well that there was no use in railing against this situation; as he had since he'd taken off from Sheremetyevo he resigned himself to the responsibility of keeping her safe, both from others who might want to kidnap her and do her harm, and from herself.

"In that you and Alli are alike," he said. "She seems to lack the ability to know what's good for her, or maybe it's her own self-hatred that pushes her to seek out dangerous situations."

Annika smiled what might best be described as a secret smile, or at least an ironic one, as if his words had triggered hidden memories.

"You see her in such a clear and perfect light, Jack, I admire that, I really do. I mean, she's such a complex person, not that most people aren't complex, but there's something about her that—"

She stopped abruptly, as if changing her mind, and her eyes seemed to drift away to another time, another place. It wasn't the first time Jack had observed this phenomenon in her, and he was struck by its similarity to what he sometimes observed in Alli. And now, as this particular Rubik's Cube shifted perspective in his mind, he began to wonder how many more similarities there were between the two women.

Her carnelian eyes came back to him, in the light of the entryway their mineral quality making them transparent. "Jack, you don't hate me for what I did, do you?"

"Did? What did you do?"

"What I said to Alli."

"No, not at all. She needs all the help she can get, even if that help is sometimes difficult for her to hear."

"I'm relieved then." She placed a hand on his arm. "After all that's happened—"

"But that's just it." Jack suddenly decided to take the bull by the horns. "I don't know what happened to you."

"What? I told you."

"But you didn't, not really. When I first saw the scars I decided not to ask you how you got them because I thought it might be an invasion of your privacy, but now I'd like to know."

"Why? Why is it important now?"

"I've already told you, you have a particular affinity for understanding a young woman you met just days ago. I want to know how that works."

Soft echoes of footfalls, of muffled voices came to them now and again. Since their arrival the mansion had come alive as if it had been waiting for them. A number of cars were parked on the generous expanse of gravel outside and the interior exhibited the air of expectancy, the bustle of hastily arranged preparations.

"It works," Annika said, "because we're both broken."

Her mineral eyes studied him with a frightening intensity. In those eyes it was possible to get lost, moreover, to want to get lost. Jack felt himself losing his sense of time and place, and he enfolded her in his arms, felt the slight tremors of her emotions firing along her bare arms.

"It works," she said, "because, like her, I was taken. It works because I'm just like her."

"DARLING, YOU'VE only taken one bite of your stollen," the widow Tanova admonished. "Did I put in too much cinnamon?"

Dyadya Gourdjiev smiled vaguely. "No, Katya. I was just thinking about the past."

Katya Tanova came and sat beside him at the dining room table. They were in her apartment, which was smartly furnished in the latest Western style. She was not a person to become stuck in amber like so many of her friends who had not moved on from the things they had liked in their thirties and forties. Their homes were like museums or mausoleums, depending on your level of cynicism. Katya's public persona—cool, proper, even a bit formal—was in stark contrast with her private demeanor, or at least her behavior with Gourdjiev, which was very private, indeed. With him she was like a young woman, coquettish, bantering. She often threw her head back and laughed, or else she engaged him with an intellectual rigor he found positively erotic.

"For most people that's not so good, darling, but for you it's terrible."

He nodded with gravity. "That may be true, but I can't help it."

"She came to see you, didn't she? You saw Annika."

He stared out the window at the hideously bare branches of a tree.

Katya wore a sleeveless flowered dress short enough to show off her strong legs, but not so short as to be unseemly. She had kicked off her shoes when she sat down. Her feet, wrapped in sheer stockings, were quite beautiful.

"You always become so melancholy when you see her. And the past—"

"Sometimes I can fool myself into thinking I'm happy, or satisfy myself at being so clever at this game or that. Once in a very great while I can even feel young again, but it always fades, this feeling, and then I realize that I've simply deluded myself. I expend so much energy trying to ignore the past, or forget it or—and this would be best of all—erase it, but it comes back to haunt me again and again." He turned from the window with a bleak smile. "How can it not?"

"But, darling, how can you keep blaming yourself, when—"

"It wasn't my fault? I should have known, I should have foreseen—"

"How could you, you're not a sorcerer."

"If only I were, I could obliterate the past, alter it with a wave of my hand!" he cried in anguish. "Such a terrible ending. No one deserves that."

"Especially not Nikki. She was your wife but she was my best friend, we both miss her terribly." Katya put her hand over his. "But we're not really talking about Nikki now, are we? She's dead and gone, beyond pain, beyond suffering. But Annika—"

"I cannot quantify Annika's suffering, because to this day I don't know what happened to her."

"And if you did know, of what possible use would it be to you, except to bring you more heartache and self-recrimination? And, darling, you are full up on those things already." She pushed the plate of stollen closer to him. "Come now, have something to eat, you'll feel better."

"Dammit! Nothing's going to make me feel better!" He pulled away from her, in almost the same movement rose, and in rising, swept the plate off the table. It crashed to the highly polished floor, where it burst into a hundred pieces. Crumbs of stollen went everywhere.

He stood against the wall, biting his knuckle, while Katya's Siamese crept out from under the sofa, where she had slunk at the instance of commotion, and with her head down and shoulders working, began to methodically eat the pastry.

Katya said nothing. She went into the kitchen, returned with a broom and dustpan, and knelt down.

"Don't," he said. "I'll do it." Stooping, he very gently took the implements from her hand and spent the next several minutes cleaning up. The cat came up to him and, arching her back, rubbed herself against his leg. When he was finished there wasn't a shard of china, a crumb of stollen left on the floor. The Siamese, licking her lips, didn't seem to mind; she'd eaten her fill. Katya had trained her to be dainty in her eating habits. A genuine little lady.

"I'll wax the floor tomorrow," Katya said, gesturing for him to sit down opposite her after he had returned from emptying the dustpan.

He did as she bade, sat silently with his hands clasped between his legs like a schoolboy caught making mischief.

"Darling, listen to me, there are some things in this life we aren't meant to know, some questions, though asked over and over, that have no answer. You must try to accept this, though I know better than most this cuts across the grain of your personality. You're a man born to find the answers to the thorniest questions, and when this becomes the norm, it isn't easy to look at a blank wall and say, Is this all there is? Because, yes, that's all there is, darling. When it comes to Annika there are essential secrets in her heart you cannot know. The darkness behind that wall is hers, not yours, no matter what you may believe. I know you've taken this as a failure—'I should have known, I should have foreseen'—these are the words of the seeker. As Apollo brought light to the world each day you find answers—but because you don't have the answer to what happened to Annika—"

"I should have protected her."

"In a perfect world, yes," Katya said, "but, darling, in a perfect world you wouldn't *need* to protect her." Her eyes found his and she smiled. "This world is far from perfect, however, and nothing is easy or quick or the way we want it to be. The world is incomprehensible, and the harder we strive to understand it the more mysterious it becomes. And do you know why? Life is all moral compromises, and with each compromise we make a tiny piece of us gets lost. And when it isn't compromises that we must make, it's sacrifices, and sacrifices change us irrevocably, until we look like that tree outside.

"Consider what you have sacrificed for Annika—you have gone to the edge of the world, the place where even maps fail, where the devil resides, in order to keep her safe. I beg you to ponder that the next time you feel compelled to say 'I should have known, I should have foreseen.'"

"Yes, yes, it's true," he said in a voice that betrayed him, for his mind thought one thing and his heart felt another. It took some effort to return her smile, but by the look on her face he knew that she appreciated it. "Everything you said is true." He looked around as if awaking from a dream. "I'll buy you a new plate."

"Thank you, but don't bother. That wasn't the first one you've smashed and it won't be the last." She laughed. "That's why I put out this particular service, it was a wedding present from my mother and

I never did like it. It's so, I don't know, Victorian. Very her—not me at all."

"Your mother and her lies," he said, with a rueful shake of his handsome head.

"Lies are what drew you and me together," she said. "Lies we had to create and then, far worse, perpetuate, in order to go on living. And these lies required both moral compromises and sacrifices that, while regretting, we wouldn't change. I lied to my husband and you lied to Batchuk. I became friends with my husband so he would never find out how much I loathed him, and his money allowed me the freedom to live my life. For him I did not exist as a sexual object, or, if I did, it was only for a matter of months, if not weeks.

"As for you, my darling—" She leaned over and kissed his cheek. "You made your peace with Batchuk because everything in your world depended on your alliance with him. It took all your skill and charm to convince him that you were sincere, since he knew very well that you had every reason to want him destroyed. How did you manage it, I wonder? I wouldn't have been able to pull it off, even though I've certainly honed my acting skills over the years."

"He made a request of me and I complied," he said. "There was someone in his way, someone he couldn't touch, couldn't even get near. I could. Simple as that."

He stood up and, hands in his trousers pockets, stood staring out at the gnarled tree.

"You of all people, darling, should know that nothing is simple," Katya said, "especially when finding an answer brings an end to a life."

"I know you're not judging me, because you know very well what was at stake. When he made the request he knew I'd have to comply, which is why he enjoyed asking me. The idea of giving me an order appealed to him. It must have given him immense satisfaction knowing I would do it, knowing that he was causing me pain at the same time he was ridding himself of a thorn in his side he couldn't pull out himself."

"It was that death that kept Annika safe, is that what you're saying?"

He nodded, but didn't turn around. "What Batchuk did was monstrous, unspeakable, depraved. It's as if Stalin has risen from the grave."

Katya rose, then, and went to stand by his side. "You're not thinking about anything foolish, something that could get you killed, are you? Leave matters the way they are."

"It's too late, events have been set in motion. Batchuk is here in Kiev. He is looking for Annika."

"You trained her well."

"Because I was forced to make a deal with the devil. Are you saying I should withdraw my protection?"

She slid her arm around his waist. "Look at that tree. It has withstood drought, hailstorms, lightning, and torrential rains that turned the ground around it to a river of mud. But there it is. Its roots never gave way, it was never split asunder. It may be ugly and leaning, it may not be as tall as it once was, but it abides, darling, it abides."

"Time," Miles Benson said, standing in the doorway to the shadowed study. The brightest light came from Aaron's iPhone. "Mr. Secretary, it's imperative that we finish our conversation now." But so fierce was the glare that Claire gave him he had no recourse but to take a step back, just as if she had pushed him.

"All right," Paull said, but he never took his eyes off his daughter, who, it seemed to him now, had never looked more beautiful. She had been a child when she had left him; now she was a mature, self-confident woman. How the devil had that happened, he wondered. Seven years wasn't that long a time; on the other hand, it was a lifetime for small creatures, an eternity for others. Claire had made the most of those seven years, and what had he done with the time?

"Wait for me," he said to her. "I won't be long."

"Even if you are," Aaron said, his bright, transparent eyes serenely regarding his newly discovered grandfather, "Mom and I won't leave without you." He looked up at Claire. "Right, Mom?"

MORGAN THOMSON was waiting for them. He had opened the glass doors to the library and when he saw them approaching, said with a sweep of his hand, "Let's take a walk."

There was a Japanese-style footpath made of slate-colored stepping stones, each slightly different yet related to one another, that led down to the pond and the moon bridge. As they neared the water Paull could see flashes of black, white, silver, and orangey-gold beneath the surface as the ornamental carp swam into the sunlight and out. Much to his surprise Benson took out a handful of dry food and sprinkled it on the surface. The greedy carp rose, their mouths open and gasping to suck in the food.

Assuming the professorial demeanor he so adored Thomson said, "Believe it or not this accord is going to consolidate President Yukin's power both inside and outside Russia."

At once Paull thought back to his conversation with Edward Carson in the limo on the day they had buried Lloyd Berns. Carson had voiced consternation that Brandt was trying to push through the accord despite the president's unease. Paull assumed an expression of bland attention.

Thomson's hands were clasped behind his back, his head tilted slightly upward as if he were sniffing the air for eavesdroppers, or clues to their ultimate fate. "As you no doubt know, since Yukin has been in power the government's ownership of companies comprising the Russian stock market has ballooned from twenty-five percent to forty percent."

"If that isn't totalitarianism," Benson said, staring down at the swarming carp, "I don't know what is."

"He has also made a mockery of the state governors' races," Thomson continued as if Benson hadn't spoken. "No one can get on a slate unless expressly endorsed by Yukin."

"Or his lord high executioner, Oriel Jovovich Batchuk," Benson said without apparent irony.

Thomson shrugged. "It amounts to the same thing. Batchuk is deputy prime minister, he's thrown in his lot with Yukin, he rises and falls on the strength of Yukin's power. But in a sense Miles is correct: In his own right Batchuk is a formidable opponent."

"A fucking latter-day Stalin," Benson said. "There's so much blood on his hands they say he lives in an abattoir."

"Very funny," Paull said.

"He's a Russian," Benson said levelly, "so who the hell knows, it might be true."

"He's a clever bastard, this Batchuk." Thomson's eyes met Paull's. "More clever, even, than Iosif Vissarionovich." He meant Stalin.

"Where is this all leading?" Paull asked.

"An excellent question." Thomson began to move, and the other two men followed him as he mounted the moon bridge. At the apex of the arc he stopped and, placing his forearms on the railing, stared down into the depths of the pond. "General Brandt has made some sort of private deal with President Yukin, the details of which we have no idea, but I can tell you unequivocally that the moment we discovered the fact we severed all ties with him. Nevertheless, Brandt is out there operating on his own, taking the law into his own hands, and we have no way of stopping him."

"BATCHUK IS in charge of *Trinadtsat*," Kharkishvili said to Jack, "which is a secret cadre—"

"I know what *Trinadtsat* is," Jack said.

"You surprise me at every turn, Mr. McClure, you really do." Kharkishvili's eyebrows arched. "But possibly you don't know this:

Trinadtsat was created by Batchuk for one reason—a secret discovery of an enormous deposit of uranium—possibly one of the largest in the world—in northeastern Ukraine, very near the Russian border. Add to this the fact that the Kremlin has determined Russia's own inground supply of uranium is far smaller than had been thought, and you have a major crisis in the making.

"What is crucial to understanding why the current situation has become a crisis is that Russia is firmly committed to nuclear power," Kharkishvili continued. "We—that is, the members of AURA—were and are just as firmly committed to keeping the nuclear power industry in private hands in order to mitigate the Kremlin's expansionist plans. We fought Yukin as long as we could, but he consolidated his power too quickly and too well. With Batchuk's help he got inside our defenses, accused us of fiscal malfeasance or, in cases when that didn't work or wasn't for some reason sufficient, outright treason. He seized our companies and would have sent us to Siberia if we hadn't been warned and fled here to Ukraine."

Heavy weather had blown in off the Black Sea, and rain was beating at the windowpanes as Jack, Annika, and Alli sat at an enormous gleaming wood table in the vast dining room of Mikal Magnussen's manor house. Four members of AURA sat at the table, big-shouldered men with guileful eyes but a singular lack of delicacy. Between them lay platters of food and cut-crystal flasks of vodka, slivovitz, and soda water, a feast for more than a dozen, but not one was eating.

"Now the worst has happened," Kharkishvili continued. "With us gone, Yukin has nationalized the uranium consortium, just as he did with Gazprom. Yukin has come to the same conclusion we did almost a decade ago, that Russia's dependence on foreign oil—especially Iran's—puts it at a strategic disadvantage. That's why he's agreed to this U.S.-Russian accord. He doesn't mind making concessions as far as his traditional business ties with Iran as long as he has a steady supply of uranium."

"But without the huge Ukraine uranium strike he won't have it."

They all turned as a man entered the room. He was darkly handsome with the rough-hewn features of a Sean Connery or a Clive Owen. His hair was shot through with gray, the color of his eyes, as if he'd trekked through a snowstorm to arrive here. And, who knew, there may have been a number of metaphorical snowstorms in his past.

He turned to Jack. "I'm Mikal Magnussen, I apologize for not being available when you arrived." He paused now, waiting while an aide appeared at Kharkishvili's side and whispered briefly in his ear. Kharkishvili shot Annika an involuntary glance, which was so quick, so circumspect, it was possible that only Jack noticed it.

"So Yukin means to steal it," Magnussen said, "using soldiers who are *Trinadtsat* personnel."

"It's my understanding that it takes a decade to get a uranium mine up and running," Jack said. "I don't understand how an incursion into Ukrainian territory is going to accomplish anything."

"Ah, well, here's the true genius of Batchuk's plan." This from Malenko, another of the dissident oligarchs. Burly and bald, making him look like a tenpin, he had the prominent jaw of a carnivore and tiny ears absurdly low on his skull. "The troops will be sent in under the guise of aiding Ukraine, but once they're in the area they won't leave. Instead, they'll set up a perimeter so that Russian tanks can roll in across the border."

"It'll be a fucking mini-Czech," Glazkov, another oligarch, said, referring to the Soviet Union's 1968 invasion of Czechoslovakia, "except the Russians will stop at the border to the uranium discovery."

"They can't just invade Ukraine on any pretext," Jack said.

"They will, just as they did in Georgia, where their troops are still deployed," Kharkishvili said.

"The economic situation in Ukraine, particularly the east, is dire, so much so that riots have broken out in several cities and are gaining momentum throughout the country." Magnussen had talked to the table, but remained standing. "Experience tells me that Yukin will use this economic crisis to doubtless claim his troops are there to protect both Russian and Ukrainian interests."

"But our problem—and yours, Mr. McClure—is not only the Kremlin," Kharkishvili said, "but one of your own countrymen. Yukin is being aided by an American by the name of Brandt. A general in your military, an advisor to your president."

"General Brandt is the architect of the current accord being hammered out between Yukin and President Carson," Jack said. "Carson's success as president is more or less tied to the accord being ratified by both sides."

"That security accord is pure poison. Once it's signed Yukin and Batchuk will send their *Trinadtsat* troops across the border into Ukraine, Russia will take possession of the uranium strike, and because of the accord with the United States no one will dare to stop him."

"The United States itself—President Carson—will stop him."

"Do you really think so?" Magnussen said. "You know very well that the prime reason for President Carson agreeing to the accord is to get the Iranian nuclear card off the table. In this particular matter Yukin will be as good as his word. He has decided to throw Iran to the wolves in exchange for this massive uranium strike, which will serve Russia's burgeoning nuclear power plant needs for decades to come."

Jack's mind was working furiously. "If Carson lifts a hand against the Russian incursion into Ukraine, he risks Yukin reinstituting its nuclear commerce with Iran. And of course he doesn't dare do that; the entire architecture of the accord is to neuter Iran's nuclear program."

Kharkishvili nodded. "You have it entirely."

All of a sudden Jack's mind gave him a different view of the situation. "This is about General Brandt, isn't it?" he said. "Brandt has a private deal with Yukin; in return for getting the accord done he's going to receive a piece of the action here in Ukraine."

There was absolute silence in the room. Kharkishvili turned to Magnussen and said, "You see, Mikal, I was right to entrust this part of our plan to Annika." He turned to her. "You found us the perfect person, my dear. Congratulations."

"SO AS you can see," Thomson said, "the problem is Brandt. He has moved beyond our control. We have no power in this administration, but you do."

Paull took a deep breath. "Let me get this straight. You recruited Brandt and now you want me to clean up his dirty work, and yours?" He laughed. "Why on earth would I do that?"

"Because if you don't," Benson said, "your president is going to end up with egg on his face—egg that won't be easy to scrape off, I can assure you—when the deal Brandt has made with Yukin comes to light."

"After which, he can kiss a second term good-bye." Thomson was still in professorial mode. "You and Edward Carson have a personal relationship, don't you? I mean to say you're friends."

"'Friends don't let friends drive drunk,'" Benson said, quoting the oft-heard TV ad. "Bottom line, General Brandt is driving the president's car and he's very, very drunk."

Paull ran a hand through his hair, but he kept his expression neutral. He felt as if he were walking on eggshells around these two. Right now he needed to take a step back in order to assess the rapidly shifting situation with a clear eye and a calm mind. It was apparent that these two men made their living feeding off other people's weaknesses and mistakes, but now they themselves had made a mistake or a miscalculation. Or they had seriously underestimated Brandt. From the evidence they had put forward so far this was a possibility that they had overlooked, and Paull was not about to bring their attention to it. The two choices as outlined were, one, General Brandt had gone Kurtz, as Benson so colorfully put it, or, two, he had cleverly outmaneuvered them, using their resources to forge his relationship with Yukin only to abandon them as the metaphorical clock ticked close to midnight. Yukin and Carson were about to sign the historic accord that, if Thomson and Benson were telling the truth, would give the world the picture of a high-level American military man, one of the president's closest advisors, in league with the president of Russia.

There was, of course, the other possibility, standing out as surely as a black swan: that the two of them were working a con on a massive scale in order to get him to stop Carson from signing an accord that would do the very thing the president and everyone in his administration was praying for it to do: pull the plug on Iran's nuclear program. Without Russia's imported parts, fuel, and expertise the Iranians would have no choice but to drastically scale back the program, or shut it down entirely.

This was the enigma presented to Dennis Paull, the web from which he needed to extricate both himself and the president without damaging the president's reputation or jeopardizing the security accord. It reminded him of the classic conundrum of an explorer traveling through a country inhabited by two tribes. The members of one tribe always tell the truth, the members of the other tribe always lie. The tribe that always lies are headhunters and cannibals. The explorer comes across a tribal hunting party, which quickly surrounds him. However, he is unable to distinguish which tribe they represent, and now he understands his dreadful predicament. He needs to ask two questions: the first is, Which tribe are you from? The second is, Will you eat me? But whichever tribe the men belong to they are going to give the same answer: We're from the tribe that never lies, and we're not going to eat you. And yet the outcome will be polar opposites, either the explorer will be safe or he will die a horrible death.

Paull was now facing a similar situation, lethal in the political sense with no room to be wrong. Were Thomson and Benson members of the tribe that tells the truth or the tribe that lies? If he acted on their information and they were in fact lying, he would jeopardize not only Edward Carson's presidency but the future security of America. But if they were telling the truth and he *didn't* act, out of a belief that they were lying, the same terrible scenario would come about.

"Why did General Brandt order a sanction on Jack McClure?" Paull asked.

"We don't know," Thomson said, "except to say that Brandt must feel that McClure presents an immediate danger to his private deal with Yukin."

Now Paull knew he had to tell the president, get the sanction rescinded before Jack was killed. He wished with very fiber of his being that Jack McClure were with him. Jack would unravel this seemingly no-win situation, because he'd be able to see the sides of it Paull could not. But Jack wasn't here, and Paull knew he'd have to make the crucial decision as to what to tell Carson himself. He racked his brain to find a way out, or at least to swing the odds from fifty-fifty to a percentage that was more favorable to him and the president.

What was clear, what he had hard evidence proving, was that General Brandt had seriously—terminally—overstepped his authority. This fact—the only one Paull had—argued that Thomson and Benson were telling the truth. That conclusion was far from certain, but what in this life, he asked himself, was ever certain? He had to trust these two, but only as far as he could throw them.

"All right," he said, breaking the lengthy silence, "I'll call the president."

Twenty-Six

ORIEL BATCHUK sat in the ultrabright, candy-colored confines of the Baskin-Robbins in the Globus shopping center on Maidan Nezalezhnosti, which rose on one side of Kiev's Independence Square. He was surrounded by bubbling Ukrainians dressed in Tommy Hilfiger or Pierre Cardin, trying their hardest to be American.

His mind, drifting, returned to the past, to his confrontation with Dyadya Gourdjiev, an encounter he had hoped never to have, but that he saw now, with the perfect clarity of hindsight, was inevitable. Their relationship was bound to end in tears, as the British were wont to say, because it was all artifice, meticulously constructed by the two of them out of lies, fabrications, disavowals, and obfuscation. The truth was they had both made compromises and, yes, sacrifices—not so very difficult for men who lacked a moral compass—in order to live in the world with one another, in order not to tear the other limb from limb. The emotions that ran between them, that bound them together in a private arena, were both lava hot and ice cold, how could it be otherwise, considering the hideous stroke of fate that had befallen them?

But of course now that he looked around the Technicolor store with blind eyes he realized that it was no coincidence that he had ordered the rendezvous here at this particular place, because it was on this very spot, long before Globus was even an idea in the mind of its developer, that he had first seen Nikki. She had been walking with Gourdjiev, he remembered the moment as if it had been transferred from his retinas, seared into his brain, an image that could neither fade nor crumble. That first sight of Nikki transcended time, existed outside it, as if he had caught a glimpse of a creature beyond human ken. For Batchuk, who had never before allowed himself an emotional connection with another human being, the response to Nikki was galvanizing. In fact, he was forced to sit down, though it was not yet time for his meeting with Gourdjiev. He watched, transfixed, as Nikki, arm in arm with Gourdjiev, floated at his side. Then she detached herself and, running past startled shoppers, flew into the arms of a tall, regal-looking man with black hair and hazel eyes. The man, laughing, lifted her up, whirling her around while Gourdjiev stood by, a fatuous grin on his face.

When Nikki planted a kiss on the man's lips a tiny, involuntary noise escaped Batchuk's mouth, terrifying him. It was as if an ice pick had been shoved into his belly. He felt sick and dizzy, and was thus at a disadvantage when Gourdjiev left the blissful couple and came to where Batchuk was slumped over in his chair.

"Are you ill?" Gourdjiev said as he slid onto a chair opposite Batchuk. "You're sweating like a pig."

"An excess of vodka last night," Batchuk improvised, "or I should say this morning."

Gourdjiev laughed as if he didn't have a care in the world. "Your partying will be the death of you, Oriel Jovovich, of that there can be no doubt."

This was in the days before Batchuk had been named deputy prime minister, before Yukin has ascended to his self-styled throne, but the two were already close, stars rising in tandem through the perilous firmament of the Russian political chop shop. In fact, it was Batchuk who had introduced Yukin to Gourdjiev, who was then already the éminence grise in the power politics of Ukraine, in all of Eastern Europe, in fact. At that time it was essential to have Gourdjiev's backing and influence in order to rise to the first tier of power. Batchuk, who loved Roman history, thought of his friend as Claudius, a man who had decided to step away from the bloody turbulence at the center of Eastern European politics, but not from the corridors of power, where he manipulated people and events from deep within its shadowed recesses. Like Claudius he was an unprepossessing man, a man you assumed to be in the twilight of his life, who, like the generals of antiquity, was content to gaze out over the Palatine hill to the magnificent centurion cypresses, dreaming of past glories. Until you came in contact, or perhaps conflict was the correct word, with his astonishing intellect.

For many years Batchuk had stood in awe of Gourdjiev, dealing with Yukin and others as the older man did, with discretion, shrewdness, and diabolical foresight, but try as he might Gourdjiev's mind was always six or seven steps ahead of him, and in denying the lack in himself he began to envy Gourdjiev, and this malice slowly and inexorably curdled their friendship.

"Who is that man with Nikki?" he said almost as soon as Gourdjiev sat down. He had not meant to, but to his dismay—or, more accurately, horror—he couldn't help himself.

"That's Alexsei Mandanovich Dementiev," Gourdjiev said.

It disgusted Batchuk that he could not take his eyes off her. He'd heard about her, of course, but until this moment Gourdjiev had kept her away from him. Was it by design, he wondered. He watched Nikki and Alexsei, absurdly jealous that they seemed to fit together like two pieces of a jigsaw puzzle, as if their births were also the birth of a shared destiny. They cleaved to one another, so blissful only a cataclysm, he was certain, could separate them. He said naively, stupidly, "They're seeing one another?" and immediately despised himself for it.

"You could say that." Gourdjiev laughed again. "He and Nikki are getting married next month."

With a start, Batchuk returned to the unpleasant present. The candy-colored world of the Baskin-Robbins, with its yammering kids and harried-looking parents, turned his stomach. Sick to his soul, he rose and stalked out, only to return and glare at them all.

"I'LL CALL the president," Jack said, "and tell him what's going on. He'll take the appropriate actions as far as General Brandt is concerned."

"He may, indeed, do that," Magnussen said, "but do you really think he will hold up the signing of this historic accord based on your say-so?" He shook his head. "We have no hard evidence of Brandt's personal involvement."

"But I know he ordered a sanction on Annika," Jack said. "That, surely, is overstepping his authority."

"It may or it may not, we have no way of knowing," Kharkishvili said. "But the thornier issue, the conundrum that we cannot even begin to solve, is if someone is behind General Brandt and, if so, who it is. This is why we need you. Because getting rid of Brandt, even stopping the signing may not be enough to keep Yukin and Batchuk from ordering their troops across the border. You have no idea how desperate Russia is for new energy sources, how far Yukin is prepared to go in order to obtain them."

"Either way," Jack said, "I'm going to have to inform the president."

Magnussen nodded. "We understand that, but before you do we

needed to let you know the immense stakes. If Russia moves across the border into Ukraine without that treaty being signed it will trigger a regional war that will quite rapidly escalate, dragging your country into it."

Jack looked from Magnussen to Kharkishvili. "In other words we're all damned if the accord is signed and doubly damned if it's not."

Kharkishvili nodded. "Unless you can come up with a solution. Annika was right from the beginning: I think you're the only one who can."

"What if there is no answer?" Jack said.

"In that event I fear we're all doomed." Kharkishvili looked around the room at each of the faces, each one grimmer than the last. "Then everything will come to an end, the greed of wealth, the lust for power. In that final moment, everyone will fall, even the kingpins of empires."

PRESIDENT EDWARD Carson had just returned from the Kremlin, having received Yukin's full agreement to the accord. To Carson's mild surprise the Russian president did not object to the time of the signing tomorrow evening at eight o'clock, local time, noon back home—more than enough time, after the Internet sites and the blogosphere had their say, for all the major news feeds to have developed think pieces that would be popping up on TV just in time for the six and seven o'clock newscasts.

He was sitting down to the first decent meal he'd had in days when his cell phone rang. His entire entourage, including the press secretary, jumped to attention because he was sitting across the table from the senior political correspondent from *Time*, who was about to engage him in a major interview that would be the magazine's cover story next week.

The president took the call because it was from Jack. Excusing himself, he stood and whispered into the press secretary's ear, then hurried out of the hotel dining room, accompanied as always by his Praetorian guard who, in this instance, was loaded down with equipment designed to jam any attempt at electronic eavesdropping.

"Jack, what progress?" Carson said. "And is Alli okay?"

"Alli's fine, better than fine, in fact."

"Well, then, it seems that being with you is the best medicine for her." Carson was immensely grateful. Whatever flicker of jealousy he might have felt was extinguished by Jack's revelations. His voice seemed to bore through Carson's head like a power drill.

"Let me get this straight," Carson said, as he stared through one of the hotel's plate-glass windows at the snow piling up in Red Square, "you're telling me that General Brandt has some kind of private deal with Yukin regarding a uranium strike in northeast Ukraine?"

"That's right, sir."

"But what about Alizarin Global?"

There was a pause before Jack's voice buzzed in his ear. "I never heard of Alizarin Global."

"Neither did I until ten minutes ago when Dennis Paull called." A young woman was struggling across the vast expanse of Red Square, bent forward into the wind. Carson was happy he wasn't outside, but at this moment that was about all he was happy about. "It's some kind of multitentacled conglomerate that has employed both Benson and Thomson. They, in turn, hired Brandt to help them make a deal with Gazprom. According to what they told Dennis, Brandt has made this side deal with Yukin. They fired him the moment they found out, but he's ignored their communications. He's acting in his own interest, not theirs. They're convinced he's gone insane."

"Edward, I suppose I don't have to point out that we're talking about your political enemies here. What makes Paull think he can trust them?"

"He doesn't, not really. But, concerned about intelligence leaks,

he's been immersed in a sub-rosa investigation of everyone in my inner circle, during the course of which he found evidence that Alizarin did, indeed, fund Brandt's winter trips to Moscow. Now Brandt is
so out of control he authorized a sanction on you. Naturally, I canceled it the moment I got off the phone with Dennis."

"Is anyone left in the field?"

"No," Carson assured him, "all the agents have been successfully
recalled."

There was a short silence while, Carson supposed, Jack absorbed
the shocking news. At length, he said, "I can see how I'd be a threat
to him, but what I can't understand is how he'd know it. How would
Brandt have knowledge of where you sent me and what I've been doing?"

"A good question," Carson said. "I think you'd better find the
answer."

"I'm trying to do just that," Jack assured him. "What about the
accord?"

"From what you've just told me there doesn't seem to be an easy
way out of signing it, Jack," Carson said bleakly. "If I refuse to sign it,
or even move to postpone the ceremony after Yukin has bent over
backward to meet all our demands, I'll not only look foolish, but I'll
destroy whatever political capital I've gained during the run-up to
the signing.

"No, unless you can come up with another solution, the signing
will commence at eight tomorrow evening."

JACK, PUTTING away his cell phone, was running the multiple vectors of the information the president had given him. Much of the
information seemed contradictory or an outright lie. He didn't for a
moment think that Benson and Thomson had anyone's best interest
in mind except theirs. According to the president they didn't want
the accord with Yukin signed. It was their contention that both the

accord and its chief architect, General Brandt, were a danger to the country, but were they telling the truth? From the damning evidence that Paull had discovered it seemed they were telling the truth about Brandt. Were they then lying about the danger inherent in the accord? He already knew from Kharkishvili the likelihood of events if it was signed tomorrow. If he was to find a way out of this damned-if-you-do, damned-if-you-don't conundrum he had less than twenty-four hours to do it.

His musings were interrupted by Kharkishvili striding purposefully toward him.

"Mr. McClure, I'm glad I caught you. I've received some alarming news."

At once Jack's mind sprang backward to the aide bending over Kharkishvili, whispering in his ear, and that strange, circumspect look Kharkishvili had given Annika.

"Annika's uncle Gourdjiev has shot one of AURA's members, a dissident oligarch and a friend of mine by the name of Riet Medanovich Boronyov."

"I find that difficult to believe," Jack said. "What on earth would cause him to murder one of your people?"

"I have no idea," Kharkishvili confessed. "Nevertheless, he shot Boronyov in front of two of Batchuk's men and gave the body over to them, this was confirmed by an eyewitness." Kharkishvili appeared genuinely distraught. "This is a disaster, because Boronyov was one of the dissidents who, as far as Batchuk and *Trinadtsat* were concerned, were dead. We made certain of that. Now Batchuk knows better, and it's a fair bet he'll check on the others who were supposed to be dead, all of us here, me included."

Now Jack gleaned another piece of the puzzle: Like Annika, Dyadya Gourdjiev was a part of AURA, but if so why had he killed a man who their enemies already thought was dead?

"Perhaps Boronyov was a double agent," Jack said, "secretly working for Batchuk."

Kharkishvili shook his head emphatically. "Impossible. We met as young strivers, I ate Sunday dinner with him and his family, we shared business deals."

"All of which proves nothing," Jack pointed out, "except that he was a perfect candidate for a double." He'd already thought of the reason this could not be true, but before he had a chance to speak, Kharkishvili shook his head even more vigorously.

"No, I fear it's Gourdjiev who's the traitor. He and Batchuk have a long history together, longer, closer even than the one I had with Boronyov. For years, he has pretended to be Batchuk's friend, but what if that was also a ruse, what if they're actual allies, working hand in hand?"

"There is, or was, no double inside AURA," Jack said with authority. "If Batchuk knew you were alive all the time you'd all be dead by now, there would be no AURA to oppose him and Yukin."

"And yet Gourdjiev must be in league with Batchuk now," Kharkishvili said. "There is no other explanation for his action."

"You don't like Dyadya Gourdjiev, do you?"

"What?"

Jack could see that Kharkishvili's annoyance was masking both shock and consternation, and he knew that he had hit on something vital. "You don't like Gourdjiev and I'd like to know why."

"So would I."

The two men turned to see Annika, who had come up silently behind them and was now standing with her feet slightly apart, arms crossed over her breasts, between Kharkishvili and the relative sanctuary of the dining room.

GENERAL BRANDT, sitting in an arcade off Red Square that had an unobstructed view of the brooding walls and towers of the Kremlin, wondered what it would be like to be all energy. Watching the snow falling in endless curtains he tried to imagine the world from a snowflake's point of view: the pure cold, the clean symmetrical design, the absolute quiet. Who wouldn't want that time to think undisturbed by civilization's anxieties, tensions, and clumsy attempts at manipulation. The urge to maintain control was unknown in a snowflake's world, and it was better off for it.

Every hour of every day control was slipping away from him. He could no longer bench press twice his weight, his arthritic left knee made it impossible for him to run a mile a day as he had for decades since he was thirteen, his hair was becoming fine as well as thin, he could no longer eat chili dogs or Tabasco without suffering the consequences, and there were nights when he gazed at young girls with the detached wistfulness of an old man. There was no doubt about it, his body was deteriorating at an alarming rate, coming apart at the seams, as it were, and more and more he found that he no longer wanted to be a part of it or, more accurately, in it. How much easier it would be to be pure energy, not to have to worry about his rotting flesh, which continued to betray him at every turn.

He was at a loss to say when this nihilistic worldview had come over him, perhaps he'd always had the seed of it deep inside his pragmatic, highly regimented mind. With a paranoid's unmatched cunning he suspected the seed had started to take root the moment he retired from the military, which had been his stern father and his comforting mother for over forty years. The world outside the military seemed a strange and unpleasant place for him, until he learned to back away from it just enough so that it lapped at the fringe of his reality and nothing more. Being a talking head on TV was an excellent way to insulate himself, to remain unapproachable, solitary, hidden in plain sight. The more he appeared on TV, the more the idiot anchorpersons asked their fatuous questions, the further he receded into himself. All glory is fleeting, to paraphrase George Patton, one of Brandt's patron saints, but that was fine because he had had enough of glory, TV had made him sick of it, or more accurately, what passed for glory in this postmodern age. Now all he craved was security, which his pension did not assure, especially because his Down's syndrome son needed care far above and beyond what his health insurance was willing to pay. It seemed odd, not to mention unfair, that after spending his entire adult life in the service of his country he had become obsessed with money, something that in his younger days he didn't think about at all because his housing, food, and travel expenses were all paid for by the United States Army.

He looked at his watch now as the waiter brought him a double espresso with a shot of vodka, which he drank quickly with a sharp tilt of his head like the old, grizzled Italian fisherman he'd met in Key West. He liked the Keys; it was his long-cherished dream to move to Marathon or Islamorada and fish, bask in the sun, and get stone drunk at ten in the morning whenever the hell he felt like it.

As soon as he finished his heavily fortified coffee he checked his watch again and frowned. It was past time for Yukin to call him via his encrypted line. He signaled the waiter for another double, and sat brooding, his head sunk between his bony shoulders, glowering at the spotlit facade of the Kremlin as if he could will Yukin to call him. The silence was deafening, mystifying, which required drowning in alcohol and caffeine. He downed his second drink as fast as he had the first, so fast, in fact, that the waiter hadn't yet left the table.

"One more," Brandt said in excellent Russian. "And bring the bottle."

The waiter nodded and departed without comment.

And that was another thing, Brandt thought gloomily, Moscow was too fucking cold, even in April—I mean, snow, for chrissakes! This furtive spring might as well be January. Unconsciously he rubbed his palms down his thighs in an attempt to bring more circulation into them. At least the drinks had warmed his belly.

The waiter arrived at approximately the same time as his cell phone buzzed. He let it ring, his heart heavy in his chest, until the waiter had set the coffee and the bottle of vodka on the table and left.

"Yes," he said, the cell clamped to his ear.

"Everything is sealed and delivered, it's just wanting signing," Yukin's familiar voice said in his ear. "He loved that I caved on all those provisions I never wanted. You were quite correct; causing him to focus on the minutia of the accord was the way to get it done."

The General drained half the cup in one swallow, then unscrewed the top of the bottle and poured an imprudent amount of vodka into his espresso. And right then and there he felt the intense hatred for the Russians—not just Yukin and Batchuk—he'd always felt but had suppressed for so many years, that had caused him unnumbered ulcerous bouts and sleepless nights as soon as he had been taken out of the field in order to deal with them face-to-face. A faceless enemy, he'd been taught, is the best enemy because he's the easiest to hate, but the Russians put the lie to that lesson with a big, emphatic exclamation point. They were children, really, inasmuch as children haven't learned how to act in civilized society, but who act out all the naked and embarrassing whims and desires of their ids without thought of either propriety or consequence.

"The accord is everything we could have hoped for," Yukin said, sounding jollier and jollier. "Thanks to you, I've got everything I want, everything I need, and so will you, we're in the home stretch, be sure of it, and I'll tell you why. Do you remember the man you met here in December, Kamyrov?"

Indeed the General did, a hairy, slope-shouldered ape of a man with the manners to match. Brandt had a vivid memory of a dinner with the two men on a gelid, snowy night, Kamyrov expounding on methods of bringing antagonistic men to heel, his face gleaming with grease, unchewed bits of red meat lodged between his teeth. "The man you installed as president of Chechnya."

"Homicidal maniac is more like it," Yukin said. "I sent him in there because of his reputation as a strongman, because I needed to get control of the terrorist insurgency there. Since he's been in power he's ordered the murder of a dozen former military men, political challengers and their bodyguards—bodies are turning up all over the place: Budapest, Vienna, Dubai—it's becoming embarrassing, the local police chiefs are understandably pissed off at having to scrape our offal off their streets, but Kamyrov is doing such a terrific job of neutering the insurgents I have no choice but to keep him there. But what the hell, it seems that these people have an appetite for destruction. Me, I just feed that appetite.

"I bring this up because eastern Ukraine has fallen into a severe economic depression, there have already been riots there as there have been in Moldavia and parts of Germany. This expanding civilian unrest is just the excuse we need to move our troops into northeastern Ukraine and keep them there, and after the accord with the United States is signed no nation will dare rise up against us. Thank you, General. As requested by President Carson's press secretary, I have scheduled the formal signing for eight o'clock tomorrow night in order to get the maximum exposure on American television. When we sign the accord in front of a thousand news cameras your part in our little play will come to an end and your account in Liechtenstein will be filled to overflowing with gold bullion.

"Tell me, General Brandt, how does it feel to be a wealthy man?"

"ORIEL JOVOVICH."

The sound of Limonev's raspy voice brought Batchuk back to the present, back to the eyeball-searing interior of Baskin-Robbins.

"A strange place to meet."

"Let's go." Batchuk rose to his feet. "I have a job for you." As usual, remembrance of things past had turned his mood sour; he felt no inclination toward small talk.

"You could have texted me the way you always do," Limonev said as they rode the escalator to the underground garage. "I sent you the number the minute my new cell was activated."

"This one's different," Batchuk said without looking at him. "It demands a different level of security."

Limonev said nothing more until they had walked between the ranks of parked cars and were comfortably settled in the deputy prime minister's luxurious Mercedes sedan.

"We're going together?"

"It's a two-man job." Batchuk guided the Mercedes up the ramp and out onto the busy street. Twenty minutes of battling traffic at either a dead crawl or flying along at insane speeds brought them to the Ring Road, which Batchuk took around to the northeast, where he swung off the exit to the slums and Skol'niki Park. He pulled over at the park's outskirts and they went into it, heading down a gentle slope to the lake known as Pulyaevskiye prudy. It was too cold and snowy for the homicidal gangs and addicts to be out; in fact, this particular area of the park was all but deserted. Snow continued drifting out of the hard, porcelain sky, swirled and blown sideways by gusts of damp wind that seemed to make the snowflakes expand, grow heavier, as if they had turned from frozen water into silver or glass tiles.

At the edge of the lake Batchuk glanced at his watch. "He'll be coming soon. He has an appointment on the other side of the park."

Limonev squinted through the snow. "Perhaps in this weather he won't come."

"He doesn't give a shit about the weather."

"I'll need to be able to recognize the target." Limonev glanced in every direction to ensure that there was no one close to them. "As usual a photo of him would be best."

"Of course." Batchuk slipped a snapshot out of the breast pocket of his black leather trench coat. "This is the man I want you to kill."

Limonev looked down at the photo of Riet Medanovich Boronyov, his eyes closed, his face waxen and gray. There were flecks of blood on his lids and along one cheekbone.

Batchuk had already produced an MSP internally silenced, blunt-barreled pistol. Now he shoved it against Limonev's chest and fired a round.

Limonev lost his balance and fell to his knees in front of Batchuk. One hand, shaking as if palsied, fumbled for his gun, but with an almost negligent wave Batchuk knocked it away.

"Unfortunately I gave you the same order fourteen months ago." Batchuk took the assassin's chin in his hand. "How many?" he said. "How many of the oligarchs are still alive?" He raised Limonev's head and stared into his bloodshot eyes. "Kharkishvili, Malenko, Konarev, Glazkov, Andreyev—you claimed you had killed them all. Did you, or are they as alive as Boronyov was until a few hours ago?"

Limonev licked his lips, opened his mouth, and spat into Batchuk's face. With a sound of disgust Batchuk pushed the face away and, raising the MSP, fired the second round point-blank between Limonev's eyes.

"I never give the same order more than once," he continued, as if his companion were still alive. Pocketing the MSP, he threw the other man's gun into the lake, retrieved the photo from Limonev's grasp, and then, bending over, dragged him into the water and left him there.

"IF IT'S true that Gourdjiev and I don't always see eye to eye," Kharkishvili said, "it's also true that we also have nothing but respect for one another."

"Tell me something," Jack said. "Who is AURA's leader, you, Magnussen, who?"

"There is no leader," Kharkishvili said. "We reach agreement by consensus."

"That sounds both unwieldy and impractical," Annika said with an obvious measure of skepticism. "Just look at the United Nations, which eats up so much time and money without ever managing to get much of anything accomplished."

Kharkishvili brushed his fingertips across his forehead, as a sign either of impatience or of annoyance. "We're not the United Nations—and I assure you I'm not set on a road to character assassination. AURA would never have been possible without your *dyadya*. I and the other oligarchs would not be here, in all likelihood we wouldn't be alive if it weren't for him taking on the dangerous task of informing us in advance that the FSB was coming for us."

His eyes seemed to have retreated into the depths of their sockets, where they lay hooded and troubled. "I know he found out about the government's move against us from Batchuk, and I must tell you that I cannot for the life of me fathom how he is so successful at playing both sides of the fence."

"That's only a part of his genius," Annika said with more than a trace of pride. "But it seems both odd and counterproductive for you to have a problem with a relationship that provides you with such vital information."

"If you don't mind my saying it," Kharkishvili said, "it's the other side of the relationship that I find disturbing."

"I do mind you saying it," Annika said. "You certainly had no problem when the information he got from Batchuk saved your life and the lives of the other AURA oligarchs. He would have been summarily executed had Batchuk found out." Her ire aroused, she took a step toward Kharkishvili. "In addition, I wonder what AURA would have done if he hadn't engaged Magnussen and his multinational task force of engineers and surveyors to test and report on the feasibility of mining the uranium strike?"

Jack's eyes went out of focus as his brain began to give him another view of the puzzle that had been resolving itself piece by piece from the moment Edward had informed him of Lloyd Berns's death on Capri when he should have been here in Ukraine. For the first time he understood that there was the possibility or probability of a double agent inside AURA, and if there was, he suspected who it might be, though something about the setup didn't track, and he knew there was more information needed before he made any accusations that could backfire on him and Alli.

"DO YOU think he was convinced?" Miles Benson said, one hand on the quivering flank of the British Labrador.

Morgan Thomson blew on his chilled hands. "I know Dennis Paull. He loves Edward Carson, he'd throw himself under a bus before he'd let anything untoward happen to him." He shifted the shotgun from one shoulder to the other. "Whether or not he believed us I really can't say. It doesn't matter, anyway, because as far as he's concerned, by calling Carson he did the right thing."

The two men crouched in a thatch blind they had built themselves at the eastern edge of the Alizarin Global property, waiting patiently for dawn and the flights of ducks that would come with it. For them duck hunting was more than a pleasant pastime, it was a way to blow off steam, to release themselves from the pressure-cooker of their professional lives. Other men might have availed themselves of the services of an upscale brothel, or even something more exotic, but these men had extensive experience with entrapment. How much graphic, even obscene, incriminating evidence they had gathered on their enemies over the years was a subject for statisticians.

"The General has outlived his usefulness." Benson's gaze was fixed on the tenuous band of pink that wavered on the eastern horizon.

"Not quite. He was the mark from the beginning," Thomson said as he put his shotgun to his shoulder and aimed it. "Now he'll become our scapegoat." He pulled the trigger, the bird fell through the sky, and the Lab took off like a shot. "Our dead duck."

"I'd feel a whole helluva lot better," Benson said, squinting like Clint Eastwood, "if we had heard from our man in the field."

"He had instructions to maintain communication silence when he was in place."

"Yes, but I want these last obstacles to be taken care of."

Thomson watched with pleasure as the Lab returned with the duck in its mouth. There was blood on the dog's dark muzzle and its eyes were alight with the ecstasy of doing what it was born to do, what it had been trained to do.

As it set the duck gently down at Thomson's feet, he said, "You worry too much."

"I'm paid to worry too much," Benson said sourly.

WHILE ANNIKA met with Magnussen and Kharkishvili, Jack and Alli walked through the manor house. It was some hours after the AURA session had broken up. Since his conversation with Edward Carson, Jack had been trying to fit all the disparate pieces together to form a coherent whole—he knew it was out there, he could feel it forming, coalescing, the problem was it kept changing shape and scope as it was appearing to him.

Over the years he'd discovered that his mind was often at its best when he walked or ate, mechanical functions that allowed his brain to digest and reorder the seemingly random bits of information it had picked up. There was a great deal of pressure on him both from Edward and AURA to find a way out of the escalating crisis, but he'd made Kharkishvili and Magnussen promise to leave him alone until he had need of them.

"Jack," Alli said, "I'm hungry."

He nodded. "Me, too. Let's find the kitchen."

Was it his imagination or had she grown up in the last couple of days, did her features seem more set, had the last vestiges of her girl-hood been swept away by the intense events compressed into the short time they'd been together? It was as if she had unlocked an invisible door and, having stepped out into the light of day, or in this case, the ample lamplight of the manor house, was at last allowing herself to be seen, instead of cowering in the shadows of her misery and anguish.

Like everything else in the manor house the kitchen was vast. Bubbling with activity just before and at mealtimes, it was manned now by a sous-chef and a couple of servers who doubled as kitchen assistants. They were going over the recipes for tomorrow, and paid Jack and Alli scant attention, but when they approached the enormous double refrigerator the sous-chef broke off his discussion and came over to them, asking what they'd like to eat, there were plenty of leftovers from dinner. Neither of them wanted the rich food they had already rejected so they both settled on vegetable omelets.

There was a plain wooden table where, Jack suspected, the kitchen staff ate at odd times. He and Alli pulled out chairs and sat while the sous-chef broke eggs into a stainless steel bowl and began to whip them with a bit of water and heavy cream.

"How did you manage at the meeting?" Jack asked.

"That sleazeball Russian I was sitting next to, Andreyev, wanted me to come to his room tonight because I owed my life to Ivan Gurov," Alli said.

Vasily Andreyev, with skin the color of putty or suet, and the black button eyes of an evil doll that, having been shunted aside for newer playthings, harbored the need for revenge.

"Don't give me that look, I can take care of myself." She tossed her head. "I tuned him out by thinking about what you said before, and I know you're right. I've been so intent looking over my shoulder for death to steal up behind me, I was already half dead. When I was taken . . . that week might have been a month or a year, I didn't know, I became unmoored from the present, or maybe from time itself. Nothing felt right, there were periods when time passed at a glacial pace and at other times it seemed as if hours were compressed into seconds."

Jack put his elbows on the table, leaning forward, listening to every word she said. With the crackle of the frying eggs no one could overhear what she was saying.

"When I went to Milla Tamirova's apartment, when I went into her dungeon, sat in the restraint chair, I began to realize that the feeling of being unmoored, of being outside time never left me during the months after you rescued me. Now I think it has, now I want to look ahead, to experience the new, and even the old, which will feel like new to me, just like I've been doing since we got here."

The eggs arrived, sided by thick slices of the dense Ukranian brown bread. The sous-chef placed the plates in front of them, along with silverware, and went to pour tea out of a large, ornate samovar standing on a corner of the work counter.

Alli took up her fork and dug into the glistening eggs. "In the middle of hearing about what flawless skin I had," she continued, "it dawned on me that the only time I've been happy—really happy—since Emma's death is when I've been with you and Annika. The adrenaline rush of the present annihilated the past, at least for a short time, but it also began to resurrect my sense of time and place."

Jack chewed on a slice of bread, which was intensely flavorful, slightly sour, and slathered with salted butter. "You feel more yourself now."

"I don't know about that, because I was only beginning to learn about myself when Emma died." Alli looked thoughtful. "What I feel is *different*, as if I've just thrown all the sandbags off an air balloon and now I'm rising up toward. . . ."

"Toward what?"

"I don't know, exactly, but I think now that I have a kind of gift.

When I listen to you talking to other people, or when I listen to them talking among themselves, if the conversation goes on long enough, I have a sense of what they mean, not what they're saying necessarily, but what they're trying to get across or, more often, what they're trying to hide. And, it seems to me, that the longer the conversation goes on the clearer their real purpose becomes, or maybe I mean how important their lies are to them." She cocked her head. "Do you see what I mean?"

"I think so." Jack was wolfing down the omelet. "But give me an example, anyway."

"All right, let's see . . ." She screwed up her face in thought. "Okay, here's one, that Russian sitting next to me—"

"Andreyev, the lecher."

She laughed softly. "That's right. Well, when I mentioned that we had met Dyadya Gourdjiev he started talking about him, and though there was nothing negative in what he said—quite the opposite, in fact—I began to sense that he was lying, that he didn't like him at all, and when he mentioned Kharkishvili—and only in passing—I just knew that Andreyev had aligned himself with him."

Jack was thinking of his recent conversation with Kharkishvili, who had denied any kind of rivalry between him and Gourdjiev. If Alli was right in her observations then Kharkishvili deliberately lied to him and the situation within AURA was more complex than he had been led to believe, which in all likelihood might lead to difficulties in his dealing with these people even if he did come up with a solution to the problem of how to defuse Yukin's plan. He resolved to test her belief at the earliest opportunity.

At that moment Kharkishvili came into the kitchen, opened the refrigerator, and took out a bottle of beer. He nodded at Jack in a stiff, almost formal manner.

"I need to ask this guy some questions," Jack said, rising. "I'll be right back."

He was halfway to where Kharkishvili was standing, working an opener under the crenelated cap of the bottle, when the floor began to tilt under his feet. He took a step to correct it and felt as if his knees had turned to jelly. He began to pitch over, but before he hit the floor he heard Alli screaming. Then he plunged headlong into oblivion.

TWENTY-SEVEN

IT WASN'T often that Dyadya Gourdjiev thought about Nikki, in
fact there were entire months when she never entered his mind. She
was, however, never far from his heart. The essence of her filled his
mind now as he stepped off the plane into Simferopol North Airport.
He'd made no secret of his plans, booking the seat and traveling under his own name. He thought this would make it easier for Oriel
Batchuk to follow him; he didn't want anything to impede his
enemy's progress.

Gourdjiev took his time even after he picked up his weekend bag
from the luggage carousel and walked outside to the long-term lot
and got into the car he always left there when he was on his way back
to Kiev or, every once in a while, Moscow. It was an ancient Zil that
wheezed every time he stepped on the brakes, but he loved it anyway.
It smelled like home.

He could not get Nikki out of his mind, perhaps he didn't want
to because thoughts of her brought him back to Batchuk. He recalled

with startling detail the moment Batchuk had first seen Nikki because that was the moment death had attached itself to him, and from that moment forward a shadow followed in Batchuk's wake. Other people would experience it as intimidation, but Gourdjiev was not so easily fooled, because when he looked into Batchuk's eyes all he saw was catastrophe and death.

From time to time he had mentioned Nikki to Batchuk—after all, there were occasions when it was impossible not to—but he had bent over backward to make certain the two never met. He made dates for Batchuk to come over to the house for dinner only when he knew that Nikki would be busy with her girlfriends or, latterly, with Alexsei Mandanovich Dementiev, to whom he had introduced Nikki at a gala at the State Opera House. He had no notion as to whether they would take to one another, but he was immensely relieved when they did, and it was only when Alexsei asked for her hand in marriage that Gourdjiev contemplated allowing Batchuk to catch a glimpse of her.

In fact he had orchestrated their meeting so that Batchuk would see Nikki and Alexsei together, see how much in love they were, and no matter what he thought of Nikki would understand that that path was closed to him forever.

Now, driving away from the airport in the Crimea, Gourdjiev could scarcely believe the lengths to which he had gone to keep Nikki and Batchuk from meeting. Had it been a dream, a premonition, or simply intuition, he could no longer remember. But it seemed to him that he had awoken in the middle of the night with a vision of Nikki and Batchuk together, Nikki weeping bitterly, inconsolably, and it was as if he had been afforded a glimpse of a tragic future so that he could ensure that it would never happen. He knew Batchuk's taste in women, knew just what he liked most to look at and to feel, and there was no doubt in his mind that Nikki fell right into that category. What she might have felt about him he couldn't say, but over and over again he had seen Batchuk pursue what he wanted, persistent, implacable until he got it. It might be an exaggeration but Gourdjiev had come to believe that there was scarcely a woman Batchuk wanted who would not eventually accede to him. Long experience had taught him that the only way to view Batchuk was through a cynic's eyes because Batchuk was at his most dangerous, his most disingenuous when it appeared that he was being sincere.

He swung onto the highway without it fully registering. His mind was back at that meeting when he'd seen the dreadful expression on Batchuk's face as he watched Alexsei swing Nikki around outside the mall jewelry store. *Good Christ, that was very nearly the worst moment of my life*, Gourdjiev thought. He wished to whatever god existed that it had been, everything might have ended differently.

Watching Nikki, Batchuk had the look of an angel, as if an ethereal glow were illuminating him from the inside. Gourdjiev knew that meant trouble on whatever level, but he pushed the thought aside as people will terrifying nightmares or worst possible outcomes because the human brain won't allow it. It was like contemplating your own death—the incomprehensible end of all things known and comforting—the level of fear was simply too great to maintain. Some benign circuit breaker in the brain turned off that possibility, or shoved it so far back into the realm of unreality or fable that it faded from consciousness. This is precisely what happened to Gourdjiev when he saw Nikki's image fill Batchuk's eyes to overflowing. Some part of his brain switched off, saying: No, no, no, let's get on with the real, the present, the pressing now, and for the next twenty minutes the two men talked about their plans as if nothing untoward had happened.

And yet it had, Gourdjiev thought, as he accelerated toward the coastline and, beyond, the violent and turbid Black Sea. The malevolent seed had been sown despite his best efforts, and immediately began to germinate, cracking open and springing to life in the black soil of Batchuk's mind.

Gourdjiev neared the coast with its high, dark, bruised-looking clouds, trembling with thunder and rain. He did not have to glance in the rearview mirror to know that he was being followed, he had felt it the moment he had arrived at the airport, the sense that someone was watching his every move. There was a vehicle behind him, of this he was certain, he was being followed, either by Batchuk or by someone Batchuk owned.

One glance in the mirror would tell him. He knew Batchuk so intimately that he could pick out his outline even through the rain-spattered windshield. And yet he kept his gaze on the road ahead as it wound through the landward incline of the brooding cliff face. The truth was he preferred not to look, preferred to be unsure of the identity of his pursuer, of one thing at least, because everything else was laid out before him as if it had already occurred, as if he were locked into a trajectory that, no matter how he tried to twist away or fight against it, would lead him to some final place filled with tragedy.

FIFTEEN MINUTES after Dennis Paull drove out of the Alizarin Global compound with Claire beside him and Aaron heavy-lidded and drowsing in the backseat, he found a spot by the side of the road where, this late at night or early in the morning, he was certain he could not be observed. He got out of the car, went around, and opened the trunk. He fired up the laptop and within minutes found that it had been hacked. Because of the safeguards he had installed the hacker's electronic fingerprints were all over the file system; Paull knew that he had made a complete copy of the information on the hard drive.

That was fine by Paull, he'd expected no less. Despite what he'd told the president he had used insecure servers to gather information. He needed stone-cold proof as to the identity of the man in Carson's inner circle who was passing on classified information to Benson and Thomson, and if he didn't have the time to do it himself he was determined to let the culprit do it for him. When he had exited the Residence Inn that morning he had known that sooner rather than later someone would be coming for him. That's why he'd planted this dummy laptop in his trunk days ago. His real laptop, the one with all the hacked information, was stowed in a secret compartment below the spare wheel well that he opened now by the light of the small, recessed bulb on the inside of the trunk lid.

He turned it on, and plugged in a 3G Wi-Fi card. Almost at once his private, shielded network was activated. He had a good signal, even out here. He inputted information and set up the parameters of the various Internet searches he wanted the automated software to perform, then closed the trunk and got back behind the wheel.

"Tomorrow I promise we'll be off to do some celebrating." He was looking at sleepy Aaron, but he knew Claire understood he meant it for both of them. "Would you like that, kiddo?" He used to call Claire kiddo when she was Aaron's age.

"I sure would, Grandpa." His grandson looked around and yawned. "Where are we gonna celebrate?"

Paull grinned at Aaron's image in the rearview mirror as he put the car in gear. "It's a surprise."

"BEFORE I saw you and Aaron this afternoon," Dennis Paull said, "I thought it was all slipping away from me, everything I had ever wanted out of life, that even before I died there would be nothing left, nothing to live for. Everyone had left me prematurely: your mother, you, and Aaron, who I'd never seen before today."

The three of them were in the spacious room at the Mandarin Oriental Hotel on Maryland Avenue where he was putting Claire and Aaron up for as long as they wanted to stay after the funeral. His first instinct had been to invite them back to the house, but on second thought he decided it was presumptuous. The house where he and Louise—mostly Louise—had raised Claire was crammed with too many memories, good and bad, for both of them. Better, he felt, to take it slow.

"But you had your work," Claire said without rancor, as she closed the door to the bedroom where she had put Aaron to bed, "and it seemed to us—Mom and me—that was all you cared about or needed."

Paull felt as if he had been set on fire by his own guilt. "Yes, I can see how I must have given that impression so many times." He took her hand. "I'm so very sorry, Claire."

"Don't be sorry, Grandpa." Aaron stood in the doorway, speaking with the meticulous seriousness only a seven-year-old could display. He was wearing Buzz Lightyear pajamas. "Mom and I will take care of you."

This elicited a burst of laughter from Claire. "Oh, Aaron." She went over and kissed him on the cheek. "Now go on back to bed, honey."

Paull bit his tongue so that he wouldn't say what he was thinking: No, I'll take care of you and your mother, because he knew Claire would hate that. He had to get used to her being grown up, an adult who could take care of herself.

"We'll make the arrangements for your mother's funeral tomorrow and do the service early," he said. "I promised Aaron a celebration."

"You've changed." Claire could not keep a touch of wonder out of her voice.

"Surprised?"

"Frankly, yes, Dad. I didn't think you could, or rather that you might want to." She sat in a plush, upholstered chair. "What happened?"

"I got older and wiser." He perched on the corner of the coffee table as if to reassure her that this was her room, her space. "That may sound facile or a cliché, but in my case it's true. I guess I had to get to be a certain age to understand what I was missing, to understand what I'd done wrong, but until today I didn't know what to do about it."

"You mean the president doesn't need you twenty-four-seven?"

"No, he's got Jack McClure for that." Paull took a quick glance at the bedroom door, which was still slightly ajar. "Besides, even if he did I'm with my family now."

This was absolutely true as far as it went; however, and most unfortunately, at the moment catching up with Claire and his grandson weren't the only things on his mind.

"I think it's time for you to get some sleep."

"I'm not tired."

"All right," he said, "then tell me what your life has been like these last seven years."

She sighed and put her head back against the cushion. "We're living in Baltimore, which I don't particularly like."

"Then why are you there?" Paull asked.

"I have a good job—great, really—that pays really well. I create greeting cards that are sold over the Internet."

"Surely you can do that anywhere," Paull said. "You could move back here."

The instant the words were out of his mouth he regretted it. Claire's face clouded over and her gaze went to the closed drapes through which, at any moment, the first light of dawn would seep. "I'm not sure that would be a good idea, Dad."

"Sure, stupid of me. You and Aaron have your own lives."

"But we don't have much family, do we?"

Both father and daughter looked at the little miracle of Aaron who, standing in the doorway, his pajamas emblazoned with the phrase TO INFINITY AND BEYOND! was apparently far too excited by the events of the long day to sleep or even to lie in bed. And now

Paull wondered whether Claire's self-imposed exile to a city she did not like was punishment not only for him, but for herself.

He thought she was about to respond, he wanted her to respond, but at that moment his cell phone vibrated. He wanted to ignore it, did his best to ignore it, in fact, but a moment after it stopped, the vibration returned, this time in a different pattern, and he knew that he had no choice. Excusing himself he padded across the carpet to the bathroom, but even before he got there he had his phone out and was reading the text message.

It was one of three that he had prewritten in the event of new information being picked up by any one of the three programs he was running on his laptop. This one was from the proprietary search engine he had a part in developing. Unlike others available to the general public, this one had the ability to dig through corporate filings and other ephemera to come up with answers to questions such as the one Paull had given it this evening: Who owns Alizarin Group?

It seemed the program had the devil's own time plowing through a mountain of labyrinthine document filings, shell companies that led nowhere, phantom bank accounts, and the like. Nevertheless, it persevered, as he had designed it to do, but now he knew the privately held company was owned by seven partners. He had no idea what to make of that; he knew of only one man who could.

ORIEL BATCHUK, driving along an unfamiliar highway in the Crimea, would have been shocked if Gourdjiev wasn't aware that he was being followed. He did not appear to care, which did shock Batchuk. He had no idea what his old friend and foe was up to, just as he couldn't fathom what had motivated Gourdjiev to shoot Boronyov, a man whom Limonev had assured him was already dead. Gourdjiev had told Batchuk's men that finding the fugitive oligarch was why Annika was in Ukraine, but Batchuk hadn't believed that tale for a moment. Gourdjiev had a plan, that much was certain—not knowing what it was worried him.

Gourdjiev, always so mysterious, so circumspect, was nothing of the sort now. It was when people started acting out of character that the real problems started, Batchuk knew from cold, hard experience, the first instance of which appeared with Nikki. Through his twenty-minute talk with Gourdjiev he had become increasingly enraged first that Gourdjiev had deliberately blocked any possible meeting with her, and second that when it did happen, he made certain to push her impending wedding in his face. The cruelty of Gourdjiev's actions was not lost on him, and the reverberations from that affront had never ceased.

That day Gourdjiev had acted out of character, he had indicated through deeds rather than words that Nikki was off-limits, that she was better than Batchuk and so deserved better than him, a man named Alexsei Dementiev.

Ahead of him the filthy Zil Gourdjiev was driving turned off the highway onto a secondary road that appeared to lead to the coast. Batchuk made certain that he never lost sight of the car; he was on the lookout for a quick switch, where a second car and driver waiting by the side of the road would allow the drivers to switch vehicles, thus throwing off any pursuit, but no such vehicle was in evidence.

Batchuk returned to his contemplation of the past. He was powerful enough even at that time to start an investigation into Dementiev's life and, if necessary, manufacture evidence that would disgrace him or put him behind bars. But Batchuk quickly determined that neither of those outcomes would do him any good because Gourdjiev would know what he had done and would not only come after him but also put Nikki out of his reach forever. He would not have that. In his confused state he didn't know what he felt for Nikki beyond a potent erotic attraction, but he did know that getting to her, fucking her until she couldn't walk, was all he wanted, all he could think of now. How strong a component revenge was even he couldn't say.

He could see the Black Sea through a sudden squall of rain, ominous clouds hanging low on the horizon. Not for the first time he considered the possibility that Gourdjiev was leading him into a trap, that either the shooting of Boronyov or Gourdjiev's loaded remark to his men was the bait. This thought caused him to recall their most recent confrontation, when he had stepped out of the shadows of Gourdjiev's building, confident that he had the upper hand, when their escalating emotions had driven him to lay down his ultimatum: *"I came to warn you, or more accurately, to give you the opportunity to warn Annika. I'm coming for her—me, myself, not someone I've hired or ordered to do a piece of work. This I do personally, with my own hands."*

And now, for the first time, it occurred to him that the trap might have already been sprung, that possibly it had clamped him in its teeth the moment he had gone to tell Gourdjiev that his—what had he called it?—his burnt offering would not save Annika this time. What if, he asked himself now, that entire heated conversation had been choreographed by Gourdjiev? He was more than capable of such a Machiavellian stratagem.

It was a stratagem that he had used himself with Nikki and Alexsei Dementiev years ago, in another, simpler world, driven only by emotion, pure or impure. He had been invited to the wedding and he had gone, taking one of his many women, he could no longer remember which one. He kept away from the couple of honor. Not surprisingly Gourdjiev's eyes were upon him the entire night, but even if he hadn't been under scrutiny, he had resolved to keep his distance as a first step in his stratagem. Patience was his ally when it came to Nikki, he knew this in his bones, though his flesh felt like it was on fire every time he caught sight of her. And when she danced, in the center of the ballroom floor, his heart nearly stopped.

In the weeks that followed he did nothing at all but go about the

business of following in Yukin's shadow and, like his mentor, amass-
ing more and more power as he rose in prominence and influence. It
was just over two months from the wedding date that he contrived to
cross paths with Alexsei Dementiev in a perfectly natural way so as
not to arouse Gourdjiev's suspicions. It was hardly difficult; Dementiev worked as a state prosecutor, his whereabouts known and docu-
mented by any number of ministries with which Batchuk had powerful
contacts. Batchuk made it vital that Dementiev depose him for an
important case he was prosecuting for Yukin. Afterward, they went
to lunch. Having committed to memory every fact aggregated in
Dementiev's government file, Batchuk invited him to play tennis, a
sport the young man adored, at the indoor facility owned and oper-
ated by his club. Dementiev wasted no time in accepting, and in this
way, among others cleverly devised by Batchuk, the two men became
friends. And so it came about that Alexsei Dementiev himself introduced Batchuk to Nikki when he brought him home for dinner, the
first of many nights that the three of them—and sometimes four because Batchuk was careful to bring a date now and again—spent together, eating, talking, and drinking the excellent vodka Batchuk
was sure to bring.

Early on in his relationship with Dementiev, when they had
gone out drinking after a tennis match, Batchuk had determined
that the prosecutor did not have the capacity for alcohol he himself
did. One night, eight months later, when the three of them were alone,
they drank so much that near midnight Dementiev passed out, obliging Batchuk to help Nikki carry him to bed, after which the two of
them returned to the living room, where a welter of dirty plates and
servers awaited them. Batchuk obligingly helped her clean up. Space
in the kitchen was at a premium, and more than once their bodies
brushed against each other.

Nikki was not the kind of woman to fuck a friend while her husband lay insensate in the next room so Batchuk didn't try, though he

had to summon up all his willpower not to take her forcibly and relieve the demonic itch that afflicted him like an allergy or a response
to poison. When it came to Nikki's effect on him poison was not too
extreme a word. When he was in her presence—and, eventually,
even when he wasn't—he felt ill, disoriented, dizzy as he lost track of
who and where he was. It was only when he was alone with her, so
drunk he could taste, or thought he tasted, his heart in his mouth,
that he was comfortably numb. But then the gray morning would
come and his mind would be beset by the thought of what Alexsei
Dementiev had, what he didn't have, and it was all he could do not to
tear his hair out.

Patience, he counseled the raging part of him. Patience.

And then one day his patience was rewarded.

Batchuk's mind snapped back into focus as he saw Gourdjiev's Zil
turn off the secondary road, down a gravel driveway that led to a
high wall into which was set an electronic gate that opened for the
car, then immediately closed behind it.

Beyond the wall, set on a rocky promontory, he spied a large and
imposing manor house that he knew he must penetrate. He pulled
over his car, doused the lights, and began to formulate a plan.

Twenty-Eight

Jack, bent over a toilet, was retching, his eyes watering, his guts still spasming.

"It's all right," he heard a voice say from behind him, "it's all out of his system."

A pair of strong hands pulled him upright, led him over to the sink where he washed out his mouth and put his head under the cold, gushing water. Then he was being dried off with a towel. He heard the toilet flush and had a sense that that sound had been going on for some time. There was a terrible taste in his mouth, part supersweet, part salty, that made him shudder. He heard the toilet seat being lowered and then he was seated on it, the damp towel over his face, another one, rolled and soothingly cool, at the back of his neck.

"Tell them he's all right," the voice said. "I'll bring him out in a minute, just be patient."

He felt ill and exhausted, as if he'd just returned from a fifteen-round boxing match where his midsection had been systematically pummeled by Lennox Lewis. Pulling the towel off his face he looked up and saw Kharkishvili grinning down at him. Kharkishvili handed him a glass of water.

"Drink, my friend. After puking up your guts for twenty minutes, you're seriously dehydrated."

Jack drank the water, feeling better with each swallow; however, his head thundered and his throat ached. He handed back the glass, which Kharkishvili refilled from a nearly full pitcher.

"What happened?" His voice was a thin, ugly rasp, as if his throat and vocal cords had been seared.

"Poison," Kharkishvili said. "You were poisoned." He refilled the glass, handed it back. "Good thing I was in the kitchen when it happened, I've had some experience with poisons." He chucked darkly. "You know, in my line of work—which, I assure you, the less you know about the better for both of us—you need to know many ways to skin a cat." He waved a sausagelike hand. "The important thing is I got you to swallow water with sugar and salt, which caused you to expel everything in your system."

"I don't remember."

"You wouldn't, you were raving but not, fortunately, unconscious." Kharkishvili nodded. "Now drink up and return fully to the land of the living."

A sudden fear pierced the slowly dissipating fog in his mind. "Alli was eating the same food I was, is she all right?"

"Perfectly. She's outside, everyone was evacuated while we interrogated the kitchen staff. Please keep drinking." Kharkishvili refilled his glass. "It wasn't the food that was tainted, it was your fork."

"How?"

"Arsenic, an old but reliable methodology."

"Who, the sous-chef?"

Kharkishvili shook his head. "One of the assistants, we have him in custody."

Jack drained his glass; he was feeling better with every moment that passed. "How long ago was he hired?"

"I inquired of Magnussen; he was hired six days ago."

Kharkishvili was proving to be a good man. Jack's brain, which had felt as if it had been encased in jelly, was functioning again, enough, at least, for him to remember his conversation with the president, who had assured him that, the sanction canceled, no more government agents were in the field.

"I want to speak with him," he said. He rose, took two tottering steps, and sat back down.

Kharkishvili frowned, making him look something like the ogre in the story of Jack and the beanstalk. "In your condition I don't think that would be a good idea."

"Please have Ivan Gurov come in, then bring the poisoner here," Jack said, a certain snap returning to his voice. "We don't have time to worry about my condition."

Kharkishvili nodded and left.

When, in due course, Gurov poked his head in the doorway and asked how Jack was feeling, Jack said, "Ivan, the assassin who followed us here, the one you blew off the road, do you know anything about him?"

"I checked with Passport Control at Simferopol North. His name was Ferry Lovejoy."

"A government-assigned legend."

"Ah, yes." Gurov nodded. "A false name to go with the false papers the American government gives its agents overseas. But, no, I checked with FSB in Moscow. Neither Mr. Ferry Lovejoy nor anyone matching the surveillance photo I took of him is in their database."

Jack's mind was working at such speeds that he felt momentarily dizzy. "It's now more imperative than ever that I speak with my would-be murderer."

"Mr. Kharkishvili has him outside."

"Good. But first, please have Alli come in, would you."

While Kharkishvili went to fetch Alli, Jack put a hand on the porcelain sink and levered himself up. For a moment he stood swaying slightly. He spent his time slowing his breathing in order to get his heart rate back to a normal level. All the while his mind was running full tilt. He now had almost all the pieces to the puzzle, though there were still important gaps to fill in. He hoped he could do that before the deadline of tomorrow night, or was it already tomorrow? He glanced at his watch, but his fall had shattered the crystal face and it had stopped working.

He pulled out his cell phone and that was when he saw that there was one voice mail message. It had been flagged URGENT.

ALLI EMBRACED him. "Are you all right?" She had arrived before he could pick up the message.

"I'm fine."

"Then what are you still doing in the bathroom?"

He smiled. "It makes an excellent interrogation cell." He pulled her closer to him. "Now, listen, in a moment Kharkishvili is going to bring in the man who tried to poison me and I'm going to talk to him. You'll watch him, listen to him, assuming he says much of anything, which is doubtful. That shouldn't matter to you, you'll evaluate his facial and body movements, which will tell me a lot. Okay? Think you're up to it?"

"Of course I'm up to it." Her eyes were large and liquid. "I'm just . . . I can't believe you'll trust me with this."

Jack brushed back the fringe of hair from her forehead. "It's not my trust you can't believe, Alli, it's your trust in yourself."

A moment later Kharkishvili appeared with a slight, dark-haired young man who Jack recognized as one of the kitchen assistants.

"This is the sonuvabitch," Kharkishvili said, manhandling him through the doorway. "His name is Vlad, so he says." He glared at Vlad. "He's Ukrainian, that much is for certain, the accent is unmistakable."

"Sit down."

When Vlad made no move, Kharkishvili pushed him roughly down onto the closed toilet seat.

"You can do whatever you want to me, I'm not going to talk," the young man said.

Jack ignored him. "Vlad, I'm going to tell you a story. This happened a long time ago, in seventeenth-century Italy. A Neapolitan woman named Toffana marketed a cosmetic, Acqua Toffana. It was a face paint that, as was the custom of the time, made women's faces very pale, almost white. This Acqua Toffana proved astoundingly successful among the married women of the area, who were counseled by Toffana herself to make sure their husbands kissed them often on both cheeks while they were wearing the makeup. After six hundred of these unfortunate men died, turning their wives into rich widows, the authorities finally discovered that the main ingredient of Acqua Toffana was arsenic. It was the arsenic that gave it its white color."

He shrugged. "But being an expert poisoner I suppose you know the history of arsenic. However, not expert enough, it seems, because I'm still here."

Slouched on his uncomfortable plastic seat, Ivan looked at him, trying to seem bored. As befitted his profession he had a thoroughly unremarkable face, except for his eyes, which, when Jack looked closely, were yellowish and slippery as oil. They stared out at the world with what seemed a false stoicism, as if they were lying in wait for the enemy to appear.

"Who do you work for?" Jack said. He waited for an answer, but Vlad said nothing. His surface was as bland, as blank as the surface of polished marble, calm and curiously unconcerned by his incarceration.

"I know it's not the United States government, Vlad, so do you work for the FSB?" Jack paused again to allow Alli to make her assessment. "Perhaps it's the Ukrainian Security Service who employs you."

Another pause; the silence from Vlad was deafening.

He leaned in suddenly, careful not to block Alli's view. "I know you and Ferry Lovejoy work for the same firm." He knew no such thing, but he wanted to observe, and wanted Alli to observe, Vlad's reaction.

Vlad's brow furrowed convincingly. "Ferry . . . ? I'm not familiar with that name."

Jack smiled, using his teeth. "You work for Alizarin Global, so did Lovejoy, but he's dead now. Ivan Gurov blew him off the road to this manor house, didn't he?"

Kharkishvili grinned wolfishly. "Absolutely."

"Is that supposed to frighten me, because—"

"Okay, we'll dispense with the formalities," Jack said, standing up. "I have neither the time nor the inclination to interrogate you further, so I'm going to hand you over to the Russians, Vlad. Let them deal with you. Believe me, whatever information you have they'll squeeze out of you."

Jack made a motion with his head and Kharkishvili hauled Vlad to his feet.

A look of contempt hardened Vlad's face. "You won't hand me over to the Russians, you won't be allowed to do it."

"Allowed?" Jack said, pouncing on the word. "By whom? Who do you work for, who inside AURA?"

"It's Andreyev, isn't it?" Alli had stepped up to stand beside Jack. "You're taking orders from Vasily Andreyev."

Vlad spat onto the floor. "Vasily Andreyev is an old fool."

Kharkishvili cuffed him hard in the back of the head.

"Manners," Jack said, but Vlad had already revealed as much as he was going to. "Take him away," he said to Kharkishvili.

When he and Alli were alone, he said, "Tell me what you observed."

Alli considered. In that moment Jack saw no trace of the overprotected, narcissistic young woman who had been abducted at the end of last year.

"I'd say he definitely works for a private company."

"What seemed to frighten him, anything?" Jack asked.

Alli's face tensed in concentration. "One thing: being turned over to the Russians."

Jack nodded. "That was my impression also, which tells me that the company he's working for isn't American, or at least not primarily American." He gave her an encouraging smile. "Okay, what else?"

"I got the feeling that he doesn't know Ferry Lovejoy, whoever he is."

"The assassin who Ivan Gurov killed." Jack had come to the same conclusion.

Also, who or what was going to stop Jack from handing Vlad over to the Russians?

"And what's the deal with this mysterious company that sent them?"

"I'm not sure," Jack said, "but I intend to find out."

DYADYA GOURDJIEV parked his comfortably rumpled Zil outside the front door of the manor house just as the first pallid streaks of dawn light cracked open the black-and-blue dome of night. Getting out of the car he shivered in the damp chill air and steeled himself for what was to come.

Magnussen, Glazkov, and Malenko had emerged to welcome him, but not, predictably, Kharkishvili. Though clearly startled by his unplanned visit they nevertheless were warm in their greetings.

As he walked into the entryway he felt himself transported back to the past, back to when he became aware that Oriel Batchuk was spending an inordinate amount of time at Nikki's house. That, in fact, was why he had come over unannounced that night, he had hoped to surprise Batchuk and, in front of Nikki, tell him in no uncertain terms to stay away from her and from Alexsei. Batchuk had easily seduced Alexsei with his power, privilege, and his ability to obtain for him the plum cases that had advanced his career, and would continue to do so. By virtue of Batchuk's magnanimous helping hand the couple had moved out of Alexsei's cramped one-bedroom into a spacious, light-filled two-and-a-half-bedroom in a luxurious building within walking distance of Red Square. Gourdjiev had also taken note, not without some alarm, that Alexsei had begun wearing made-to-measure British designer suits and Nikki was dressing in the latest Western fashions.

But that night Batchuk was nowhere to be found, instead he walked in on a screaming fight between Alexsei and Nikki. At first no one answered the door, but when he became insistent Nikki opened the door a crack.

He was stunned to see her looking disheveled, her face pale, her carnelian eyes fever-bright. There was a snarl on her lips that she was too upset to hide or modify as she stared out at him. She hadn't wanted to let him in, had begun to close the door on him when he'd planted his foot on the lintel. Then he'd leaned into the door and pushed it open, stepping inside.

At once Alexsei rushed out of the bedroom where, it seemed, their argument had escalated into a full-scale battle of harsh words, hurled invective, insults, and accusations.

"It's him, isn't it!" Alexsei shouted. "How dare you let him in?" When he saw that it was Gourdjiev standing in the entryway, he turned away, but he was hardly mollified. "Now you call your father to take your side."

"I didn't call anyone, Alexsei."

"Liar! You call Oriel all the time!" he shouted as he whirled around.

"He calls me," she said, "it's not the same thing."

"It is if you accept the call." Alexsei's lips were drawn back from his teeth.

"You're making something out of nothing," Nikki said.

"Do you deny you see him during the day?" he snarled. "Go on, deny it, it would be just like you. Deny it and I'll have my proof of what sort of woman you are, because I've seen you two."

"You've been spying on me?"

"I saw the two of you having lunch, bent over the table together, your foreheads were practically touching, I saw it and there were other prosecutors there as well."

"Alexsei, think for a minute, if I were having an affair with Oriel would either of us be stupid enough to meet in public, let alone at a restaurant frequented by your colleagues?"

"I know him, he wants to throw the affair in my face, he's out to humiliate me, he wants everyone to know that he's taken you away from me."

"You speak of me as if I were a horse or a sack of wheat."

That was when Gourdjiev turned on his heel and left. No good would come from him inserting himself between them, especially when emotions were running so high. It was only when he emerged from the building and saw the spotlit domes of the Kremlin that he knew there was only one place for him to go.

"Is everything all right?" Magnussen said now, wrenching Gourdjiev back to the present. They stood in the villa's entryway. "We didn't expect you."

"Yes, I know," Gourdjiev said, "but there was no place else to go."

BATCHUK WAS inside the perimeter of the manor house before he saw a guard. The brick wall surrounding the property was high but not particularly difficult to scale or to get over. The real difficulty was in keeping his silhouette from being seen in the gloaming of dawn. There were no trees on the cliff top, no foliage to mask his movements, but luck was with him, a light fog was billowing in off the water in ghostly waves.

Dropping down off the top of the wall he heard faraway barking and he crouched down, still as a rock. If there were dogs on the property, particularly hunting dogs, they would present a problem. With the onshore wind they would already have picked up his scent, or would at any moment. Close to the front of the house he saw the Zil. As he watched, a guard emerged from the house and drove the Zil around to where a number of other cars were parked.

As soon as the guard was back inside Batchuk ran as fast as he could, zigzagging, still bent over, heading for the left side of the manor house. He reached it without incident, but now he heard a chorus of barks, close enough for him to identify them as belonging to Russian wolfhounds. Wolfhounds were not in themselves dangerous, they liked people too much, but they would certainly sound the alarm for those inside the house. Any moment now other guards would come pouring out, following the dogs who, he was now certain, had picked up his scent.

He knew the feeling, he'd had a hound coming after him the night Nikki told him that she couldn't see him anymore, that Alexsei had found out about them and was causing a terrible row. She told him unequivocally to stay away when he said he was coming to make sure she would be safe.

"I don't need you to feel safe," she had told him. "I don't need you at all."

"You do need me," he had replied like an idiot, as if he were seventeen, "I know you do, Nikki, no matter what you say you can't hide it from me."

"You are so deluded," she shot back, "I was a fool, weak and sad, and you caught me in that moment, you took advantage of me and climbed all over me."

"Don't give me that," he said, "you loved every minute of it, it was you who climbed all over me, if memory serves, you couldn't get enough."

"Shut up, shut up, shut up!" she shrieked, clearly terrified.

"I did what you wanted me to do, nothing more."

"Liar! It was what *you* wanted."

"You can't fight it, Nikki, I don't understand why you even try."

"Idiot, because I'm married."

"You'll divorce him, I'll make it easy for you."

All at once she sounded desperate. "I pledged my heart, my life to Alexsei, don't you get it? But, no, I don't suppose you do, why would you? You have no soul, no humanity, you're heartless, pitiless, you want what you want, that's the beginning and the end of it."

"Then why did you give in to me? Why did you scream over and over in ecstasy?" He barely got out the last word when she hung up on him.

An hour later Gourdjiev came for him, baying at his door, and he had had no choice but to let him in, no choice because Gourdjiev knew he was home, and if he'd ignored the repeated knocking he'd become a prisoner in his own apartment. He had plenty of power, it was true, but so did Gourdjiev; he had no wish for an all-out war that would bring an end to both their political careers, he had too much on the line to take that risk. And so he opened the door, accepted his medicine, the righteous indignation, the affronted anger, the howl of the animal that feels its offspring threatened.

Visibly chastened, he did not argue, he acquiesced. Whatever Gourdjiev wanted of him he did without argument or protest, let him win this battle, let the war wait in abeyance, all the players frozen in place, until the moment when he himself dictated that the next act would begin.

———

BUT THE dogs would not wait, the wolfhounds came tearing through the carefully manicured foliage—sculpted boxwood and cotoneaster, as close-clipped as a general's hair—to where Batchuk had crouched under the eaves at the back of the house, but he was no longer there, and they ran in dizzying circles, barking and yelping, their nostrils full of his scent, but with nowhere to go.

"That badger again," one of the guards said, after he and his companion had had a thorough look around, "or maybe this time an opossum."

JACK WAS just finishing up his call with Dennis Paull, having at last found the time to answer his urgent voice mail, when he caught sight of Annika. She was in the entryway, talking with Dyadya Gourdjiev, of all people, obviously just arrived, as he stood in his water-beaded overcoat. At this hour, as misty dawn light crept slowly up to the manor house, everyone should have been sleeping, they should have been in bed hours ago, sleeping through the small hours of the morning, when the country was quiet and indolent, dreaming of yesterday or the day after tomorrow, when sorrow's heartbeat was stilled at last, overcome by hope. But Vlad's attempt on Jack's life had turned the world within the manor house upside down; at Kharkishvili's urging several of the guards had hustled the inhabitants outside while Ivan Gurov and his crew interrogated the kitchen crew, discovered Vlad's treachery, and slowly, feeling shaken, chilled, and desolate, everyone had filtered back inside, where they puddled in the library, knocking back glasses of slivovitz and watching each other with ambushed eyes.

Jack told Paull his location and said, "Now have my would–be NSA assassins turn their skills to good use," before he disconnected.

Dyadya Gourdjiev had seen Jack, and Annika turned and ran toward him, flung her arms around him, and held him tight.

"I was so frightened for you," she whispered in his ear. "I was terrified they had succeeded."

"They?" he said as he held her at arm's length. "Who do you mean?"

"The Americans, of course." Her carnelian eyes studied him with complete candor. "The Izmaylovskaya's reach doesn't extend to the Crimea. At least you're safe from them, if not from your own despicable people."

She had put him in danger the moment she had lured him into the alley behind the nightclub in Moscow, but there had been no real danger from Izmaylovskaya revenge, she was with him, and the supposed dead Ivan Gurov, loyal, brave, and more clever than he appeared, had been watching over both of them. Then the game had unexpectedly opened up, as General Brandt sent NSA agents after them, and now, after those agents had been withdrawn from the field, another—Vlad the Poisoner—had been dispatched by Alizarin Global. For what reason? Why did Alizarin want to kill him? Time to find out.

"Annika, listen, I need to speak with Vasily Andreyev, but I want you and Dyadya Gourdjiev with me as witnesses. I know Gourdjiev just arrived and he must be tired, but can you see if you can convince him to do that now?"

"All right." She nodded and went back to the entryway, where Gourdjiev was immersed in what appeared to be a heated discussion or argument with Kharkishvili, who had stopped on his way out.

She touched his arm and, though reluctant to cut short the discussion or argument, he could not refuse her. She spoke briefly in his ear and he glanced at Jack, who stood ready and waiting. Then he nodded, said something curt to Kharkishvili that, to Jack, looked something like, "Don't forget what I've told you, we'll continue this later." Kharkishvili stalked out as Annika and Dyadya Gourdjiev approached him.

Having taken a stroll around the main level with Alli, his brain had automatically memorized the floor plan as a three-dimensional space. He therefore knew that the best place for privacy was the old-fashioned drawing room. It had mullioned leaded-glass windows out to the west side of the house and only one entrance, double doors that opened onto the short corridor that ended with the kitchen, pantry, and back door.

Jack found Andreyev, his hair disheveled, his black button eyes furtively glancing at Alli every chance he got. A glass of slivovitz in one hand and a cigar in the other, he stood against the mantel; either he or it required propping up. The other oligarchs were now nowhere to be seen, Andreyev said that Magnussen had suggested they go for a walk to clear their heads before breakfast, but he hadn't felt up to it. So that's where Kharkishvili was off to. Two guards and, of course, the three Russian wolfhounds had accompanied them. By Jack's count that left Alli and two guards remaining on the property. Gurov was gone, transporting Vlad the Poisoner back to Simferopol North Airport for delivery to the FSB. The emptying out of the manor house suited Jack's purpose.

Andreyev accompanied Jack and Alli out of the library, down the rear hallway, and into the more private drawing room, where Annika and Dyadya Gourdjiev greeted them. Jack saw in Annika's face a sense of great expectation, of a mystery about to be solved. As for Gourdjiev, he had his usual sphinxlike expression, calm and unruffled, despite the tension of the moment.

"You should have told me you were part of AURA," Jack said as he clasped the old man's hand. His grip was still firm and sure.

"No need to burden you with something you didn't then need to know." He gave Jack a grandfatherly smile. "Annika tells me that you will solve the dilemma of the uranium field, of Yukin's land grab, the specter of a spreading conflagration."

Jack's eyes flicked to her and back. "Annika puts great faith in me."

"She does," Gourdjiev acknowledged. "She has from the very beginning; she is an unerring judge of character and, just as importantly, of potential." He paused, waiting expectantly.

"May I ask," Andreyev said in his furtive manner, "why you have brought me here, Mr. McClure?"

"Certainly." Jack put him firmly under his gaze. "I am extremely unhappy with the unwanted attention and inappropriate advances you have made on my daughter."

"You must be mistak—"

The beginning of Andreyev's transparent denial was cut off by two short bursts of semiautomatic fire. Jack, racing to the double doors, was about to thrust them open when they opened from the outside. Oriel Batchuk stood in the doorway, an OTS-33 Pernach machine pistol in his hand. Reacting immediately, Jack chopped down on his wrist, knocking the Pernach to the floor, but Batchuk shoved past him, raised his left arm at Andreyev as if he were accusing him of being alive. The lethal dart struck the oligarch in the neck. Clawing at it, he fell to his knees, the terrible clicking sound of massed insects coming from his throat before he pitched over, dead.

"Step back." Batchuk swiveled his arm. "Step back or Annika dies next."

Jack did as he said, and Batchuk, crouching down, plucked the Pernach off the floor. "All right," he said, standing and pointing the machine pistol at them. "Time to disarm yourselves."

"TIME TO disarm yourself," Batchuk said.

"I will kill you now." Alexsei Dementiev was silhouetted in the doorway of his apartment, in which Batchuk was already standing, a Makarov pistol in his hand.

During one of his earliest evenings there before his affair with Nikki began, Batchuk had made a wax impression of her key, had a copy made so that he could gain entrance any time he chose. Though he was not given to introspection, he nevertheless understood that the complete domination of her privacy was essential to his conquest. At work, at court, inside the Kremlin, or elsewhere in Moscow, it pleased him to know that he was always, in one way or another, intimate with her.

"I'm not joking or bluffing," Alexsei said.

His face was drawn, deeply etched with tension and misery. To Batchuk he looked ten years older than when they had first met at court, only eighteen months ago.

"I'm quite certain you're not, I assure you that I take the threat quite seriously." But by the way Alexsei held the pistol Batchuk knew he was no expert in firearms. In fact he wondered whether Alexsei had ever fired a Makarov, or any pistol for that matter.

"You deserve to die." Alexsei was growing tenser, more anxious. "For what you have done to my wife I will be justified in taking you out with the rest of the garbage."

"Tell me, Alexsei," Batchuk said, "have you ever killed a human being?" He cocked his head. "No? As someone who has killed many men, let me assure you it's no easy thing, no, not at all. You never forget the face of the first person you kill, the look in his eyes as the light goes out."

"I'll welcome that look in your eyes."

"That expression haunts you, Alexsei, follows you down into dreams, into the deepest recesses of your mind, lodged there like a lesion or a tumor that can't be treated, can't be eradicated no matter what you do."

Something flickered in Alexsei's eyes, some disturbance or doubt roiled up by Batchuk's words. In that instant of doubt or hesitation Batchuk lunged at him, slapping him across the face so hard that Alexsei, totally unprepared, reeled back against the door frame.

Batchuk ripped the pistol from his hand. "You're a buffoon, Alexsei, a patsy. I used you to get to Nikki. Do you really think I'd be friends with someone like you, someone who lets his wife be taken away from him?"

Alexsei, enraged at both his rival and himself, came at Batchuk, roaring like a bear. Indolently, almost carelessly, Batchuk swiped the barrel of the Makarov across Alexsei's face.

"That's right, she was going to leave you, leave your poor, pathetic life behind to be with me."

Alexsei would not stop, he continued to grapple with Batchuk until Batchuk had no choice but to take Alexsei's head in one hand, his neck in the other, and twist in one powerful motion that broke the vertebrae.

DYADYA GOURDJIEV, glancing briefly down at the handguns he, Annika, and Jack had placed on the carpet of the drawing room, heard Batchuk say, "Now sit down, all of you, and I'll outline the situation."

As they sat, Batchuk continued, "The two guards are dead, the others are away with the dogs, so that leaves just us, not that I have much time, but then killing doesn't take much time."

"Whatever you do, leave the girl out of it," Jack said, indicating Alli. "She has nothing to do with this."

"She's here, isn't she, she's seen my face." Batchuk shook his head. "No one is exempt."

"Oriel, your battle is with me, let the others go," Gourdjiev said sharply.

"I told you I was coming after Annika, I told you she had overstepped even your protection, did you think I didn't mean it?"

"HE'LL COME after me, I know it," Nikki said as she lay in the hospital room.

"Have no fears on that score," Gourdjiev said soothingly, "I'll protect you come what may."

"And the child."

Gourdjiev took her hand. "Of course the child, she's the product of your and Alexsei's love."

Nikki closed her eyes. "He's coming soon, Papa, when I'll be weak and helpless." Her eyes flew open. "Oriel has an instinct for knowing when people are most vulnerable. Promise me you'll keep her safe."

"I swear, Nikki, calm yourself."

"Her name is Annika, I want to call her Annika."

She was a perfect baby. Gourdjiev remembered holding her in his arms, so tiny, so pink, so Annika, and the world seemed all right again. But then five years later everything came undone, Nikki had killed herself, Annika was gone, and Gourdjiev knew that he had failed daughter and granddaughter both.

"I HAVE an instinct for knowing when people are most vulnerable," Batchuk said, "and now that I've caught up with you both it's time to end our decades-long game of charades."

"I prefer to call it a game of cat and mouse," Gourdjiev said.

"Call it whatever you want," Batchuk leveled the machine pistol, "it's over."

At that moment, Alli moved.

"Keep still, girl!" Batchuk shouted so loudly that Alli jumped and he almost shot her.

Jack took a step forward, Batchuk swung his machine pistol around, and Annika rushed him. She buried her fist in Batchuk's belly while Jack wrested the Pernach away from him.

"His left arm!" Gourdjiev shouted, leaping to his feet. "He's got a dart launcher!"

Indeed Batchuk, through eyes streaming with tears, struggled to level his left arm at Gourdjiev. Jack knocked it sideways an instant before the dart was launched, causing it to embed itself harmlessly in the crown molding that joined wall to ceiling.

"Let me go," Batchuk said. Though he was being restrained by Jack, he addressed Annika, as if they were alone in the room.

"Why would I do that?" she said. "You're a monster."

"It's your grandfather who is the monster. I swore never to talk about it, never to tell you, but what are oaths now, in the end the promises we make all fail, they're meant to be broken."

"How evil you are," Annika said. "You're rotten with malevolence, nobody knows this better than I do."

A peculiar light shone in Batchuk's eyes. "You think you know the meaning of evil, but you don't, Annika, because it's your grandfather who's truly evil."

Gourdjiev took a step toward them. "Don't believe a word he says, Annika."

"Yes, not a word of it, but here is the truth of it: Nikki and I were in love, she was the only woman I cared about, to this day that's the truth."

"You wouldn't know the truth if it came up and bit you," Gourdjiev said.

Batchuk kept his gaze firmly on Annika. "It was your grandfather who schemed to keep us apart. He never let me even meet your mother until it was too late, until she was already engaged to Alexsei."

"No," Annika said, "my mother and father were in love."

"Alexsei loved her, of that there can be no doubt." Batchuk shook his head. "But as for Nikki, no, she thought she loved Alexsei until we met, and then she knew the truth of it. Even though she was married neither of us could help ourselves, we became lost in each other—nothing, no one else existed."

"What he's saying is nonsense," Gourdjiev said. "He's simply try-ing to justify his actions."

"Annika," Batchuk said, "it was our love, your mother's for me and mine for her, that caused Alexsei to feel so threatened. If we'd just had a quick tumble, if our connection was purely physical, do you think he would have become so maniacal with her? No, he knew, just as she knew that her love for me meant that their marriage was over."

"You killed him," Gourdjiev said. "You broke Alexsei's neck."

"He gave me no choice, he was out of control, nothing less would have stopped him from tearing me limb from limb."

"So now you claim the murder was self-defense," Annika said.

"Yes." Batchuk nodded. "Absolutely."

Gourdjiev took another step toward him and at last his antagonis-tic intent was unmistakable. "And that same night was it self-defense when you raped my daughter the moment she came home while her poor dead husband was bundled in a closet?"

Batchuk's face filled with blood. "I did no such thing!"

Annika's eyes were full of shock and rage. "Did you? Did you rape my mother the night you killed my father?"

"I never raped her," Batchuk said. "There wasn't a time I touched her when she didn't want it, didn't beg for the release only I could give her."

Annika slapped his face, very hard, the energy rising in her from her lower belly through her arm into the tips of her fingers, the im-prints of which could be seen on his cheek white on red, and then an instant afterward, red on pink.

Gourdjiev kept moving in, as if for the kill. "And what do you call it, also self-defense, when you stole Annika away from her mother?"

"You mean from you, Annika was never Nikki's child, she was yours, you tried with all your power to make sure of that," Batchuk said. "But yet it most certainly was self-defense. I took her from you, from your clutches, because she's mine." He turned to Annika. "You were conceived the night I killed Alexsei Dementiev in self-defense, you were conceived after he died, in the frenzy of passion your mother and I shared."

TWENTY-NINE

"Is THIS true?" Annika said to Gourdjiev, breaking the stunned silence. "You knew?"

"Not right away, of course not."

Jack could see that the old man was on the defensive now, which was just where Batchuk wanted him. He risked a glance at Alli, who had come off her chair and was standing very near Gourdjiev as if to stop him if he leapt to throttle Batchuk. He could tell that she was totally absorbed in the psychological fireworks.

"But gradually, as your mother's mental condition began to decline, I got some inkling. At first I thought her depression was a result of Alexsei's death, but then, as the months turned into years I grew convinced that something else was eating her alive. Finally, five years from the day of Alexsei's murder, I got it out of her, how she had come home that night to find not Alexsei waiting for her, but him, Oriel Batchuk.

"I was out of my mind with rage and anguish, all I could think of was how to revenge myself on him, so much so that I lost sight of her, I failed to realize just how deeply in the grip of her depression she had sunk. That night I stayed with her and with you, and that night she slit her wrists, silently, on the bathroom tiles, while you slept and I plotted revenge."

"There you have it," Batchuk said, triumph creeping into his voice, "the anatomy of true evil."

Annika put the machine pistol to the side of his head. "Move away, Jack," she said.

"Annika." Alli had moved from Gourdjiev's side to Annika's. "Don't, he's your father."

"You don't know what he did to me, the years I was with him."

"I did what you wanted me to do, nothing more."

"Liar! It was what *you* wanted."

"You're wrong, I kept you safe," Batchuk said, "safe from *him.*" He glanced at Gourdjiev.

"I didn't need you to keep me safe."

"Annika, no matter what he did in the past, no matter what he is now, he helped bring you into the world," Alli said. "Without him you wouldn't exist."

"At this moment," Annika said, "I wish I didn't exist."

"You don't mean that," Alli said.

There were tears in Annika's eyes. "I'm going to blast his god-damned skull open."

"Don't, Annika, don't. You'll never be able to live with yourself."

"It doesn't matter, I want to die, but before I do I will see his blood spattered all over this room."

"I hate my father, too." Alli was pleading with her. "But I couldn't bear the thought of him dying."

"Whatever he did, it couldn't be anything like what this man—"

"Your father."

"—did to me."

"Crimes are crimes," Alli said. "Whether they're of cruelty or of neglect what matter does it make, they've changed us, and they can't be taken back or absolved or forgotten, but the cycle has to end somewhere, so why not here, why not now, with you?"

"You're right." Annika smiled at her, a slow, sad, rueful smile. "It has to end." Then she pulled the trigger. Batchuk's blood, brains, and bits of bone flew outward in a hail of red and pink, an explosion so violent its human shrapnel covered them all, so massive it seemed as if he had detonated from the inside out.

BENEATH A gauzy and indistinct sky Dennis Paull stood with his daughter and grandson at Louise's grave site just across the Chesapeake in Virginia. He and Claire had each dropped a shovelful of dirt onto the lowered coffin.

"Mom, why did you and Grandpa put earth in the hole with Grandma?"

Tears glittered in Claire's eyes. "So part of us can stay with her and love her always."

To Paull's surprise and immense pleasure Aaron stepped forward, stooped down to grab a handful of earth, and dropped it on top of theirs.

Even though they had come here to bury his wife his thoughts weren't diminished by her death and loss, rather they were filled with the return of his family. How, he wondered now, had he deserved this miracle? Had he been a good man, righteous, strong in his convictions, repentant for his sins? And what did the answers matter, the universe didn't care, every event was random, chaos ruled, there was no answer for any question, large or small, only compromises and, perhaps, if one was as lucky as he was, sacrifices.

His arm was around Claire's shoulders, his eyes were on Aaron, who was perhaps dreaming of the promised celebration later this afternoon, but for Dennis Paull the celebration had already begun.

A DEAFENING silence now engulfed them all, made their legs numb, their hearts thud in their chests, numbed their minds. What remained of Oriel Jovovich Batchuk lay half in, half out of the drawing room, his blood was all over, but not a single drop of Vasily Andreyev's had been spilled.

"So, it's over at last," Gourdjiev said, breaking the awkward silence. "Annika, I'm so terribly sorry you had to hear that." He went to her, tried to put his arm around her, but she shrugged it off.

"Don't," she said, moving away from him.

Jack gingerly unwound Annika's fingers from the machine pistol. When he took it from her she made no protest, instead she took Alli's hand and held it tight.

"I knew you were right, I wanted to . . . but I couldn't."

"It's all right," Alli assured her, "it's all right."

Annika stood staring down at her grandfather's nemesis—her father—with a kind of terrified disbelief. She was holding Alli's hand so tightly their fingers were white. Jack knew it wasn't healthy for any of them to remain in this abattoir.

"We need to clean up," he said.

Annika nodded, but she didn't move. There were bits of bone stuck to her cheeks and nose, oblique smears of blood elsewhere on her chest and face, including her lips. Gourdjiev stepped agilely over the body and stood in the hallway waiting for them, silent, wrapped in his own enigmatic thoughts. He did not look at his bloody hands.

"How are you?" Jack asked Annika.

Her carnelian eyes were pale and bleak, as if all the mineral quality had leached out of them. "I haven't the faintest notion, my mind is numb, I feel lost and alone."

"You're not alone," Jack said. "Come on, you and Alli need to clean up."

He nodded to Alli, and she guided Annika out of the drawing

room, past Gourdjiev, stoop-shouldered and gray, and into the bathroom. Jack led the way into the kitchen, where he and Gourdjiev cleaned up as best they could, using the kitchen sink.

Jack watched warm water sluice the muck off his hands. "It's true, isn't it, everything Batchuk said."

Gourdjiev stared out the window over the sink. "Most of it, anyway."

"So for years you knew he was her father."

"Yes."

"But she didn't."

"Not until a few minutes ago when you heard about it yourself."

"It's no wonder she killed him."

"To be shot to death by your own child." Gourdjiev turned back into the kitchen, slowly washed his hands as if reluctant to part with the tangible evidence of Batchuk's death. "I wish I could say that I felt satisfied, but I fear that revenge is not all it's cracked up to be; in fact I'm finding it's rather meaningless. His death won't bring my Nikki back, it can't mitigate her pain, and now I think it's very possible that Annika is lost to me as well. If that happens I'll have nothing."

Jack, aware that Annika and Alli had come into the kitchen, their faces and hands clean if not their clothes, said, "Not to worry, you still have Alizarin Group."

"What, I didn't hear you."

"You heard me well enough," Jack said. "I know you own Alizarin Group. There are six other partners, but you're Alizarin's guiding hand."

"I'm afraid you're sadly mistaken, young man."

Jack hefted Batchuk's machine pistol. "The only thing you should be afraid of is me."

"I don't understand."

During this exchange Gourdjiev was gradually transformed from an old beaten-down grandfather to a stern, ramrod-backed business-man with the keen, knowing eyes of an expert poker player. No wonder he had outsmarted Batchuk, Jack thought. And he knew that he had to guard against succumbing to the same fate.

"The man who poisoned me was employed by Alizarin Group, your company."

Annika stared at him. "Dyadya, is this true?"

"What nonsense, of course it isn't."

"He's lying," Alli said. "I was with Jack when he interrogated Vlad. He works for Alizarin Group." She and Annika stood close together, as if they were sisters standing up to their parents. "Anyway, when Ivan Gurov delivers him to the FSB the truth will come out."

"That's not going to happen." Gourdjiev sighed. "Ivan Gurov's vehicle was intercepted on the way to the airport and Vlad was res-cued. Unfortunately, Gurov chose to put up a fight and was killed."

"What are you saying?" Annika looked as if she had about hit her breaking point. "Your people murdered Ivan?"

"He gave them no choice, Annika. He wouldn't let Vlad go."

She stared at him, dumbfounded. "Then it was you who ordered Jack killed?"

"Not killed," Gourdjiev corrected, "poisoned by arsenic, debili-tated, perhaps hospitalized, not dead, never dead."

"But why?"

Dyadya Gourdjiev turned to Jack and said just as if he were asking for the time, "Do you want to tell her, I'm certain you have figured it out by now."

Jack hesitated, not because he didn't know the answer but because he wasn't sure he wanted to play Gourdjiev's game. Then he shrugged mentally. "It was Alli, she really threw a wrench into your plan. It's a joke, funny when you think about it, but that's how life is, Gourdjiev, a spur-of-the-moment decision, something from out of left field you couldn't possibly have anticipated. Given her real identity you couldn't afford the scrutiny from the American government that would be the inevitable result of my bringing her here, so you thought up a way to take the spotlight off her and put it on me. My government would be so busy trying to find out who had tried to poison me they'd forget all about Alli and what happened to her here, that was why you risked exposure to rescue Vlad, why your people killed Gurov. He recognized them, didn't he, or at least one of them. You couldn't allow either Gurov or Vlad to talk, now neither of them will."

Dyadya Gourdjiev nodded as if immensely pleased with a prized pupil. "And of course you figured out my plan."

"It seems that you've been playing both ends against the middle. You were never going to share the astronomical profits from the uranium strike, either with Yukin or with AURA. You wanted it for yourself."

"Not at first." Gourdjiev kept one eye on the muzzle of the machine pistol. "I put AURA together to go after the uranium strike, but rather quickly I saw that AURA was going to fail, principally because Kharkishvili turned against me, he split the AURA members, it was becoming ineffective." He shrugged. "So I decided to have Alizarin step into the breach."

"But there was a problem," Jack said, "a seemingly insurmountable one, which is where I come in."

Now Gourdjiev laughed. "I very much regret that I ordered Vlad to dose you, you have a remarkable mind. Unique." He nodded admiringly. "I've known the president of Ukraine, Ingan Ulishenko, since he was a young man. I went to him with our proposal, but all he saw was sovereign land, potential profits being taken away from him. He refused to believe that there was an imminent threat from *Trinadtsat*, from Yukin and Batchuk. He would not allow us to buy the land."

Jack had not raised the weapon, had made no threatening move against Gourdjiev. "What you needed was an outside source to confirm what you'd told him, someone unimpeachable, someone Ulishenko could neither ignore nor refuse."

"An American in government, close to the president, but who was totally apolitical."

"Someone Ulishenko would be sure to trust."

"No one else fit the bill, Mr. McClure."

"Which is why your grandfather would never kill me," Jack said to Annika. "He needs me and, as it happens, I need him. I'm going to make sure Alizarin Group gets the uranium field."

The solution had come to him sometime when he was washing Batchuk's grisly debris off his face. He had tried to come up with an alternative, but it was no use, his brain told him that he'd found the only one, even though it wasn't perfect—wasn't even, to his way of thinking, good—but there was no other path to take, and now he wondered whether Gourdjiev had hit upon it before him.

"The accord with Yukin must be signed, President Carson made that perfectly clear. But if he does sign it Yukin will move into Ukraine and use the accord to stay there. That isn't acceptable, either. I talk to Ulishenko, tell him what Yukin is planning. He'll have no choice but to sell the uranium field to Alizarin Group. Alizarin is a multinational corporation that Yukin can neither touch nor attack, so as to his energy ambitions in Ukraine he's stymied. Plus, he now must abide by the accord he will sign tonight with the United States."

Jack turned back to Gourdjiev. "In addition to the purchase price, Alizarin Group will pledge fifty percent of all profits from the field to the Ukrainian government."

"Ten percent," Gourdjiev said.

"Don't make me laugh. Forty-five percent or I tell my government what you've done. They'll shut Alizarin Group down like a toxic waste dump."

"Twenty-five percent or I walk away and let Yukin have his way."

"Without me to confirm to Ulishenko the imminent threat posed

404   Eric Van Lustbader

to his country by Yukin you and Alizarin are dead in the water," Jack said. "Thirty-five, that's my final offer."

"Done."

Dyadya Gourdjiev held out his hand.

"Jack, you're not really making a deal with him," Alli said.

"I have no choice."

"There's always a choice," she said, "you taught me that."

"Not this time." Jack grasped Gourdjiev's hand, and at that moment they all heard the clatter of rotor blades descending.

"What's happening?" Gourdjiev said.

"The cavalry," Jack said, "has arrived." Just as Dennis Paull promised.

THIRTY

FROM THE back of the immense, ornate salon in the Kremlin, Jack watched as Alli stood on one side of the First Lady, Lyn Carson, Mrs. Yukin on the other, as President Edward Carson and President Yukin used pens specifically designed for the historic signing of the U.S.-Russian security accord. Alli was wearing a long sapphire blue dress that made her look very grown-up. While video and still cameras dutifully recorded the momentous occasion Jack's gaze fell on Yukin's face, alight with pleasure and a certain amount of secret triumph, the origin of which only he, Carson, Annika, and Alli knew. An hour from now, when Ukrainian national television broadcast Dyadya Gourdjiev and President Ulishenko jointly announcing that the tract of land in the country's economically ravaged northeastern section was sold to Alizarin Group, Yukin's demeanor would change markedly. Alizarin would pledge thirty-five percent of the profits to Ukraine and immediately begin hiring thousands of unemployed citizens to work the largest uranium strike in Asia.

After the signing, the seemingly endless photo ops and interviews began, neither of which Jack chose to be a part of, despite Carson's requests to the contrary.

"I can serve you best," Jack told the president, "by remaining in the shadows."

Uncharacteristically Alli had agreed to stay by her parents' side during this tiring and dreary process, or rather, Jack reflected, it was a new characteristic, one that spoke to her recent adventures, insights, and sense of herself. As he watched her move about the room with the Carsons and the Yukins he felt a great surge of pride for who she was and what she might now become.

He spent the time with Annika, who had flown back with him and Alli from Kiev, where the helicopter manned by Paull's people had let them off.

"I don't think I'll ever speak to him again," Annika said.

Jack knew she meant Gourdjiev, a man whose name she no longer spoke, much less called *dyadya*.

"He was trying to protect you."

"Really, is that what you think?" She looked at him skeptically. "Or are you just trying to make me feel better?" She held up a hand to forestall an answer she did not care to hear. "The truth is he was trying to protect himself. As long as I remained ignorant of the facts of my conception he didn't have to answer awkward or embarrassing questions."

"It seems odd that Batchuk didn't tell you he was your father when you were with him."

They were standing by a window that must have been fifteen feet high. She looked away from him, out onto Red Square, where it had begun to snow again, according to the weather forecasters the last snow of winter.

"The truth is as simple as it is ugly: He didn't want me to know I was his daughter, not then, anyway. He was too busy mourning my mother's death and staring into my eyes—studying my face brought her back to him as nothing else could. And, of course, there was the other thing." Tears glittered beneath her lashes. "To tell me that he was my father would have destroyed the sexual bond he tried to establish between us."

Jack felt a sudden chill render him all but speechless. "When you were five?"

She continued to stare out at the snow, she neither answered nor moved her head, there was no need.

She wiped her eyes with her forefinger and turned to him suddenly with a thin smile. "I'm sorry, Jack, sorry for lying to you, deceiving you, putting you through the wringer with Gurov's supposed death, but it was necessary."

Was it, he wondered. He supposed that depended on your point of view. He could begrudge her her elaborate deception, but to what end? He had seen firsthand how Sharon's rage at him had destroyed not only their marriage but Sharon herself. As long as she held on to that anger she would never be able to trust anyone, she'd be alone and in anguish for the rest of her life. That was a path he had turned away from some time ago.

"There's one other thing I can't fathom," he said now. "How did you know I'd follow you to the alley that night?"

She put the flat of her hand against his chest. "You're a decent man, you weren't going to let me walk into an ambush where you were convinced that I would surely wind up dead."

He shook his head. "I'm not buying that answer. You could never have been certain that I would come, even after you were careful to tell me in the hotel bar that the Moscow police were worse than useless."

Her smile was cunning, which had the startling effect of turning her into a sexual creature he did not want to resist. "I studied you, Jack. I knew what had happened with Emma, I knew how your ex-wife blamed you, how you blamed yourself, how, to compensate and to try to make amends you couldn't resist someone in peril, especially mortal peril." When he made no comment, she went on, "Tell me you didn't think of Emma when you made the decision to leave the hotel and come after me."

"You're right," he said, after a time, "Emma was all I thought about that night."

"Once again, I'm sorry."

"Don't be." Leaning forward, he kissed her. "I don't want to hear you say you're sorry again."

"Don't worry," she put a hand behind his head, caressing him, "you won't."

Jack saw the Carsons coming and remembered that Edward had invited him to dinner after the ceremonies.

"I'm going to have to go," he said, reluctantly breaking away from her.

"Meet me tomorrow," she said, "in the lobby of the Bolshoi Ballet at seven forty-five."

And then she was gone, vanishing in the dense swirl of people.

"I hope I didn't scare off your lady friend," Edward Carson said. "I was going to invite her to dinner."

"That's all right, sir, I don't think she cares much for this place."

Carson looked around. "Who the hell could?" He put his arm around Jack's shoulders. "Once again I owe you a debt I can never hope to repay."

"No need, sir."

"On so many levels," the president continued, "not only me, not only Lyn and me, but the country itself. Dammit, Jack, no one else could have figured out a way to make this damnable security accord a success."

"I appreciate your faith in me." Jack didn't want to talk about a success that involved Dyadya Gourdjiev getting everything he wanted. Instead, he looked around. "I haven't seen General Brandt."

"And you won't. He's being held incognito and in strict isolation aboard Air Force One. The Justice Department has been notified and will deal with him in due course, as will every other knotty problem of state, when we arrive home tomorrow." His smile was broad and, for once, relaxed. "Tonight we eat, drink, tell jokes, and best of all, listen to the stories you and Alli have to tell about your adventures in Ukraine. For this one evening we've all earned the right to forget about the difficulties of yesterday and whatever may come the day after tomorrow." He took Lyn's arm and nodded in Alli's direction. "Now how about you escort Alli back to the hotel; everything has been prepared for us in my suite."

THE NEW day dawned just as it had ended, with snow. The presidential motorcade set out for Sheremetyevo, where Air Force One was fueled and waiting. Jack, sitting beside Alli in the limousine directly behind the one carrying the president and First Lady, was looking forward to interrogating the General. Carson had promised him an hour alone with Brandt before anyone else had a crack at him. The president was of a mind to grant Jack pretty much anything he asked for.

"Sorry to be going home?" Jack asked half in jest.

"As a matter of fact," Alli said, "I am."

They had reached the Ring Road, coming up on the exit that led to the airport. The snow had lessened and, according to the latest forecast, would be nothing but a memory in an hour or so, but the night had been frigid, and with the overcast predicted to hang around for the next couple of days the sidewalks and roads would remain slick. Jack thought about Annika and the date at the Bolshoi for tonight that he would not now make. He'd called her and left a message on her voice mail telling her of his change in plans. Carson had been expected to stay another day, but the itinerary had abruptly changed because of embarrassing difficulties Ben Hearth, the newly appointed Senate whip, was having keeping the conservative wing of their party in line.

"I miss Annika," she said, "do you?"

"I wish we were staying longer." Jack looked out the window at the bleakness of Moscow. "I wanted to see the Bolshoi."

Alli smiled. "But not with me."

He smiled in return. "No, not with you."

Alli was silent for a moment, staring at the motorcycle cops flanking their limo. "Maybe she'll come to Washington, maybe you'll come back here."

"Maybe." He put his head back; he was suddenly very tired. The moment he closed his eyes he saw Emma. He smiled at her but something was wrong.

Alli must have seen the change in his expression because she said, "Don't be sad, Jack."

"I'm not sad, exactly, I—"

The rest of his thought was cut off by her scream. His eyes snapped open to see everything in frantic motion. The presidential limo had skidded, most likely on a patch of black ice, and was now veering off the roadway. Still spinning, it plunged down the verge onto the median, where it struck something buried under the snow. It flipped over as it slammed into a high-tension pole. The cables broke free and swooped down like black crows out of an icy sky, striking the limo, sending a powerful charge through the car.

Alli was still screaming and Jack was out of their limo, running with the Secret Service agents toward the wreck. Sirens were wailing, people were shouting, the entire motorcade had come to a halt, the press corps piling out and running, too, cell phones out, calling, texting, Twittering, whatever means would get the news out the fastest, spreading it to all four corners of the globe even before those on the scene could determine the condition of the president and the First Lady.

Alli caught up with Jack as he waited for the two agents who were closest to swing the cable off the limo. The moment it was safely aside, he wrenched on one of the rear doors. The limo was resting on its roof, there was a welter of security personnel, both American and Russians. Because the Russians were being turned back, their commander decided his men should form the perimeter, keeping back the howling press corps.

By this time Jack had wrenched the door open. He took one look inside and handed Alli to one of her detail.

"What's going on?" she cried. "Jack, tell me what you saw!"

Putting his head back inside Jack saw Lyn Carson cradling her husband's bloody head. All the personnel in the front were mangled, clearly dead. Defib Man checked on the president, shook his head, and started to cry.

"Mrs. Carson," Jack said, "Lyn, we've got to get you out of there now."

She did not move, did not respond, and Jack climbed in over the body of his good friend. When he began to pull her away, Lyn screamed. Her eyes were wide and staring, she was clearly in shock. Then there were other hands helping him, and slowly the Carsons were separated. That's when he saw that the front of Lyn's coat was soaked through. At first he thought it was Edward's blood and, indeed, some of it undoubtedly was, but when she passed out as they tried to extricate her he knew that something was very wrong.

THEY TOOK the president and First Lady—Edward and Lyn—straight to Air Force One, where the president's trauma surgeon was standing by in the plane's operating room for Lyn Carson, who had sustained abdominal damage. The American medical team worked on her for six hours, and even then the team leader could not give a definitive long-term prognosis. She was, however, stable enough for Air Force One to take off. By that time the snow had ceased, and a silver sun briefly showed its face through a crease in the thick cloud cover.

During those six hours Jack stood holding Alli, who, after asking him what he had seen, had said not a word. She stared down at her father, gray as ash, shiny as a melted candle, without an outward sign of emotion. This continued for so long that Jack grew worried. He spoke to her several times in halting phrases; his tongue felt as if it were swollen. He himself needed time to grieve over the loss of Edward Carson, but it had not yet become a reality, it was too immense, too unthinkable to take in so quickly. How could Edward Carson, the President of the United States, die in a car crash, how could he be dead? He couldn't be, no one believed it except the Secret Service detail, because they had been trained for this moment, hoping it would never come, but prepared for it mentally and physically nonetheless. Dick Bridges, the detail's leader, was dry-eyed and stoic, there was never a moment when he wasn't in command, when everyone wondered whether they could count on him. After he had supervised the loading of the agents who had been in the lead limo into the belly of the aircraft he returned to the president's body as a member of the Praetorian guard stands by his Caesar, even in death.

Jack had not heard from Annika and he did not now expect to. It was just as well; he wouldn't know what to say to her, how to respond, his mind was here by the side of his fallen friend, his leader, and Alli.

Just before the doors closed Jack left Alli's side and stepped out onto the moving stairs. He was surrounded by grim-faced Secret Service agents, silent in their sober grieving. Their regret was so palpable he felt buffeted by it. There was nothing special to look at, Sheremetyevo was much like other airports in other countries, and yet to him it was utterly unique.

Everything comes to an end, he thought. Love, hate, even betrayal. The accumulation of wealth, the scheming for power, the barbarity, the cruelty, the endless lies that capture what we think we want. In the final moment, everyone falls, even the would-be kings of empires like Yukin, even the princes of darkness like Dyadya Gourdjiev. In the silence of the tomb, we all get what we deserve.

While he was thinking these thoughts, while he was taking his last breaths of the chill Moscow air, his phone vibrated. He almost didn't take it out of his pocket, almost didn't look at who was attempting to contact him at this inopportune moment. He both wanted and didn't want it to be Annika. Compelled to look down at the screen he saw that she had replied to his call via an e-mail. He opened it up and read:

> Dearest Jack,
>
> My grandfather warned me not to tell you, but I'm breaking protocol because there's something you have to know; it's the reason I haven't come, why I won't come no matter how long you wait, why I'm not being melodramatic when I say that we must never see each other again.
>
> I killed Lloyd Berns. I sought him out in Kiev and then in Capri, where, free of his official escorts, it was easy to do what I wanted with him. I ran him down. He had made a deal with Karl Rochev—two stubborn birds of identical corrupt feathers—that threatened AURA's plans. My grandfather knew the president would open an investigation into Berns's death and suspected that he'd assign you because Carson trusted you, and only you, and you were already with him in Moscow.
>
> I know you must hate me, I've been preparing for that since the moment I built up the file on you. There is little point in reiterating how desperately my grandfather and I needed your unique expertise, no one else could have unraveled the Gordian knot that had stymied and bedeviled us. So you hate me now, which is understandable and inevitable, but you know me; what I can't stand is indifference, and now, no matter what, you'll never be indifferent to me. So, in that regard, I'm content, though certainly not happy. But,

then, it seems to me that I'm not destined to find happiness, or even, perhaps, to fathom its nature, which is as mysterious to me, or maybe alien is the correct word, as prayer.

Whether or not you choose to believe it, we all run afoul of forces we cannot see, let alone understand. This is not to excuse, or even to mitigate what I did. I don't seek absolution; I don't know its meaning and I don't need to. I neither regret what I did nor feel pride in it. In peace as in war sacrifices must be made, soldiers must fall in order for battles to be won—even, or perhaps especially, those that are waged sub-rosa, in the shadows of a daylight only people like us notice.

Dyadya Gourdjiev and I won our battle over Oriel Batchuk and America got what it wanted from Yukin and the Kremlin. That's all that matters, because you, me, all the pieces on the chessboard have no meaning without it.

Annika

"Mr. McClure." Dick Bridges tapped him on the shoulder. "Everyone is waiting. I must ask you to go inside now and take a seat, the captain has received clearance for immediate takeoff."

Jack took another look at the e-mail, as if on a second reading the words, the meaning would change, as if this time he would not find out how terribly, how deeply, how completely Annika had betrayed him, how she and her grandfather had spun lies and deception in concentric circles, layer upon layer, each one inside another, protecting each other, like Russian nesting dolls.

He gazed out at the last snow of April. Alli had said, *"Maybe she'll come to Washington, maybe you'll come back here."*

It was possible that one or the other of those futures would come to pass, but today as he ducked back inside the sad, lonely, silent plane, he very much doubted it.